Hawk gently raised her fingers to his lips.

♡

"My father hasn't exactly been easy on you, has he?" The intensity of his eyes mesmerized her.

Carrie was acutely aware of his nearness and disturbed by it. Why did he have to affect her this way? "I don't want your pity, and I don't need your passion!" she cried. "Leave me alone."

As she quivered with fury and another unnamed emotion, he drew her slowly, unprotestingly into his embrace. "You may not want my pity, but as to the other..."

He lowered his mouth and kissed the silken column of her neck. "Firehair," he breathed softly, as she instinctively threw her head back. He pulled the pins from the bright flaming tangle and let it tumble down.

"No," she gasped, but he took her open mouth, softly at first, then with searing intensity. Her heart raced and every nerve in her body cried out to him. Never had Carrie felt anything like this fire. Hawk's hand roved downward on her back. His need was as obvious as her own, and he growled out an unintelligible word of passion...

Captive The Sun

W9-CLG-280

Also by Shirl Henke

Golden Lady
Love Unwilling

Gone to Texas Trilogy:
Cactus Flower*
Moon Flower*
Night Flower*

Published by
WARNER BOOKS   *forthcoming*

ATTENTION: SCHOOLS AND CORPORATIONS

WARNER books are available at quantity discounts with bulk purchase for educational, business, or sales promotional use. For information, please write to: SPECIAL SALES DEPARTMENT, WARNER BOOKS, 666 FIFTH AVENUE, NEW YORK, N.Y. 10103.

ARE THERE WARNER BOOKS
YOU WANT BUT CANNOT FIND IN YOUR LOCAL STORES?

You can get any WARNER BOOKS title in print. Simply send title and retail price, plus 50¢ per order and 50¢ per copy to cover mailing and handling costs for each book desired. New York State and California residents add applicable sales tax. Enclose check or money order only, no cash please, to: WARNER BOOKS, P.O. BOX 690, NEW YORK, N.Y. 10019.

Capture The Sun

Shirl Henke

WARNER BOOKS

A Warner Communications Company

WARNER BOOKS EDITION

Copyright © 1988 by Shirl Henke
All rights reserved.

Cover design by Barbara Buck
Cover illustration by Max Ginsburg

Warner Books, Inc.
666 Fifth Avenue
New York, N.Y. 10103

W A Warner Communications Company

Printed in the United States of America

First Printing: February, 1988

10 9 8 7 6 5 4 3 2 1

For John and Sylvie Sommerfield,
the best agents and friends
any writer could have.

Acknowledgment

Plot problems are worked out in diverse ways by writers. My associate Carol J. Reynard and I were planting blackberry bushes in her backyard when she untangled a mystery for me and set up the clues for Mathilda Thorndyke to uncover. I had puzzled over how to handle that central plot problem for weeks before Carol supplied me with the answer one sunny afternoon in Michigan.

Our weapons expert, Dr. Carmine V. DelliQuadri, Jr., D.O., moved his search forward thirty years from the 1850s to the 1880s for *Capture the Sun*. The longarms and shortarms handled by gunmen such as Hawk, Kyle, and Caleb had to be the best. Thanks to Carmine, Carol and I are certain that they are.

Author's Note

When I first conceived the story idea for *Capture the Sun*, I was confronted by a series of unique research challenges. I knew only that my half-breed hero must live in a time and place where white civilization, in the form of large cattle empires, clashed with the Indians' free hunting ranges. However, the emergence of the cattle barons usually occurred only after native Americans had either been driven to extinction or had been completely subdued and herded onto reservations. I needed an Indian culture still intact, although menaced by the whites, a tribal society in which a few of the younger members were able to roam and raid.

Having read Mari Sandoz's poetically majestic masterpiece *Cheyenne Autumn*, my natural inclination was to make my hero a Northern Cheyenne. But the Cheyenne, northern and southern, ranged a thousand miles from the Canadian border all the way to the hot country of Nebraska, from which Sandoz's beleaguered protagonists fled. In rereading her book, I discovered that a tiny handful made it back to the Yellowstone country of eastern Montana. I dug into a number of additional sources on the Cheyennes: *Wooden Leg: A Warrior who Fought Custer*, interpreted by Thomas B. Marquis, rich in firsthand narration about Cheyenne life; Edward Adamson Hoebel's *The Cheyennes*, and in collaboration with Karl Nickerson Llewellen, *The Cheyenne Way*, careful, scholarly studies of the complex and highly organized social system of these most impressive of all the Horse Indians of the high plains. By then I had Iron Heart's band fixed in my imagination.

Next, I turned my attention to the villains, the cattle barons. The only place and time when the Cheyenne, with their Sioux allies, coexisted autonomously with a fairly well-developed cattle industry was during the era of the late 1870s and early 1880s in eastern Montana. Granville Stuart, a Yankee, and Conrad Kohrs, a German, were wonderful prototypes for my ruthless cattle barons. The railroad was only then inching its way toward Miles City, Montana, bringing white civilization, and with it, a slightly more organized law and order to replace vigilantism. Men like Stuart and Kohrs manipulated both kinds of justice, or injustice, depending on how one prefers to view history.

I found an excellent resource in the Time-Life Old West Series, *The Cowboys*, text by William H. Forbis. This put me on the trail of several excellent secondary sources dealing with ranch life on the high plains such as *The Rawhide Years* by Glenn R. Vernam and *The Great Range Wars* by Harry Sinclair Drago. The finest primary source on a fascinating man is *Pioneering in Montana*, Granville Stuart's rather sanitized but highly informative account of the foundation of his empire. For delightful anecdotal material on cowboy life and humor, Ed Lemmons's *Boss Cowman* and *The Cowboy Reader*, edited by Lon Tinkle and Allen Maxwell, were superb.

From this rich tapestry of western lore I wove my tale of Hawk the half-breed gunman and Noah Sinclair the ruthless cattle baron, each intent on possessing a spirited and beautiful eastern woman who defied them both. All the characters in *Capture the Sun* are fictional, but they are often based loosely on composites of people who lived in the old Montana Territory, where I found men and women more heroic and more villainous than any sweep of the writer's imagination could ever envision.

PROLOGUE

The Black Hills, 1869

The fierce Dakota sun beat on the tiny willow lodge
that sat isolated in a clearing. Not even a scrub pine
offered shelter, although many grew a scant hundred yards
away. Inside the cramped hut lay a slim youth, his body
glistening with sweat. The narrow confines of the lodge
barely accommodated his long frame as he panted in the
blazing heat. The night would soon bring its cooling
touch, cooling the perspiration on his bare skin until he
shivered. Thus he had waited the past four days, alternately
enduring heat and cold, with no food, no water, no
complaint. Sharp pebbles and twigs bit into his back as he
lay supine, but his mind paid no heed to his body. His
spirit soared far above the low roof, high in the brilliant
blue freedom of the sky.

*This is the fourth day, the last day. It must happen now,
before Grandfather returns at sundown. Perhaps no sacred
vision can come to me.* He forced the disquieting thought
from his mind and drifted back into his semicoma. Once
again his fevered mind pictured the face of his mother,
radiant as she lavished her love upon a small boy. Gradually
her image blurred. When it cleared, she was no longer clad
in a buttersoft buffalo-skin dress. Rather, she wore the stiff
garments of a white woman, with long skirts and cinched
waist. Laughing Woman was gone. In her place stood

1

Marah. Marah, wife of his white father, as full of bitterness as the missionary name she had been given. Her arms slipped from the boy she had held fast only a moment before, leaving him cold and alone. He cried out to her as the vision faded. Her tight *veho* dress seemed to bind her, holding down her arms as they strained to reach for him. She was gone.

Another figure entered his trance. He Who Walks in Sun stood staring intently as if peering into the soul of his only manchild and finding it wanting. Of course, he would always think it so; he always had. Nothing was ever good between them.

The youth shook his head to clear the weight of sorrow from it. Then he tensed. A new figure appeared beside that of the father he could not banish. This one the days and nights of feverish dreaming had never before revealed. She was *veho*, a white for certain, yet supple and slim despite the foolish clothing she wore. Her face was blurred, the features indistinct, but the fiery red of her hair was as brilliant as the rising sun. *Who is she to stand next to my father?* His mind slipped into oblivion once more.

The keening of a Cheyenne death chant—high, thin and clear—reached him in the darkness of sleep. In his mind's eye the strong, lovely face of a Cheyenne woman appeared, imploring him for something—he knew not what. Her liquid eyes were filled with wistful sadness. He groaned as a deep pain crushed his heart, stopping his breath until she vanished from his trance. The death chant faded with her.

He awakened, yet did not stir. He had been forbidden to move from his prone position until the sacred vision came. These troubled nightmares, peopled by his parents and the two unknown women, were not the message from the Powers for which he had fasted and prayed. Time was running out.

Again he sent his mind high, reaching toward the vast clear sky beyond the lodge. He felt the hairs on the back of his neck prickle in anticipation of something that would change him, direct his life, give him his destiny.

Suddenly in the open sky a hawk soared powerfully and effortlessly against the canopy of brilliance. Just as the sun was setting, or rising—he could not tell which—the hunting bird swooped downward to rake its sharp talons through the dense coat of a wolf, leaving deep bloody furrows. Then once more the hawk soared skyward, this time with a newborn wolf cub held alive in its possessive grip. The last thing he saw was the outline of the bird's wings as it flew into the fierce orange rays of the sun.

St. Louis, 1869

Hearing her daughter cry, Naomi Patterson rose and slipped into Carrie's bedroom. The child was having a nightmare, unusual for the sunny-natured, calm seven-year-old.

"Shh, baby, it's only a dream, a bad dream," Naomi crooned, stroking the springy red curls and holding the girl to her breast.

Carrie's eyes widened as she recognized her mother and the familiar room. "Oh, Mama, it was awful! A dog with mean gray eyes was tearing me up, and then a big fierce bird came down, and they wrestled—"

Before she could relate anymore, Naomi interrupted, "It's all right, darling, don't worry. Papa and I will never let any wild animals hurt you. You're safe. Nap time is over. Get up and enjoy the lovely afternoon. Just remember that there are no wild dogs in St. Louis. This is a clean, modern city. You're protected."

Suppressing a hiccup, Carrie let her normally cheerful disposition triumph over the dark dream. She was loved and secure. What could happen on such a beautiful summer day?

The Black Hills, 1869

The old Cheyenne laboriously climbed the hill, then knelt at the opening of the hut. "The four days are ended, my son. What have you learned?"

The face of Iron Heart was strong and seamed with

years, yet handsome in its granite austerity. His eyes mirrored an openness of soul that had won for him his name signifying courage. Now those black eyes looked down expectantly at the awakening youth. The old one never doubted the boy would experience his medicine dream. Others in the band scoffed, saying the Powers would not grant such a blessing to one of mixed blood who lived with the *veho*. Iron Heart knew better.

The boy sat up disorientedly, taking the outstretched hand that pulled his weakened body from the tiny hut. He shivered in the cool air of sunset until Iron Heart placed a robe of soft buffalo hide around his thin shoulders and offered him a drinking horn brimming with water. When he had regained his voice, scratchy and uneven from thirst, the youth told the vision to his patient mentor.

The old man's eyes were shuttered. He was surprised by the description of the stolen wolf cub. That he must ponder. For the rest, it was clear.

"What does it mean, Grandfather? Why would a hawk attack a wolf? Such a thing does not happen." The face was earnest, not yet a man's face, but now more than a boy's.

"What is not real in the world out there," he gestured to the hills surrounding them, "can be quite real inside the soul." He touched his tong-scarred breast. "First consider the he-wolf brought down by the hawk. Was not your father once a killer of wolves?"

The boy nodded uncertainly, always uncomfortable at the mention of He Who Walks in Sun, as the Cheyenne called his golden-haired father. It was true, his father had once been a wolfer, killing the sacred and beautiful animals for their pelts and bounty. But that was long ago when the People were many and the *veho* few. Now he was a wealthy rancher; the whites were many and the Cheyenne few.

"Then who is the hawk who dares hunt the wolf and steal from him?" The boy considered the animal metaphor carefully as his grandfather sat silently, waiting for the youth to supply his own answers. "I am the hawk! I dare to challenge him!" His jet eyes flashed and his nostrils flared as he realized the full implications of his medicine dream. The chiseled features turned hard and shuttered, revealing his Indian ancestry. Yet the arrogance of his expression was an inheritance from his white father rather than from his Cheyenne mother.

Iron Heart nodded in approval. "Yes, you have judged rightly. From this day you shall be called Hunting Hawk."

CHAPTER 1

St. Louis, 1880

"What do you mean, Gerald, you *can't* marry me?" A note of suppressed hysteria sharpened Carrie Patterson's voice while a tinge of color blossomed in her cheeks. The young man sitting next to her in the closed carriage cringed.

"We set the date for this very spring, as soon as you finish your term in medical school. Isn't it a bit late to be getting cold feet?" Carrie pulled her small clenched fists from the larger hands enveloping them and sat stiffly against the leather seat cushion. For several moments the only sound she could hear was the clop-clop of the horse's hooves as the carriage threaded its way through the elegant brick streets of Lafayette Square near her home.

Gerald Rawlins, a tall, slender young man with thick sandy hair and bright blue eyes, nervously cleared his throat. This morning he had finally worked up the courage to confess. He had to get it all out, by damn, and tell her! Of course, Carrie wasn't making it any easier for him. Not that he could blame her. He listened to the monotonous drum of hoofbeats on the bricks, swallowed hard, and took a deep breath. Not daring to look at her bewitching face, he stared straight ahead at the front wall of the coach. He must not weaken now. Patience and Hiram Patterson would never give him a second chance.

"I can't marry you, Carrie, because I have agreed to marry your cousin Charity at the end of summer!" There, it was out. He felt her stiffen and draw in a sudden gasp of breath, but he dared not face the blazing green fire in those eyes.

"Charity! I might have known. She's been making cow's eyes at you since we were sixteen. But why, Gerald? Why? I don't mean to sound vain, but I know I'm better looking than she is." That was certainly true. Carrie was unfashionably tall for the ideal of feminine perfection, but her figure was well proportioned with slim, soft curves, her face delicately sculpted into strong, elegant features. She had dark green eyes and a great mass of red hair that glowed like a living flame when touched by the light. Her cousin Charity was a tan-blonde with watery blue eyes and a dumpy figure.

"Of course, you're beautiful and Charity is, er, merely pleasant." He sighed. Strictly speaking, that wasn't even the truth. God knew Charity's disposition was far from pleasant. It bordered on downright shrewishness when she did not get her way!

Haltingly, Carrie ventured, "Do—do you love her, Gerald?" She turned and looked squarely at his handsome profile.

He still could not meet her eyes. "I fear, my dear, love has little to do with a practical marriage. I must be brutally frank with you, Carrie. When I graduate from St. Louis University Medical School I'll need a good deal of capital to set up a practice. You know how hard it's been, scratching out a bare existence on my inheritance from Grandfather. Well, it's run out now, and I find myself in debt for this past term's expenses. I didn't want to worry you with such gross monetary concerns, but there it is." He flashed the boyish, engaging grin that had always melted women's hearts. It wobbled a bit when he looked at Carrie's face.

"There it is, and there was my Uncle Hiram, I'll just bet! My rich uncle, desperate to marry off his eldest, spinster daughter, never mind if he had to buy a groom, even steal him from his niece! How much, Gerald? How much is it worth to you to endure Charity for the rest of your life?'' Her voice dripped scorn as she valiantly hid the ripping in her heart.

He attempted to take her cold, slim fingers in his grasp and pull her to him, but she stiffened and wrenched away. Then she methodically removed a faultless white kid glove and slipped the small silver ring from her finger. "Here is your ring. My felicitations to you and my cousin. I hope you have joy of her!''

With that she pressed the ring in his palm. The carriage had conveniently stopped in front of the large brick house where the Pattersons lived. Before Gerald could gather his scattered wits, Carrie was pulling on the coach door.

Frantically, without thinking, he blurted out, "Don't leave like this, darling! Let me explain. Oh, Carrie, we can still have a life together. Don't you see? Once I get established and build up a good practice, I'll be a wealthy man. Then I can do as I please. I'll take care of you, Carrie. Charity need never know—''

When the full implication of his rash proposition struck her, she felt ill. With a whimper of frenzied pain, she slapped his pale handsome face with all her strength. Her other hand still held the door latch tightly. Furiously she yanked it open and fairly tumbled out of the coach before the embarrassed driver could assist her.

With Gerald's voice still echoing in the cool March air, Carrie fled toward the sanctuary of the house. She rushed around the side, using the back door, wanting no one to witness her distress. She could well imagine Aunt Patience's satisfied smirk upon seeing her in tears.

"Might as well use the servant's entrance. That's all I am here anyway, an interloper, a surrogate maid to Charity and Faith on Tilda's day off."

Having reached her third-story room without encountering anyone, Carrie lay across her narrow bed. The room was stifling in humid St. Louis summers and freezing in bitter St. Louis winters. Today in the brisk sunny March weather, it was bathed in golden light, enriching the faded wallpaper and the thin bedspread tossed carelessly across a lumpy mattress. Her fingers clenched and unclenched, bunching the scratchy fabric into a mass of unsightly wrinkles. Her thoughts ran riot in confusion and pain.

"Oh, Gerald, how could you? We would have managed together. We didn't need their money, only each other." The hoarse whisper seemed louder than it really was in the still room.

Downstairs in the front parlor, a plump, gray-haired woman stood by a window overlooking the street. Patting a curl on her elaborately coifed but faded hair, Patience Patterson smiled. The malevolence of the expression on her righteous, potato-faced countenance would have shocked even her closest confidants. It was an unmasking she allowed few people to see. Patience, as her name suggested, was a skillful planner, one to outlast the competition. Along with a sizable dowry from her father, that cunning endurance had helped her to snare Hiram Patterson. Now she plotted for her eldest daughter. From the moment Charity had set eyes on the winsome young medical student Gerald Rawlins, she had been smitten. Of course, it had taken some doing to convince Hiram that the penniless youth was worthy of his daughter, but she had managed it. After all, he was a Rawlins, and if sponsored in his profession he could become quite prominent, perhaps the city's leading physician.

After watching her distraught niece flee the carriage in front of their doorstep, Patience was certain Gerald had told the girl of his and Charity's future. It was all working out splendidly! She glided across the floor toward the small cherrywood table in the corner and again perused the letter. Yes, it would happen just as she envisioned last year. Her cousin Noah was coming east for a business trip and a visit. He was also in the market for a wife now that he was free of that terrible Jameson hussy. And, of course, Patience had the perfect wife for him—young, educated, healthy, and most especially, damn her, beautiful!

Patience had watched in growing horror as Carrie matured beside her own daughters, like a blossom among thistles. Where Charity and Faith were short and tended toward plumpness, Carrie was statuesque and slender. While their hair was lank dishwater blond, Carrie's was a riot of fiery bouncing curls. With her green eyes and flawless complexion, she fairly glittered, an outstanding beauty in any roomful of St. Louis belles. Then, too, there was always that air about her, the veiled defiance, the spirit Patience had never completely been able to break. Well, she knew Noah Sinclair, and he would finish what she had started.

He was arriving tomorrow night. It was perfect. She and Hiram would put his suit to Carrie while she was still prostrate over Gerald's betrayal. Patience would take no chance on Carrie's catching any of poor mousey Faith's beaus, nor leading the still-besotted Gerald to disgrace his new fiancée with infidelity. No, she would send Carrie away from her family, to the far reaches of Montana, over one thousand miles distant. Once again Patience read Noah's letter with a triumphal glitter in her lead-gray eyes.

"My dearest Cousin Patience," it read, "I will be arriving on March fifteenth and look forward to meeting your niece. She sounds most adequate for my needs . . ."

Carrie stood in front of the mirror, making a last perusal of her toilette. Her bright hair was piled high on her head in an elegant pompadour with wispy tendrils escaping alongside her high cheekbones. The new dress, a surprising gift from Aunt Patience, fit her to perfection. The moss-green watered silk molded around her breasts and fell simply from the fashionable bustle. Tailored to accent her superb figure, it was the style of dress she loved most.

"I guess it's her token peace offering now that she's won Gerald for Charity." Carrie shrugged, trying desperately to feel some of the light insouciant air she affected. It was no use. She felt used and cheated. Gerald had been her first love, her knight in shining armor, her means to escape the hopeless cold existence of this bleak house. Now all that was ended. Since they had bought off Gerald, what did the Pattersons intend for her? Spinsterhood? No, that would mean Uncle Hiram would have to support her for the rest of her life. Surely his miserly soul could never abide that. Then, what?

As she descended the long flights of stairs to the front hall, Carrie heard voices, her aunt and uncle, her two cousins and another male voice, an unfamiliar one. When Charity had come to tell her to wear her new dress for dinner, a strange light of excitement had shone in her usually lackluster eyes. Was it something to do with this stranger?

Quietly she walked to the walnut sliding doors that divided the front parlor from the hall. The unknown man was tall and lean. Carrie judged him to be around fifty or a little older. She was sure he had once been handsome, but now his face was harsh and bitter, set in cruel lines. His hair was still golden, except for the encroachment of gray at the temples, and his face was darkly tanned by the sun. Fleetingly she compared it to Gerald's blond pallor, Gerald who never ventured outdoors. It was obvious this man had spent a lifetime under a merciless sun.

Her scrutiny was suddenly interrupted when Aunt Patience caught the glimmer of Carrie's bright green gown from the corner of her eye. "There you are, tardy girl." With a falsely fond smile, she glided over to take Carrie's arm and escort her into the big, cluttered room, filled with bric-a-brac and expensive Victorian furniture.

"Carrie, I would like for you to meet my *dear* cousin, Noah Sinclair, from Montana Territory. Noah, here is Carrie." Was there just the faintest touch of veiled meaning in the way she worded the introduction?

Uncertainly, Carrie smiled and made her curtsy. Noah's cold blue eyes seemed to rake her with a scorching fire from head to foot before he spoke.

"I have been looking forward to this meeting for a long time, my dear." The lips smiled, but the glacial eyes did not.

Carrie's puzzlement changed to alarm and a prickly warning inched its way up her spine when she glanced from Noah Sinclair to Charity. Her cousin looked as if she had just been selected Veiled Prophet Queen of 1880, the highest debutante honor in St. Louis. Why should Patience and Charity want this stranger to meet her? Carrie could not remember her aunt ever mentioning a cousin from some godforsaken place in the Far West.

Later that night, as Carrie passed the library on her way upstairs, she heard the voices of her Uncle Hiram and Mr. Sinclair. Dinner had been an agony of strained conversation, with her aunt's cousin contributing little to lighten the tense atmosphere. Charity and Faith were their usual coy, fluttery selves. Noah mostly ignored them, concentrating what little attention he gave to the women on Carrie and Patience. Her aunt's deference to the man was almost nauseating to Carrie.

Sinclair answered questions in monosyllables or with forceful opinions if his interest was piqued by a particular query. When Hiram mentioned the railroad's progress into the West and intimated it could not go as far north as Montana, Noah immediately interrupted to pronounce that a line would be completed to Miles City within the year. Carrie felt that Noah Sinclair was a man well accustomed to getting his way, and probably quite ruthless when crossed.

After a miserable night spent tossing and turning, Carrie awakened early to the sound of hard spring rain dashing against the glass panes of her window. Unable to fall back asleep, she sat up and rubbed her eyes, preparing to arise and slip downstairs for an early breakfast in the kitchen. As often as possible she avoided formal meals with her relatives, preferring the kinder company of the cook and gardener. She especially wanted to avoid Noah Sinclair this morning.

Thinking about him once more, she shivered. All last evening he had watched her, like a wolf stalking its prey. His cold blue eyes took in everything, although he said little to her. She shook her head to drive away the absurd fancy. "Wolf, indeed! He's just a lecherous old man, every bit as unpleasant as his kinswoman. I will simply avoid him until he's gone."

With that she began to dress, donning an ugly gray

muslin gown. Even in her plain wardrobe, it was exceptionally unbecoming. "I certainly don't have to dress for any man's fancy anymore, now that Gerald—" Carrie cut herself off. No self-pity. She was well shut of any man who could be bought, but the ache of betrayal remained.

As Carrie descended the stairs on her way to the kitchen, she heard voices coming from the parlor. The heavy sliding doors were ajar, and Aunt Patience and Noah Sinclair's voices carried into the hall.

"She'll come around quickly enough, Noah. No need to fear. The poor child has just suffered a terrible shock. You see, she was quite infatuated with the young man my Charity is going to marry. When their wedding date was announced the other day, well, it took Carrie rather by surprise. Of course, there was no doubt that Gerald Rawlins would choose my Charity over her! All the more reason for her to be grateful for your suit, Noah. You're here at a most opportune time."

Noah snorted in derision, imagining exactly what had induced a man with normal eyesight to pick that fat tan wren over her flame-haired cousin. "Yes, I imagine my arrival has been timely. The point is, Patience, that I have but a few days before I must leave for Miles City. I can't play the ardent swain. I wasn't interested in doing it thirty years ago, and I'm not about to start now."

"Never fear. After all, while she's prostrate by rejection, she'll be in a receptive mood for a secure match with a wealthy older man. Any young woman with sense and no money would be insane to turn you down! If you want her, she's yours, dear cousin."

"Oh, I want her right enough, Patience."

The slow drawling chuckle that followed left every hair on Carrie's head standing on end. Her breath froze in her throat and her hand clamped on the newel post at the bottom of the stairs. They were plotting for her to marry him! The nerve—the insane, vicious nerve of that woman! Furiously, Carrie drew several breaths to ease her trembling limbs. She must think rationally. Her first impulse was to storm into the room and refuse then and there in front of the conspirators. However, reason quickly prevailed. Aunt Patience would exact terrible revenge for such an unthinkable breach of decorum. No, she would wait until her uncle came home this afternoon and reason with him.

When her parents, Josiah and Naomi Patterson, had been killed five years ago in a riverboat explosion, she had found herself alone and virtually penniless. Her father had invested his wealth none too wisely and had been skirting on the edge of bankruptcy at the time of his death, a fact her aunt and uncle reminded her of all too often. Grudgingly he had taken in the bright, indulged child of his only brother. Although he never took her side against his wife, Carrie was sure her uncle would not expect her to quickly marry a man she had only just met.

"But, Uncle Hiram, you can't be serious!"

The stricken way Carrie's voice broke when she spoke almost made Hiram Patterson weaken. He was rather put off by Patience's cold, arrogant cousin. He could see why the girl did not favor him. But a man must be practical. His investments in the past few years had not been good, and he could not afford the expense of a debut for his wastrel brother's daughter as well as both his own. Then there was the matter of all that money for Rawlins's schooling and setting him up in practice. Damn Patience and her plotting! Rawlins wasn't the son-in-law he needed to take over his bank when he retired. He was furious with his wife, indeed with all women, at the moment. Carrie's tearful pleading was becoming increasingly irksome, and he wanted the interview terminated.

"I'm sorry, my dear, but there's nothing to be gained by this unseemly display. Noah Sinclair has done you the honor of asking you to marry him. He is a very rich man. He'll make a fine husband for you."

"He's old enough to be my father—my grandfather even," Carrie sputtered through her tears. "I don't love him. I don't even know him!"

"It's been my observation that courtships and romantic matches are often ill-fated. You'll get to know him after you're married. It's much more sensible, really."

"Yes, I'll get to know him, thousands of miles away from home, among wild Indians and grizzly bears! Well out of Gerald's reach! That's it, isn't it, Uncle Hiram? You and Aunt Patience want me gone so Gerald won't renege on his bargain! Well, I won't do it. I won't marry Noah Sinclair. You can't make me." She clenched both fists tightly and stood her ground in the big, dusty library.

"Don't be too sure of that, missy!" Patience's voice cut in venomously, causing Carrie to whirl in surprise when her aunt entered the room from the hall doorway. In exasperation she glanced at her husband. "I might have known you couldn't control her, Hiram."

"Now see here, Patience. I told her in no uncertain terms she should be most honored to marry Noah." Hiram's face was florid with anger and his voice raised an octave as he addressed his wife.

"I am not honored, and I won't be sold! You can't do this to me." Carrie stubbornly faced the divided ranks of aunt and uncle.

"Tell her, Hiram! Tell her what will happen if she refuses this generous offer." All the years of jealousy, seeing Carrie's loveliness alongside the homeliness of her own girls, goaded Patience. Now she'd have her revenge.

Hiram's face took on a waxy pallor, in sharp contrast to its reddened tinge of a moment earlier. He gripped the edge of his cluttered walnut desk as if to give himself courage, and then spoke slowly and deliberately. "Either you will marry Noah Sinclair the day after tomorrow or your aunt and I will be forced to disown you. You are penniless, with no other relatives. If we cast you out, no good family will receive you in their home."

"You'll end up a prostitute, down on the levee," Patience put in viciously. "That flashy red hair should make a nice advertisement for your wares!"

Carrie saw black flecks swim before her eyes and had to take a step back, bracing herself against one of the chairs by the window. Patience glided across the room to stand next to Hiram. Together they faced Carrie down, unified now in their heartless purpose.

"Be reasonable, Carrie. You'll be a wealthy widow

someday. There are some benefits to marrying an older man. Noah will leave you well provided for.''

Hiram's calm practicality defeated her even more than Patience's blatant cruelty. There was nowhere to turn. She took inventory of her resources, realizing Patience's assessment of her fate was probably right. No one would take her in if the Pattersons disowned her. She had no skills that could enable her to earn a living. Factories hired only sturdy girls from lower-class families. She couldn't cook or operate a sewing machine. She had an education, but no references with which to get a governess's job. Besides, the disgrace that Patience would heap on her name would effectively bar her from obtaining such work. Carrie had no doubts now that her aunt was capable of the most outrageous lies. No decent employer would hire her. She'd starve or freeze or, worse yet, end up in one of those places her friends from school had whispered about.

"You leave me no choice whatsoever, do you? You may inform Mr. Sinclair I accept his gracious proposal," Carrie forced a glacial smile and then walked from the room like a wooden doll.

During the two days prior to the ceremony, Carrie saw her future husband alone one time. Faith, her fifteen-year-old cousin, came to her room to announce with an irritating titter that Cousin Noah wanted to see her in the library. Dreading the confrontation, Carrie was nonetheless oddly curious about how he would act now that she had succumbed to his proposal.

Carefully she soaked her tear-swollen face with cold towels, refusing to give them the satisfaction of seeing the evidence of her distress. Obdurately, Carrie donned the ugly gray dress once more and braided her hair into a tight bun on the back of her head. Looking much more formidable than she felt, she marched down to the study and knocked on the walnut door. When Noah bade her enter, Carrie took a shaky breath and walked in, carefully closing the door behind her.

She looked for all the world like a cornered fawn, frightened and ready to strike out at anything around her,

Noah thought to himself. He eyed her gray dress with obvious distaste. "If that's a sample of your day dresses, you can leave them all here. I'll buy you better."

One hand went instinctively up to her throat, smoothing the scratchy lace collar as she felt an embarrassed flush creep up her neck to her face. "Since everything has been arranged between you and my uncle, I hardly thought I needed to dress to entice you." The minute the words were out, she could have bitten her tongue. *Stupid girl! This is no way to placate the man who is carrying you off to the wilderness day after tomorrow!*

His sharp bark of laughter caught her off guard. "Good! You do have some spirit. I like gumption in a woman as well as beauty. You were quiet as a churchmouse last night. I assume your presence here means you've accepted my proposal?" When she made no move to affirm or deny the fact, he continued arrogantly, "I could have come, hat in hand, on bended knee and played a lovesick fool, but that's never been my way. Besides, I don't have time for such nonsense. I have to be in St. Paul in a week to close a stock-feed deal, then back home to the Circle S as soon as possible. Speaking very plainly, my dear, I need a wife. You have just been jilted by an impoverished suitor and need a husband to salve your wounded pride. I'm a rich man and prepared to be generous to you."

Carrie's eyes flashed a warning green fire, and she burst forth impulsively, "It's deplorable to buy a husband for a woman as Uncle Hiram did for Charity, yet quite all right for you to buy a wife. Well, I'm not interested in your money."

His face darkened beneath its deep tan and he gripped the crystal glass he held in his hand. Forcing himself to be calm, he spoke in measured tones laced with sarcasm. "I am ever so glad for your assurances that you are no fortune hunter, Carrie. You are educated, bright, and beautiful. I am a man of wealth and influence in Montana Territory, and I want a woman with your qualities. You may be the wife of the next territorial governor." His blue eyes gleamed fiercely as he said the words, evoking a long-cherished dream. "I want a woman to stand by my side who I can be proud of, to give me children, sons to run a ranch bigger than some eastern states. Together, Carrie, we can found a dynasty!''

The intensity of his craggy features and harsh voice seemed to compel a response from her. Yet nowhere in his grandiose plans had he ever mentioned love. A flood of hopelessness washed over her, but Carrie had made a bargain and it was useless to renege now. ''I don't know what to say, Mr. Sin—Noah.'' The name seemed awkward on her lips, but she would get used to it. If he called her Carrie, she would address him as an equal. ''I'm afraid I know nothing about the West, not even where Montana is located.'' She could not bring herself to broach the subject of having children with this stranger, this man more than twice her age.

Smiling tolerantly, Noah walked toward her, his long-legged stride betraying the rolling gait of a man who had spent a lifetime on horseback. ''Montana borders on Canada, the Dakota and Wyoming Territories. It's almost twice the size of Missouri. The journey to my ranch in the southeastern part of the state is over a thousand miles. It'll take us nearly three weeks, including my stopover in St. Paul. So you can see why we have to get on our way soon.''

As he spoke, he guided her to the door. Uneasily she followed his lead, resenting the perfunctory dismissal yet glad to be free of his overbearing company. In one decisive movement he reached in his suit pocket and extracted his wallet. Pulling out a thick sheaf of bank notes, he pressed them into the startled girl's hand, then shoved her out the door with the admonition, ''I expect you to spend it all on some fashionable dresses and other accessories. Do all the shopping tomorrow. I've told Patience what clothes to order for you, but I don't think much of her taste. I'll trust your judgment now that you don't have to answer to her for what you choose, or to Hiram for the cost! Oh, yes, burn that damn gray shroud as soon as you have something to replace it!''

Carrie stood in the hall outside the library, stunned into immobility for a few seconds, staring dumbly at the wad of money held in one slim hand. The nerve of the man! Her shock turned quickly to outrage. He had indeed bought her. Here was tangible proof! Then her fury dissolved in tears of frustration and impotence. What was the use? The rapid shift of emotions that she had just experienced left her exhausted. She trudged limply upstairs and sequestered the money in the bottom drawer of her bureau.

CHAPTER 2

Standing on the deck of the Diamond Jo Line steamship, Carrie Sinclair smoothed the wrinkles from her new peach silk dress and waved spiritlessly to the crowd. As the craft left the shore, she could see Uncle Hiram's tall, paunchy figure standing beside that of his short, plump wife. Both waved in immense relief, overjoyed to have the unwelcome responsibility of their niece taken from them so neatly. Faith's small drab form melted into the press of the crowd as she gave a listless farewell salute to her cousin. Charity and Gerald were attending an afternoon tea at the Rawlins home. Mercifully, Carrie did not have to face her ex-fiance now that she was married to Noah Sinclair.

Noah. For one hour he had been her husband. They had been married with only time enough to rush to the levee and board the big riverboat that would carry them to St. Paul. Nervously, Carrie looked up at him, observing his hawkish profile while he gazed at the receding waterfront. The big steamship strained against the power of the mighty river, slowly propelling itself upstream, north to Minnesota. She was alone, married to this stranger, going to an alien land. Carrie felt powerless, cut adrift like the floating pieces of debris in the muddy waters, swept along with the current. Where was he taking her? How would they deal with one another for the rest of their lives? His harsh features gave her no clue. Other than their one brief and unsatisfactory confrontation in the Patterson study, they had not been alone together until now.

Carrie had spent all day yesterday assembling her trousseau. Her lavish shopping spree had given her some satisfaction. Charity and Faith had acconpanied her, gazing in sullen wonderment and open jealousy as she spent Noah's money. From the perky little feather hat on her head to the soft kid slippers on her feet, Carrie was completely outfitted in the latest fashion. Several trunks were secured below, full of silk dresses, lacy undergarments, handsomely fitted shoes, and sheer night rails.

Noah had indeed been generous, but now as her thoughts turned to the thin batiste gown laid out for her in the cabin, she was gripped by panic. Tonight would be her wedding night, and she knew nothing of what to expect. Her school friends had giggled and exchanged a few whispered remarks in vague terms about *something* that men and women did when they married, but her actual knowledge was nonexistent. Aunt Patience had been far too distant and hostile a figure to approach about such a delicate matter. There was no one else.

All Carrie knew of lovemaking she had learned when Gerald kissed her. The pain of his betrayal still knifed at her dully as she recalled the feverish but brief embraces stolen on carriage rides or in secluded gardens. When he had held her and pressed his lips to hers, she had reveled in the warmth of his dear familiar body. The thought of having a complete stranger take her in his arms was unimaginable. Yet it—and more—would surely happen in only a few hours. Her stomach lurched nauseously, protesting the vibrating of the steamboat deck.

When they were clear of shore, well in the vast main channel of the mighty river, Noah turned his attention to the slim form of his new wife. She looked fragile and ladylike, dressed in a pale peach dress that flattered her porcelain-clear skin and bright hair. She had exhibited natural good taste in her choice of the wedding dress. He felt confident the money he had given her was well spent. This marriage would go as he planned. *It's about time one did*, he thought angrily to himself.

Just then Carrie lifted her eyes to Noah's face and saw his fierce, scowling expression. God, what had she done now! Seeing her uncertain look, he suddenly smiled and took her hand in his, leading her toward the interior of the elaborate sternwheeler. As they walked, he spoke.

"I must commend your taste, if this gown is a sample of what you purchased, especially considering the short time you had for shopping."

"I—I'm glad you like it. You were most generous."

She felt so stiff and unnatural conversing with him. Outside their wedding vows, she had had only a few perfunctory exchanges with him about the logistics of moving their luggage aboard the boat earlier in the day. What did you say to a new husband during your wedding supper, just before he took you to bed? Noah seemed not to mind her reticence; nor was he especially interested in talking himself. She had heard westerners were boisterous braggarts who loved to spin tall tales. Her husband was obviously an exception.

Yet she felt compelled to make an attempt to know him, to have some idea of what her future with him held. She knew only that he was a wealthy rancher involved in territorial politics. At age fifty, surely he must have been married before. When did his first wife die? Were there any children? What was his ranch like? Was the house primitive or comfortable? Were there savage Indians nearby? Her mind reeled as the realization sunk in: *I am married to a man I know virtually nothing about*. Preoccupied, Carrie ignored the breathtaking, high-ceilinged room with its elegant clerestory windows and deep Persian carpets. Noah had chosen the most comfortable and ostentatious steamboat on the St. Louis–St. Paul run, but Carrie was in no frame of mind to appreciate the selection.

Noticing her disoriented manner, Noah assumed it was a combination of tiredness from the hectic past few days and virginal fearfulness about the night to come. He smiled tolerantly, anticipating her initiation into the physical delights of marriage. There was no doubt of her innocence. He had Patience's assurance, and she would never risk crossing him with such a deception.

"Why don't I have a steward show you to our stateroom so you can rest and freshen up? I'll be down to escort you to dinner at seven." He looked at her with a smiling face and deliberately kept his tone of voice solicitous.

However, Carrie decided something in his eyes was not right. They were cold and gleaming, almost feral. She forced a return smile and nodded in acquiescence, grateful to escape and collect her thoughts.

I'm being fanciful, like a fifteen-year-old schoolgirl. Oh, damn, I just don't want it to be him, *that's all.* Carrie's thoughts skittered in all directions as she lay on the bed in their spacious cabin.

For a riverboat stateroom it was quite large—nearly fourteen feet square with gleaming brass lights and rose velvet-flocked wallpaper. Thick carpets repeated the muted rose tones combined with soft deep blues. The delicate French Provincial dressing table was set against a huge mirror. However, none of the opulence of the room consoled Carrie.

Tonight she must share this bed with Noah Sinclair. Forcing herself to confront her fears, Carrie acknowledged the undeniable facts. *I made the bargain; now I have to make it work. I must stop imagining things and make an effort to get to know him. Once I do, things will look better.* She recalled one of her father's most cogent lessons to her as a child: Nothing is as bad as the unknown. Face any fear and it will never be as terrible as cowardly imagining. Upon rising, she began to dress for dinner.

When Noah opened the door and found her waiting in the stateroom, his earlier feelings about her innocent loveliness were doubly confirmed. Carrie had chosen a dinner gown of rich gold satin, with a somewhat fuller skirt than current fashion dictated. The low décolletage was quite dramatic on her tall, willowy frame. The color picked up amber flecks in her eyes and the fiery glow of highlights in her hair. She wore her only good jewelry—a small pendant and drop earrings of topaz. They matched the gown perfectly and their very simplicity added an aura of innocence to balance the creamy swell of bosom and the sophistication of the dress. Her hair was piled high on her head, with a few artful curls tumbling onto one shoulder.

Noah studied her from head to foot with a harsh, possessive stare. "You're beautiful." His voice was surprisingly hoarse. Then he extended his arm as she murmured her thanks and placed her slim pale hand on his expensive broadcloth sleeve.

After they were seated at a table with a splendid view of the river, Carrie looked around the elegant dining room. Dazzling white damask tablecloths covered the round tables, with crystal bud vases gracing every one, each filled with a delicate blood-red rosebud. The ornate silver and fine bone china gleamed in the flicker of the lights. The room gave the illusion of endless space. Every wall was covered with mirrors, and the dark woodwork was ornately carved and lustrous.

For the first time since embarking on the journey, Noah felt his new wife was aware of the magnificence of her surroundings. "The food is as superb as the decor. I've traveled with the Diamond Jo line often. Do you like it, Carrie?"

Hearing her name on his lips gave her a soft flush of unexpected pleasure. Here was her opening. She must draw him out so they could really talk.

"It's beautiful beyond anything I've ever seen, Noah. I—I've been rather preoccupied, I guess, since we boarded. I didn't mean to be rude or unattentive, please believe me. It's just that . . . well, we really know so little of one another. Could—could we try to become acquainted . . . on our honeymoon, I mean?" She hated her voice. It broke and quavered in all the wrong places, making her seem girlishly immature.

Noah smiled and nodded, patronizingly it seemed to Carrie. "All right, my dear. Tell me about yourself. I can see you have good taste in clothes. The topaz jewelry is lovely. Was it your mother's?" Considering its insignificant value, Noah cynically surmised it was allotted to Carrie by Patience, whose greed for expensive jewelry would have left nothing of any real worth for her niece.

Carrie's face lit up. "Yes, these belonged to my mother.

I have only a few things left, but I dearly love them." She fingered the frail chain across her delicate collarbone as she spoke. Briefly, sparing his kinswoman much, Carrie told Noah of her life since she was a thirteen-year-old girl come to live with Patience and Hiram. Considering how sheltered her life had been, and considering how much of her aunt's behavior she had to omit, Carrie felt her discourse sadly brief and colorless. She said nothing of Gerald either, assuming Patience had told Noah everything about her infatuation with that fortune hunter.

He asked few questions and seemed only moderately interested in her simple narration. Still, she felt a desperate need to continue their first real conversation.

"Have you lived out West all your life?" There was a long pause, as if Noah was weighing his words before he replied. Carrie fidgeted nervously as their soup course was faultlessly served by two waiters.

"I came to Montana Territory with my younger brother Abel about thirty years ago—from Tennessee. Just a kid wanting to make my fortune. There was a gold strike in 1852. We hit a pretty good vein, but after getting a small stake, it played out. For a while we bought trail-worn horses and cattle from settlers heading west, fattened them up, and resold them to others coming later. We roasted charcoal, did some blacksmithing. Anything to make cash money. Got together a good amount—hoarded it actually. Then we bought prime stock and staked out the land that became Circle S. From there on it was pure hellish work to get where I am today."

Carrie intuited he left out so much more than the brief sketch told. "Is your brother at your ranch?"

Noah's face closed over abruptly, and he said in a flat voice, "Abel was killed by Crow Indians twenty years ago. Don't let's talk about it anymore."

Carrie flushed, feeling both sorry and embarrassed for bringing up painful memories. "Tell me about the Circle S."

Noah finally warmed to the subject, describing the unimaginable distances in the basin, the tens of thousands of cattle from Oregon crossbred with newer Hereford and

shorthorn stock. He described the main house of stout oak
and ash, built sixteen years ago. It sounded spacious and
comfortable.

The question almost asked itself, ''You must have built
such a lovely house for a family. Were you married
before?''

If the question about his dead brother was met with
reticence, this was met with stony silence. The seconds
seemed to tick into infinity as Carrie watched Noah carefully wipe his mouth with a snowy napkin, meticulously
set it on the tableside, and then regard her with a glacial
stare that fairly pinioned her to the chair.

''You are young. For that I will forgive you this once for
such a breach. Never again inquire about any predecessors, Carrie. Considering my age, obviously I've been
married before. I was not married when I met you. That is
all that need be your concern. That and the fact that I
require an heir. You, my dear, are here to see to that rather
significant matter. Now, shall we enjoy the main course?
The beef is done to a turn and quite superb, I assure you.''

The waiter approached the table, bearing a huge silver
tray, redolent with prime beef ribs. They were well done,
not pink as Carrie preferred. Noah seemed to relish the
overcooked meat, but Carrie ate mechanically, drinking
more freely of the accompanying red wine than was her
wont.

His cold dismissal earlier had cut her to the quick, but
even more, she was frightened by his unwillingness to
share with her anything of his personal life. All he cared
about was an heir for his cattle kingdom, and she was his
breeding heifer, his brood mare, his . . . Her mind choked
back the repugnant thoughts even as her throat choked
back the badly overdone beef. She reached again for the
wineglass. What was happening to her? Where was she
heading? A blackish light reflected off the crosscurrents of
the river outside her window, swirling downward, ever
downward.

The room was barely lit. Only the dim flicker of a
bedside candle broke the quiet—that and Carrie's painful

breathing. She lay tense and shivering, trying desperately to force her unwilling limbs to relax. Just then Noah entered the chamber. He had waited for her to disrobe, allowing for her expected virginal modesty. She was safely tucked under the covers of the large bed.

Wordlessly, he strode over to the bedside and began to undress with precise care, laying his suit coat and pants over the chair. The soft rustling of garments caused Carrie's eyes to wander in spite of her terror. She could barely catch sight of Noah from the corner of her eye without turning her head to stare openly, an unthinkable breach of decorum! When she saw him turn to gaze on her, she closed her eyes tightly. Even then, she could feel his patronizing amusement as he continued the methodical strip, silk shirt rustling, underwear unsnapping.

Noah finally pulled back the heavy covers cloaking Carrie and knelt with one knee on the bed. She jerked her eyes open abruptly when the cold air hit her through the thin batiste fabric of her night rail. Then, quite unintentionally, she looked at his naked flesh. He was darkly tanned from the waist up, and pale below. His whole chest was covered with thick gold-gray hair that traveled from his tanned skin to the lighter area below, where she did not allow her eyes to dwell. His flesh was corded with long, sinewy muscles, yet his midsection was paunchy, showing the effects of the recent years' indulgence in food and liquor. The thickness looked strangely indecent on such a spare frame. The dim uneven candlelight seemed to bounce off the harsh contours of his face, accenting every line and sag. When he climbed onto the bed and bent over her, the loose skin of his belly seemed to hang suspended.

Carrie shivered anew. *He's really old*, her mind registered in shock! Disguised in expensively tailored clothes, his body was quite presentable, but now every harsh year of frontier life seemed etched on his flesh.

Noah looked down at her pale, frozen face. Ignoring her innocent state of nerves, he drank in her youthful beauty. Slowly he ran a calloused hand from her shoulder to her slim flank, relishing the swell of breast and narrowing of waist. He could see through the sheer white cotton garment. Her skin was milky with pink nipples and bright red fur at the junction of her legs. His breath caught, then accelerated. This was going to be good, better than he had imagined even. Dimly he heard Carrie speak through his thickening haze of lust.

"I—I don't know what to do, Noah." Her eyes were wide and so dark green they looked liquid black, like the river at night.

"I should hope you don't! That's to be expected. I'm the one who'll do what needs to be done. All you have to do is lay back and let me . . ." He let out a soft hiss of pleasure as he pulled up the hem of her gown and caressed a long, elegant leg.

"Take that gown off." It was said rapidly in a flat, commanding voice, hoarse with a desire Carrie could neither understand nor reciprocate.

Blushing in humiliation and feeling like a filly on the auction block, she knelt awkwardly and pulled the night rail off, tossing it quickly on the floor, then sat huddled in the center of the bed while he looked at her. She could not meet his icy-blue gaze, but she could remember those eyes and feel them sear her flesh, like branding a calf on a roundup. Bits of their dinner conversation about the ranch came back to her idiotically now. *I'm your wife, not one of your cows*, she wanted to cry out. But she did nothing, choking in silence, awaiting his next move.

He stared at the proud uptilted young breasts, the breathtaking curve of her slim spine covered by the blazing tangle of hair hanging down her back. He took a fistful of curls, raising her to her knees. Then he moved nearer as he drew her into an embrace.

The contact of their bodies was shocking to Carrie. He felt strangely cool against her flesh, and his sinewy frame scratched and tickled her soft skin. He toppled them both abruptly back onto the length of the bed, crushing the air from her lungs when his long, heavy body rolled on top of her. She could feel the pressure of his paunch against her ribs and something else below, hard and probing. Carrie closed her eyes and struggled to remain calm, to catch her breath as he thrashed about. His hands and mouth pillaged everywhere, rapidly, roughly. Then he quickly reached between her legs and she flinched. Some instinctive subliminal intuition told her what would happen next as he pushed her legs apart and guided himself to enter her. At first it was only a humiliating pressure, then suddenly, as he broke through her maidenhead, pain blossomed deep inside her body.

Noah was aware of the sharp gasp from her and felt the tearing. Good, she was as pure as she seemed! He gloated while he plunged in again and again, losing himself in swift, intense pleasure.

It was over quickly, at least there was that. When he groaned and rolled away from her to lie panting on his back, spread-eagled across the bed, Carrie tried to cover herself with the tangled sheets. He seemed oblivious of her now. She lay very still, willing the shivers of revulsion to abate. The wounding, tearing soreness would not go away so easily. This coupling had been rough and cold, devoid of love. Could there be no love, ever?

Carrie lay dry-eyed and frozen when Noah finally reached over and doused the candle. Then he pulled the covers over his lower body, paying no further attention to his wife. *Best to let a shocked virgin cool her indignation. Damn shame good women have to be so wooden. Give me a good whore for fun anyday, but a wife—that's another matter. Well, she'll never be a lively piece in bed, but then, I can fill that need elsewhere. At least she won't laugh at me or compare me to other men, like Lola did.* Silently he cursed that bitch and then turned his thoughts to the young beauty lying next to him. He'd have her breeding in a month or two, damn him if he wouldn't! On that positive note, he fell into a deep dreamless sleep while Carrie watched the dark reflections of the Mississippi ebb and flow against the ceiling.

Noah was always an early riser, and the day after his wedding was no exception. He looked down at his sleeping wife. Her eyes were darkly shadowed and her face pale. He had slept soundly and was unaware that she lay awake for hours. Considering how childlike and frail she looked now, he decided to let her rest for a while. No reason to tax her too much too soon. He must school himself to be patient and let her become accustomed to his ways. *Once she's pregnant, she'll be content, and then I can turn my attentions to other matters,* he thought complacently. Quietly he left the room.

Hearing the door click, Carrie awakened, as if climbing out of a dank, menacing cave. She was disoriented as only an exhausted and depressed person can be. Gradually, the previous night came back to her. She shuddered, then sobbed aloud, letting the dam break on the roiling emotions she had held in check for the past several days.

I am married to a coldhearted stranger whose bed I must share each night. Oh, it was so rough and degrading. How could I ever have thought . . . Her thoughts dissolved in a startled gasp of pain when she slid across the bed to put her feet on the floor. He had hurt her! When she gingerly stood up and looked at the faint smears of blood on the sheets, she whitened. A quick examination of her gown told the tale of their origin.

"I must have a bath! Oh, God, I have to be clean!" As if someone had read her mind, there was a discreet tap on the door. Carrie answered, "Who is there?"

"Steward, ma'am. Your husband requested hot bath water and a tub. We've brought them."

In a few short moments Carrie was blissfully luxuriating in the hot scented water, restoring her bruised and torn flesh. Youth imparts a certain resiliency, and Carrie found she possessed more of that quality than she had ever suspected. Once she took inventory of her body and assured herself that she would mend, her mind turned to her benefactor. Well, at least he had been thoughtful enough to send the bath. She was grateful, but she was also apprehensive of the coming night.

Maybe it wouldn't be so bad if I could learn to care for him. Perhaps it isn't just the difference in our ages. Even if I'd married Gerald I might have been just as unhappy with . . . bed. Even in her innermost thoughts Carrie couldn't bring herself to say the word "sex," and she could certainly see no reason to call it "making love"!

If only she'd had a female confidante. Her aunt's mores had given her the notion that women weren't supposed to enjoy sex. Perhaps they *could* not do so even if they were base enough to try.

However, Carrie remembered her parents and how much they had loved one another. When she had believed herself in love with Gerald Rawlins, she had certainly enjoyed his kisses. Love. That must be the key to it all. If there could be love, then even if the physical aspect of marriage was not enjoyable, it might at least be bearable.

By the time she had finished bathing and dressing for the morning, Carrie's resolve was firm. Noah had been considerate in sending the bath. It was a good sign. She would just have to try harder to breach his defenses, to learn what he was like, to learn to love him. If she could do that, might he not learn to love her as well?

Eagerly she looked in the mirror to check her toilette one last time. Her face was a trifle pale, but her fiery hair was piled elegantly high on her head in a sophisticated style that made her look older. Her dress of tan silk trimmed in brown satin was tasteful and beautifully tailored. The matching chocolate hat, slippers, and parasol completed a picture of refinement. Yes, she would do, Carrie decided.

"At least I have the wardrobe to impress him. If he likes the way I look and dress, it's a beginning." Firmly she opened the door and stepped outside into the bright promise of midmorning sunlight.

When Noah saw Carrie moving along the railing, he started to intercept her, then stopped to admire the picture she made and the way the people around her reacted. Male passengers looked with open admiration and women with ill-disguised jealousy. Small wonder. The sun highlighted the dazzling fire of her hair like living tongues of flame, flashing out from beneath her hat. Her delicately sculptured brows arched above bright green eyes, and her pink lips parted in a generous smile as she nodded graciously to fellow passengers. The warm tan and brown tones of her ensemble accented her exotic coloring, enriching the pale ivory complexion and warm red hair.

*Just wait till the cattle barons in Miles City see her. I
could take her to the governor's mansion or even Washington.*
Once more Noah congratulated himself on his choice of an
aristocratic and refined woman to stand by his side. Yes,
she would do, Noah decided.

Carrie watched her husband stride across the crowded
deck toward her, wending his way by the passengers who
were enjoying the invigorating spring sun. He looked
robust and commanding as his strong white teeth flashed a
striking smile. She returned it.

Through breakfast they chatted of inconsequential things.
He told her more about Montana, the ranch, and Miles
City, which was the nearest town of any size. It was easy
to get him to discuss his empire.

"You'll like Montana, Carrie. It's a land of men who'll
appreciate a woman of your obvious breeding and refinement. Real ladies are still rare and treasured. I'll be proud
to show you off as my wife."

The words were superficially meant as a compliment,
she was certain; however, Carrie couldn't help but feel
there was an underlying proprietorial tone to his voice that
made her uneasy. Before she reconsidered it, she spoke
out, "I'm only human, Noah, and not all that refined,
really. I'd like to be your helper, your companion, someone you could learn to love. I don't want to be on a
pedestal—"

Before she could go on, he fixed her with a stern glare
while that patronizing schoolmaster look came over his
face once more. "Love." He fairly sneered the word.
"Let me make one thing clear in that vacant, beautiful
little head of yours, my darling. Love is for moonstruck
boys and flighty old ladies. It's a myth. A wife need only
be concerned with providing heirs for her husband and
acting as his gracious hostess. In return for your loyalty
and duty to me, I'll provide handsomely for you. I'll see to
your every material need and leave you and our children
well provided for when I die. Forget the love nonsense and
accept what I offer you—a fine social position, wealth,
comfort, security. That's what life is really about."

Carrie sat very still during his discourse, trying to

discern some cause for the bitterness she sensed in his cold, logical proposition. "Have you never loved anyone?" She couldn't seem to stop herself as she whispered the question.

Noah looked exasperated for a second. Then he paused briefly and considered. "Never the romantic dribble you're thinking of. When a man spends a lifetime on the frontier building an empire to bequeath to his descendants, he is forced to give up some things. All the people I cared for died long ago. I'm too old to begin again. Don't ask that."

Sadly, she looked at his piercing blue eyes and harsh expression. "I'll have to accept your terms in other words. But if—if we have children, they'd need a father's love . . ." She let her words trail off, uncertain and embarrassed to be discussing such a personal thing, recalling the night they had just shared.

"I shall do my best to be a dutiful father, Carrie. But first, you shall have to be a fruitful wife, won't you?"

Something in his tone of voice was even more lewd than the veiled suggestion about her fertility. She felt patronized and cheapened beyond measure. Her temper, repressed for years in Patience's house, flared now. "How dare you! I'm not some piece of livestock—a . . . a horse!"

Noah was out of patience and determined to quickly bring this romantic fencing of hers to an abrupt end. "Ah, yes, my dear, you are precisely that—a brood mare—to be well ridden!"

Carrie blanched, both appalled at his crudity and devastated at his cruelty. She could not meet his eyes. Gripping her coffee cup securely in both hands, she raised it to her mouth and took a steadying gulp of its scalding strength. So, she would be his ornament and his brood mare, the two "duties of a lady." How foolish she had been to quest for love.

CHAPTER
3

After the humiliating setdown from Noah that morning, Carrie confined herself to their cabin for the duration of the day. Noah demanded a command performance for dinner at the captain's table that evening. Her withdrawn, spiritless demeanor when he came to their stateroom made him furious, as did her simple light-blue muslin gown with the sprigged embroidery around its high collar.

"Take off that washed out, fluffy, little girl's dress and wear something with class." He ran his long fingers rapidly across her gowns, hanging neatly in their narrow wardrobe by the bedside, and produced a brilliant turquoise silk. It had long, tapered sleeves and was cut very low in front, with sparkling jet beads trimming the bustline, waist, and skirt. The dress was so daring and sophisticated that Carrie had decided not to buy it, but a clever saleswoman must have seen the same potential Noah did, for she had convinced Carrie it was perfect for her.

With his eyes boring into her trembling body, she stripped off the simple blue and donned the turquoise. When her fingers fumbled nervously with the buttons, he perfunctorily turned her around and efficiently fastened them up the back. She endured his ministrations silently.

"I will not present a sullen, spoiled child as my wife at the captain's table tonight. You will act like a refined, gracious woman." He finished the buttoning and turned her around, holding her shoulders in his hands, willing her to face him.

His fingers felt like claws, she thought in revulsion as she forced herself to look at his face and acknowledge his command with a nod. The tenor of their relationship for the duration of the trip seemed set from that moment on.

Noah had not exaggerated the length nor arduous nature of the journey. The comforts of the steamer were soon forsaken for a brief overnight stay in St. Paul, Minnesota, the end of the Diamond Jo Line's run upriver. Carrie spent a lonely day sitting in a plush silk chair by the window of their hotel room, overlooking the rushing currents of the mighty river she had just left. She wanted desperately to float back south to St. Louis—but to what? Home was lost to her now. Really it had been lost when Naomi and Josiah had died five years earlier. She must continue her rocky journey with Noah Sinclair to his distant kingdom. He concluded his business the following day and finally deigned to take her out for dinner.

The next morning they boarded a Northern Pacific Railroad car for Dakota Territory. It was noisy, jarring, and unbelievably dirty. After a scant few hours of inhaling thick, sooty coal smoke, Carrie knew she'd never be clean again. The windows of the passenger cars had to be opened for ventilation, but the soot from the train's engine whipped inside and enveloped everyone, allowing little freedom to breathe.

The physical misery of her passage west was compounded by psychological pain inflicted by her husband. Whenever they were permitted the privacy of a night's rest in a stopover hotel or roadhouse, Noah insisted on bedding her, coldly and perfunctorily, almost as if it was an onerous task. She endured his attentions woodenly, in aching exhaustion. It seemed to Carrie that he derived more satisfaction from breaking her spirit than he did from his sexual release in her flesh. Whatever his motivation, she was being defeated.

After a grinding five days on the train, they were forced to resort to stagecoach for the last days of the journey into Montana. The rails had not been laid that far yet. Baths in wayside inns were crude, skimpy affairs at best. The beds were lumpy and frequently inhabited by lice and other even less appealing creatures. After two weeks on the road, her body was abused and sore, her mind numb.

In the past few weeks Carrie had taken in more than her sheltered eighteen years allowed her to assimilate. The vast distances of the Dakotas awed and cowed her secure Midwestern sensibilities. At the far western edge of the territory the jagged peaks of the Black Hills stood like sentinels defying invaders. This was the sacred medicine land of Sioux and Cheyenne, Mandan and Blackfoot. Its wild stark beauty both frightened her and called to her, as if from some strange, long-forgotten dream. She shivered uneasily as she looked out the window, wishing they were safely at the Circle S. *At least I'll be safe from savage red Indians there*, she thought, trying to find some consolation in her plight.

The night they arrived in Miles City, Carrie was too exhausted to even notice the bustling little cow town. Noah helped her from the coach and headed straight for the Excelsior Hotel, where he'd wired ahead for rooms. The young clerk's eyes widened in surprise at Mr. Sinclair's beautiful wife, obviously an easterner and obviously much younger than the cattle baron. No one in town had been told that Mr. Sinclair was getting married while he was in St. Louis. Respectfully the clerk, Jubal Akin, led them to the best room in the house, holding his curiosity at bay. Noah was too tired to take her that night. Carrie was grateful, and they both slept soundly.

The next morning, while Noah and Carrie were finishing breakfast in the hotel dining room, a tall, lanky man with leathery dark skin and a startling shock of snowy-white hair ambled gracefully toward their table. He was dressed in range gear, expensive but well worn, and carried a lethal-looking gun on his hip. When Noah saw him, he motioned curtly for the stranger to approach their table.

"Frank, figured you'd be here right on the dime."

The thin man's long, callused hand grasped Noah's outstretched one, and his bright blue eyes crinkled at the corners. "I had ta ride out afore th' nighthawks come in ta git here on th' dime." He let out a chuckle, and the toothy smile he gave Carrie made a startling white slash in his dark, angular face.

Carrie never had seen such a dazzling set of teeth. Frank gave his full attention to the beautiful young woman seated at the table, almost ignoring Noah. Flourishing his hat in one hand, he bowed in a rough facsimile of chivalry.

"Ma'am, welcome ta Circle S country." His wide smile was infectious, and Carrie found herself returning it.

"This is my general foreman, Frank Lowery, Carrie. Frank, meet my bride, Mrs. Sinclair from St. Louis." Possessively, Noah rested his hand on her shoulder as he made the introductions.

Forgetting the weight of his grip, Carrie found herself drawn to her husband's contemporary. Unlike the majority of people on their long journey who were openly curious about the May-December honeymooners, Frank's shrewd but kindly gaze reassured her and asked no questions.

As she rode on the bumpy supply wagon to the Circle S, Carrie listened attentively while Noah and Frank discussed the operation of the ranch. Before they left town, Frank and four Circle S hands loaded up the big rig with what seemed to Carrie enough food staples and seeds to supply an army garrison. One of the young cowboys, Hank Allen, was assigned to drive the wagon on which Carrie was a passenger. Noah and Frank rode close alongside and the other three men took up the rear. Were they guards? Nervously she asked the shy youth who drove if there was any danger from Indians.

He grinned. "Nope, ma'am. Nearest Cheyennes is over 'cross th' basin now. They move around a mite, but they's peaceful. Onliest one's givin' trouble lately is Sioux, and they's north mostly, in Canady."

His answer, rather than reassuring Carrie, alarmed her, since it was obvious the territory was aswarm with various tribes, all of them in a state of perpetual migration.

If only Montana were not so big, Carrie thought in awe. The limitless sky stretched off the far horizons in every direction, its blinding azure melded into the fresh-kissed

green of the prairie grasslands. There seemed no shelter,
no place to hide in the thin clear air of the high plains. It
was utterly alien to Carrie, who had been brought up in the
mud-rich humidity of the Mississippi River Basin. The
vegetation here was as different from Missouri as the
topography. Buffalo grass grew tall and wild, incredibly
thick and hearty despite the extremes of heat and cold,
drought and flood. Even the sparse outcroppings of conif-
erous trees stretching to reach the dome of heaven were
taller and starker than those back home. It seemed as if
everything in nature here was larger than life, as if all the
hilly, gentle greenery of the lower Midwest was merely
pretty stage scenery compared to the titan landscape of
Montana.

Bunches of fat cattle grazed randomly, sprinkled across
the undulating plains. Carrie noticed that they were shorthorned and thickly built, not at all like the wild, stilt-
legged longhorns she had seen pictured in books. She
decided to put her feelings of misgiving aside and learn
something of her new home. "Are these cattle longhorns?
They don't look like the drawings in my books."

Hank turned to her and grinned. "No, ma'am, them's
scraggeldy tough critters, pure mean, 'n' all horns 'n' tails.
Texas's where they run. Montana cattlemen mostly raise
good shorthorn breedin' stock, lots o' it from Oregon,
some from as fer east as Ohio."

"I've never seen so many herds of cows, all running
loose. There must be a lot of ranchers around here,
although I've not seen a barn or house since we left Miles
City." Carrie scanned the horizon. "How soon until we
reach Circle S land?"

Hank looked mildly surprised, then considered that she
was a tenderfoot. "Been on it fer th' past couple o' hours,
ma'am. All them cows is Mr. Noah's. Hisn's th' biggest
spread in th' eastern part o' Montana Territory. We'll be at
th' big house by sundown, never fret. Guess yore a tad
tired from all this bumpin' 'round. A horse's a lot easier
than this hard seat."

Carrie flushed, feeling as out of place as a carpetbagger
at a cotillion. "I'm afraid I'm consigned to the hard

wooden seat, at least for now. I never learned to ride a horse.''

If she had told the boy she never learned to walk, she couldn't have produced more amazement. Lordy, what a greenhorn the boss had brought west! But then again, she was so nice and pretty, Hank thought he would purely love to teach her to ride, yessiree.

When they arrived at the main ranch house toward evening, Carrie was much surprised to see how large and handsome it was. Even Noah's boasting had not prepared her for this gleaming whitewashed structure. The house contained at least a dozen rooms, she guessed as her eyes spanned the wide two-story porch that ringed the front and both sides. Rustling aspens and oaks shaded the beautiful structure from the warm spring sun.

Both Noah and Frank watched Carrie's face. Frank was pleased that the quiet, sad young woman liked her new home. He sensed something was amiss between her and his employer, but was too discreet to ask. Noah's chest swelled with pride for the grandeur of the edifice to which he brought his bride.

"If yew like th' outside, jist wait till yew git an eyeful o' th' inside!" Frank said as he dismounted and assisted Carrie down.

Still stunned by the elegance of the house in the midst of such primitive wilderness, Carrie nodded, anxious to see what lay within.

Noah appeared quickly by her side to take her arm and usher her up the wide front steps onto the deep porch and then in the front door. The interior was as Frank had intimated—startlingly beautiful. Thick Turkish rugs lay on the polished hardwood floors in the long entry hall. Pale blue-and-gold French wallpaper blended in with the deeper colors of the carpet. Off to the left, beyond a gleaming dark oak door, left partly ajar, lay the front parlor with delicate Queen Anne furniture. To the right was the formal dining room, dominated by a long dark oak table and carved sideboard. Crystal candlesticks were set with fat honey-colored candles on both massive pieces of furniture. A huge glass-faced breakfront full of delicate china was barely visible on the far wall. Carrie had thought Hiram and Patience's house in St. Louis grand! By comparison with this, it was merely vulgar.

Immediately Carrie knew a woman had decorated this place. But who? Whoever, she had exquisite and expensive taste.

Noah let Carrie stand in awe for a brief moment and then began to speak. "You'll want the grand tour, I'm sure, after we see if the staff is prepared for us."

Before he could say more, a reedy, tall woman dressed severely in brown appeared at the end of the long hall. Her face was pinched and angular, and her dark gray-streaked hair was pulled tightly into a knot on top of her head, as if the tightly pinned hairdo could tauten up the lines of age in her harsh face. She did not smile as she welcomed her employer and his bride.

"This is Mrs. Thorndyke, my housekeeper. You'll find her a trusted and invaluable paragon of many skills. She keeps all the domestic workers doing their jobs efficiently. Mrs. Thorndyke, my wife."

"I'm pleased to welcome you to the Circle S, Mrs. Sinclair." Her flat tone of voice and cold gray eyes seemed to be anything but pleased or welcoming.

Carrie instantly sensed she had an enemy, but had no idea why. Before she could frame a reply, the housekeeper dismissed her from her attention and turned to Noah with a blaze of anger in her eyes. "You should know, Mr. Noah, *he* is back. Rode in only minutes before you."

Noah paled and then swore in amazement. "Damn, if I didn't think the son of a bitch was dead down in the Nations! Where is he now, Mathilda?"

"I'm not sure. You know how quiet and secretive he is. I guess he went up to his old room."

Carrie observed the exchange silently, trying to make sense of it. Before she could glean anything, Noah turned to her abruptly.

"Go and make your own inspection of the downstairs, Carrie. I have to attend to this first. Then I'll join you." With that he began to climb the steep, thickly carpeted steps at the side of the hall while Mathilda Thorndyke vanished like a specter.

Well, since I'm deserted, I will look on my own, she thought, glad to be free of the hostile older woman. As if Noah wasn't enough to adjust to, she was also to be faced with a phalanx of loyal and jealous servants! As she stepped into the parlor, Carrie was once more enchanted by the lovely silk damask chairs and elegant sofa. "I wouldn't have chosen blue, but it is tastefully done," she murmured aloud to herself, running one hand along the back of a carved rosewood chair beside the heavy marble mantel.

"You're right, blue doesn't suit you, but Lola was blond, and she picked the color."

Carrie gasped at the low, gravelly voice that spoke so softly behind her. She whirled to confront a man standing in the big oak doorway. He was very tall, nearly filling the high doorframe as he lounged negligently against the sash for a minute, then uncoiled to glide silently into the room.

At once she knew this stranger was the "he" Noah and Mrs. Thorndyke spoke of. He was very dark-skinned, with shoulder-length blue-black hair that fell across his high forehead, shadowing deep-set jet eyes and thick black brows. His cheekbones were high and his nose long and straight with full, handsomely sculpted lips beneath. It was an arresting face, startlingly handsome when he smiled, revealing straight white teeth. Yet there was something alien about the face, about him. Carrie's eyes quickly dropped to his clothes. He wore an elaborately fringed buckskin shirt, loosely laced across a wide expanse of chest with thick black hair curling through the openings. His long legs were encased in tight breeches of the same soft tan leather, and on his feet he wore moccasins. On one slim hip a low-slung gun hung, and on the other a wicked-looking knife was sheathed. It was the sort of outfit she'd seen trappers and rivermen wear on her westward journey. The expensive, exotic-looking gold and silver rings on his hands were unique, however. He was different from any man she had ever met—untamed, barbarous looking. Yes, barbarically handsome, like a savage, an Indian! She took a step backward as he took a step forward.

"Who—who are you?" She hated the frightened squeak in her voice that made her appear juvenile. He took another couple of measured steps toward her, that savage smile once again in place as his gleaming black eyes perused her.

God, she is a fetching little bitch with a beautifully molded body and flashing green eyes. The hair was the thing, though—like living flame surrounding that delicate pale face. Young, not even out of her teens. *Noah sure robbed the cradle this time.* Then he reconsidered and wondered who had done the robbing. *I'll just bet she's got an eyeful of this place already. Probably knows what the silver's worth.*

"Who are you?" he asked aloud, throwing her question back at her although he'd already heard from Feliz that Noah was bringing a new bride with him from St. Louis.

"I'm Carrie Sinclair, Noah's wife. Now, would you be so good as to answer my question, since I inquired first?" She was proud of the steadiness of her voice, especially since he now stood a scant three feet from her, towering over her slim frame so that she had to arch her neck back to address him.

"I'm Hawk, Hawk Sinclair. It seems we're kin of sorts now." Again the predatory grin.

Suddenly Carrie knew. There had been something familiar in the long, rangy frame and harshly chiseled features. The difference in coloring and costume threw her. He was Noah's son!

"You're Noah's son! But you're an Ind—"

"Cheyenne," he cut her off coldly. "Indians live on the Asiatic subcontinent on the other side of the world. Stupid of the white explorers not to know where they landed four hundred years ago."

Carrie felt her face flame as brightly as her hair. She'd never met an actual savage, never even seen one at a distance until they passed through western Minnesota. Now one stood right next to her calmly speaking in an educated voice, giving her a geography lesson!

"I didn't mean—"

"I know exactly what you meant, *Mrs*. Sinclair." He stressed the title contemptuously. "My mother was the first Mrs. Sinclair, and she was a full-blooded Cheyenne. I am what is not affectionately known out west as a half-breed."

"Evan, there you are. I see you and Carrie have met." Noah's voice cut like a knife, slicing through the crackling tension between the man and woman in the center of the room. He quickly walked over to Carrie's side and took her arm as he inspected his only son with flinty blue eyes.

"You look well, especially considering I heard at least a dozen rumors to the effect that you'd been shot."

"You should know how hard I am to kill, Noah. You only *hoped* it was true."

Carrie let out a small hiss of breath as the veiled animosity between her and Hawk shifted to open warfare between father and son. What was she caught in the midst of?

"Let's adjourn our discussion to a more appropriate time, Evan," Noah said with a nod to Carrie.

"My name is Hawk. I don't use Evan, not since I was fourteen." He ground out the words with rigid control. "Your missionaries may have turned my mother from Laughing Woman to Marah, but I earned Hunting Hawk, and I'll keep it."

Carrie watched the predatory fierceness in his flashing black eyes and studied the powerful profile. Hawk. Yes, it fit him perfectly, she thought with a shiver as she watched him stare Noah down. It was the first time since she'd met her husband that she had seen him back off.

"All right, *Hawk*. I don't know a good reason to fight it anymore, since no one calls you Evan anyway," Noah snapped angrily. "Dinner is at seven, as usual. You know where your room is. I'm going to show Carrie to hers."

"Until dinner, Mrs. Sinclair." That deadly white smile flashed once more. "Oh, never fear, I do know how to use a knife and fork." With that sally, Hawk went swiftly and silently out the door.

Carrie was stunned into silence as she allowed Noah to show her to her room. Pleading a headache, she asked to

be left to nap before dinner. Noah seemed relieved not to
have to answer her questions, and quickly left her with a
terse nod.

Her room was lovely, with a French door to the outside
veranda that ran the length of the house. It was light and
airy, with soft lavender curtains and bedspread, a thick
navy-blue rug, and dainty cherrywood furniture. There
was even a rocker in one corner by a window, a perfect
spot for curling up to read on cold winter days.

Carrie sat down dazed in the rocker to contemplate this
latest piece in the puzzle of Noah Sinclair's life. A son, an
Indian wife. What had Hawk called her—Marah? Then a
second thought hit her. Good Lord, was his mother still
alive, off with those savages? Was her own marriage
legitimate? Or was Hawk a bastard and the so-called
marriage of his mother to Noah some primitive tribal
sham?

Her temples pounded as questions whirled about in her
aching brain. She must somehow get Noah to tell her the
truth. What else lay hidden in his past?

The first dinner in her new home provided more answers
than Carrie wanted to hear. At quarter to seven she walked
into the parlor expecting to find Noah waiting to escort her
to the table. Instead she found Hawk brooding by the open
window. He turned abruptly, sensing her presence with a
savage's instinct, no doubt, since she had entered very
silently. While he looked her over, he posed indolently,
leaning one long arm against the mantel, a drink in his
hand.

"Very fetching. Redheads always look good in yellow.
Soft and warm, like butter 'n' honey." His words were soft
and faintly suggestive, but his black eyes were what really
alarmed her. He looked at her like a critical predator,
debating whether or not the prey was worth the effort of
swooping down to snatch it. Carrie had taken special care
with her toilette. She chose a simple but chic dress of deep
yellow silk. Tailored in straight lines, it accentuated her
coloring and flattered her height.

Indeed, she noticed how very tall Hawk was, even more
so than Noah, who stood at six feet. Hawk appeared to be

several inches taller, making her five-foot-seven-inch frame seem tiny by comparison. She was used to looking men eye to eye and didn't like being at such a disadvantage.

Hawk had bathed and shaved, and was dressed differently than before. No guns or knives were visible on his person. However, in spite of his crisp linen shirt opened at the throat, well-tailored gray suit and gleaming boots, he still looked dark and dangerous. Oddly, she felt a thrill of perverse fascination when she looked at him.

"Are you always so quiet, or is it just my presence that freezes up that pretty little tongue?" Those relentless eyes continued to skewer her.

She blushed. "I—I just don't know how to respond to you, er, Mr. Sinclair. You see, until I arrived here, I never even knew you existed."

He barked a sharp laugh, and then his face lost all traces of humor. "I just bet you didn't! Most western men who go east seem to conveniently forget their half-breed relatives in polite society. I ought to know. I spent a good part of the past decade in eastern schools being a curiosity. Ever seen an 'Indian' before, Carrie?" He used her given name like a taunt, as if he was aware of her uncertainty about how to address him and taking advantage of the fact.

Carrie was on unsure footing, but highly indignant at his hostility. She couldn't help it if she had never seen a savage before she came west! "I thought you were a Cheyenne, not 'an Indian,' Hawk." Good. She plucked the name of his tribe from the recesses of her memory.

"So I am." He raised his glass in salute, seeming to approve of her spunk and her use of his given name. "Red men are divided into many nations, as are the whites, who my mother's people call *veho*, which means spider in Cheyenne," he added, baiting her.

Trying to change the topic of conversation, she asked, "You've spent a lot of time in eastern schools, you said. Where?"

"You mean I speak educated English without accent? I even know the rudiments of political science and geography? Quite a prodigy for a savage, but then consider that I was kicked out of at least three or four of the best schools in Massachusetts, not to mention leaving Yale in my sophomore year. Something about my background seems to upset easterners.'' Black humor was reflected in his face as he spoke.

"Why are you so bitter? If your father sent you to such good schools, you had advantages most white children never have.'' As soon as she spoke, she regretted it.

"Yes, white children—like my father expects you to give him, no doubt. For now, he can use me, or my guns at least, but I'm only half white, and that's not good enough to inherit all this.'' He let his hand sweep the opulent room in a dismissing, scornful gesture.

Carrie was saved from responding to that impossible statement by Noah's entrance.

"It's time for dinner, Carrie, Hawk.'' His eyes swept from her to his son and back, sensing that some exchange of hostility had just transpired between them. He dismissed it and took her pale hand on his arm, leading her to the dining room. When he felt her trembling, he smiled.

Carrie sat across from Hawk, and Noah took his place at the head of the imposing dark oak table, set with delicately patterned china, gleaming silver, and sparkling crystal. The meal was served by a dark-haired young maid. Carrie was amazed at its delicacy, a wine-sauced chicken dish with spicy ham and cheese in the center of the plump breasts. Crusty bread, fresh garden peas, and a delicate white wine accompanied the main course. Despite Carrie's appreciation of the cook's skill, however, she had too much on her mind to do the food justice.

Again and again through the course of the meal Carrie's gaze strayed to Hawk. It was as if she couldn't help herself. He was right; his table manners were impeccable. The slim dark fingers held delicate china cups and thin French crystal with careless ease. He had obviously inherited his Indian mother's love of jewelry. The rings on his hands glistened in the candlelight, and he had a silver medallion suspended on a rawhide thong around his neck. Intricately worked, made of many fine strands of silver interwoven into a star design, it nestled in the thick black hair of his chest like a softly winking star. She found herself wondering if he always wore it.

Unwillingly, her eyes traveled up to his face, where the strongly chiseled features looked almost satanic in the flickering candlelight. *A splendid barbarian.* Where had she read the phrase that popped suddenly into her mind?

He caught her staring, and his amused black eyes scorched her cheeks, turning them aflame with a humiliating girlish blush. Carrie had never felt so young and socially inept in her life.

Table conversation did not help ease her case of nerves. Noah opened the offensive, breaking the strained silence under which they'd begun the meal. "Why'd you come back? Things get too hot down in the Nations?"

Hawk picked up his knife and meticulously cut a small slice of the chicken breast before replying, "At least I arrived in better condition than last time. Aren't you grateful I'm not bleeding all over your Aubusson rugs?"

Carrie gasped in shock. "Bleeding?"

Noah cleared his throat in warning to her. Damn her childish curiosity. Grudgingly he said, "Last time my son arrived home more dead than alive. Shot in a gunfight."

Hawk let out a harsh, low chuckle. "Yeah, Lola was furious with Kyle. When he dragged me in I ruined the carpet in the entry hall. Thoughtless of me to hemorrhage in such an inconvenient place."

That was the second time Carrie had heard the name Lola. Who was Lola? Was she the former housekeeper? A sister?

Noah glared at his son with such intense hatred that Carrie thought it would shrivel any ordinary mortal. "Leave that tramp out of this conversation!"

Hawk looked unconcerned by the menacing posture of his father as he turned to Carrie.

"Another skeleton in the closet. Poor girl, you really should check out a man's family connections as well as his bank account before marrying him."

Carrie let out a little gasp of indignation, and Noah's face darkened.

Before either of them could say a word, Hawk continued. "Lola Jameson was the second Mrs. Sinclair."

This time Carrie blanched.

"Ah, you didn't know you're number three? Well,
maybe three's a charm. Luck!" With that he raised his
wineglass to her in a mock toast and then drank deeply.

The silence was oppressive for several minutes, then the
maid came to clear the plates and bring dessert. By the
time the servant finished her duties, Carrie had gathered
her scattered wits. "I *assume*," she stressed the word,
"that both my predecessors have passed on?" Damn,
she'd get one thing straight!

"Marah died sixteen years ago, when Hawk was nine.
Lola is still alive." Noah stopped short, leaving the
distinct implication that he wished the latter fact to be
otherwise. Rather than elaborate, he bit into a slice of
blackberry pie, dismissing Lola from further consideration.
He was sure his son would enlighten Carrie.

"Lola and Noah are divorced, Carrie. Last year while I
was gone, I believe. These things take time and political
influence." He paused here, then added, "And enough
money." With that cryptic comment he, too, lapsed into
silence and took a few desultory bites of the pie.

The conversation turned to safer ground when Noah
inquired, "I suppose Hunnicut's with you?"

Hawk shrugged. "Kyle's here. We both seem to have
more lives than a cat, I guess. You want to hire his gun?"

"Might. Tell him to see Frank in the morning. But,
Hawk—this time he'd better not slope off without notice
like he did last time. Way that man drifts, I'd swear he's
part Cheyenne, too." He took a slug of the steaming black
coffee.

"Maybe that's why we've hung together for so many
years." Then, in offhand deference to Carrie, Hawk added,
"Kyle Hunnicut's an old friend. Saved my life down in the
Nations four years ago."

"You keep mentioning the 'Nations.'" Carrie felt so
ignorant of even the most basic facts in this strange new
world.

CAPTURE THE SUN   49

"The Indian Nations, Oklahoma Territory, south below Kansas, Carrie," Noah answered.

Hawk cut in. "You mean the dumping ground where the government has imprisoned over a hundred different tribal groups from every part of North America." His voice was tinged with bitterness and anger. Then abruptly he stood up. "If you newlyweds will excuse me, I've had a long ride today and I'm short on sleep." Moving as silently as a cat, he went up the stairs.

Carrie turned to Noah. "Will he be staying now?" She didn't feel at all comfortable sleeping under the same roof with this educated, embittered barbarian. Enough to deal with the father, much less the son.

Noah considered before replying, lost in thought. He was upset by this unexpected resurrection, more than he wanted to let on to his bride. "God only knows," he finally said in disgust. "He's come and gone like the wind since he was a small boy. I've never been able to understand him. Smart as hell, but all he ever wanted to do was run off to his mother's people again and again. I should've let them have him!"

Feeling the anger and frustration in his voice, Carrie asked hesitantly, "Why didn't you?"

Noah affixed her with a haughty stare; once more the mask of pedantic superiority slipped in place. "He is my only son. Mine. No one ever takes anything away from me. There's a lesson in that for you, Carrie. Heed it."

While Noah and Carrie shared uneasy postdinner conversation, Hawk went up to his old room, situated at the far end of the long hallway on the second floor. Hawk preferred the privacy. The big, dented old brass bed with its sagging mattress stood by the far wall. An elk head with a magnificent spread of antlers hung on the other wall. Noah had shot the animal when Marah was still alive and prized the trophy back then. When Lola redecorated, it was far too western and crude to remain downstairs. His room, a junk repository of sorts, inherited it. Likewise the scarred oak washstand and chest. Dust stood thick on everything. Mrs. Thorndyke never wasted her energy here, he mused wryly. Not that she'd have dared to enter his domain

anyway. They had hated one another ever since Noah hired
her sixteen years ago. So far she'd outlasted two Sinclair
wives. Unlikely she'd outlast this young one.

Hawk pulled back the musty covers and stretched his
long-legged frame across the familiar contours of the bed.
He considered his father's new wife. His first impression
in the parlor earlier that afternoon had been that Carrie was
a bigoted, money-grubbing tart who had latched onto a
rich old man. After watching her at dinner, however, he
was not so sure. Of course, a beautiful woman that young
married a man of fifty-five only for his wealth, but she
wasn't nearly as hard or clever as he'd first given her
credit for being. The way she stared at him with a mixture
of fascination and revulsion angered him, but also indicated that she was not very skilled at concealing her emotions. The blushes and quick anger also betrayed her
youthful inexperience. He got her to rise to his baiting
with ease.

Hawk also observed how cowed she seemed around
Noah. *It isn't the coy act of a scheming woman trying to
butter up an old fool,* he mused to himself. *No. She's got
herself in deep water with Noah Sinclair. It'll be interesting to see how well she can swim.* He chuckled.

That thought led him to picture her drenched in the
creek with that yellow silk dress clinging to every curve of
her body, that tall, willowy body with its high, pointed
breasts and slender, flared hips. He swore and pounded the
pillow in self-disgust, only to be greeted with a huge puff
of two-year-old house dust.

*Give that randy old stud six months and she'll be fat as
a buffalo, ready to drop a calf.* However, the image of
Carrie pregnant with Noah's child did not appeal to him
for a variety of reasons, only one of which he wanted to
acknowledge. He finally drifted into a fitful sleep, promising himself a visit to the best cathouse in Miles City
tomorrow night.

CHAPTER 4

Carrie awoke suddenly from a disquieting dream. It was the nightmare that had first occurred when she was only seven years old. It had recurred at infrequent intervals over the years, but since her marriage, it was fast becoming a regular thing, one she dreaded. Dazedly she sat up in bed and looked through the big French doors of her room to see a breathtaking sunrise. How eerie! The last scene of the nightmare was always dominated by a blazing sky, either sunrise or sunset, she could never tell which.

"Well, I can't just lay abed and be morbid," she whispered to herself in grim resolution as she flung off the covers and rose. At least Noah had left her alone last night to sleep in peace. Today she vowed she would get acquainted with all the domestic staff. If she was going to be mistress of this vast household, she had a great deal to learn.

After meeting with Mrs. Thorndyke, Carrie began to realize just how formidable her task might be. The older woman stopped marginally short of being rude. Carrie collided with her in the front hall when she descended the stairs to go to breakfast.

"Good morning, Mrs. Thorndyke." She offered her most winning smile, wanting to thaw the cold reserve that inexplicably seemed to be a part of the woman's attitude toward her.

"It's scarcely morning anymore, Mrs. Sinclair. On a working ranch, people are up before the sun. The bunkhouse cook rousts the hands at four-thirty. In the big house we have breakfast at six, midday meal at noon, and dinner at seven.'' With that terse and inflexible bit of information imparted to the dumbstruck young woman, Mathilda Thorndyke turned on her heel and swished away, pausing only long enough to call over her shoulder, ''If you need breakfast, go ask Feliz to get you something. She's in the kitchen.''

The hallway from the front to the back of the house seemed endless to Carrie. As she slowly traversed it, she felt more like an unwelcome outsider with every step. In St. Louis, arising at seven was considered unfashionably early. How was she to know the beggarly hours of this wilderness? Quelling her insecurities, she decided she must be far more forceful with Mrs. Thorndyke if she was ever going to take her proper place as employer and put the housekeeper in hers as employee.

The smells emanating from the kitchen were heavenly. Everything seemed to run like clockwork here. Even the food was superb. For a panic-stricken moment Carrie envisioned herself as a useless ornament, flitting through the beautiful house with nowhere to go and nothing to do, ignored by everyone including Noah. He had already made it clear to her that her primary function was to breed for him. What would she do?

''Get ahold of yourself, Carrie.'' She ground out the words through clenched teeth, forcing her imaginings and her trembling to abate. With a steady hand she opened the door to the kitchen and stepped inside. A short, rotund woman in a bright red dress and full white apron was busy at the oven in the far corner of the large, well-equipped kitchen. Her black hair was liberally streaked with gray and pinned in a frazzled bun. She was pulling large, fragrant loaves of bread from the oven, one after another. Suddenly she caught sight of the bright hair and blue dress from the corner of her eye and turned. She held a wooden paddle with a steaming golden loaf still securely on it.

Her round face creased into a big welcoming smile, and her chocolate-brown eyes glowed warmly. ''You are the new Señora Sinclair! I am so pleased to meet you.''

Carrie smiled in return, overjoyed to have someone welcome her to this hostile household. "I'm Carrie Sinclair, and you must be our wonderful cook. Your dinner last night was excellent. Ah." She sniffed in pure delight. "The bread smells divine. I'm sorry to have missed breakfast. I overslept, I guess. We don't get up so early in St. Louis."

As she deftly slid the loaf from the paddle onto a cooling rack, the older woman made a gesture of dismissal. "*No es importante*. I am Feliz Mendoza, Doña Carrie. I will fix you whatever you want to eat."

Smelling the coffee and eyeing the hot bread, Carrie replied, "Just a slice of that with some butter and a cup of hot coffee would be lovely, thank you."

As Feliz poured a steaming mug of rich black coffee, she laughed. "I hope you like it, señora. I try not to make it so strong as the bunkhouse cook, Turnips, does, but Don Noah likes it the way most western men drink it, thick enough to float a horseshoe in."

Carrie tasted the aromatic brew. It was hearty but not at all bitter as so much of the coffee on her western journey had been. "It's delicious, and I don't think we ever need to try the horseshoe test, do you?"

Her youthful grin was infectious to the older woman, who had been uncertain about yet another Mrs. Sinclair. The previous one was terrible. This one she liked.

As Carrie devoured the hot crusty bread with thick creamy butter melted across it, they became acquainted. "Mendoza is a Spanish name, isn't it? How did you get so far from home, Feliz?"

The cook's wide face split in a smile, revealing beautiful small white teeth. "I am Mexicana, but you are right, it is still a long way from home. My husband, God rest his soul," she crossed herself perfunctorily and went on, "he came north with Frank Lowery from Texas. We grew up in a little town near the border, and my Carlos was a vaquero for a big rancho. He wanted a better life for us. When his amigo Frank asked him to make the long drive with cattle to Montana, he went, then sent for me. It has been a good life, even if the winters are cold. I have two sons who are vaqueros for Don Noah, and a daughter who works here in the house.''

''The girl who served our dinner last night? She's very pretty, Feliz. Your husband, has he passed away?'' Carrie asked gently.

Reassuringly Feliz replied, ''Sí, he was killed five years ago in a stampede on a trail drive. I miss him, but I am grateful for all our blessings while we were together, thirty-two years.''

Carrie started at that, imagining herself and Noah married that long. Why, she'd be fifty and Noah would be—

As if reading her mind, Feliz inquired, ''Did you know Don Noah long before you married?'' The difference in age was startling to Feliz, and it was hard for her to imagine them as a couple.

Carrie hesitated for an instant and then decided to speak openly to this guileless woman. ''No. It was an arranged match, I'm afraid. Noah's cousin Patience and my uncle Hiram are married. They were my guardians, and decided I should accept his kind offer.'' She hesitated again, then plunged on when she saw a leap of sympathy, even pity, in Feliz eyes. ''I am sure we will be happy, but everything out west is so new and strange to me. I just need some time to learn all the customs. Then perhaps Noah and I can grow closer. Right now, you're my first friend, Feliz.''

''Gracias, señora. I am proud to be your friend.''

''Please call me Carrie, Feliz.'' Carrie reached out her pale, slim hand and grasped the plump, brown one. Instantaneously, a bond was forged between the two women.

Feliz chatted about the help at the ranch, explaining to Carrie what the names and duties of all the domestic workers were.

Carrie said, ''It certainly is a big place, even larger than I could imagine when we arrived yesterday. I'm overwhelmed by all the new faces.''

Feliz smiled and then added knowingly, ''Sí, so many people to know. And having Hawk home, that was a surprise, too.'' She was certain neither was aware of the other's existence before yesterday afternoon.

Carrie's guilty flush gave her away once again. ''More

than that, I fear. I never knew Noah had a grown son, and I certainly didn't expect to meet him the way I did. Is he always so . . ." Carrie searched for words, "so caustic and menacing?"

Ah, so they had tangled already, had they? Feliz was not surprised. "You cannot blame Hawk for being bitter, Carrie. He came home after being away over a year. He left to escape that woman Don Noah had married. She was evil. Each time he returns, he never knows what kind of welcome to expect."

"Certainly not a replacement for the old stepmother, I bet," Carrie burst out in stung pride, recalling his rudeness.

"No, he did not. But then, you know what you represent to him, don't you? If your husband has a white son by you, he will disinherit Hawk, Carrie."

Carrie was taken aback. She had not thought of it that way. Of course Noah wanted her to give him children, but he already had one son. "That can't be true, Feliz! Hawk is his firstborn. Even if they don't get along, he is still Noah's son. Surely he wouldn't . . ." Her words trailed off as she realized the obvious. How stupid of her! Hawk was a half-breed, a drifter and gunman, for all his education in the white world. If Noah could get pure-blooded children from her, he would discard Hawk ruthlessly. She did not doubt it for a minute. Then another thought occurred to her.

"Feliz, were . . . were Marah and Noah married—I mean legally, by white custom, not Cheyenne?"

Feliz smiled serenely, going back to a long ago time. "Sí, they were married by a missionary minister. It was not a tribal ritual, Carrie. Marah was a beautiful young woman of sixteen when she met Don Noah. Hawk has her fine features and coloring, and her free spirit and love of the land. He has much to be bitter about, Carrie, but he is a good boy."

Carrie arched her brows. Somehow she could not think of that menacing gunman as a boy. "Frankly, I find it hard to imagine his ever being a child, Feliz."

Feliz laughed as she recalled one of Hawk's boyhood pranks. "One day when he was seven I baked his favorite ginger cookies. He sneaked up to that window and pulled himself on the sill where he could reach in and grab them. Since I had just taken them from the oven, he burned his fingers, but he told me it was little enough pain for the honor of counting coup on my kitchen.''

Carrie smiled as she saw the obviously fond memories Feliz had of Hawk's boyhood.

''Frank told me about a time when Hawk was out on the range with him looking for stray steers. Hawk was maybe nine years old by then. They came across a Sioux chief's burial lodge. These are like big woven beds, set high in the air on four long poles. One of the vaqueros decided to climb up and see if the old warrior had anything valuable to steal. Well, Hawk slipped off from the men and came around from behind. He got a long stick and sneaked under the lodge with it. When the vaquero was rooting through the dead chief's medicine bag, Hawk pushed the stick through the woven mat and propped the dead body up. Frank said the men back at the bunkhouse could hear that grave robber yell. He fell backward off the ladder and hurt his leg. All the other men laughed so hard no one could give him help. He just lay there, flopping around on the ground while they hung on their horses and laughed.''

While Feliz reminisced with Carrie about Hawk's childhood, Hawk was busily at work. He had arisen in time to join the bunkhouse breakfast at four-thirty and renew old acquaintances with a few of the men who were his friends.

Kyle was sleeping with the hands. He had always hated Noah's elegant house and preferred rough camaraderie to the formal manners required to eat at Noah's table. Kyle had been born in a Texas whorehouse and never knew his father. Hawk often told him he was lucky. But because Kyle knew he lacked education and refinement, whenever they returned to the Circle S, he chose to keep his distance from the big house.

Later that morning they rode out, ostensibly for Hawk to reacquaint himself with the stock and see what improvements had been made in the operation of the place. In fact, it enabled the two men, both of whom had been range detectives, to take a look at the rustling situation firsthand.

"Yore pa offered me a job o' work, Hawk," Kyle said as they rode, then lapsed into silence.

"You take it?"

"I reckon I like the view up north fer a change. Yore fixin' on stayin' awhile. Thought I'd lope along here fer a spell. If'n I'm gonna git shot at, Montana's as good as anywheres else."

"It is a good day to die," Hawk said softly, a quirk of a smile lingering around his mouth.

"Don't yew go hexin' me with thet Cheyenne death song, Longlegs. I figger on dyin' in bed, with a woman on each side o' me, ta kinda get me ready fer all thet heat down there below. Nah, these here bastards're plumb dumb as sheep. Cuttin' out a few head o' stock an' runnin' it off whilst yore pa's away. All's he has ta do is hire a few trackers with guns an' them varmints'll skedaddle."

"It appears to me he just did that," Hawk said dryly.

"Since when's the old man hirin' his own son? Yer still sleepin' at the big house, ain't ya?"

"Yeah, Kyle, I still have a room. They even let me eat in the dining room with them," Hawk said. The sarcasm couldn't mask the bitterness lying beneath it.

"Reckon I know whut burr's under yore blanket, Longlegs, an' she's got red hair, I hear tell. Ain't seen 'er yet, but Frank says she's a real looker."

"White women are poison, beautiful or not."

"All women er pizen, my friend, but whut a way ta die, huh?" He laughed a bit, then sobered and looked over at the tall, silent rider beside him. "Ya figger he'll cut yew out if'n she foals him a nice white boy?"

"Always did. I never really thought I'd inherit Circle S, Kyle. One way or another, Noah'd keep me from it. He knows I'd open the land for the People to hunt on. Buffalo are gone, but there are antelope, elk, deer. Better than they've got on that so-called government land where the White Father promises food and starves them into submission.

"Only question was how he'd acquire another heir. As long as he was married to Lola, there wasn't a chance.

This time he's picked very carefully. She's out of her depth. He'll make her heel to his every command, or I miss my guess. But she's young and healthy, a good breeder.'' He laughed grimly. ''Yeah, she'll earn her money with that old bastard.''

''Whut ya figger ta do, Hawk? I'm game fer leavin'. We cud head up ta yore ma's people an' visit fer a spell.''

''I'll visit Grandfather and the others soon, but for now I just want to stay here and devil the old man. As long as he can use my gun, he'll keep me on. Besides, I'm anxious to see just how he'll go about telling me when the time comes.''

''Ya figgerin' ta throw his money in his face when he offers yew a chunk ta ride off in the sunset.'' It was not offered as speculation but as a bald statement.

''You know me pretty well, old friend. . . .''

Carrie had spent the morning gleaning as much information as she could from Feliz, the repository of all Sinclair family information. Noah had been out on his land since daybreak, and Carrie did not see him until the midday meal. He was preoccupied and paid little attention to her, eating quickly and heading back to the corral.

Carrie tried to bring up the problem of Mrs. Thorndyke's rudeness and independence, but was unable to get more than a perfunctory and exasperated, ''She's run the house perfectly for over sixteen years. I won't disturb things that work well.''

In other words, Carrie concluded disconsolately, she could wander around, a stranger in her own house, or take charge of it without Noah's support. Pondering that, she conceded that she would at least get some help from her husband with her other obvious problem: she could not ride a horse.

Noah had been horrified when Carrie told him she had never been on horseback in her life, that in an urban area like St. Louis, horseback riding was not a popular diversion for most young ladies. Noah immediately took charge in characteristic fashion by announcing he would select her a gentle mount and have it outfitted with a sidesaddle. She was to report to Frank Lowery for her first lesson on the morrow.

Nervously, Carrie did as instructed, dressing in a simple riding habit she had bought as part of her trousseau. It had been a request of Noah's and she had honored it without confessing that she did not ride. She smoothed the brown skirt and decided to brave the corral with no more procrastination. Anything larger than a sheepdog terrified her. Pray God whoever Frank selected to teach her would have the patience of Job!

As she approached the corral, Carrie sighted Frank's snowy hair easily because he stood nearly a head taller than any of the other hands. He was surrounded by men taking morning job assignments and then moving off in groups of twos and threes to saddle their mounts and set to work. Patiently she waited until he was finished discharging his responsibilities. She was uncomfortable with the curious and occasionally leering stares of the motley assortment of men who passed by her. Some tipped their hats in deference, some blushed and looked down at their boots, and a few eyed her far too boldly for her comfort.

Finally, as the press thinned, Carrie caught Frank's eye. He flashed that toothy smile and loped toward her. "Right early fer ya ta be up, ma'am. What kin I do fer ya?"

Carrie was taken aback. "Didn't Noah ask you to find someone to go riding with me? I—I don't know how to say this to a Texan, but I never rode a horse before, and I'm under orders to learn." She smiled uncertainly, and he returned it broadly.

"I do apologize, ma'am, but Noah musta plumb fergot. Ya see, soon's he got down here, word come 'bout some stock bein' stole down by th' Mizpah fork. I reckon he had some fierce worries. Fact is, soon's I post the day's work, I—"

A drawling voice cut in, "Know yer right pushed fer time, Frank. Be real proud ta show th' missus th' ropes. Yew know no one's better'n a Texan ta teach a tenderfoot ta ride." Kyle Hunnicut's bandy-legged gait carried him around the corral to stare eye to eye with Carrie. He was barely taller than her, despite his high-heeled riding boots.

A thick thatch of frizzy reddish hair stuck out from beneath a wide-brimmed, battered hat and an equally unruly patch of freckles was liberally spread across his face. A nose, long ago displaced in a Texas bar fight, fell sharply to the left side of his cheek while a strong set of teeth, yellowed by chewing tobacco, flashed her a warm grin. He could have been as young as thirty or as old as forty-five. It was that kind of a face.

Frank laughed good-naturedly and spoke up. "Mrs. Sinclair, meet Kyle Hunnicut. This here rascal's th' best stock detective north o' th' Platte, ma'am, an' I reckon a fair rider, too."

Carrie nodded, returning the greeting of the wiry little man who wore a deadly Colt strapped to his hip as naturally as had his friend Hawk. "I'd be grateful, Mr. Hunnicut, for any pointers you could give me. I'm quite a novice, I'm afraid."

The crooked grin again. "Nothin' ta it, ma'am." Kyle patiently saddled a small mare for Carrie, then helped her into the sidesaddle. Once up on the horse, the ground looked far down, and she immediately transmitted her nervousness to the animal, causing her to skitter. After a few minutes of patient instruction and reassurance by Kyle, they set out.

"You're a 'stock detective,' Mr. Lowery said. What does that mean?" Carrie still felt as though she was in a foreign country.

Kyle grinned and began to roll a cigarette as he explained. "Wall, ma'am, thet's really a fancy name fer a good tracker who doubles as a hired gun. Fact is, I kin foller most any stolen cow's trail an' deal with th' varmints thet took 'em."

"Is there much theft around here? I thought my husband was so powerful that no one would dare steal from him." Carrie was taken aback at his casual reference to violence, but tried not to show it.

"Fact is true, Noah Sinclair's got him th' biggest spread in eastern Montana, but thieves is a peculiar lot. They purely don't care. Thet's why Noah kin use us fer now."

"Us? You mean you and Hawk, don't you?" For some

inexplicable reason Carrie found herself bringing up his name when she knew she shouldn't.

He nodded in agreement and corrected the position of her hand on the tightened rein.

Here I am out in the middle of nowhere, calmly riding around with a hired gunman, she thought in disbelief, making yet another resolution to adapt, no matter what.

As if sensing her unease, Kyle said, "Yep, Longlegs 'n' me, we go back a piece. He run off from school 'n' come ta th' Nations lookin' fer some way ta survive. I cud see he's a nat'ral with a sidearm. Sorta quiet an' moved real quick. Guess th' Injun blood gave him thet."

"So you trained him," Carrie supplied, intrigued despite herself.

"Yes'm, I did thet. Never had me a breed fer a pardner afore. Ya might say he trained me in a way, too." He lapsed into silence, remembering.

"Why did you offer to teach me to ride, Mr. Hunnicut?" He was Hawk's friend. Why was he being kind to her?

"I'd be obliged if'n ya'd call me Kyle, ma'am. Onliest ones whut calls me 'Mr. Hunnicut' 'er fellers in bars tryin' ta cadge a drink off'n me."

Carrie laughed. "All right, Kyle." She waited for him to answer her question.

He considered for a minute, then said, "It seems Hawk's got one idee about yew, 'n' Frank's got another. Figgered I'd see fer myself."

"Well, Kyle, how do you vote?" Carrie was abashed at his forthrightness and decided to be equally bold.

"I ain't rightly decided yet. Got ta think on it fer a spell. I'll let yew know." He grinned toothily.

Carrie was sure this strangely honest ruffian would do just that and surprised herself by hoping that she'd pass his inspection.

By the end of her first week at Circle S, Carrie was used to early rising, despite Noah's nightly visits to her bed. Pushing that unpleasant thought from her mind, she headed toward the corral for her morning ride. Frank and Kyle had taken turns squiring her around and answering questions about the daily workings of the big ranch. Both were easygoing and possessed a rough Texas charm that she found relaxing. *I will learn to fit in here*, she thought to herself, recalling the vast store of western lore she was absorbing daily. Even her horsemanship was slightly improved, although she dreaded being balanced precariously on the back of a bouncing, pitching beast, prey to prairie dog holes, scratchy brush, and sudden noises that might cause the half-controlled horse to skitter and unseat her. Nevertheless, Kyle had actually complimented her the day before when she had doggedly kept her seat after her horse stumbled.

So pleased was Carrie in recalling her success that she approached the big barn by the corral almost eager to mount. Then she saw Hawk leading her small tan mare and immediately changed her mind. However, before she could turn and flee, his long-legged stride caught up with her. A thin, sardonic smile hovered about his lips.

"You're late." The voice sounded bored rather than accusatory. He stood still, letting the mare's reins trail negligently in one hand while he inspected her outfit from head to toe. It was her particular favorite, a long, full riding habit made of rust-colored broadcloth.

The smirk turned to a disgusted scowl. "Lady, you have too many clothes on." With that startling pronouncement, he proceeded to slip his wicked-looking knife from its sheath on his left hip. He dropped the reins and stepped closer to her.

Carrie was frozen. Unless an earthquake swallowed her, there was no way she could move of her own volition.

In one lightning movement, he grasped the train of her long riding skirt from her hand where she held it to keep it from dragging in the dust. Just as swiftly he fanned it out and sliced off the whole thing in a neat incision, leaving the skirt one even length, just above the ankles.

Fright quickly turned to fury as she watched him calmly slip the knife back into its resting place and heard him say in a low silky voice, "Now, why did I just know that you wouldn't scream?"

"You sadistic brute!" Looking down at the unhemmed

ruins of her expensive habit, she ground out the words, wishing her vocabulary were equal to the situation.

A blinding white smile slashed across his dark face, and he laughed as he picked up the filly's reins. "You couldn't ride this while carrying all that." He gestured from the saddle to the excess of her skirt piled in a rusty heap on the ground.

For the first time Carrie noticed the saddle on Taffy Girl. It was a regular western stock saddle, not the sidesaddle she had been using.

As if reading her mind, he said, "If you want to look ladylike on a dangerous contraption like that sidesaddle, you can fall and be dragged, breaking your beautiful little neck for all I care. But if you want to ride like western women do, I'll teach you. Kyle told me how you nearly fell when Taffy shied yesterday."

"But I didn't fall, and he praised me for keeping my seat so well," she retorted hotly, perversely angry that his common sense should so closely parallel her own thinking about women's riding gear.

He stood patiently, looking at her as if she were a half-bright child being indulged in a temper tantrum. Without a word she grabbed the reins from him and stomped over to the left side of the mare. When she reached one booted foot up and placed it in the stirrup, she felt his hands span her waist as he effortlessly lifted her into the saddle. Grudgingly, she admitted feeling a foot in a stirrup on each side of the horse gave her a sense of security. However, his hands on her waist did just the opposite.

"Two stirrups feel comfortable, don't they?" That damn echo of her thoughts again! When she failed to respond and sat mutinously still, chin pointed determinedly forward, he shrugged and turned to swing gracefully on his large bay stallion.

They rode in silence, broken only when he issued a few terse commands to her about how she pulled on the reins or distributed her weight in the saddle. *Nitpicking*, she sniffed to herself, but made the necessary adjustments.

Finally, uncomfortable with her own silence and the

feeling of his eyes on her, Carrie turned to look at him and said, "Why did you volunteer to take me riding today?"

He turned his face in profile, looking straight ahead as he replied levelly, "Maybe I wanted to see if you scare easily, or maybe I wanted to keep you away from Kyle." He turned to meet her stare head-on now and stated, "He's become rather smitten, or hadn't you noticed?"

That shocked her, and unwittingly she let out a small "Oh," before she could stop herself. "That's absurd! Kyle's a smooth-talking, forthright Texan, not some lovesick college boy." Thinking of the tough bandy-legged Hunnicut next to Gerald Rawlins, she almost laughed at the ridiculousness of the comparison.

"You underestimate your charms, Carrie." He paused before he said, "Then again, maybe you don't. After all, what's one crude Texas cowhand for the baron's wife to take notice of?"

Carrie flushed in fury for the second time in an hour. Damn the hateful man! He was insufferable, unbearable! She groped for a word that was adequate. *Bastard!* There, she'd found a good word. Now, if only she had the courage to say it out loud!

After seething for a few hundred yards, she realized he was enjoying taunting her, reveling in her temper and embarrassment.

She decided to go on the offensive. "Why do you have such a low opinion of me? I understand about the inheritance, that Noah might cut you out if I have children . . ." She found the last words difficult to say. *Lord, I don't want Noah's children!* She quickly continued, "But I'm not to blame for what he does. I didn't even know he had a son before we arrived at Circle S. I'm only a pawn in his game, just like everyone else." *Like you.*

Hawk's face was stony. He grated, "Next I suppose you'll tell me you married a man over twice your age because you respected him so much. Maybe he reminded you of your daddy! How gullible do you think I am, lady? He's a *rich, old* man. You thought you could wheedle and manipulate him, but, baby, you're sitting in a high-stakes game with a penny-ante poke. He'll flay your pretty gold-digging hide and hang it out in the sun to dry."

So he thought she had ensnared Noah for his money and then been beaten into submission! The gall of the man, the abysmal ignorance! Yet a small voice taunted her: *It is true that you act like a whipped dog around Noah.* Had he truly broken her spirit? With these confusing thoughts tearing at her, Carrie dug her heels into Taffy Girl's sides and rode ahead, ignoring the insensitive oaf who would never believe the truth.

For the next couple of weeks Carrie saw little of Hawk except at unavoidable dinner-table encounters. One riding lesson sufficed. Once having drawn the battle lines, it seemed father and son decided on a wary, unspoken truce, at least in her presence. They discussed the rustling, the new shorthorn cattle Noah had brought from Oregon, weather, roundup, all the usual things she supposed that cattlemen talked about. She was seldom included in the conversation, but learned a great deal from listening.

Hawk and Kyle would ride off together and be gone for several days at a stretch. Sometimes a few other men rode with them. Carrie was uncertain about the nature of their mission, but suspected it had to do with the livestock thefts. She wondered what they did when they apprehended a criminal.

If she saw less of Hawk and the other hands, she saw far more of Noah than she wanted, for he visited her room every night. After arising at dawn to ride out and oversee the vast ranch, as well as making frequent overnight trips to Miles City, how did he have the energy left to bed her?

Perhaps she would not have minded it as much if only he would have paid some attention to her in other ways, done something to show her he at least considered her a person instead of a brood mare. However, he did not. She was left to her own devices daily. He ignored her every attempt to show him how she was adapting to western life.

Frank confirmed Hawk's statement that many western women rode astride. Every day after her dramatic lesson with Hawk, she rode Taffy Girl, accompanied by Frank or one of the other hands he assigned, and she always rode astride.

Carrie never told Noah about her newly acquired skill, practicing until she was sure she could acquit herself competently. Perhaps this was the way to make him proud of her. She had to try something. As it turned out, she had chosen the wrong thing.

"Ladies ride sidesaddle! Indian squaws ride astride! Where the hell did you get that rig, and who taught you?" Noah's infuriated accusation rang across the stableyard. Several hands overheard, but they quickly pretended they had not and hurried off to do chores in the farthest reaches of the barns and stables.

Tears welled up in her green eyes, but they were as much from sheer frustrated anger as from disappointment. She had planned to surprise him with her western skill, but he wanted her to be a proper eastern lady. Now, if she confessed where she learned to ride astride, it would only start more fighting between Hawk and his father. Suddenly a thought struck her. What if Hawk knew how Noah felt about women riding astride? Had he set her up deliberately?

Well, damn them both! She was fast becoming a good rider, and she wouldn't go back to the old way for anyone. "I see nothing wrong with my using a safe saddle. Last week when we were in Miles City I even saw a pattern for a split riding skirt in the modiste's book. I was thinking of ordering several." She spoke quietly, amazed at the steadiness of her own voice.

Noah's face darkened to a fuchsia red as he looked down at the set determination in the eyes of his slim, beautiful young wife. Where had the frightened little tenderfoot gone? God, he would have no repeat of Lola's defiance.

He grasped her right arm with an iron grip and carefully propelled her toward the house. Carrie flinched from the pain of his grip, but refused to demean herself by making a scene. Woodenly they walked back to the big house to argue in private.

CHAPTER 5

The sun cast an arc of pink and red light across the eastern sky, followed by deep, hot yellows and golds bathing the lodges of Iron Heart's people in warm summer light. Like all Cheyenne villages, this one was constructed with the tepees in a horseshoe shape. The open end of the horseshoe faced the rising sun, as did the door of each lodge.

It was nearing the summer solstice, and more and more bands were meeting on this warm plain for great feasting and solemn ceremonies, but the hunt was not as good as it had been in years past. The great masses of shaggy buffalo were thin, and thinning even more. So were the People. Smallpox and cholera decimated them while the bullets of the *veho* destroyed the sacred buffalo. Still, it was once more summer, and those who were left rejoiced.

Iron Heart, now in his seventy-sixth year, was still a robust man, having survived the ravages of the white man's diseases, a Crow arrow, and several bullets from both Indians and *veho*. Age had not stooped his shoulders nor dimmed his vision. He stood six foot four inches, and his black eyes were as piercing as they had been when he first counted coup as a boy of fifteen. Standing in the door of his lodge, he stretched while he watched the birth of a new day. It never ceased to awe him, as the mighty hands of the Powers sundered the blackness and thrust in the light each morning.

He heard a procession of giggling young maidens, some from his village and some from adjacent bands, venturing in search of summer berries. Iron Heart continued to watch the eastern sky expectantly. It was not only the sunrise that held his attention, but something more. He had had a dream last night, and his dreams were seldom wrong. Hunting Hawk was coming back to his people. He felt it in his bones. It was time.

By midafternoon the old man's vigil was rewarded when a lone rider appeared on the horizon. Even before he could distinguish the tall rider he recognized the huge bay stallion of his grandson.

Hawk looked at the village, spread across the rich grassy prairie in a neat geometric design, clean and orderly, in union with nature. In his mind he contrasted it with the ugly sprawl of Miles City. Kneeing Redskin gently, Hawk rode briskly into the embrace of the lodges and their people. Many had come out to greet the half-blooded grandson of Iron Heart. Most were friendly, but a few of the young bucks in the warrior societies were hostile. Hawk was bareheaded and dressed in a simple buckskin shirt, pants, and soft moccasins. He wore only his knife, no sidearms, as a symbol of respect for the village he entered as a brother. The big bay carried no saddle. In Cheyenne society, only the women and old men rode with saddles.

Hawk slid effortlessly off the stallion and stood face-to-face with Iron Heart in front of the elder's lodge. They clasped arms gravely. "It is good to be home, Grandfather."

"It is good to have you here, Hunting Hawk." There was a look of peace in the old man's eyes as he ushered his daughter's only son into the lodge. This would be a private reunion. Time enough for feasting tonight. There were things that must be said.

"The village looks prosperous. I counted ponies like waves on the sea as I rode in, even buffalo and elk hides drying in the sun." Hawk looked at the clean, functional interior of the tepee with its hard-packed earthen floor, soft grass-stuffed beds, and willow backrests. The cooking pot outside had been full of a thick antelope stew. He was relieved hard times had not yet struck this band.

"For now, it is good, but never like before. In the old days, the buffalo darkened the plains and shook the earth. No more. They are few. Even the elk and deer grow scarce. For one more summer we rejoice, but trouble comes." The old man sat down gracefully on one of the thick beds and reclined against the willow backrest, motioning for Hawk to do likewise.

When they were comfortable, Iron Heart prepared and lit his pipe, a ritual of welcome he greatly enjoyed. He offered it to Hawk, who accepted the honor and took a pull on its length.

"You speak of trouble. I know the game grows less as the whites grow more. I fear for the People." Hawk's eyes were clouded with a worry he was powerless to dispel.

"It is more than these things that have been happening slowly. Since I was a young warrior I could see our fate."

"What do you mean, Grandfather?"

The old man paused, measuringly. "You have been away to the south for many moons. You have not heard. It concerns He Who Walks in Sun."

At the mention of his father's name, Hawk stiffened. "What has he to do with the trouble?"

"The bad medicine wagons that run on wooden trails are coming closer to our lands. Already this spring word has come from the sacred lands of Dakota that the white men build more wooden roads. They stretch ever closer to the sunset. Within a year they will be on this hunting ground."

Railroads this far west! Hawk swore in English. Damn! The rails of the Northern Pacific had stopped in the middle of Dakota Territory back in '73 when old Jay Cooke went bust. Who the devil had resumed construction?

"I have not heard this news. When I returned to the ranch, no word was spoken of it. Are you sure Noah is involved?"

"He sends his cattle herders to set up their little wood huts on pieces of the land to the east, all in a straight line.'' Iron Heart's eyes were shrewd as he looked at Hawk.

They both knew what it meant. In order to bribe the railroad into using a route near his ranch, a cattle baron would have his cowboys purchase homestead tracts from the railroad. The railroads had supposedly paid the Indian Bureau for the land ''held in trust'' for the plains tribes, from whom it had really been stolen. The red men never saw any money from the Indian Bureau. However, once the cowboy had built a crude shack as ''proof of intent'' to farm the land, he simply turned the actual use of it over to his boss, who had paid for it in the first place. Thus the intent of the Homestead Act was subverted, with both small farmers and Indian tribes the losers, especially the Indians. Once railroads ran into an area, towns followed and game became scarce. With no means of sustaining their food supply, the hunters of the plains were starved onto reservations, pitiful little tracts of land the whites did not yet want.

It was happening here, so far north. Hawk had hoped the inevitable could be forestalled, at least a little longer for the Northern Cheyenne. He was hardly surprised that Noah wanted a railhead in Miles City, a shipping point for his beef to rich eastern markets.

He sighed in resignation, knowing nothing could stop the march of the rails. How close they came to the lands around the Circle S was another matter. ''I will see what Noah plans, Grandfather.''

''You are the one who will one day claim his land. It would be good if you could stop him from doing this thing now.''

Hawk's face hardened in grim lines. ''No. I will not be the one, Grandfather. Noah has taken a new wife, a young one.''

Iron Heart pondered that news. ''Is she a second wife? The barren one he married before, she still lives? I thought white men were not allowed two wives.''

Hawk quirked a crooked half-smile. ''Yes, Lola still lives, but Noah has divorced her. If a white man does that, he may take a new wife.''

"Then you will live with the People, not with him. It is a bad thing to drift alone, coming and going from one place to another, belonging nowhere. Our lodges are open to you, and our hearts."

Hawk felt a tightening in his throat as he looked at the earnest old man who loved him. Yes, Iron Heart would welcome him, and so would many of the others, but he would still be a half-blood, one used to the other way of life, not quite fitting in. Several of the younger men had already made that plain. His own feelings were not clear either.

"I will think about it, Grandfather. I do not know my own heart. If I can stop Noah in some way, I must try. Then . . ." He let the thought trail off unspoken. Truly, he did not know what course he would take.

There was feasting that evening, for Iron Heart was an honored chief of the Cheyenne and his grandson was welcomed home.

As they sat around the blazing fire in the center of the encampment, Hawk watched a maiden with a group of women on the other side of the leaping flames. She was young and delicately built with fine features, not the strongly hewn ones that were characteristic of the People. The bold sculptured faces of Cheyenne men were strikingly handsome, but the counterpart on women made most of them too heavy-featured for Hawk's taste. This young woman was distinctly enchanting, however.

He recalled seeing her that afternoon when he left Iron Heart's tent. A sharp war cry had been sounded, and all the young men had quickly rushed out of camp as if to do battle. However, it was not a real war. Hawk recognized the false warhoop that was made by a girl. Often, as a sort of courtship ritual and for just plain fun, the young women on their way home from a day's food gathering would issue the war cry. The single men then rushed to respond, and a mock battle ensued. The maidens pelted the braves with turnips and other roots they had gathered; the braves responded by returning the vegetables and then "capturing" the invaders.

From the sidelines, he had watched them come gamboling

back into camp in groups of two, three, and four, laughing and teasing innocently. The girl across the campfire had caught his eye then as she broke free of several attentive young men and rushed toward the lodges across the way. She had collided with him in her flight and seemed startled, knowing he was Iron Heart's half-blooded grandson. Yet she had lingered for a fleeting moment when her eyes met his and saw his appreciative look.

"Grandfather, the maiden who stands next to Calf Woman, who is she? I do not remember her." Hawk's curiosity was piqued by the lovely Cheyenne.

The old man's eyes lit up. Yes, it might be a sign. It would be good. "Her name is Wind Song. She is, the daughter of Standing Bear. He went to her mother's band when you were a small boy. Now, since her mother is dead she is returned among us with her father. Few of Black Reed's people are left alive. The remnants are among our lodges."

Hawk nodded in understanding. Smallpox had virtually wiped out many bands of Cheyenne. "She is very lovely, Grandfather."

The old man smiled. "Perhaps the blood calls you."

Hawk looked quizzically at Iron Heart, who chuckled and said, "Her grandfather was a French trapper who came to live among her mother's band in the old days. She, too, has a small bit of white blood in her."

Hawk shrugged, not wanting to confront his mixed heritage despite his grandfather's goodwill.

That night he dreamed of Wind Song with her delicately blushing dusky cheeks and gleaming black braids. Were her green eyes a legacy from her French grandfather? What was so familiar about those eyes?

Hawk was not the only dreamer that night. Wind Song had watched him from across the campfire in rapt fascination. So this was the great warchief's half-blooded grandson who lived much of his life among the *veho*. Sitting tall and straight, dressed in beautifully beaded buckskins, with his strongly chiseled features and dark eyes, he looked every inch a Cheyenne warrior. Yet the unbraided shoulder-length hair, the faint shadow of a beard, and the dense hair on his chest proclaimed him a white man, for all Cheyenne men wore long braids, did not need to shave and, indeed, possessed virtually no body hair. He was a curious blending of the red and the white, and to her eyes he looked good. She vividly recalled how they had collided that afternoon when she could not seem to free herself from his laughing black eyes. That night she dreamed of him bringing presents to her lodge and sending an intermediary to ask her bride-price of her father. With the morning's awakening, she hoped it was an omen. Such things often were.

The next day more of the bands arrived for the summer ceremonies and the air of excitement in the camp grew. Always inveterate gamblers and lovers of fleet ponies, the young men of the Fox Warrior Society organized a horserace.

"Will you join the competition, my friend? I know your big red pony to be fleet as the wind." Stands Tall, one of the chiefs of the Fox Warriors, came to invite Hawk. Indeed, the race was basically a competition between members of the various warrior societies—Fox, Crazy Dog, and Elk—but even men not affiliated with any group were welcome to participate. Stands Tall was a longtime friend of Iron Heart and a gentle, courteous man of great dignity. Hawk had always liked him.

Smiling, he replied, "I would be honored to race my bay, although I have already seen many swift ponies in the camp who might outdistance him."

Before the race began, Hawk rubbed the blood bay down until his coat gleamed like polished bronze. He had raised the great beast from a colt, a foal out of one of Noah's best mares. He trained it to be ridden with a saddle or bareback, mounted from left or right side. Making Redskin both a white man's saddle mount and a Cheyenne war pony appealed to his sense of irony as well as providing him with another way to aggravate his father. Noah had been scornfully certain no blooded animal would take to such training, and he waited, assured of his willful son's failure. He did not count on Hawk's uncanny way with animals. Redskin became not only the most intelligent cow pony on the Circle S, but the fastest racing horse

as well. That he was accustomed to either Cheyenne or
white men's style of riding was an added benefit to his
proud owner.

The day was hot. Like most of the men participating in
the race, Hawk stripped to accommodate the heat and to
lighten his weight. He wore only a breechclout and moccasins. His silver medallion gleamed against the bronze of
his bare chest. The necklace had belonged to his mother, a
gift from her beloved brother who was killed in battle
before Hawk's birth. Originally it belonged to Iron Heart
himself. It was Hawk's link to the past, to his Cheyenne
heritage.

He clubbed his hair back to keep it out of his eyes in the
wind. Nothing was more dangerous than being blinded
during a fast turn in a race. Now he envied the other
braves their long hair that could be easily braided and kept
out of their faces, but on the whole he preferred the
coolness and comfort of shorter hair.

When all the contestants finally arrived at the starting
point of the race, wagers were thrown down at the betting
tree by the racers and the onlookers. The tree was simply a
tall pole erected in a clearing of flat ground designated for
that purpose. Colorful jewelry, finely fashioned pipes, and
warm buffalo robes were wagered. The prizes for the
winners would be rich indeed.

While the mounted men lined up and the course of the
race was agreed upon, the maidens watched from the
sidelines. Since many bands were gathered for the summer, the unmarried girls had a splendid assortment of
prime young men to admire. A great deal of preening went
on among the braves and giggling among the maidens who
watched them.

Wind Song came to the race with her younger sister
Sweet Rain. While the twelve-year-old gazed in wide-eyed
wonder at all the milling confusion as the finest horsemen
from each band assembled, her older sister searched the
ranks of blacks, chestnuts, and spotted ponies for a distinc-
tive blood bay and its rider. She saw him just before the
signal was given for the race to begin. Wind Song was
fascinated as she gazed on his nearly naked body covered

with an exotic furring of dark hair. How would it feel to run her hands over the thick, curling hair on his chest? A little shiver of excitement tinged her cheeks with color at the unmaidenly thought. She noticed that the shadow of a beard, which had been visible in last night's firelight, was gone now. How did he do that? Wind Song had never seen a white man shave.

The race began abruptly with a flurry of dust and the low thunder of hooves. Just before he took off on that huge red horse, Hawk looked over at Wind Song and caught her staring at him. He flashed her a grin and winked. She immediately cast her thick black lashes down until his face was turned and the race was on. Her heart hammered like the thud of hooves across the dry prairie grass.

Judging by the field of horses, it was going to be a fast race. Stands Tall rode his lightning-quick little paint, Angry Wolf was astride a big gray with a ground-devouring stride, and Little Reed had a likely looking black in the running. After the first mile or so, Hawk suspected Angry Wolf's gray was the one he had to beat. The huge stallion quickly outdistanced all his competition. At first Hawk held back, trying to gauge the endurance and second wind of several of the other horses in the field. The gray might tire and the black or the paint win in a last-minute blaze of speed. He had ridden in enough wild free-for-all races from Montana to Texas to know the front-runner doesn't always finish first. In this case, with nearly two dozen horses to consider, anything could happen. The gray was holding on to the lead with dogged tenacity and showing no signs of tiring. Hawk inched closer and waited.

It would feel good to beat Angry Wolf, a childhood companion whose bullying and hateful nature had made a younger half-blooded boy's life a misery. Yes, Hawk would relish this victory. He had also noted the way his old foe looked at the lovely green-eyed maiden before the race. She did not favor the big Cheyenne, but instead cast her eyes on Hawk. The win would be doubly sweetened if he could make it. As they neared the homestretch, he gave Redskin a quick rake with his moccasined feet, and the big bay plunged forward in a sudden lunge that pulled him

abreast of the gray. Angry Wolf was laughing as he
sighted the end of the race, a stand of alders by the banks
of the Tongue River. When he saw Hawk and Redskin out
of the corner of his eye, he let out a guttural oath and
leaned forward to whip his horse with a rawhide strip,
urging it to greater speed. The long, sharp leather lashed
out, narrowly missing Hawk and his mount as well. Angry
Wolf never did play fair, Hawk remembered grimly.

However, flaying his horse did not help Angry Wolf. By
the time they neared the alders, Hawk pulled into the lead
and the bay flashed by the crowd of waiting onlookers.
The gray with his sullen rider came in second, several
lengths behind the bay.

As he slid smoothly off Redskin, Hawk was greeted by
Iron Heart, pride worn like a banner across his face. "You
have done well, Hunting Hawk. I am pleased."

He was not the only one pleased. Wind Song stood near
the edge of the crowd, looking at Hawk's sweat-soaked
body as he gratefully took the soft cloth proffered by the
old man and began to towel off his face, neck, and upper
torso.

Her hypnotic gaze was broken when Angry Wolf came
stalking up to her. He could see where her eyes were
turned. "So you look on the half-blood. He is not Cheyenne.
He will not stay with our people. Like the summer rains,
he comes and goes without warning. Best beware lest you
lose your chastity to his spiderish ways and end up on the
prairie!"

At this, Wind Song let out a furious gasp of indignation.
Casting a woman out on the prairie was a degrading
punishment reserved for women caught in repeated adultery, almost unheard of in their band. Without speaking a
word to the hateful man, she proudly walked away to
rejoin several of her young women friends and her little
sister. She held her head high to show her disdain for his
filthy suggestion.

Morality among the Cheyenne was uncommonly strict
by either white or Indian standards. Sexual relations between unmarried men and women was strictly forbidden,
and adultery punished with public disgrace and ostracism.

Divorce was possible but rare. In all the bands Wind Song had observed at summer camps, she had only heard whispered talk of three or four women who were known to be common harlots. No honorable man would ever offer them marriage, and they lived a degraded, meager existence on the periphery of tribal life.

She wondered how the *veho* were different, having heard rumors about their loose morals. Surely the grandson of Iron Heart would never dishonor her. Certainly she would never allow herself to be used so cheaply. Wind Song thought about the vast world beyond the sunrise, that place full of *veho* cities. She heard some of the old men speak of it, those chiefs who traveled to the east to meet leaders of the whites. Hunting Hawk had been part of that alien unimaginable world. Was he like them or like the People?

Sunrise. Hot orange light filtered across the high plains as Hawk stretched and awakened instinctively. He had been unable to sleep past daybreak since his earliest memories, no matter how late he stayed up at night. Always this oneness with the birth of morning was his. Today he would go hunting with his grandfather and Stands Tall.

They split up, the three men, each taking a different track. By midmorning Hawk found fresh signs and silently crept to a nearby watering hole to wait. Within an hour his patience was rewarded. A young buck elk silently picked his way to the clean pool and cautiously scanned his surroundings. Sensing no intruder, he dipped his head to drink. Hawk took careful aim with his rifle and fired one shot. The big elk crumpled, hit solidly in the chest. As Hawk tied the elk across a wooden travois, Iron Heart admired the clean kill. It would be a good pelt, and the teeth on the young buck were beautiful, perfect for the elaborate trim sewn onto ceremonial dresses by Cheyenne women. He thought of one maiden in particular.

"The meat will roast tender and sweet," the old man greeted him.

Hawk nodded absently as he worked. "Yes. Calf Wom-

an will make some fine stews as well, I imagine.'' Calf
Woman cooked for Iron Heart.

The old man cleared his throat, then spoke evenly. ''I
have much meat already in my lodge. Everyone has been
generous to an old man. There are others in the village
who could use it more . . .'' He let his words trail off.

Hawk picked up the cue. ''Tell me who, and I will take
it as a present to his family.'' Such generosity and mutual
help between families of the People was always the custom.

''Standing Bear has grown old and infirm. His daughters are alone and have no one to hunt for them. Wind
Song and Sweet Rain could use the elk meat.'' He looked
expectantly at his grandson. Hawk grinned. ''Then to the
beautiful green-eyed Wind Song it goes. Even the teeth to
decorate a dress.''

''Hrumpf,'' the old man grunted, satisfied.

Wind Song was in her father's lodge, removing food
bowls from behind a willow backrest when she heard
Hawk's voice outside, speaking with Standing Bear. Quickly
she smoothed her braids and adjusted her leggings. Feigning
a trip to the stream for water, she grabbed a big bucket and
casually stepped toward the tepee opening.

''I have killed an elk. My grandfather has already
received from others more than an old man alone can use.
I offer it to you and your family, Standing Bear.''

The old brave was palsied and frail, far from the robust
specimen Iron Heart was, even though Hawk's grandfather
was far the older of the two men. Standing Bear nodded
gravely, indicating that Hawk should untie the game. ''For
a sick old man and his two maiden daughters, your gift is
most welcome.''

As if on cue, Wind Song emerged from the lodge.
''Father, I—'' She stopped short, her eyes widening as the
tall, lean man effortlessly dragged the elk from the travois
and deposited it in front of their lodge. He smiled in silent
greeting. Hating herself for it, she blushed in response,
then forced her voice under control and spoke. ''I was
going to fetch water. I will send for Sweet Rain to help me
with the elk. We are most grateful to the grandson of Iron
Heart for his generosity.''

"I am called Hunting Hawk." Once more the disarming grin appeared, making the harsh lines of his handsome face soften.

"And my elder daughter is called Wind Song." Standing Bear supplied the rest of the introduction. "Will you stay and eat with me? I would be honored."

In response, Wind Song moved to spread a buffalo robe next to her father's side so Hawk could sit. Nodding gravely, Hawk squatted effortlessly on the soft cover as the lithe girl slipped inside the lodge to bring food. She completely forgot her ruse about the need for water. As she was preparing dried fruit and strips of meat, Standing Bear began another coughing spell. Setting the food down quickly, she rushed outside to find Hawk supporting the old man's weight. Standing Bear struggled to breathe.

"It is better if he lays down with his upper body raised." She began to help her father rise, but anticipating her need, Hawk lifted him up and carried him inside the lodge. Gently he stretched the pain-wracked man across a pile of robes, propping him against a backrest to ease his labored breathing.

Wind Song quickly mixed a small amount of the potion she had received from the medicine man and forced it between her father's bluish lips. His coughing subsided and his breathing became slower and deeper. Soon he slept.

Silently the two young people slipped from the tepee back into the day's bright grasp. "Thank you for helping. The attacks grow worse. I fear for another cold season." Her voice was infinitely sad.

Hawk realized the truth of her words. Standing Bear could never survive another winter on the plains. "It is the white man's consumption?"

She nodded. "For the last two seasons he has grown thinner and the cough stronger. He was at Fort Robinson when there was not enough food or blankets. The white man's lodges are not as warm as ours. He came home sick and broken. Then my mother died and he just gave in to it." Her voice was haunted by all the tragedy visited upon her young life, all brought by the spider people.

"Do you have other kin in my grandfather's village?" Hawk felt a wistful sympathy for this lovely girl of mixed blood.

She shook her head. "No, only my sister and I are left now."

The other solution was obvious in Cheyenne society. She looked to be sixteen or seventeen. "Is there not one fine young warrior who you favor? Surely you have had many offer your bride-price."

She blushed, recalling the elk in front of the lodge. "No man has offered who I would choose, yet." She could tell her cheeks were hot with color, and was relieved when Sweet Rain burst in on their conversation.

"Oh, Wind Song, I was told to come help you with an elk. It is beautiful!" She looked at the big beast on the ground in undisguised pleasure. "Maybe this time I'll get my elktooth dress and one for you, too. If only you had not refused the elk Angry Wolf brought you yesterday!"

Unaware of the implications of her speech, Sweet Rain went inside and began to gather sharp adzes and skinning knives for the task at hand.

Hawk's black eyes took on a speculative gleam as he looked from the child to the flustered young woman who stood in acute embarrassment. Gently he said, "I must go now. Whenever you need my help, just send word, Wind Song. I will come." With that he quickly took Redskin's reins, turned the empty travois, and left her standing silently in front of the lodge. She busied herself immediately with dressing the elk, afraid to look around and see if he was watching her.

Early the next morning Wind Song really did need to go to the stream for water. Still pensive over her meeting with Hawk and distraught over her sister's teasing about his gift, she wandered down a seldom-used path to the river. It was overgrown with alder trees, but she could hear the rushing of water from behind the seclusion of greenery. Wanting a peaceful place to think in private, she wended her way through the bushes to the edge of the stream and knelt to fill the bucket.

Sweet Rain's taunts about Angry Wolf still burned her

ears. He wanted to marry Wind Song, but she had refused him. Her father agreed that she did not have to marry a man she disliked, but how long could she wait? Already Angry Wolf had staked a claim on her by frightening off several other young braves who had courted her. Everyone was afraid of him. Hateful bully! She detested him, but if her father died and she was left without a protector, the chiefs would meet and give her to whoever they deemed best, probably Angry Wolf. It was selfish of her to cause her father and sister to suffer this way. If she married Angry Wolf, her family would be well provided for because he was a good hunter and a rich man. Still her heart rebelled. She lost track of time, kneeling in silent misery, hidden by the tall grass at the edge of the water. Just then her twisted thoughts were interrupted by a sharp oath of pain from a male voice that spoke in the *veho* tongue.

"Damn!" Hawk had just knicked himself with a dull razor. He cursed for not taking time to hone it—and for needing it in the first place. Cheyenne men were certainly better off. What few chin whiskers they had they could easily pull out. He eyed the thick black stubble covered by the soap lather on his face and swore at his white blood. Just as he looked in the mirror to finish the shave, he heard a twig snap and a small gasp from the trees behind him. Wind Song's frightened face appeared in the glass. She was standing in the thick undergrowth by the water's edge, bucket clasped awkwardly in one hand, staring in wide-eyed amazement at his soap-covered face.

He grinned crookedly and put his thumb to the nicked place on his jaw as he turned to greet her. "Good morning, Wind Song."

Nodding, she lowered her gaze in mortification. "I did not mean to intrude. I was getting water and wanted to be alone, so I wandered farther from camp than I should have." Then her eyes lifted, curiosity overcoming shyness as she looked at his face. His smile was warm and heartened her. "What—what is it that you do?"

He chuckled. "It may look as though I am bleeding myself, but I am really trying to shave off my whiskers. I do it badly, I'm afraid." With that he turned and continued to scrape the lathered beard off with sweeping strokes of the razor. Finishing, he wiped his face with a rag and turned back to her.

Now his countenance was smooth and hairless. So that was why some white men had great bushes growing on their faces and others had none.

"There, you see, smooth as any Cheyenne."

"Until tomorrow," she said with a smile curving her lips. "You must do this every day? It seems a great lot of trouble."

He grunted in agreement, then changed the subject, not wanting to dwell on his white heredity. "You must have been deep in thought; you were very quiet back there. What troubles you, Wind Song?"

Hesitantly she looked up at him. How could she explain it to him? She was already embarrassed enough by what her sister had said yesterday. "Our father grows weaker each day, and I am the elder daughter. It is my responsibility . . ."

"To marry a strong provider to care for your family," he supplied for her. "And Angry Wolf has offered, yet you do not like him. Surely there are others?"

"He has driven them off," she spat furiously. "There is no other brave enough to stand against that one."

Now it was her turn to eye him speculatively. When he looked back at her levelly, she lost her boldness and stooped to pick up the sloshing water bucket, refusing to meet his gaze any longer. "I must go. My sister will be calling for me."

Despite his unwillingness to be drawn into Iron Heart's matchmaking, Hawk was attracted to the maiden and sorry for her plight. "Do you come here often—to think?"

She smiled dazzlingly as she began to walk toward the clearing, hefting the large bucket effortlessly. "Every morning," she replied, adding to herself, *Every morning from now on.*

For the next several days Hawk came to the stand of alders to shave each morning, and Wind Song came to fill her water buckets. If accidental and infrequent, such casual encounters between young women and men were permissible under Cheyenne social customs. However, the regularity and premeditation of their meetings was a serious breach of tradition. Hawk knew he was taking a real risk of being trapped into an unwanted marriage. Nevertheless, he found Wind Song's innocence and beauty captivating. He was scrupulously careful to keep the relationship on a conversational level, never allowing it to move toward anything physical. But the attraction between them was a palpable thing, and he knew he could have her if he wished to pursue her. Hawk held himself in check, honoring the strict morality of the People and the trusting naiveté of the maiden.

"What are white women like?" Wind Song asked him one morning as she lowered her bucket into the clear rushing water.

Hawk paused with his razor in midstroke. "Depends. Some are all right, I guess. Some are evil. I am afraid I have spent more time with the bad ones than the good. Fine ladies avoid half-breeds, you see."

Sensing the bitterness in his voice and puzzled about his life in the white world, Wind Song said, "You are the son of a powerful white man. You have been to their cities and schools. You must look like a white man when you dress in his clothes. Why would these women not find you pleasing?"

He smiled at her unconscious compliment. "Oh, I have a good education by Noah Sinclair's standards, but despite it, the easterners know me as an Indian. Anyway, most white women want a rich husband. I have been a drifter and gunman, Wind Song."

"But you are his only son . . ." she said in puzzlement.

Hawk gave her a pitying glance, realizing how little she could imagine of the twisted, hateful ways of the *veho*. "I am his son, but for the last five years of my mother's life he never acknowledged her as his wife. He was ashamed of her. He and I always fought. We never understood or loved one another, even when I was a boy. I never expected to inherit his riches. Neither did any of the women in the territory think I would. I am a terrible prospect for a husband."

"That is not true—" She stopped short as a crimson flush stole up her neck and over her face. "I—I must go. My father will be wanting to sit outdoors on this warm day. I must attend to him."

He moved quickly to her side before she could pick up the heavy bucket and took her lovely face in one hand, tipping her chin up and looking into her green eyes. "I am sorry, Wind Song. I did not mean to embarrass you. You are innocent and honest. You do not know how to dissemble. Stay that way." He kissed her softly on the lips, a chaste, tender gesture that was over quickly. Then he let her go.

Trembling both for what he said and did not say, she scooped up the water and fled with his kiss and warm breath still caressing her mouth.

Hawk swore and turned to gather up his gear from the ground. "Time to be moving on. You may just have outstayed your welcome, at least if you don't marry that girl," he muttered under his breath, uncertain of what he should do, or even of what he wanted to do.

He knew he must confront Noah about the railroad land being bought by Circle S men and find out what that greedy fox was after. Then what? He was as confused as ever, still wondering if he had a true home anywhere.

CHAPTER 6

As he rode back to the Circle S, Hawk recalled his last conversation with Wind Song. He had told her he was returning to Noah's ranch to try and help the People escape the ravages of the railroad, making it clear that he was uncertain of when he would return. He could promise her nothing. They had spoken of their mixed blood and what it meant to each of them.

"I never knew my grandfather, the Frenchman. At times I do not feel I have any white blood in me, yet I know I am different. My eyes are the strangest color and my hair curls at the ends when the weather is damp."

"Your eyes are beautiful, like a clear pool after a summer rain, like the ocean," Hawk responded.

"You have seen this . . . this great water—the ocean? I have only heard of it and of the big cities of the whites stretching along its side. And of boats that cross it to more great cities on the other side. Are there really so many tribes of white men?" Her eyes were wide with wonder and curiosity.

He smiled sadly. "Yes, too many tribes, all warring among themselves. The only thing they agree on is that all of them should exploit the red men. Sometimes I fear the People are doomed, Wind Song."

"We cannot fit in their world, but you can. Why do you not go and live among them?" She said the words hesitantly, unwillingly, but she needed to understand the answer.

He considered. "I have spent my life between worlds, I guess. Part of me wants to be here, part of me cannot let go of the white ways instilled in me as a child. I really do not fit in either society. I still look for my place, I suppose."

"The People will welcome you. You will always belong here, but it is up to you to choose if you want to be Cheyenne. The whites may not give you this choice. Do you want them to?"

Hawk pondered her question as he rode back to Circle S. He was sure Noah would never offer him a place in his world on any terms, but with friends like Frank and Kyle the young man already had acceptance. What else was there? Nagging thoughts of Carrie surfaced, her green eyes and Wind Song's melding together. What made him suddenly think of Noah's little fortune-hunting bitch of a wife? He swore and gave Redskin a kick.

At least he could salve his conscience about the lovely Cheyenne. Before he left the village, he asked his grandfather to take Wind Song and her sister under his protection when Standing Bear died. With the considerable influence of Iron Heart, she would not be forced into an unwanted marriage with Angry Wolf or anyone else. Of course, Hawk knew Iron Heart hoped his grandson would return to the People and marry Wind Song. The maiden wished it as well. He could feel it during the last weeks they had spent together, but his own desires were in turmoil.

What did he want? To be Cheyenne? To be white? An honored warchief or a respectable rancher? He scoffed at the probability of the latter. Carrie, beautiful green-eyed bitch, would see to it that he never inherited Circle S. He considered. No, in all honesty, Noah would cut him out of the will whether or not Carrie gave him white heirs.

It was hot, the sun seeming to stand still in the brilliant azure sky at midday. Carrie shrugged and pulled the sticky yellow cotton blouse away from her breasts where it clung, wet and itchy. "How I'd love a nice, cool bath in that pool," she thought aloud.

After having another argument with Noah, she had

ridden all morning. In spite of his rough, loathsome
nightly attentions, she still did not quicken. He had questioned
her in humiliating detail about her monthly courses, which
had begun again last week. Even if she hated him—and
she was beginning to—it might be better to conceive a
child of his. If she were breeding, at least he would leave
her bed and give her peace. He would go back to his
whore in Miles City. Noah had already made it clear that
he found his wife's lack of response most unsatisfactory
and told her she was a child in a woman's body.

Carrie shivered in revulsion, thinking of his wrinkled,
flabby flesh and those clawlike, cruel hands roaming over
her. Suddenly she was cold in the noonday heat. What
might it be like if a young, lithe male caressed her instead
of her old husband? *What made me think that?* Even
though it was only a private thought, Carrie fairly twitched
in outraged embarrassment. Of course, it was a thought
that frequently haunted her in past weeks. *If only I'd been
able to choose my husband, a man my own age . . .*

Dejectedly she let Taffy Girl pick her way toward the
edge of the water. It was a small lake, one of several on
Circle S land, clean and sweet, wonderfully inviting in the
heat of an August day. The surroundings were quiet and
beckoning. No one was about to disturb her. *Well, why
not?*

She answered her question by quickly slipping off her
horse and vanishing into the thick willows by the pool's
edge to shed her clothes. Young ladies in the cities of the
east were never allowed to swim, but Carrie had learned
when she was a child, still living with her parents. Her
mother's cousin had a farm in St. Charles, a small town on
the Missouri River. Carrie, a mere six or seven to her
second cousin Hildy's ten, would slip off to a small pond
behind the apple orchard. There Hildy taught her the
unladylike art of doggy paddling, diving and playing like a
young otter in the warm Missouri water.

The clear spring-fed Montana lake prompted memories of
carefree childhood. *Why, oh why, did Mama and Papa have
to die? Life was such fun back then.* Sighing, Carrie lay
back and floated in silent reverie.

Suddenly her peaceful haven was disturbed when a horse whickered. It wasn't Taffy Girl who was tied on the opposite side of the alder trees. At once Carrie was alert, silently treading water over to a partially sunken log, lodged against a small finger of land that jutted out in the middle of the pool. Behind the leafy cover the log afforded, she could watch undetected and see who had intruded on her private domain.

The minute she sighted the big red horse tied by the bank, she knew who it was. Then she saw him next to Redskin, in the process of stripping methodically. His gunbelt and knife already lay gleaming evilly on the lake bank. In wide-eyed wonder she watched as he slipped a buckskin shirt over his shoulders, baring the broad expanse of his furry chest. Dark coppery-colored skin rippled with lean muscles as he bent over and pulled one, then the other moccasin off. When he straightened up and began to unfasten his breeches, Carrie knew she must look away. But she did not. Never in all her young life had she watched a man undress. When Noah came into her room he did so under cover of darkness, shedding his robe by her bedside. Strange, she had never possessed the slightest curiosity about male anatomy—until now. Certainly she had never before seen such a specimen—in or out of his clothes!

Hawk stood still, stark naked in the warmth of the noon sun, then stretched like some barbarous bronzed god, worshiping and being worshiped by the sensual beauty of the hot day. He was long-legged and muscular in a lean, hard fashion, with black curly hair covering his chest, forearms, and legs. Quickly she let her eyes skip over the core of his maleness and looked at his face; his eyes were closed as he raised his chiseled features and let the sun caress them. His shoulder-length hair gleamed with raven's-wing luster as he shook it and then began to stride deliberately into the inviting water.

In fascination, she watched his copper-colored body gradually submerge until he began to swim in bold, strong strokes across the water toward the opposite bank. Then suddenly he vanished beneath the water while in the middle of the pool. Surely he was not drowning, she thought in panic! What should she do?

Carrie treaded water, holding onto the scratchy log, frantically considering what had happened. Just as suddenly as he had vanished, he surfaced—directly beside her!

"Oooh!" Releasing the log, she dropped deeper into the water, hiding the tips of coral nipples from his view.

Laughing as he slapped a mass of midnight hair from his face, Hawk said, "Careful, you might suck in half the lake and lower the water level. Then I'd see what you're trying so hard to hide."

Spluttering more, she backed against the log and crouched even lower. He looked at her as if his eyes could penetrate the blue-green depths. "I recognized your horse, but couldn't believe a nice city girl like you would be skinny-dipping in a pond, much less spying on a man while he undressed, Carrie. Shame, shame."

She felt the heat of the flush stain her neck and face despite the cool kiss of water lapping over her shoulders. "You had no right! If you saw Taffy you should never have come in here, Hawk Sinclair. No gentleman would ever invade a lady's privacy like this!"

"I'm no gentleman, remember. Besides, no lady would be naked in the first place. You are naked, aren't you, little firehair?"

With that, he made a lightning move across the water separating them and clasped her around her waist. With a shriek, she fell thrashing into his arms, her body pressed intimately to the length of his.

"Yep, mother naked," he breathed as he ran trespassing hands down her back and over the curve of wet silky buttocks. Then he raised one hand beneath the blanket of water and cupped a full round breast whose nipple had inexplicably puckered into a hard point.

Carrie could feel the scratch of his hairy torso against her belly—also that male part of him, hard and probing between her legs. Her breasts tingled and her whole body quivered. Was it fear or anticipation? It was not the cold revulsion she felt when Noah touched her. Her thrashing protests stopped and she looked into his jet eyes. Her own green ones were puzzled and expectant. *Why don't I scream?*

An eternity seemed to pass in the shady pool as he held her with one long arm and silently explored her body. Hawk felt his breathing accelerate and his temperature rise. His hand was soft, slicked with water, his fingers cunning and deft as he traced the rounded curve of her breast where it joined to her ribs, then moved downward over the slim swell of a hipbone, then back to cup the soft cheek of her derriere. All the while he held her pressed closely to him with an inflexible arm, aware of the pounding of her heart and trembling of her body.

Carrie's hands were flattened on his chest, pressing against him but not pushing him away. Her palms were incredibly sensitive as she felt the flexing of his muscles beneath the heavy mat of his chest hair. The instinctive desire to rub little circles across his hard body was irresistible. She desperately wanted to feed the hunger of her own questing hands and almost gave in to it. But then he broke the spell.

"How old are you? Eighteen? Maybe nineteen? Have you ever been with a young man? Have you ever had a real lover, Carrie?" He sensed her increasing arousal that matched his own, and despised them both for their carnal weakness. "Too bad you got more than you bargained for with Noah. He may not be good, but I bet he is thorough."

All the breath seemed to leave her body at his cruel taunt, unexpectedly reminding her that she was a married woman, most unhappily so. Furiously she pushed at him in earnest now, and he let her go. She stumbled backward, cringing against the log. "Get away from me! I want to get out of the water!"

"I won't stop you," he said in smirking amusement.

"Turn around and swim across to the other side so you can't watch me," she ordered through clenched teeth. Now the chill of the shadowy water was taking its toll. Deprived of his body heat and frozen in shame, she shook with cold.

Shrugging in acquiescence, as if supremely indifferent, he rolled over and began to swim leisurely toward the center of the lake. Quickly Carrie climbed out of the water and grabbed for her clothes on the open bank. She could still hear his even strokes cleaving the water, but when she looked up, her horrified green eyes locked with his hot black ones. He was swimming away all right, but he had changed to a smooth, even backstroke, all the while watching her emerge from the shelter of the water. She clutched a sheer camisole to her breasts, glaring at him, not able to think of anything vile enough to say.

"Turnabout's fair play, Carrie. You watched me strip. I get to watch you dress," he called out, then stopped swimming and treaded water while his eyes raked over her pale-pink skin, that length of slim elegant leg, sleek flair of hip, and swell of breast that he had felt only a moment ago. He swallowed a groan of frustrated misery. Dammit, she was beautiful, perfectly, magnificently beautiful.

Snatching up her blouse, boots, and pants, she yelled furiously over one shoulder, "You—you half-breed! You bastard!"

His voice mocked her as she vanished into the cover of the bushes alongside the bank. "Guilty on the first count, Firehair, but not the last. My mother was married to Noah Sinclair just as legally as you are!"

Damn him for putting it that way, for reminding her! He was her husband's son. She felt suddenly in need of a bath in spite of her long swim in the clean, clear water.

Hawk rode up to the corral, where Kyle Hunnicut was slowly removing the saddle from his horse. Without seeming to acknowledge his friend's arrival, Hunnicut grunted as he swung the heavy load across a fence rail. "Yew been gone long 'nough. Find yew a woman with yer ma's folks?"

Hawk grinned as he slid off Redskin. "Not the way you think, amigo. We'll have to go to town for that. Man'd get scalped in Iron Heart's band for fooling around with the women."

"Too damn good fer their own good if'n ya ask me," he grunted, dragging the saddle into the big tack barn next to the corral.

After both men had stowed their gear and rubbed down their horses, Kyle gave Hawk a level look and said, "Somethin's eatin' at ya, Longlegs. Wanna palaver?"

"How in hell do you read people so well, Kyle? Hell, I don't know. A lot of things are bothering me." His face darkened as he recalled the feel of Carrie's wet skin that afternoon. After she had left, he had dressed and ridden around aimlessly for several hours, trying to suppress the unexpected surge of desire she'd elicited from him. No, he couldn't confess that encounter—not even to Kyle!

"You're right in part, I guess. There is a girl in Grandfather's village. He'd like me to marry her and live with them."

Kyle looked at the anguished face of his friend, understanding the tearing of his soul, perhaps better than anyone. "An' yew cain't rightly decide whether ta be red er white." It wasn't a question. He had long known of Hawk's divided loyalties. He spat a wad of tobacco and said, "I reckon if'n ya marry Cheyenne, thet burns yer bridges, don't it? Ya got unfinished business here, though."

Hawk looked up abruptly. "What do you mean—the rustling?"

"Railroad. I heerd some talk from Noah's ole hands. Seems he's got 'em becomin' sodbusters. Leastways fer a while." He spat again in disgust.

Hawk's eyes blazed. "That's what Grandfather told me. You're right, as usual, Kyle. I have to do whatever I can for his band, to secure their lands here before I ride off Circle S again, this time for good."

Kyle assessed his friend's predicament shrewdly. "Yep, I figgered ya'd leave fer good this time, whut with thet new filly o' Noah's. She ain't all bad, though. Fer a tenderfoot, she's got real spunk. Rides out ever day—astride, even though th' ole man pitched a real bitch 'bout it." He chuckled. "Whenever he's off ta Miles City politickin', she gits out her pants 'n' takes off on Taffy. Why, today—"

Hawk cut in abruptly, "I know you fancy yourself in love with that redheaded baggage, but let her and Noah settle their own problems. I'm interested in who's buying up homestead lots along Circle S property. Get me a list of names, Kyle."

"Whut ya fixin' ta do? Yew cain't stop th' railroad. It's acomin', Longlegs, damn if'n it ain't."

"I know that. Question is, where will it be routed— through the southern Yellowstone country or north on Krueger's land? The farther away from Cheyenne summer hunting grounds, the better. I'm going to snoop in town at the clerk's office. You check things around here. Then I'll decide what to do about Noah's schemes. Any more stock missing?"

"Old man's madder'n a biled owl. Figger it's Krueger's men." He chuckled, remembering the fat herd on the east range lost last week. It was Krueger all right. He looked measuringly at Hawk. "Yew figgerin' whut I think yew are?"

Hawk's smile did not extend to his cold black eyes. "That Karl Krueger and I might have a common enemy?" He nodded slowly.

After telling Feliz she had a headache and needed to rest, Carrie spent the afternoon in her room. In truth, she tossed fitfully on her bed, awash in humiliated misery over her encounter with Hawk Sinclair. How could she ever face him again? Noah would know at once that something had transpired between them. Even worse than her husband's wrath was her own gnawing sense of guilt and confusion over the feelings Hawk had awakened in her.

As a schoolgirl in St. Louis, she had found some young men attractive. When Gerald had kissed her, she had thought she was in love with him, but time and maturity had made her realize how shallow the infatuation had been on both their parts. After her first weeks around Hawk, she had developed a growing sense of uneasiness that really had nothing to do with his Indian blood, but much to do with his magnetic maleness. Until today she had not faced that fact. Now that she had done so, she could not deal with the shame it engendered. And the worst part was his mocking indifference to her. He had let her go. With her face flaming, Carrie admitted to her tortured soul that if he had pressed his suit in the water, she would have welcomed it. "What kind of harlot am I? Has Noah's callous depravity driven me to this, or was I always destined to be bad?" Silent tears seared her cheeks as she lay alone in her room.

That night at dinner Carrie was composed, at least on the surface. Painstakingly she had soaked her ravaged face with cold water and then had applied one of Feliz's cucumber facial remedies. With clenched teeth she had decided to show Hawk the stuff Carrie Patterson was made of. She would be calm and beautiful, as unconcerned over the afternoon's debacle as he. Having selected a dress of deep-green crepe, she then washed and curled her hair and applied a dab of artful rouge before donning the sleekly elegant gown. It picked up the color of her eyes and made her look older and more sophisticated. Noah would like it. Perversely, she hoped Hawk would, too.

He did. Entering the parlor for a before-dinner whiskey, he took in the fire-haired vision dressed in dark green. She stood with her profile to him, facing Noah and toying with a crystal stemmed glass filled with wine. Feeling a sudden rush of desire, Hawk took iron rein on his emotions and forced himself to saunter silently to the bar for his drink.

Noah ignored him, since they had exchanged testy words earlier that afternoon about his visit with the Cheyenne. Carrie looked past her husband's shoulder at the immaculately attired young man who was transformed from a sweaty savage in buckskins to a barbarously handsome stranger in tailored black broadcloth. His dark face split in a sardonic smile. In a mock salute to her, he raised his glass behind Noah's back. A ruby ring winked insolently from his hand as he quaffed the whiskey.

Mrs. Thorndyke announced dinner stiffly. The meal was strained, but somehow Carrie managed to eat and drink calmly and even offer a few words to the desultory conversation.

Noah and Hawk talked about the rustling and the progress of the railroad. She sensed an undercurrent between father and son over the details of where the rail line was to be laid, but did not understand enough to dare ask questions. She would talk to Frank about the matter tomorrow.

Frank Lowery had quickly joined Feliz as Carrie's staunchest ally. Perhaps it was their common animosity toward Noah that drew them together. Frank intensely disliked his boss. Several times she had wanted to ask why, but felt it was presuming too much. For now she was glad to have someone who would ride with her and teach her about the operation of the ranch. Frank, who was Noah's age, treated her like an adored daughter, which was balm to her wounded spirit.

Early the next morning, as soon as Carrie was sure Noah and Hawk were both gone for the day, she put on her most comfortable riding pants, really a split skirt that Feliz had fashioned for her, and headed to the corral where Taffy Girl waited.

Frank was just issuing the last instructions to a couple of bronc busters at the breaking fence when he spied her and waved. He watched the graceful ease with which she now rode. In a few short months she had become an accomplished horsewoman. The youthful flush of vivacious joy on her face as she trotted Taffy up to him tugged at Frank's heart. Despite the difference in appearance and culture, Marah and Carrie were both so alike, so in love with life's simple pleasures, so kind and desirous of pleasing others. Why did Noah treat them so rottenly? Swearing to himself, Frank decided some men had all the luck and deserved none of it.

"If'n ya kin wait up a spell, we'll ride ta th' line camp 'n' I'll show ya th' fat bunch o' calves there." His broad, toothy grin was infectious.

Carrie also grinned. "You have a deal!" Just then she caught sight of Hawk and Kyle as they rode away, heading to the north. Her face darkened.

Frank watched her reaction. It was not the first time that he had noticed her flush of anger and something else indefinable when she looked at Hawk Sinclair. He was afraid to speculate about what her feelings were, but felt she needed guidance.

While he saddled up, they talked. She questioned him about the railroad. "Why is Hawk against the railroad? Surely it means more schools and business, a better life for everyone here. More food and medicine can be shipped to the reservations for his own people if the rails are nearby."

Frank shook his head sadly. "Wish thet was th' case, honey, but it purely ain't. Ya see, them crooked Injun agents mostly skim off th' supplies an' sell 'em ta who-ever's got th' cash ta buy 'em. That is, whut little th' bigger crooks in Washington don't already pocket afore th' railroad even ships it west. Naw, rails only mean th' Injuns real source o' food gits drove off. More rails means more cattle, more sodbusters, jist more white folks. All thet means less buffalo, deer, elk. All biles down ta starvin' Cheyenne, Sioux, Araps, all th' rest. Damn shame!"

Gravely Carrie considered his words. "I see. You really sympathize with the plight of the Indian, don't you, Frank?"

"Anyone with a lick o' human feelin's ought ta. 'Course, they's two sides ta ever' story. Sioux's still warrin' on ranchers, 'n' Crow'll steal ya blind 'n' run back ta their reservation. Reds's like whites, I reckon. Some's good, some's bad," he concluded.

"Noah seems to hate all Indians now. I never under-stood. After all, he married a Cheyenne woman. Now he hates his own son." As she spoke, Carrie watched Frank's face darken.

"Noah's a fool! He had him a good, lovin' wife and th' finest son any man could want. Trouble goes back ta Able, I reckon."

"Able," Carrie echoed in bafflement. "Noah's dead brother?"

"Kilt by Crow when Hawk wuz jist a tyke," Frank put in. "After thet, wal, it seemed like everythin' went sour fer Noah. He blamed all Injuns, not jist th' Crow, but even Laughin' Woman's people—his own wife and son! 'Course, by then, more white folk's movin' in, too. All respectable like, with their uppity white wives an' daughters. Seems like ole Noah reconsidered. Even though she loved him more'n life, he was ashamed o' her, damn him!'' The fierce blaze of anger in his eyes masked a more tender emotion.

Carrie said gently, "You loved her, didn't you, Frank? That's why you stayed with Noah all these years. To watch over her son and his birthright.''

Frank's eyes were suspiciously shiny as he looked at Carrie. "Reckon I did and reckon I do kinda care fer thet young hellion o' hers. But Noah never figgered ta leave Circle S ta her son. Hawk knowed it 'n' so do I.''

Hesitantly Carrie spoke up. "Frank, I hope you don't blame me. If I—if Noah and I . . .'' She stammered to a blushing halt.

Frank looked at her with a kindly, sad smile, soothing her embarrassment. "If'n yew have another Sinclair son fer Noah, he'll get Circle S, yep. But I don't figger ya wanted it thet way an' even if'n yew wasn't here, someone else would o' been. After he got shut o' thet tramp Lola he might o' done a heap worse'n yew, ma'am.''

Carrie was touched by his perception and consideration. She also wanted to understand about Lola Jameson Sinclair. "Everyone seems to have disliked the second Mrs. Sinclair. Why, Frank?''

He considered how to explain it delicately to this young girl who, unlike her predecessor, was so obviously a lady. "Ma'am, Lola was everthin' Noah thought he wanted after Laughin' Woman died. She wuz from a high-society family back east in Chicago. Dressed real fancy an' talked even fancier. Looks that'd knock a man off'n his horse—yeller har 'n' blue eyes. Yep, I reckon he took one look at Lola Jameson an' thought he had jist th' ticket.'' He paused grimly. "Wal, he wuz purely wrong. She wuz as wicked on th' inside as she wuz purty on th' outside. First thing she wanted wuz fer thet dirty Injun kid ta be sent away— back ta his ma's folks 'er east ta school. Didn't make no niver mind ta her—jist so's he wuz gone. Noah obliged her. Sent Hawk off when he wuz only a tad, nine er ten's all. But she never had any youngun's o' her own. Feliz said she had ways not ta, if'n ya take my meanin, ma'am.'' Frank colored at this and coughed. When Carrie nodded in vague understanding, he continued. ''She wanted Noah's money right 'nough, but she didn't want ta live in 'this godforsaken wilderness'—whut she called Circle S country. Even Miles City wuz jist a dirty ole cow town ta her. She spent money like water runnin' over th' Tongue River Falls in a spring thaw.''

''I knew she decorated the house. It's exquisitely beautiful but very costly, too.'' Carrie recalled Hawk's mention of Lola's taste.

Frank made a sound of disgust deep in his throat. ''Hell, he built th' house fer her! Like one o' them fancy places back east. Afore thet, Noah and Laughin' Woman lived in a purty lil' place, over west aways. Her things'er still there. . . .''

''I thought the big house was built in 1862. That was before Marah died,'' Carrie said in puzzlement.

Frank nodded. ''Yep, he built it, but it wuz ta be fer a *white* wife, even if'n he hadn't picked her out yet. Laughin' Woman never lived in it. Thet ain't even th' worst o' it. I figger if'n yore gonna hear this, ya might's well hear it all. Sooner 'er later, things kinda got them a way o' comin' up anyhow.''

''Go on, Frank,'' Carrie said, almost afraid of the rest.

''Seems like after a bunch o' years back 'n' forth, in an' outta a passel o' eastern schools, Hawk growed up. At seventeen he wuz as tall as he is now; fine-lookin' young feller. Lola thought so, too. Oh, she'd eyed up all th' good-lookin' young studs 'round hereabouts, an' more then jist looked at 'em, yew kin betcha. Noah niver caught on, cuz he wuz always busy gettin' richer, leavin' her alone.

''One night Hawk came ta me all shook up—Injun mad, I always called it. She'd tried ta lure 'em ta her bed whilst Noah wuz in Miles City overnight. Th' dirty Injun kid wuz real appealin' ta her all o' a sudden. Now, Hawk wuz young, but he warn't dumb. He wanted nothin' ta do with thet schemin' female, her near old 'nough ta be his ma. He lit out fer th' Nations thet night.''

''Why didn't he tell his father what she'd done?'' Carrie

was revolted by the whole sordid mess, for more reasons than she cared to think about.

Frank looked at her levelly. "Do ya think Noah'd a believed him?"

She shook her head. "No, I guess not."

"A couple o' years went by. By then, Noah'd took Lola's measure 'n' wanted shut o' her. Then Hawk turned up agin. Kyle brung him, more dead 'n' alive. First Lola wuz madder'n a biled owl fer him being laid up, clutterin' up her fancy house—till he got well enough fer her ta git interested. Thet time Noah seen whut wuz happenin'. Hawk wuz all fer light'n' out soon's he cud sit a horse, but I talked some sense inta thet stubborn Injun skull. Got him ta go east fer a spell ta one o' them fancy colleges. After thet, wal, yew know th' rest."

"Finally last year Noah got the territorial legislature to give him his divorce and free him from Lola." Carrie finished the sorry tale, adding to herself, *Just in time to come to St. Louis and entrap me.*

"I jist wanted ya ta understand 'bout Hawk 'n' Lola. It warn't his fault, ma'am. He wuz only a boy."

Carrie thought grimly to herself, *He was a boy then, but he's a man now.* She did not want to consider what that made her.

CHAPTER 7

Carrie came in early from her daily outing. Since Noah did not usually return from the range until evenings, the midday meal for the household was informal. Sometimes Carrie had a tray sent to her room, but often, like today, she dropped in Feliz's kitchen to share a light luncheon with her friend.

"*Buenas tardes*, Carrie." Feliz's round face split into a broad smile. "I have some cold fried chicken and bread fresh from the oven for you. Did you have a good ride?"

Carrie returned the smile. "Yes. The day is so lovely, not so hot as it has been. Here, I'll get the chicken. You slice the bread. Have you taken time to eat yet?" Knowing full well the tireless cook seldom took a break since she spent the day feeding each passerby in the kitchen, Carrie admonished her, "You've done enough for two days in one morning. Sit."

The mock fierce command worked. Sighing resignedly at her young friend's concern, Feliz pulled a rough wood bench up to the table and they both sat down to devour the golden chicken, fresh fruit, and crisp hot bread smothered in butter.

As they laughed and chatted, a sudden crash sounded from the dining room. Then the shrill voice of Mathilda Thorndyke echoed through the long halls of the ranch house, followed by a girl's muffled sobs.

Feliz's face turned from laughing to somber at once.

She knew it must be her daughter Estrella, who was the present victim of Mrs. Thorndyke's venom. The chief housekeeper was exacting in her demands on the domestic staff to the point of being a petty tyrant. All the maids and even the men who did heavy chores around the house lived in terror of her lashing tongue.

Mrs. Thorndyke and Carrie had coexisted for the past months with a hostile truce of sorts. Carrie consoled herself for her lack of assertiveness; even the formidable Lola Jameson had left Mrs. Thorndyke alone! However, when Estrella burst into the kitchen, tears streaming down her flushed cheeks, and flung herself into her mother's arms, Carrie's temper rose. Feliz crooned consolations to the girl, who Carrie knew was bright and industrious.

When she had calmed down, Carrie asked her, "Estrella, what happened? It's all right to tell me."

Carrie's warm smile and Feliz's urging brought a hiccuped response. "Oh, Mrs. Sinclair, I was dusting one of the big crystal candlesticks when she came up behind me. I—I didn't see her enter the room. She frightened me, suddenly scolding me for not working faster. As I turned around, it slipped from my hands and broke. I'm so sorry. . . ." She hung her head in misery. It would take months of wages to replace it, she knew. Mrs. Thorndyke had already told her so.

A slow, simmering anger began to build in Carrie, directed partly at Mrs. Thorndyke, partly at Noah Sinclair, partly at her whole imprisoned, frustrated life. "So she told you you'd have to pay for it, did she?" At the girl's abjectly humiliated nod, Carrie swished from the room, saying, "We'll see about that!"

This had been coming to a head for weeks, perhaps ever since she arrived at Circle S and found herself not mistress of the household, but merely an ornament and brood mare. Every time Carrie asked for his help, Noah took Mrs. Thorndyke's part. The hateful woman treated not only the owner's wife but all the staff like so much dirt beneath her feet. Knowing Noah would not back her, Carrie made some quick calculations as she marched down the hall to confront the old dragon. She must strike now while her furious anger gave her the courage.

Rounding the corner to the parlor, she found her quarry running her long bony fingers across the back of the bar to check for dust. "I must have a word with you, Mathilda." There. She had almost said "Mrs. Thorndyke," but decided to put her in her place at the onset.

The woman's gray eyes narrowed in recognition of the upcoming fray. "Yes, *Mrs*. Sinclair?" She stressed the "Mrs." contemptuously.

"I understand you told Estrella that she must pay for that broken crystal candleholder. Considering it was your fault that it was broken, I see no reason for the girl to have to do so. I shall not ask you to pay for it either. However, in the future, if you would not spy on the servants and would treat them with a bit more kindness, they might respond better." Carrie had no illusions about Mrs. Thorndyke ever being kind to anyone, but she might be less abusive.

The older woman's whole face at first whitened in shock, then froze into harsh lines of livid rage as she listened to the chit of a girl address her in such a presumptuous fashion. "I have handled the menials in this household for sixteen years without help from you. Mr. Noah has always found my work more than satisfactory. You'd do very well to leave me be and go back to riding in your mannish pants." Knowing how Noah and Carrie had argued over her riding astride, Mrs. Thorndyke could not resist jibing at her. That would show the little baggage that she knew how poorly her husband regarded her.

Carrie took a deep breath and smiled blindingly, covering her fury with icy-sweet politeness. "How astute of someone with your parochial background to realize that Noah and I are in disagreement over so many issues. However, you have to remember when everything is said and done, Mathilda, I am still his wife and you are still his servant. I'm ordering you not to dock Estrella for that candlestick. I'm also warning you that you'd better watch your step. I won't have you abusing the people who work here anymore. If one more complaint about your vicious tongue or your spying comes to me, I'll fire you."

Mrs. Thorndyke stiffened her back, trying in vain to become taller. Carrie had a good two inches on her. Glaring up into those glacial-green eyes, she hissed, "You just try it, missey, you just try it! Mr. Noah'll never let you get away with it."

Again Carrie smiled, easing over to the bar where several pieces of sterling flatware lay. She picked up a heavy, long-handled spoon and hefted it measuringly in her hand. "My husband has always been very generous to me. I have a beautiful home, furs, gowns, jewels, any pretty bauble I want. If some valuable items from the household turned up missing, he'd never blame me. I have no earthly reason to steal." Now Carrie's facial expression changed from an insipid smile to a no-nonsense glare. "But you, my dear Mathilda, are not so well taken care of. What if you were trying to, er, put aside a bit for your retirement? And what if I went to Noah and told him I caught you filching the seldom-used pieces of the sterling set? I could even hide some of them in your room. You can't guard it every minute, can you?"

Mrs. Thorndyke's face was chalky-white now. In complete shock, she found all her rage fled, replaced by amazed fear. This little nobody might actually cause her to lose her job! Who would ever have dreamed she could be so clever or so ruthless?

Carrie could not believe her own actions. However, seeing the effect her desperate little ploy had on the old harridan, she felt a small surge of exhilaration. "I think we understand one another from here on. You do your job without browbeating the staff and I'll leave you alone. Agreed?"

When Mrs. Thorndyke nodded in waxen-faced resignation, Carrie turned and stalked from the room. *Score: the witch zero, the redhead ten.*

Carrie had a dress fitting with the seamstress in Miles City, which called for an overnight trip into town. Noah had informed her several weeks previously of an elaborate dinner dance on the first of September. She had ordered a gown appropriate to her station as the wife of a cattle

baron. This was no ordinary party, but a gala political
affair, with the territorial governor, several railroad mag-
nates from Chicago, and other dignitaries. Carrie had been
instructed to spare no expense.

As she prepared for the trip to town, Carrie thought
ruefully of how she derived so little pleasure from all her
sumptuously elegant clothing. When she had been a young
girl at the Pattersons, she was constantly envious of her
cousin Charity's endless array of lovely gowns.

What do clothes matter when your life's in shambles?
she mused, steeling herself for the ride to Miles City that
morning. Frank was escorting her since Noah was away on
a trip to Wyoming Territory. Her husband's absence sat
well with her, but Hawk's offhand announcement yesterday did not. He would be joining them on their trip to
town. He had some unspecified business to take care of.
Probably at the local bordello, she sniffed testily to herself
as she smoothed and checked her silk shirt and full riding
pants for the hundredth time.

Her image in the mirror was continuously a surprise to
Carrie. The face staring back at her still had huge dark
green eyes framed by flaming hair, but the once porcelain-
pale skin was now a dark golden tan, generously dusted
with tiny freckles across the bridge of her nose and
cheekbones. Her hair, lightened from her frequent rides in
the hot Montana sun, was tied back with a brown ribbon
and fell carelessly to her waist in a riot of curls. Her
figure, too, seemed to have bloomed under the big Montana sky. Her muscles were firm and supple from hours a
day spent riding, working in the gardens, and helping in
the kitchen. The active outdoor life seemed to agree with
her.

Yet appearances were deceiving. In her yellow silk
blouse and brown linen skirts, she looked a competent
western woman, confident and serene. Who could sense
the inner turmoil and desperate unhappiness that plagued
her life? Forcing such thoughts aside, she scooped up a
flat-crowned brown hat and walked downstairs.

As soon as she led Taffy Girl outside the stable she saw
Hawk, as if sensing her presence, turn from conversation

with Frank. The blinding white slash of his smile made his face even more startlingly handsome.

"Morning, Carrie. Sleep well last night?"

She nodded, angry that his comment subtly hinted at Noah's absence from the ranch. He seemed to sense how she shrank from her husband's touch and knew she had not reacted that way to him.

She ignored Hawk and began to mount. Before she could swing into the saddle, he was there, his hands on her waist, lifting her up, his breath warm on her neck as he murmured low, "All butter 'n' honey again, I see. Yellow looks even better on you now with your skin kissed by the sun."

Without acknowledging his compliment, she kneed Taffy and took off, not waiting for him or Frank. They would quickly catch up to her.

His eyes never leaving the woman riding ahead of him, Hawk ambled over to Redskin and swung up. He could still see the open throat of her shirt, revealing the swell of golden breasts, the silk molding to her slim frame. He had fought down an insane urge to grab fistfuls of that flaming hair and press it to his face and lips, like capturing the sun. He snorted in self-derision, "Likely to get burned that way, half-breed," recalling her scathing epithets at the lake two weeks ago.

The ride to town was quiet, with Frank and Carrie chatting a bit. Hawk added little to the conversation. When the sun was high, Frank scanned the horizon for the familiar landmark of a stand of willows by the meandering bank of the Tongue River. Finding it, he indicated it was a good spot to stop for lunch.

As Carrie unpacked the lavish picnic Feliz had prepared, Hawk watered the horses and Frank talked about his overnight outing in town, a rare treat for him.

"Yessiree, I plan ta belly up to th' bar in th' Gray Mule Saloon fer th' night. They got them some good card games 'n' whiskey so strong it'll peel th' top layer off'n yore toenails. Good stuff. Grr..." He shook his head and laughed as Carrie grimaced in mock horror.

Hawk observed the warm camaraderie between the old

man and the girl. Frank Lowery, like Kyle Hunnicut, was a shrewd judge of character and did not give his friendship easily. What was it about her that won them all so handily? More than just her beauty obviously. He watched her tease and laugh with Frank and realized how readily she had adapted to what must have been an alien world. Lord knew Lola never had done so, never even tried.

As soon as they got to town, Frank stopped at Cummins's General Store, where he had to place a substantial order for supplies. Hawk mentioned he was going to the land office without explaining the nature of his business, but gallantly told Frank he would first see Carrie to Mrs. Grummond's across the street.

As soon as she was greeted by the plump, prim dress-maker, Carrie could see the woman looking over her shoulder at Hawk's retreating form, a stern frown of disapproval written across her broad, plain features. *She dislikes him. Because he's part Cheyenne?* Carrie let the question drop, deciding that even without the onus of being a half-breed, Hawk could be irritating enough in his own right to infuriate a saint.

The fittings took only an hour, and when she was done Carrie thanked Mrs. Grummond and left the shop, heading toward the general store. She needed to order another crystal candlestick. Thinking about the way Mrs. Thorndyke scurried to avoid her now, Carrie knew she had at least one thing to smile about.

When she entered the dim, overcrowded interior of Cummins's General Store, she was surprised to hear Hawk in conversation with Kitty Cummins, the owner's pretty daughter. The voluptuous brunette was flirting outrageously with him, standing alongside his tall frame and looking up at him with her huge china-blue eyes. They were back in an alcove away from the door and had not heard her enter.

"Butter wouldn't melt in her mouth," Carrie muttered low as she glanced around looking for Mr. Cummins, who was nowhere in sight. Assuming he was out back attending to Frank's order, she wandered over to the catalogues. Carrie was hidden from view by the tall bolts of cloth in the center of the room, but could clearly hear Hawk and Kitty. Obviously they were unaware of her presence.

"Meet me tonight, Hawk, out behind the supply shed after sunset. Papa and Mama are going to be over at the Jordans'. They won't be home until late." Her voice was wheedling and suggestive, whispering, as if she were speaking while her mouth was muffled.

Carrie peeked unrepentantly between two bolts of calico and saw what Kitty was doing. She was in his arms, running her mouth and hands all over his face, chest, everywhere! They may have thought themselves hidden from the front door, but anyone coming in the side would see them at once.

He stopped her playful seduction abruptly, holding her busy little hands in his. "I thought you were engaged to Thad Wallace, Kitty. That off now?"

She made a pout. "Worse luck, no. His dad owns the bank, and my parents are *making* me marry him. Oh, Hawk, he's fat and nearsighted and has the most awful nervous laugh."

"But for Miles City Savings, you'll bear him, huh?" He chuckled cynically.

"Oh, come on, you used to—"

Kitty's stage whisper was cut short by the ring of spurs and tromp of booted footsteps on the back stairs. Mr. Cummins and Frank came in before the assignation was arranged. Later, Carrie was to wonder if it ever took place. Kitty quickly stepped back, and Hawk lounged indolently against the counter.

Mr. Cummins's reaction to Hawk was no more friendly than Mrs. Grummond's had been. "Oh, it's you, Sinclair. What can I do for you?" He turned his stern glare on his daughter. "Kitty, your ma needs you over at the house to help with supper. I'll tend to the store now." Sulking, the girl left.

"Give me a couple of boxes of .44 shells, Cy, if you please." Tossing his money carelessly on the countertop, Hawk pulled out the gleaming Colt from its holster and fitted a couple of bullets into its empty chambers, then scooped up the remainder of the boxes. "Obliged." With a casual tip of his hat, he nodded to Cummins and said to Frank, "Meet you tonight. I'll go over to Grummond's and see if Carrie's finished. Might not be safe for her to walk unescorted from there to the hotel. Never know when an Indian might happen along."

If Hawk saw Cummins's livid red flush, he ignored it. Frank muffled a guffaw behind his hand and then said he had to go outside and recheck the supplies they had purchased.

Realizing she would be found out anyway, Carrie calmly stepped from behind the dry goods, catalogue in hand, and said sweetly, "So thoughtful of you to be concerned with my safety, Hawk, but as you can see, I made my way across the street unaccosted." *Which is more than I can say for you*, she added darkly under her breath.

Now it was his turn to smile. So, the little cat had been spying, had she? He hoped she got an earful and an eyeful!

As they walked out the door, after bidding a surly Cyrus Cummins good afternoon, Hawk leaned down and whispered, "You've developed a whole ration of unladylike habits since coming west—swimming naked, swearing, now even eavesdropping on private conversations."

Frostily, she replied, "You and that brazen little tart ought to be grateful I held my peace in front of her father!"

He laughed bitterly. "Nothing you could say would make Cy Cummins think less of me than he already does. Now as to Kitty, well, you probably could get her in some pretty hot water if you want to. Are you jealous, Carrie? Want to meet me behind the supply shed after supper?"

She fairly gasped, "No!"

His teasing suddenly became serious. "You know, you really should try it with a man near your age. You just might find you like it."

Without a word, she flounced ahead of him, furious that he had gotten the better of the exchange. Why did it seem he always did? Just like him to ruin that stupid infatuated girl's reputation and care not a fig for the consequences. He would certainly not marry her.

It never occurred to Carrie that Cy Cummins might not

permit Kitty to marry a disinherited half-breed, regardless of circumstances. Nor would Carrie allow herself to consider the fact that she was indeed jealous. Well, she certainly would not meet him in a tryst this night or any other!

Frank and Hawk both joined Carrie for dinner in the hotel dining room. Hawk had checked on homestead claims at the land office and found Noah had many of his hands buying up land to the south of Circle S. He and Frank surmised the railroad planned to go through the heart of the country to the south of the Yellowstone, heading westward to Helena, sending only a spur line north to Miles City.

"If they could only cut straight across from Bismarck to Miles City, then continue directly west and north, they'd leave at least a stretch of the Cheyenne hunting lands in peace," Hawk said angrily.

"Yew figger ya kin convince 'em ta do thet?" Frank gave Hawk a shrewd look.

"I can't, but maybe Karl Krueger can. His land lies north. It would be in his interest."

Carrie was only marginally listening to their conversation. She was watching the people in the crowded dining room, especially the women—the waitress and half a dozen lady customers. All female eyes were covertly riveted on Hawk. They were as fascinated as she must have been on that first encounter with him at the Circle S dining table. Several women made what Carrie felt were transparent excuses to stop at their table to chat, asking to be introduced to Noah Sinclair's wife when they scarcely took their eyes off his son. Hawk seemed uninterested in any of them, despite the fact several were very pretty. *Probably already has a woman lined up for tonight*, she thought pettishly, wondering if it were Kitty Cummins.

When the main course was finished, Hawk declined dessert and excused himself, making Carrie even more suspicious. As he left the dining room, a short, rather brassy-looking redhead greeted him in the hall and they departed together.

After watching the exchange, Carrie quirked one deli-

cately sculpted brow at Frank and said in mock sorrow,
"There goes only a tad, a poor boy, left to fend for
himself. Why, after what I've seen today, I wonder he's
not been eaten alive, Frank."

Frank gave a hearty chuckle. "Wal, ya cud hardly 'spect
'em ta stay a tad ferever. I said he growed up, didn't I?
Yeah, women er plumb took with him, how he looks 'n'
all. Used ta be thet way with his pa, too, but as he got rich
'n' powerful, it sorta soured him."

"It'll be the same way with his son, mark my words,"
Carrie responded.

"Mebee. Hawk's got more reason ta be bitter, though.
Noah had everthin' 'n' threw it away like a fool. Hawk
ain't had all thet many choices. Yew see all them purty
white females makin' eyes at him when their daddies ain't
around, but he ain't th' one's gonna git Circle S, 'n'
without it, he's jist a half-breed gunman. They might like
ta look at him, mebee even more—some o' 'em—real
secret like, but none o' them'd marry him."

Recalling Kitty Cummins that afternoon, Carrie wondered if Frank was right. Perhaps that explained his cynical
manner with all women, even her. Especially her.

Hawk did not ride back to Circle S with them the next
morning, but left word with Frank that he was meeting
Kyle and heading north to check on a matter of stolen
stock. Frank was decidedly hung over, but assured Carrie
that his poker winnings more than compensated him for his
pounding head. She was dubious. They arrived at Circle S
late in the afternoon. Bidding Frank good day and urging
him to spend the evening in his bunk, she headed toward
the big white frame structure on the hill. Her sense of
dread increased because she had seen Noah's gray horse in
the stable. He was home.

Her premonition proved accurate, for no sooner had she
set foot inside the door than he was on her, grabbing her
by one arm and yanking her into the parlor in silent,
tight-lipped rage.

"You actually rode into Miles City in that cheap costume! Not enough you cavort around the ranch in pants,
astride a horse, but now you go to town, too. Maybe you

can have Mrs. Grummond make you up a pair of satin pants for the ball next week!" His face was blotchy and livid, getting redder as he worked himself into a rage.

Carrie stood in the middle of the study, shaking but holding herself stubbornly erect, unwilling to plead or cajole him. "I've grown used to riding astride since it's safer on the open range. I never thought about doing otherwise when we went to town."

He snorted in disgust. "I can see that!"

Taking a steadying breath, she said, "If you feel it to be such a terrible thing, I'll wear a habit and ride sidesaddle whenever I go to Miles City in the future."

"So gracious of you, my dear," he said witheringly. Then he seemed to consider and said in a silky voice, "Do be sure to dress nicely for dinner. It'll just be the two of us and we can retire early tonight."

Carrie blanched in spite of herself. She had learned to stand up against his screaming tirades, but whenever he taunted her with veiled sexual threats, she turned to jelly. God, she cursed her cowardice, but loathed his touch so greatly she felt powerless to stop the trembling.

Like a leopard ready to pounce, he seized on her weakness, sneering. "You do so hate any mention of your wifely duties, don't you, Carrie? You're an unnatural woman, and worse yet, you're barren! Better start saying your prayers that you conceive soon. I'm not a patient man, and I've waited far too long already. I divorced one wife. I can do it again if I have to, but don't think I'll make a settlement on you like I did on Lola. She had an influential family. Yours already sold you to me!"

At his scathing, triumphant flush, she paled, turning to walk out the door and mount the stairs on wooden legs. Lord, she would be penniless with no one to take her in, just as Uncle Hiram had threatened back in St. Louis. She laughed at the irony of it all—she might end up the same as if she had refused to marry Noah Sinclair. How much better would it have been to face the streets without ever knowing his brutal touch?

CHAPTER 8

Hawk stood up and slapped the dirt from his hands. The campfire was barely warm and the tracks were clear. He turned to Kyle and grinned. "Looks like Krueger's been real busy."

"Purely does seem too easy. Why do ya s'pose he's got so careless in his old age?" Kyle grinned in return. "Yew fixin' ta pay him a lil' visit?" He cocked one scraggly reddish brow and waited for an answer.

"I've got all the evidence I need to cut a deal, but one thing. First, let's tree us a polecat named Squires."

Kyle whistled merrily in appreciation. "Do ya have ta take him alive, or kin I jist shoot th' varmint?"

The main dining room of the Excelsior Hotel in Miles City had been converted into a ballroom. It was cleared of its small tables, the oak floor polished to a gleaming luster, and elaborate decorations hung. Red, white, and blue bunting was looped across the walls and around the pictures of past U.S. presidents. A long, linen-draped table stood at the head of the room, bedecked with masses of fresh summer flowers and set with crystal and silver. The buffet was lavish with slabs of beef, pork roasts, fruit compotes, and, of course, those two favorites of westerners, fresh oysters and hard-boiled eggs. There was even freshly turned ice cream for dessert. A seven-piece band complete with violin players was tuning up across the floor. Orten Hobbs, the owner of the hotel and mayor of Miles City, had spared no expense in making this gala worthy of his impressive guest list.

By the time Carrie had finished her toilette and had Estrella help her into Mrs. Grummond's creation, she knew she would be late. Well, let Noah cool his heels awhile in the adjacent room of their suite at the Excelsior. He wanted her to look the part of a cattle king's queen; he could give her time to do so.

As she surveyed herself in the mirror, Carrie was startled by the face staring back at her. It seemed so much older than her scant nineteen years. It was almost hard, certainly sophisticated. Her hair was piled high in a fluffy pompadour, coiled with elaborate curls, and set with lustrous pearls. The deep midnight blue of the gown made her eyes appear almost black and her skin seem translucently pale despite months in the sun. The dress was cut daringly low, flattering her rounded breasts and tiny waist while the slender skirt emphasized her height. The rich satin was so vibrant, it required little ornamentation and was cut simply. A long elegant train and pearls sewn across the narrow shoulder straps were the only adornments. She wore matching pearls in her ears and around her neck. The luminous quality of the fabric and the jewels made her appear ethereal, yet worldly. It was just perfect.

"Then why do I dread going downstairs?" Carrie mused forlornly. She hated the thought of confronting all those staring eyes, knowing they wondered why such a young woman had married a man past fifty. Had they all drawn the same conclusion as Hawk?

Noah escorted Carrie downstairs, swelling with pride. She looked superb in her new gown. His wife would be the most beautiful woman at the ball. Even more important, not a word of scandal had ever touched her. For all his grievances against her, at least he could say that. Tonight, it would suffice.

"Smile, my dear," he said expansively, giving her hand a falsely loving pat. "Show them all how gracious as well as beautiful you are, Mrs. Sinclair."

Gritting her teeth, Carrie complied with a broad but

forced smile. She was introduced to women dressed in a kaleidoscope of colors and danced with men who were politicians, bankers, stockmen, and railroaders. After a couple of hours she had indigestion from the fresh oysters, sore feet from the clumsy dancers, and a pounding head-ache from the rudeness of Montana women who were incensed that Noah Sinclair had gone east for a wife. She asked the young governor's aide, who was her current partner, to get her a glass of punch, then slipped quickly outside for a gulp of fresh air, deserting the hapless swain.

The crowded ballroom was stifling, and the brisk September air felt immediately invigorating. She walked slowly and quietly around the back patio of the hotel, looking for a quiet bench so she could rest her aching feet when she heard the rustle of taffeta and then a low, familiar chuckle.

"If you stood half that close to me on the dance floor, Dorothea, your husband would horsewhip me."

"You know he'd never have the nerve to call you out, Hawk, but you know how folks'd talk if we danced together."

He laughed sardonically. "I see, we can *dance* together, but we can't dance together."

"Oooh, you are so naughty." Her giggle was suddenly muffled.

Carrie was furious for being caught eavesdropping by that red-skinned Lothario twice in a scant week. She quickly beat a hasty retreat back into the crowded ballroom.

Just a few minutes later she saw a tiny, voluptuous woman with jet-black hair slip in the side door, nervously patting her elaborate coiffure. "She looks bee-stung on the lips," Carrie muttered pettishly, wondering where else Hawk had trespassed on her overripe body. Then the subject of her ire came sauntering through the back entry. *I wonder what he's doing here. This sort of social thing would hardly interest him*, she thought to herself, realizing with a shock that he was dressed for the formal occasion. Even though she was well used to his dramatic appear-ance, she was shocked. In severely tailored formal black evening clothes he looked startlingly elegant. The snowy-white starched shirtfront contrasted with his swarthy com-

plexion and midnight-black eyes, but rather than emphasizing his savage ancestry, it merely added an aura of
exotic intrigue.

Something else about him was different, though, not just
the surprising clothes. *His hair,* Carrie thought with a
start. It had been freshly barbered; no longer shoulder-
length and unruly, it was significantly shorter, emphasizing
the long, carefully trimmed sideburns, giving even more
dramatic definition to the harsh planes and angles of that
arresting face.

As if daring any man in the assembly to question his
right to be there, he moved with arrogant grace. None
did. Although some eyed him with veiled hostility, most
spoke to him in perfunctory politeness, a few in what
seemed to be genuine friendliness. The noise level in the
room had not changed with his entry, but it was obvious to
Carrie that the topic of many conversations had done so.
Hawk walked casually to the buffet table and took a glass
of whiskey from Sam Waters.

The women, too, were all aware of his unexpected
arrival. A few older matrons sniffed in disgust, but most
looked at him in fascination, a few in brazen invitation,
most in concealed hunger. Kitty Cummins danced with a
plump young man with reddish hair, never casting so much
as a glance toward the buffet table, although Carrie was
certain she knew Hawk stood there, watching her with
amused black eyes. Dorothea Eldridge slipped her hand
coyly onto a gray-haired man's arm and engaged him in
intense conversation. Probably the cuckolded husband,
Carrie surmised, feeling the tension thicken despite the
sprightly music and false joviality filling the air.

Watching the assembly's reactions to Hawk Sinclair,
Carrie suddenly recalled Frank's words: *Yew see all them
purty white females makin' eyes at him when their daddies
ain't around, but he ain't t th' one's gonna git Circle S, 'n'
without it he's jist a half-breed gunman. They might look
at him, but none o' them'd marry him.* She realized how
closely Lowery had hit the mark. The men were afraid of
him and the women were attracted to him, but they all
resented his Cheyenne blood. *A half-breed gunman, in-*

deed, she thought ironically, staring at the barbarically handsome man across the room.

As if sensing her thoughts, Hawk swiveled his gaze from the dance floor and Kitty Cummins over to her. Black and green eyes locked and it seemed as if some spark of empathy was transmitted between them.

She knows, he thought bitterly, anger consuming him that she would understand his precarious position in white society. He did not choose to analyze why it should bother him so much. Kyle and Frank—even Noah—knew. With no one else did it rankle so.

Noah strode over to Carrie and proprietarily took her arm, leading her to the dance floor. "Have you been enjoying yourself? I noticed you certainly don't seem to lack for escorts," he said by way of offhandedly excusing his own lengthy absence.

"My dance card is full," Carrie responded dryly, thinking to herself how glad she was that he had chosen to closet himself with railroad men for the past hour. She positively hated the knowing smirk of the predatory females in town whenever he squired her about.

"Every man here thinks you're the most beautiful woman in the territory." He chuckled in self-congratulation. "They may even be right."

"And I'm *your* wife. That's really the point, isn't it, Noah? *Your* property!" Unexpectedly, her long-suppressed hurt over their lovelessly arranged relationship hit her with sickening force.

Noah's face flushed in anger and he tightened his grip on her, sweeping her into the waltz with fury.

As they moved in stiff, angry silence, she watched Hawk dancing with a pretty brunette she had seen in town but never met. To keep her mind off the pain Noah was relentlessly inflicting on her hand and rib cage, she speculated about who the attractive woman was as they whirled away into the crowd. Abruptly the waltz was over. As Carrie massaged her hand surreptitiously and breathed deeply, letting air back into her aching lungs, the music resumed.

Before Noah could again seize her, Hawk appeared with

the brunette in tow and made introductions. She was Evelyn Hutchinson, owner of the Lazy H, a large spread to the west of Circle S. "Evelyn here was just telling me about her new shorthorned cattle from Ohio. Thought you might like to know what luck she's had with them."

The brunette smiled devastatingly at Hawk, then turned her attention to his father. "Yes, my herd has grown quite a bit since I mixed the eastern strain with our own Montana range stock from Oregon."

"You must tell me all about it, my dear." Noah's charm was suddenly turned on, and Carrie was aware that this woman must be a rancher of some importance in the territory.

As they began to talk, Hawk edged closer to Carrie. "May I have the pleasure?"

Since Noah was already taking Evelyn's arm, preparatory to dancing, it was obviously her only graceful alternative. *From the pan into the fire*, she thought grimly, nodding in acquiescence.

He was a superb dancer. Of course, considering how graceful a horseman he was, it should have been no surprise. After Noah's harsh grasp, the way he held her seemed incredibly deft and sensitive. Shyly she looked up at his face, still amazed at the transformation in him. Her eyes ran up the faultless white shirt, across the swarthy skin of his jawline, now cleanly shaven. Then she caught sight of his right ear and noticed several tiny scars on it that his long hair had previously hidden. *Why, his ears are pierced!* Then she recalled the various Indians she had seen. All the men, even the children, wore large earrings. Oddly, it lent added attraction rather than frightening her as it might have only a few months ago. She speculated about how he would look with golden rings in his ears. Ruefully, she realized how westernized she must be becoming. The image was not at all unappealing!

Carrie was still sore from the earlier rough treatment by Noah and found it hard to relax in the crowded room where people had stared at her all night. Sensing her stiff demeanor, Hawk said in a silky, mocking voice, "What's the matter, Carrie? Don't you want to be in my arms?"

Almost in reflex reaction, she spat back, "Not nearly as much as your beloved Dorothea, I'm sure!" No more than the words escaped her lips, she winced in abject mortification. Good God, after being caught eavesdropping in Cummins's Store, now she had allowed herself to be trapped again!

He laughed as he whirled her toward the side door. Despite the press of the crowd, he did not doubt someone would inform Noah of his wife's scandalous behavior, but, perversely, Hawk did not care. He guided her out into the cool starry night before she had a chance to protest.

"Surely you don't hope for a replay of your earlier scene," she said scathingly, hating him for the effect he had on her.

He laughed. "No, but I am a little curious about how you happened onto us."

Carrie blushed in humiliation, then began once again to rub her sore hand, unconsciously. She was grateful that the darkness at least hid her flush, but it could not blanket her awareness of his tall, hard body standing so very close. "I—I just came out for some air and overheard—Oh, damn you, I'm going back inside immediately! I don't owe you any explanations. Let me—"

She whirled, like a frantic wounded sparrow trying to escape a hawk's talons. He could hear her voice break and sensed the unshed tears in it. "Wait, Carrie. Look, I'm sorry. I didn't mean to hurt you." He reached out and held her fast. Suddenly he felt disgusted with his own perverse cruelty. It was not a game anymore.

He noticed her hand then, the way she was favoring it, and recalled Noah's bruising grip earlier. Gently he took the pale fingers and softly caressed them, then raised them to his lips for a velvet kiss. "He hasn't exactly been easy on you, has he?" The intensity of his eyes mesmerized her.

Acutely aware of his nearness and disturbed by it as she remembered the scene at the lake, Carrie was in a turmoil. Why did he have to affect her this way? "I don't want your pity and I don't need your passion! Leave me alone!"

As she quivered with fury, he drew her slowly,

unprotestingly toward him. She was tall for a woman, fitting perfectly into his embrace. He was strangely gentle as he said, "You may not want my pity, but as to the other..." He lowered his mouth and devoured her neck with the most exquisite, wonderful play of his lips on that silken column. She threw her head back instinctively as he nibbled upward and captured her flaming hair in his hand. "Firehair," he breathed softly, pulling the pins free while kissing the bright silky tangle as it tumbled down, spilling pearls in its wake.

"No," she gasped, but he took her open mouth, softly at first, then with searing intensity, intertwining their tongues in a delicate dance. His warm, firm lips brushed, sucked, rubbed across hers with mesmerizing pressure. She found herself returning the erotic motions, letting her tongue travel into his mouth. For one blinding moment she prayed it would never end as she pressed her body against his and ran her hands through his thick midnight-black hair. Never had Carrie felt anything like this fire and dizziness. Her heart raced and every nerve in her body cried out to him. Breathless and beautiful sensations rioted through her. If Gerald Rawlins had pleased her, his embraces were insipid and boyish compared to what this man was doing to her. Hawk's hand roved down from her back to press her buttocks firmly against his lower body. His need was as obvious as her own, and he growled out an unintelligible word of passion. A sudden sense of desolation engulfed her. This was going too far, and she must stop it. She was married—and doomed.

Finally, achingly, she pulled away. Hawk did not try to stop her. "Please, Hawk, please let me go," was all she could gasp as her voice broke. Her eyes were dilated in the moonlight, huge and full of terror, like a fawn brought to bay by a hunter.

Wordlessly he freed her and watched her step back, fingers on her lips, numbly standing still for a second, staring hauntingly into his eyes. He could tell she was genuinely shocked by her wild response and surprised that she could feel such passion. After he watched her flee up the back stairs, he looked down at the pearls lying scattered across the stone patio, gleaming like tears in the moonlight.

By the time Estrella had repaired her destroyed hairstyle, Carrie calmed her nerves a bit. She must return to the party before she was missed. The scandal would infuriate Noah, and Lord knew what vengeance he might exact on her. Forcing down the bile that rose in her throat, she descended the stairs and searched for her husband's blond-gray head, praying a glossy black one would not fall into her line of vision.

Carrie dared not confront Hawk again tonight, but her thoughts kept straying back to him. She wondered what brought him to the gathering. Then, as if in answer to her unspoken question, a tall, thickset bull of a man came in the front door, talking in a boisterously loud voice with a slight German accent. He was expensively dressed and bedecked with flashy jewelry, but it was at the woman on his arm that people stared.

She was almost as tall as Carrie, with a full-figured body that virtually spilled out of her shockingly low-cut gown of powder-blue taffeta. Her blond hair was pale and elegantly coiffed. Glittering diamonds winked at her ears and throat. Carrie guessed her age to be somewhat past thirty, but could not be sure from a distance. Her long, thin face was carefully made up, and she was strikingly handsome rather than actually beautiful.

Piercing dark blue eyes swept the room and then lighted on Hawk, who returned her stare with a feral grimace, hostile and watchful. Slowly she began to move across the crowded floor, and this time the noise level did drop appreciably. People literally stepped aside to let her pass.

Carrie caught sight of Noah from the corner of her eye, standing by the side door with two other cattlemen and the woman rancher he had danced with earlier. His face was ashen, and he seemed frozen to the spot. The large German escorting the blond followed her toward Hawk. Both seemed to ignore Noah. However, numerous people in the crowd whispered and cast surreptitious glances toward Noah, then nervously eyed the blonde. Finally, someone signaled the orchestra to play, and the music broke the spell, raising the conversational level to normal once more.

"Hello, stranger. Don't you look good enough to escort me to Delmonico's," she said, eyeing Hawk's attire appreciatively. "Too bad we're not in New York." The blond smiled archly and placed her hand on his arm as she turned to the German behind her.

"Karl, darling, this is Hawk Sinclair. He's been, er, away for a while, as have I."

Hawk's eyes were like shards of black glass, cold and hard as his voice. "But now I'm back and so are you. I know what I'm doing here, but why you should return to the wilderness and desert New York baffles me."

"Oh, a variety of reasons. For one thing, I recently remarried. I'm Baroness von Krueger now, and my dear husband wanted to visit his younger brother Karl. We had no more than arrived when Ernst was taken ill. My sweet brother-in-law was kind enough to escort me tonight." She beamed at the formidable-looking man next to her.

Hawk smiled thinly. "You always have had a penchant for marrying rich, old men. I take it Ernst is expected to recover?"

"Naughty, Hawk. You might offend Karl, if not me." Her eyes traveled measuringly between the two men. Krueger's impassive face revealed nothing but watchfulness.

"I think I already have offended Krueger here, haven't I, *mein Herr*?"

"Then you two have met before," she interjected.

The German spoke in level irony. "In a manner of speaking, *Liebchen*. We share some, ah, common acquaintances."

"Jake Squires, for one," Hawk put in pleasantly. "Yes, I have him." His eyes skewered Krueger. "If you want him back, we need to talk somewhere in private."

The blond pouted and the German nodded warily, but before anything more could be said, Noah walked directly up to the trio with Carrie in tow.

Stiffly and deliberately he nodded to the blond and to Krueger, then, fairly pulling Carrie to his side, he said, "Carrie, may I present Karl Krueger, a fellow stockman, and Lola Jameson, late of New York, I believe. This is my wife, Carrie Sinclair.''

Carrie was mute, cursing herself for not figuring out who the showy blond hussy was. She noticed how Lola's hand curved like a talon on Hawk's forearm.

Hawk stood back, taking it all in, now suddenly amused. ''Let me bring you up to date, Noah. Lola is now Karl's sister-in-law, the Baroness von Krueger, no less. Karl and I have some private business. If you'll excuse us, ladies? Noah?''

Hawk and Krueger left the trio and retired to the hotel manager's office just down the hall from the ballroom. Without preamble Krueger began, ''So, you have Squires. What is it that you want from me, you and Kyle Hunnicut? Perhaps Squire's job? Since he was so clumsy as to allow himself to be captured, I might be willing to discuss the matter.'' Krueger's geniality did not extend to his cold eyes.

Hawk snorted. ''I may hate Noah, but I don't need to steal from him, for you or anyone else.''

''What, then?'' Krueger waited.

''You know the railroad's coming. Did you also know Noah's bought enough homestead claims to prompt the surveyors to favor his southern route?'' He withdrew a sheath of documents from his coat pocket and handed it to the big German.

Krueger smiled broadly now. ''I have heard rumors. That is why I came tonight. Already I recognize some familiar faces from Chicago in the crowd.'' He looked at the information Hawk had given him. ''But tell me, why do you want the K Bar to beat out Circle S if you won't even steal your father's cattle?''

''If it's escaped your attention, Krueger, I'm half Cheyenne. I want the railroad as far away from the Yellowstone hunting grounds as I can get it, both of your ranches be damned!''

Krueger took out a cigar and bit off the end, then lit it while Hawk was speaking. Exhaling a deep puff, he said, ''And maybe a little revenge against your father and the new bride who will give him his heir? That would sweeten any bargain, *nein*?"

When Hawk only stared impassively, Krueger shrugged and went on in a businesslike manner. "So, we agree about the route the railroad should take." He pocketed the documents. "I have every intention to talk with Herr Grossman and Herr Rogers about that tonight. What do you want for Squires?"

"No more stealing, Krueger," came the level reply. "Pay him off and send him packing, or Kyle'll kill him. I don't want a range war, and if you keep after Noah's stock, you and I both know it's bound to happen."

Krueger's cunning face split in a smile of understanding. "Now I begin to comprehend. You want what our Chancellor Bismarck would call a balance of power between the Circle S and the K Bar, to protect your red interests."

"That's right. If either of you takes all the graze in eastern Montana, every Cheyenne and Sioux—not to mention nester and sheepman—will be in danger. Just keep a snarling truce. I'll let you win this round; deal yourself in with the railroad."

Hawk started to leave, then casually turned back and said over his shoulder, "But cross me with any more hired guns, Krueger, and I'll take a lot of embarrassing information about the railroad and the rustlers to the governor. Then I'll come after you."

Noah had dragged Carrie over to confront his bitch of an ex-wife, wanting to flaunt her youthful beauty in front of the older woman and to quell the titters in the crowd. People would have made him out to be a coward if he tried to ignore Lola and Krueger. Now, watching Carrie's irritatingly unsophisticated pallor and Lola's knowing smirk, he wanted only to extricate himself from the damnable situation. What in hell did Hawk and Krueger have to talk about? Dual alarm bells went off in his head.

"So, you are the third Mrs. Sinclair," Lola said, arching one silvery blond brow in amusement. "Really, Noah, your fourth bride will be young enough to be your grand-daughter, I do believe.''

Noah bristled, tightening his grip on Carrie's arm unconsciously as he ground out, ''Do attempt some veneer of civilization in public, Lola, as much as you may scorn it in private.''

Carrie cut into the high, trilling laughter of the blond. ''In the first place, Baroness,'' she fairly spat the title in contempt, ''I won't be replaced by another wife. Secondly, I suspect you would like the age difference between you and your elderly Baron to be as great as it is between Noah and me.''

Lola's eyes turned from bright blue to whitened gray at the taunt about her advancing age. The nerve of this gawky carrot-topped child! ''Yes, you are young, nearer his half-breed son's age than your husband's.''

''You'd know more about Hawk than I would, from what I hear, Baroness,'' Carrie shot back, remembering in disgust Frank's sordid tale about the immoral woman and recalling her hand on Hawk's arm earlier.

Surprised at Carrie's venom and ability to hold her own with Lola, Noah knew he must separate the two women before a disgraceful fight ensued. ''If you will be so kind as to excuse us, Lola, Carrie and I must say hello to some old friends from Helena who just arrived.''

''I do wish the Baron congratulations—and good luck,'' Carrie said as she glided off on Noah's arm.

''How did you know Baron von Krueger was older than Karl?'' Noah was still uneasy with his wife's bursts of temper and assertiveness, as well as her continually surprising knowledge.

She smiled archly and said, ''Just a lucky guess.'' She knew only the younger sons of European nobility left home, while the oldest son inherited the title. How stupid they all must think her!

CHAPTER 9

After the ball Carrie was plagued by dreams in which she saw Lola Jameson's malevolently leering face and watched her and Hawk in a torrid embrace that faded into one of herself with Hawk. Then the old childhood nightmare about the wolf and the bird of prey returned, more vividly than ever. Noah had slept the sleep of exhaustion, reinforced with too much whiskey, while she moaned and tossed in anguish.

The next day he had busied himself with various business contacts, telling her they would spend one more night in town. That night he resumed his attentions to her in bed. Since the fateful day when Hawk had caught her in the lake, Carrie had found herself shocked by her invidious comparisons between the body of her husband and his son. Noah's flaccid, sagging flesh repelled her more than ever. After the previous night and Hawk's compelling, gentle kiss, Noah's rough, unconcerned taking of her had been wrenchingly miserable. Woodenly she had endured it, beginning to perceive for the first time just how high a price she had paid when she signed over her body in marriage to Noah Sinclair.

Furious with her coldness in bed after all the spirit she had exhibited against Lola the night before, Noah again taunted her about her barrenness, even throwing her words to Lola back in her face. "Maybe I will need a fourth wife after all, Carrie," he said.

As if to reinforce his threat, the following morning he informed her that he was going to have a physician examine her. He had proven he could have children, so obviously the fault must be hers. The implication was clear to Carrie as she sat shivering in their hotel room. If the doctor pronounced her unfit, Noah would divorce her and cast her aside, disgraced and penniless. Part of her was terrified, but another part of her rejoiced in the possibility of freedom from Noah's physical demands and unbending presence. Thus, she waited in fright and uncertainty in the hotel room.

When Dr. Phineas Lark arrived, his manner did nothing to reassure her. He was a short, pudgy man with small pig eyes recessed far into his head, giving him a perpetually myopic look. His squint took in a great deal and when he asked her to disrobe for the examination, Carrie felt unclean. He gave a curt order and left the room, giving her five minutes to comply.

Until now only Noah had seen her naked, she thought as she stripped. No, she realized with a sudden start of guilt, Hawk had seen and felt her unclothed body also. Oddly, that memory did not make her feel nearly as uncomfortable as the thought of Dr. Lark's pudgy fingers touching her. Noah waited outside the door, but his nearness did not reassure her at all. He was the originator of this new humiliation.

Lark was thorough. He prodded and poked at her, asking endless questions as she lay on the bed staring straight up at the cracked ceiling. She answered in monosyllables and he grunted in response, doing nothing to lessen her mortification or reassure her.

When he had finished the rather painful internal examination, he straightened up. "That is all, Mrs. Sinclair. You may dress." He turned to leave.

Clutching the sheet, Carrie bolted up on the bed and said, "But—but what have you learned? Am I barren or not?" He was going to confer with Noah and not even do her the courtesy of telling her what he knew!

After her subdued and frightened reaction during the exam, Phineas Lark was surprised that she would suddenly show such spirit—such unseemly spirit. He would far rather discuss this with her husband, as was fitting.

"Er, you seem to be in excellent health, Mrs. Sinclair. Your cycle is regular; you are strong and young. The birth passage might be somewhat narrow, but that should not impede conception at all." He waited, irritated that he should have to deliver his report twice.

"Then I should conceive?" Carrie was not certain if she was happy or sad at the news. Pregnancy would keep Noah out of her bed, but in the end, it would be his child she would deliver. "How long might it take me to become . . . pregnant?" Using the word was embarrassing, but she wanted to know.

"That is difficult to say." Lark certainly was not going to tell this bold chit of a girl that with an older man it often took longer because of the husband's problems! Lord, Noah Sinclair would have his hide! As it was, Lark would have a difficult enough time skirting the issue with him. If either of these two was unable to contribute to producing an heir for Circle S, it was far more likely the husband than the wife.

He whirled and fled the room, leaving Carrie feeling alone, confused, and defiled. When Noah came in, she was dressed, waiting for him to speak, hopeful the news from Lark would put him in a better humor. His brood mare was not defective after all.

Noah's face was a mask, grim and shuttered. "The doctor assures me you are in sound health, probably just not overly fertile. I might have known it would be some damnable inconclusive thing like that. If you showed a little enthusiasm in bed, if you wanted to conceive, it would probably help, but I know there's no use asking the impossible. I'll just work on it harder than before, my dear." With that acid promise he turned on his heel and departed, slamming the door.

Carrie was stunned. That wasn't what Lark had said to her. What else had he told Noah? Did her revulsion for his touch keep her from quickening? Furiously, she grabbed up a pillow from the bed and threw it across the room. "So now he threatens me with his attentions, does he!"

They did not speak on the long ride home. After her ordeal in Miles City, Carrie was actually glad to see the white frame walls of the Circle S ranch house gleaming in the warm September sun. She felt a strange sense of peace and welcome. Feliz and Frank were here. As Noah strode stiffly up the front steps, Carrie greeted Frank and walked with him toward the stables, where the buggy team would be rubbed down after the long drive from town.

Sensing the leashed anger in Noah, Frank did not press Carrie for details of their quarrel. He knew from long ago all the twisted ways Noah Sinclair could punish a woman, and his heart ached for the bright-haired girl who smiled bravely at him now.

Finally, she spoke. "Well, Frank, I met Lola Jameson the other night." At his look of goggle-eyed amazement, she had to laugh in spite of herself. "Yes, she's back, now the Baroness von Krueger, married to that cattleman's titled elder brother. I suspect he must be doddering, at least seventy."

Frank chuckled with her. "I reckon if'n he's ole Karl's *older* brother, yew might be right. Wal, since th' Baroness's gettin' up there herself, they jist might suit."

Carrie's eyes danced. "That's what I told her."

His jaw dropped. "Whut'd she say?"

"Plenty before that, not much after." Then Carrie's look darkened abruptly. "You were sure right about her fascination for Hawk. She couldn't keep her claws off him."

Frank detected more than disdain in her manner, but if it was jealousy, he would never mention it. In the past weeks he had watched the tension between the two young people undergo a dramatic change, and he feared what might eventually happen. Despite the danger, he did not want to see Hawk leave so soon after his return. Damn, there was no solution.

Unaware of his sympathetic gaze on her, Carrie continued, "You were right about the women in town, too—all the fine ladies who'll sneak off to the stables with him but not be seen in public with him! Hypocrites, all of them!"

Just then, Hawk and Kyle rode in, dismounting and

leading their horses into the area where Carrie and Frank talked.

"So, it's all settled up. Krueger'll take keer o' them railroad fellers, and I loose thet varmint Squires." Kyle's voice carried through the musty air of the stable.

Hawk started to reply, then caught sight of Frank. Carrie was hidden behind the wooden stall divider, a curry comb in her hand, grooming Jingles, one of the matched blacks of the carriage team. She looked at Hawk while he was unaware of her presence. Once more he was the tough frontiersman, clad in buckskins, wickedly armed with gun and knife. Even the barbered hair did not matter. He looked dangerous and cunning, savage. Still she recalled the gentleness of his hands on her, then shook herself in anger.

"Evenin', Hawk, Kyle," Frank said, shrewdly putting together the pieces of their previous conversation. "Treed ya a skunk, huh? Jist see ta it thet it don't soak ya good afore ya loose it. I reckon yew 'n' Krueger made a deal. I ain't interested in th' details. Onliest thing I hope is thet ya don't get shot. Thet Kraut's pure mean."

Kyle grinned. "So'm I, Frank, so'm I." Whistling, he led his buckskin toward a stall at the end of the stable, spying Carrie as he passed her place of concealment. "Well, purty lady, how's town 'n' all them fancy folk?"

Carrie stepped out and smiled uncertainly as she returned Kyle's greeting, feeling Hawk's scowl. Damn him, he still did not trust her motives with Hunnicut!

That evening at supper the air was thick with tension. While Carrie was upstairs dressing, Noah and Hawk had begun an argument that would carry into the dining room. When she entered the parlor for their usual predinner drink, both men seemed to grow more agitated in her presence.

Hawk poured a glass of sherry and handed it to her, scowling wordlessly. *He is still in a sulk over Kyle*, she thought peevishly.

Noah watched the silently antagonistic exchange, wondering if it was Frank or Feliz who had told her about Lola and his son. It rankled like a raw sore that she should

know of his humiliation by that whore. Perversely, he
blamed the boy as much as the woman. In grim humor he
thought that Carrie would never be attracted to *any* man,
much less the sullen half-breed in the parlor.

Early the next morning, after another dream-tormented
night, Carrie slipped out of the house, fortified with a cup
of coffee and a hunk of Feliz's crusty bread. She needed to
ride in solitude. Since there was no one about, she saddled
Taffy Girl herself and took off. Let Noah rail about her
riding skirt tonight. For today, she was free, and the
autumn sun was shining.

For several hours Carrie rode, soaking up the beautiful
day, thinking as little as possible. Then, her meandering,
circular course took her into a small glade where a cabin
stood in rural loveliness. With several rooms and a long
porch across the front, it was really larger than a mere
cabin. A large stone fireplace was evident on one wall and
the flower beds, although overgrown and not tended, still
yielded marigolds and mums in the warm autumn sun,
peeping their gold and white heads bravely through the
weeds and tall grass. She thought the place could be
enchanting with a bit of work. The setting certainly was
magnificent. Tall oaks and ash trees stood in a semicircle
around the cabin like guardians, and a small stream gur-
gled a welcome nearby, a tiny tributary of the Tongue, no
doubt. It was actually not all that far from the big house,
yet so artfully secluded it was like another world.

With a premonition of sorts, Carrie dismounted and
walked slowly toward the front door. It was not locked,
swinging open at her touch as if welcoming her. The main
room was lighted by three big windows, and the last
vestiges of morning sun still tinged the floorboards with
gold as it continued its westbound ascent. *At daybreak a
woman making breakfast for her family would have excellent light.*

Slowly she walked into the dusty but neat interior,
carefully closing the door behind her. The room smelled of
wood smoke and lye soap. A faint hint of lavender from an
old pomander touched her nostrils. It was a homey, pleasant blend of aromas. The furniture was mostly handmade,

rough and sturdy but not unattractive. In one corner a small dry sink with a delicate pitcher and bowl caught her eye. Next to the washstand stood a brass towel tree. As she admired the pretty white china wash set, now cracked with the fine yellow lines of age, she saw the pictures, gilt-framed ovals lined up on the oak table next to the wall. A tattered lace cloth was spread in a diamond shape across the polished wood, and the frames sat on its uneven surface.

Hesitantly, for she suddenly felt like an intruder, Carrie picked up a photo and blew the dust off. As she suspected, it was Noah, much younger, his face not graven with the harsh lines it bore now. Posed beside him was a tall, dark-haired woman with austerely handsome features, dressed in a simple print gown. Her hair was plaited into braids twisted into elaborate coils on each side of her head. In front of the couple stood a small boy with lank, dark hair falling in his face and a much smaller girl, also bearing the stamp of her Cheyenne heritage, clutching a doll. Even in childhood, Hawk's face was arresting as he stared defiantly into the camera with those fierce black eyes. Carrie wondered about the little girl. Both children looked like Laughing Woman, not just the obvious coloring of their Cheyenne ancestry, but the strong, straight noses, sensitive eyes, and chiseled cheekbones. Carefully she sat the picture back and looked at the others. One was a portrait of Marah. What wistful sadness filled those night eyes. Would life with Noah Sinclair leave her looking that way someday? Had it already?

Studying the portrait, she wandered toward the interior door and looked inside at what must have been Noah and Marah's bedroom. The bed was large, as if made for two tall people. What had once been a bright patchwork quilt lay neatly over it, now faded and crinkled with age. Sunlight spilled in from the window as she walked absently around, touching the bedpost and the high-backed chair beside it.

Suddenly a voice interrupted her reverie. "What the hell are you doing in here?" It was more a furious statement than a question.

Carrie clutched the portrait to her breast and gasped, looking up to confront Hawk's blazing black eyes. He stood over her menacingly, his hand outstretched, roughly grabbing the picture from her numb fingers.

"I asked you a question, dammit! What are you doing in my mother's house? It's all there is left of her, all he's left alone these years. You don't have any right to sneak in here."

"I—I'm sorry. I didn't mean to intrude—and I didn't sneak in. The door was unlocked. I never even knew this place existed, or that it was kept so intact. Like a shrine—" The minute she said it, she could have bitten her tongue.

His eyes flashed angrily as he whirled, clutching the picture and walking back into the main room. He carefully set it with the others. Hesitantly she retraced her steps, watching him and realizing all the wealth of memories, happy and painful, that this place must hold for him.

He looked at her resentfully. "Maybe it is a shrine. It was hers, and she loved it. Even if he'd let her, Laughing Woman would never have wanted to live in that pretentious mansion on the hill. This, this was her place." He ran his hand softly across the smooth oak table, polished by years of such touching.

"You grew up here—"

He cut her off. "And she died here. She was educated, better than any of the white women who first settled here—better than most of them now. Iron Heart sent her to the missionary school to learn the *veho* ways and act as a bridge between them and the Cheyenne. He was actually glad to have her marry He Who Walks in Sun in a Christian ceremony. Well, the *veho* God didn't bless her, that's for sure!"

So that explained her clothing and the daintily decorated cabin, Carrie thought. She had been educated as a white. But Noah was not satisfied. Noah was never satisfied, Carried concluded sadly, empathizing with his first wife.

"She lived here with you and he built another house— left her behind?" Carrie asked it softly, knowing the answer, yet wanting him to tell her in his own words. How much pain there must be locked inside him!

"More than left her behind—he hid her. He was ashamed of her! Ashamed of the daughter of Iron Heart, a great leader of the People. More white settlers came when I was growing up. They brought their white women. As Noah got richer, he got more dissatisfied. After all, the biggest cattle baron in the territory couldn't be known as a squaw man."

"Frank said he turned sour on life," she replied. "Maybe no woman could have pleased him." Her eyes were full of pain and empathy; but she hid her face from him, sensing that he would scorn what he construed to be her pity.

He looked at her in surprise, then said, "I should've figured Frank would tell you, he's so fond of you."

"He loved her, you know." She looked up at him now, and he nodded.

"Yes, Frank's a good man. I often wished—oh, hell, what's the use? What's done is done. Anyway, she loved Noah, damn him! Even when he treated her like dirt, shunned her. He waited for her to die, and she obliged him." He held the photo of his family in his hand while he spoke, his eyes staring with hate at the tall, light-haired man in the picture. "He was remarried inside the year," he rasped out harshly.

Remembering Lola Jameson's cold blue eyes and possessive manner with Hawk, Carrie could well understand his anger. Not wanting to dredge up ugly memories of Lola, she said, "The little girl in the picture. Who is she, a cousin?"

"That was my sister, Melanie. She died just after this was taken. Pneumonia." He smiled sadly at the tiny dark figure.

"I'm sorry, Hawk. No one ever told me she had a daughter, too."

"It was a long time ago. They're both gone now. This is all that's left."

"Do you come here often?" She had seen a coffeepot and cup set out on the work counter next to the fireplace. It looked like it had been used recently.

Raising his guard again, he fixed her with a hard stare. "Today I followed your trail. I hadn't intended to, until I saw where you were headed." He did not add that he had come here the day after the ball in Miles City. He needed to think about that kiss and her response. This was his tranquil haven. "Sometimes I come here to reminisce about happier days, sometimes just to think."

"I wish I had a place to go. Somewhere of my own, like Marah's place."

"Do you know what Marah means?" His curt response to her wistful statement puzzled her.

"No. It sounds biblical. You said missionaries schooled her."

He scoffed. "They picked better than they knew. Marah means bitter. Noah destroyed her. Laughing Woman was named for her joy, Marah for her sorrow." He looked at Carrie's still, silent form, standing with the light burnishing her hair, so beautiful, so forbidden. Not only was she Noah's wife, she was white, and that most of all made the barrier complete. She was one of the white women for whom Noah had deserted his mother, his sister, himself. They were all poison! Didn't he know that already?

"You better go. You don't belong here. You never can. The other house on the hill ought to be more to your taste, anyway."

If he had slapped her, she could not have been more hurt. Every time she seemed to be breaking down his hostility, he turned on her with renewed fury. Wordlessly, she whirled and fled through the front door.

When he heard Taffy Girl's hoofbeats vanish over the hill, he sat down in the rocker and clasped his hands together in front of his forehead, pondering all that had happened since he came home. Home. Circle S was not ever really his home, nor in truth was this cabin, with all its bittersweet memories rooted in the long-dead past. The Cheyenne were right. No man could ever truly own the land, any land. Everyone was an interloper. The land only lent its bounty for a brief span. He should go, but if he were to keep the *veho* from despoiling a small part of the People's space, he must stay and see it through, no matter what. He did not believe he would like the cost he must pay.

* * *

That evening Hawk did not return to the big house. Carrie and Noah dined alone. If Noah knew a reason for his son's absence, or cared, he revealed nothing to his wife. Carrie feared it had something to do with her intrusion in the cabin, but, of course, could say nothing of that to her husband.

The next morning, she came down early, hoping if she stopped in the kitchen Feliz might know if Hawk had returned in the night. On her way downstairs, she over-heard Mrs. Thorndyke talking to Cora, their timid laundress.

"It's a disgrace. He was filthy drunk, I tell you. Never should allow a savage to buy liquor, even one who's a half-breed. Lord knows what he might do. Scalp us all in our beds!"

Before the hissing whispers could go any further, Carrie glided silently into the room. "Cora, you have a mountain of wash waiting. Here are the towels from my bedroom washstand." When the woman nodded and scurried off with the linens, Carrie turned to the head housekeeper. "I would appreciate it if you would refrain from gossiping about your employers. My husband and his son may not see eye to eye, but I scarcely think Noah would want to hear his offspring referred to as a scalping half-breed who will murder us all in our sleep!"

Mrs. Thorndyke's eyes narrowed in anger. When Carrie departed, the housekeeper began to calculate. Why should she take *his* part? Was she like the last one? Wouldn't that be rich! "Just let her try to blackmail me if I catch her sleeping with that red-skinned devil!"

Not realizing what she had begun, Carrie slipped into the kitchen, where Feliz was indeed tending to a rather green-looking pair of men—Hawk and Kyle.

The Texan was crumpled on a bench, a cup of coffee clutched in a death grip between both hands. "Lordy, Miz Feliz, I'm hung over s' bad, even my har's sore." He winced as he rubbed his scalp gingerly.

"Well, it was something to celebrate," Hawk replied. "I'm not sure who put who to bed. I'm just glad we got there." He looked little better than his compatriot. Black

bristling whiskers and bloodshot eyes were the more promising features of his haggard countenance.

"I thought red and green were Christmas colors,"
Carrie chirped brightly as she walked past Hawk, her step
even more vigorous than usual for the early hour. He
propped one elbow on the table and rested his head against
it, glaring balefully at her, rather like a wet cat, but made
no reply. "What were you celebrating last night? I gather
you went to town," she queried the invalids.

"Yup, we did tie one on," Kyle ventured, then added
vaguely, "I'm not purely sure on ta whut . . ."

Hawk managed a weak smile as Feliz poured another
generous slug of coffee in his cup. "You might as well
hear it now. When Noah gets word you'll hear it from
Canada to Texas, I expect. It seems the Northern Pacific
has settled on its route. It'll take a northerly course, from
Bismarck to Helena, dropping down to link up with Miles
City, but leaving the Cheyenne lands south of here alone."

She smiled archly. "And just why does my intuition tell
me you two had something to do with such a momentous
decision?"

Kyle laughed, then winced in anguish as the vibrations
from his vocal cords reverberated in his skull. "Yew might
say we did, ma'am. Thet 'n' more." He looked at Hawk in
conspiratorial assessment.

"We ought to see a big decrease in rustling, for a while
at least," was all Hawk would say.

Carrie poured a cup of coffee from Feliz's big granite
pot and came over to sit by Kyle. Perversely, she did not
care if Hawk felt defensive about his friend or not. She
liked Kyle Hunnicut and she wanted to talk to him. "You
found out who's been doing the rustling, then?"

"Always knowed thet, ma'am. It be Karl Krueger whut's
behind it. Point is, he pulled in his horns a mite when
Hawk 'n' me nailed his big gun."

Carrie was baffled. "But Karl Krueger is a respectable
rancher, as rich as Noah!"

Both men laughed in spite of their aching skulls. Hawk
said, "Every big rancher was once a little one, Carrie, and

most swung a wide loop at least a few times. Some keep to bad habits, though.''

"But why? Krueger's rich!" Carrie simply couldn't believe a millionaire would stoop to thievery.

"Rich men always want ta git richer," Kyle said. "If'n ole Noah wuz ta lose out 'cause o' rustlers, who'd ya think'd take over east Montana?''

Carrie felt a chill of premonition. "I'm certainly glad, then, that you stopped Krueger." She looked over at Hawk, who she knew was watching her.

"I didn't do it for Noah. You can believe that." He stood up and walked deliberately from the room, saying thank you to Feliz for the coffee, nothing more to Carrie.

You didn't do it for me, either, I know, she said to herself.

CHAPTER 10

"Goddamn Karl Krueger! I knew he was at that dance for a reason. But how the hell did he know where those phony homesteads were set up? Who checked them to see they weren't proved out?" Although six of his cowhands had filed and paid for homestead land, only the most superficial things had been done to make it look like any farming was going on and, of course, each man used several assumed names to file multiple claims. The railroad, like the government, usually looked the other way. "Someone put a bee in their bonnet—Krueger!" Noah ground out the name in loathing as he paced furiously back and forth in his study while Lem Parkins stood, hat in hand.

Parkins was one of the pseudohomesteaders in Noah's employ, also the bearer of the bad news from town late that day. "Well, boss, it wharn't me—ner th' rest o' th' fellers neither. Yew know thet." He shuffled uneasily, fondly hoping Noah believed him. Lordy, he didn't want to be on the wrong side of Noah Sinclair!

Suddenly, Noah stopped pacing, absently motioning for Parkins to go. There was a lot to consider. The night of the ball, after he had such friendly assurances from the two Chicago railroad men, Grossman and Rogers, he was certain the route would be near Circle S. Then Krueger arrived and everything changed. Lola was from Chicago before she moved here. Could she and her brother-in-law be in collusion? Then he remembered Hawk and Krueger leaving him to deal with two spitting women. Hawk might have found out. Noah knew his son hated him enough to betray him. But to betray Circle S!

Noah resumed pacing. As he thought it over, it made sense. With Carrie here, Hawk had probably concluded he would never inherit. Maybe that had driven him to an act of revenge. That and his stupid ideals about those damn Indians. He would have a showdown with Hawk at dinner tonight. And if his suspicions were justified—what? His rage was murderous enough that he would wish his son dead, no doubt there. However, Hawk took some killing, as Noah well knew. His gun was deadly, and there was also the matter of Hunnicut to consider. The little Texan was as dangerous as his companion.

Compounding the problem, what was he to do about the rustling? He and Krueger had walked a tightrope for several years, barely avoiding an all-out range war for control of the region. Hawk and Kyle were trump cards against Krueger's hired killers. Noah mulled and seethed simultaneously. He would see what his damn half-breed son had to say for himself tonight.

The minute Hawk walked into the parlor that evening, he sensed Noah's stormy attitude. *So, he's going to feel me out first*, he said to himself. Hawk knew that Noah needed him and Kyle against Krueger's gunmen. And he also had the surprise card of Squires's disappearance to deal the old man. Not that Krueger couldn't hire another leader for his band of cutthroats easily enough, but that would be all the more reason for Noah to need his own guns. *It's going to be an interesting card game tonight*, Hawk thought in grim humor.

Just then Carrie entered the room, the bright yellow of her gown catching the corner of his eye. Her tall, willowy body was lushly revealed in the soft silk. Damn, what that color did for her complexion and firehair! She smiled uncertainly, not at all the jaunty, insouciant girl of the morning when they were in the kitchen with Feliz and Kyle. Noah still had her buffaloed, he thought angrily, despite her growing self-confidence around others on the ranch.

Noah poured her sherry and held the glass out to her. Hawk saw her flinch from the touch of his fingers as she accepted the drink. *God only knows what he does to her in bed at night*, he thought bitterly, more disturbed by that idea than he had ever been before.

Carrie could feel the tension the minute she stepped into the room. Noah's face was stamped in a taut, white-lipped manner that indicated wrath held in check. Hawk looked almost indolent, yet she sensed a coiled readiness beneath his facade as he lounged against the mantel, sipping his whiskey. What was going on? Then she remembered his and Kyle's celebration in town over the railroad route. So Noah had heard the news. Bits and pieces of conversation from Frank, Feliz, Kyle, and Hawk all began to come together now. What part had Karl Krueger and Lola Jameson played in this? Her head swam.

"I heard some distressing news this afternoon, Hawk," Noah began blandly. "Seems the Northern Pacific is going to bypass Circle S land and keep north, right in Krueger's lap." His cold blue eyes pierced his son as he waited for a reply.

Hawk uncoiled his long frame and stood straight, quaffing the last of his whiskey in one abrupt sip. "That so. I heard rumors about it in town last night. You always did tend to underestimate Krueger. You might take this as an object lesson, Noah." The words and the look were measured as Hawk stared at his father. Casually he sauntered to the sideboard for another drink.

"No need for that," Noah interrupted as Mathilda Thorndyke stepped in to announce dinner. A triumphant look came into her eyes when Hawk set his glass down without refilling it. He walked past the old woman as if she were invisible and entered the dining room.

Seating Carrie, Noah continued their conversation. "I never underestimate Krueger. I only wonder if he had some inside help this time."

Hawk looked at Noah with such intensity that Carrie shivered at the coldness in his black eyes. At that moment, she could see the bond of blood between father and son.

They were alike in their ruthlessness and cunning. She wondered which was the more dangerous adversary.

Then Hawk spoke. "If you think I helped Krueger, you might be right. Then again . . . you might be wrong. For now, it really doesn't matter, does it? What's done is done, and you still need me and Kyle."

"The hell I do!" Noah swore, blazing mad. "You *did* help him! Somehow you found out about those claims and told him! Why? To get revenge on me? To spite Circle S and see it go under? I'll see you dead!"

"No, you won't, Noah." Hawk's voice was ice cold and startlingly calm in the face of such open hate from his father. "As to why I might help Krueger, forget Circle S. I don't give a damn one way or the other about it or you. I want the railroad as far from the Cheyenne as I can keep it. You won't lose that much. There'll be a line into Miles City—"

Noah interrupted furiously. "Yes, a line three times as long for stock and supplies as I'd have had with the southern route—not to mention the side benefit of driving out the last of those nests of marauding redskins who murdered Abel!"

Carrie had listened to the snarling exchange and feared they might actually attack one another. Without thinking, she interjected, "But Noah, the Cheyenne didn't kill your brother, the Crow did. Starving a peaceful tribe and driving them from their rightful land just so you can get supplies and ship stock more conveniently—it isn't fair."

Hawk looked at her in flat amazement. Noah whirled so abruptly he bumped the table, causing the crystal to shimmer and tinkle from the impact. "You know nothing about this, Carrie, so stay out of it! Your place as my wife is to support me."

"Regardless of who's right and who's wrong!" Her eyes were ablaze as all her frustrations and anger at his bullying and brutality surfaced. She'd had enough!

"You are a fool!" he retorted witheringly.

"Is Frank Lowery a fool? Are the hands who work here fools? Most of them were born and raised in Montana or spent their lives around Indians. Lots of them think the Cheyenne have a right to breathe, too!''

"I might have known that bastard'd take up for the savages and fill your head with garbage as well. Your fine feelings don't mean a tinker's damn, my darling, so you can stifle them. If you ever speak up for the downtrodden red men again and humiliate me in public, I can assure you I'll make you regret it.'' By this time Noah had his blinding rage under control. He needed his wits about him, and no chit of a girl was going to deter him from dealing with Hawk Sinclair. God, how he detested the fact that this traitorous savage had a legal right to his name!

Carrie sat rigidly, defiance still radiating from every pore and flashing from her eyes, which shone like two brilliant green flames.

She's as fierce as any warrior woman! Hawk watched her confront Noah, truly taken aback by her courage. He had underestimated her. He interrupted the nasty exchange between husband and wife. "You're overlooking the main thing, Noah. Forget the railroad and the Cheyenne—and your wife.''

Noah's attention focused once more on Hawk; he took no notice of the continuing fury in Carrie's face. "I'll never forget that you betrayed me for your mother's people. You always were a lot more red than white, despite all the education and wealth I could offer you. You chose her and those dirty savages, ever since you were a child, running off to live with them every chance you got. I was a fool to drag you back, keep them from disfiguring you for life with those damn sundance scars!''

Hawk scoffed. "You wouldn't have given a damn if I died in the sundance! If I'd have gotten blood poisoning, you'd have been glad. You just didn't want a scarred savage for a son. Well, I may not have earned the tong marks, but I'll always be a savage, Noah—just remember that! And, remember, too, you need me and Kyle and our guns. We caught Squires with a running iron in his hand. I took the evidence to Krueger and made a deal. He's paid Squires off and sent him packing, but he can always replace him. You can hire other guns, too, but they might not intimidate K Bar men as much as we do. You decide. Want a range war—now while Krueger's got all the trump cards with the railroad sewed up? I think you still need me, at least for a while. . . ." He turned to his plate and attacked the steak on it with evident relish, wielding the knife with precise skill.

Noah sat down, grunting in bitter acknowledgment as he, too, turned his attention to the meal. "So, you and Hunnicut'll do me the great favor of staying on for now. I suppose I should be honored." He considered a moment, then spoke with a table knife poised in midair, gesturing at his son. "Let this be a warning, Hawk. Don't ever betray me again. Your Cheyenne aren't the only ones who pay their debts."

Hawk raised his wineglass in mock salute. "To understanding—the beginning of wisdom."

When the meal was finished, Hawk excused himself and walked down to the bunkhouse to talk to Kyle. He had a lot to consider, especially Carrie's unexpected behavior. He knew her boldness in defying Noah would not go unpunished. He also knew just what form that punishment would take. The more he thought of Carrie in Noah's bed, suffering his attentions, the more disturbing the images became. "White women *are* poison," he muttered to himself just before he entered the bunkhouse.

By the time she had prepared for retiring that night, Carrie was regretting her spontaneous outburst at dinner. Never since she had first come to live with Aunt Patience had she let her carefully trained guard down so stupidly. Then when it meant a spanking, no dinner, or the loss of a treasured possession, Carrie had schooled herself to squelch that violent temper. How much more dearly would she pay for tonight's outburst than she had in St. Louis! Shivering, she slipped her silk robe off and slid between the covers of her bed, praying Noah would be so distraught at Hawk that he would drink himself into a stupor and be unable to come to her tonight.

Her wish was half granted. Noah did drink excessively, but he did not pass out. After she had fallen into a fitful

sleep around midnight, the door connecting her bedroom
to his opened with a loud crash. Noah stood in the door
frame, his tall body filling it as he swayed unsteadily on
his feet. His robe was askew, and as he shambled into the
room, he pulled clumsily at the sash, loosening it. His
words were slurred, but the venom in his voice was
unmistakable.

"Well, if it isn't my darling wife, the Indian lover . . . let's
just pretend I'm some big, black-haired buck with greasy
braids. . . ."

Noah made a late start the next morning because of his
drunkenness the night before. He was taking a coach east
to pick up the rails to Chicago. If there was one last
chance to influence the Northern Pacific officials about the
route, he must take it. Beating Krueger and Hawk was
growing into an obsession with him—that and getting his
willful wife pregnant.

His memories of the previous night were hazy. Nevertheless, when he saw Carrie's purple-shadowed eyes and
flinching avoidance that morning, he knew he must have
dealt effectively with her. Just let her quicken and he
would gladly leave her cold bed for the lusty whores in
Miles City.

Once Carrie was certain he had departed, she went
down to the corrals and began to saddle Taffy Girl for a
ride. Aching and exhausted, she needed to ride in the
warm, clean air to cleanse the poison of Noah's touch
from her body.

"Easy, Taffy, easy. You and I will have a good, quick
ride. Just—" Carrie stopped in midsentence as Hawk
rounded the corner. What was he doing here so late in the
morning?

As if in answer to her unspoken question, he replied,
"Redskin threw a shoe. Brought him in for Jeremy to
replace it." He took in her drawn, tired appearance, trying
not to dwell on the reason for it.

With a quick "Good morning," Carrie fairly fled past
him and led her mare outside the barn. Just as she began to
put a foot in the stirrup, a pair of hands reached around her

waist to boost her up. Thinking it was Hawk, she turned to plead that he let her go. It was not Hawk, but Lew Smithers, a tall, rangy cowboy with an angular face. His thin nose and concave cheeks were red and veiny, his hands large with long, callused fingers. Smithers was unwashed, smelling of sour sweat and cheap cigars. As he nodded, one long spike of dirty blond hair fell across his forehead.

To Carrie he looked for all the world like a young, impoverished version of Noah. She paled and flinched at his unexpected appearance. "Please, I can mount by myself."

As she did just that, he let out a loud chuckle and said, "Yep, in them duds, I just bet you can." His eyes roamed across her hips and followed the curve of her split skirts down to her boots, then slid back up to her breast, now beginning to heave in agitation.

Carrie turned Taffy, but Smithers grabbed the bridle and held on. "Just a minute. What with the boss man gone 'n' all, I reckon you can use some protection. I'll ride along."

By this time, Carrie was flushed and angry. Still unnerved by the previous evening, she could not bear the proximity of this smelly young incarnation of her husband. She had to escape! "I don't want company. I ride alone."

His face darkened. "I seen ya ride with Lowery 'n' Hunnicut, even that breed. Ya mean I ain't as good as them?" Since coming to work at Circle S, he had watched the old man's beautiful young wife for weeks. If she rode out with other hands and that Indian, why not with him! He did not loose his hold on Taffy's bridle. The horse shied nervously.

"Let me go." Carrie fairly bit off each word.

Before she could say more, Hawk's voice cut into Smithers's back, low, silky, deadly. "You heard the lady, Smithers. Let her go, or this breed may decide to do something downright hostile." He was lounged against the stable door, ever so casually, but the low gun on his hip gleamed evilly in the noon sun.

Smithers quickly reconsidered, tipping his greasy-rimmed

hat. "Meant no harm, ma'am. I got no fight with you, Sinclair." With that he vanished around the corral fence.

Hawk paid the cowardly Lothario no further attention, but looked at Carrie's shaken demeanor. With a quick, choked little thank-you, she rode over the hill. He stood there, debating whether or not to follow her, thinking how frightened and vulnerable she looked. Nor did he miss the shivering revulsion she had for Smithers. *Damn you, Noah, you'll make her shrink from all men before you're done!* Just then, Kyle came up behind him.

Watching his friend's pensive stare and haunted black eyes, Hunnicut swore to himself, then spoke aloud. "It'd be smart ta fix on somethin' else, Longlegs. She'll git yew in a passel o' trouble."

Hawk scoffed. "I already said white women *were* trouble, Kyle. I know."

"It ain't her fault any more'n it's yourn. If thing's different, I 'spect yew 'n' her'd 'a'done all right. But—"

Hawk cut him off abruptly. "Forget it, Kyle! She's never been for me, and we both know it. I'm not a complete fool for you to shepherd." He considered a few seconds, then smiled. "At least, not since you carried me out of that bar years ago."

"Carried! Huh! As much lead as ya had in yew, a lil' feller like me's lucky ta drag ya." He sobered again, not wanting to avoid the issue as Hawk obviously did. "Whut ya say me 'n' yew slip off ta th' Nations agin? Ya kept th' railroad off'n yer grandpa's land. Nothin' thet *ought ta* be keepin' us here now."

"Krueger," came the terse reply. Hawk walked toward the lower corral where the smith worked, leaving a very unhappy and thoughtful Kyle Hunnicut scratching his head.

Noah had been gone for five days, and every morning Carrie thanked heaven she had not been forced to accompany him. He had considered it, but the doctor's advice about allowing her rest and a stable routine stopped him. What if she were already pregnant and the rough coach and train trip caused her to miscarry? No, he left her at Circle S and she was grateful. By the time Noah was gone a week, Carrie's monthly courses came, and she knew she was not with child. She grimaced, thinking how angrily he would take that news.

Such were her troubled thoughts when she rode home the afternoon of the sixth day of Noah's absence. She pulled Taffy up at the corral and dismounted, then stopped short when she heard a child's whimper and Kyle Hunnicut's voice trying to communicate with the frightened little one.

"Now, jist take it easy, lil' mite. Soon's Hawk gits here, we kin palaver. Lordy, do step it up, Longlegs," he muttered under his breath, all the while attempting to soothe the child.

Carrie walked quietly into the stable, adjusting her eyes to the dim interior. Then she saw the wiry little man awkwardly trying to get a small Indian girl to lie still on a hastily unrolled saddle blanket. She looked to be no more than seven or eight. Her large brown eyes were dark with terror, and her lips trembled as she whispered brokenly in a strange language Carrie had never heard before. Her long hair was bound in two shiny braids that had come partially undone and her beautifully worked deerskin tunic was ripped. However, it was the right legging that told the tale of her pain and terror. It was slashed open at midcalf, and a large gash bled profusely over the sweet hay and the blanket.

Quickly Carrie moved to Kyle's side. "She's badly hurt, Kyle. Where did you find her?"

"I wuz down a fer piece, near Cheyenne huntin' country. Heered this here little bitty cry. She's tryin' ta be real quiet. Good thing she warn't. From th' sign, I 'spect she wandered off pickin' berries an' a she bear got a couple o' good swipes at her. Dunno why it didn't finish her, but bears's funny. Niver kin tell whut they'll do."

Carrie knelt and placed a gentle hand on the girl's feverish brow. "Do you have any idea how long she lay there injured like this?" As she spoke and touched the girl, the child quieted, gazing in awe at the fiery curls spilling down Carrie's shoulder. Wonderingly, she touched one long springy bit of the hair, then withdrew her fingers as if burned.

Carrie smiled reassuringly. "It's all right." Turning to Kyle, she said, "Do you suppose she's never seen a white person before?"

He nodded. "Possible, leastways not a woman, an' fer shore not one with yer kinda har."

"If only we could communicate with her. What tribe is she? Cheyenne?"

He nodded again, then added, "Hawk should be here soon. He kin tell her we mean no harm."

"We have to get her to the house, Kyle. I'll ask Frank to send a hand into town for Dr. Lark. She needs medical attention."

"Forget Dr. Lark," a harsh voice barked out. "He wouldn't cross the street to treat a sick Cheyenne, much less come to Circle S." Hawk knelt by the girl's side, brushing Carrie back and taking the child's hand.

As if sensing their kindred blood, she spoke haltingly and he replied.

Carrie interrupted, placing her hand tentatively on Hawk's shoulder as she spoke. "We must at least get her to the house and into a clean bed so we can tend her wounds."

He looked up with a sardonic gleam in his eye. "You figure to face down Noah when he finds a filthy redskin in one of his lily-white beds?"

Her eyes flashed emerald fire. "He already has one—in *your* room! I'll take my chances. While we're arguing, this child is in pain!"

Without another word, Hawk scooped up the girl and strode toward the house with Carrie beside him. Smothering a chuckle, Kyle turned to attend to the horses.

When they arrived at the big house, Carrie calmly opened the door. Hawk carried the tiny, quaking child into the front hall. Gazing into the parlor with its high ceiling and glittering chandelier, the child's eyes glowed in fear and wonder. Just as the three moved toward the stairs, Mathilda Thorndyke materialized from the dining room, a look of horrified incredulity spread across her face.

She perched two bony fists on her spartan hips and fairly shrieked, "You can't bring that—that savage into Mr. Sinclair's house!"

Carrie cut in sharply before Hawk could speak. "You forget yourself, Mathilda! I'm *Mrs*. Sinclair, and I say I can."

Grinning evilly, Hawk added, "And I'm *Mr*. Sinclair, too, in case you forgot, Mathilda. This is my house as well as Noah's—for now." With that he swept effortlessly past the stupefied sentinel.

Carrie followed him upstairs after issuing crisp instructions. "Have Feliz boil some water and bring clean bandages to the spare bedroom on the east end of the hall. Immediately!"

Livid with rage, Mathilda Thorndyke did as she was bid. By the time Feliz arrived, Carrie had settled the child in a comfortable bed and Hawk had cut the leather legging away from her wound. The little guest room was seldom used, clean but sparsely furnished. Carrie chose it because it was small and far from Noah's room. The girl would need sleep. Already Carrie considered how she would handle Noah.

As Hawk explained to the child that Feliz was a medicine woman who was going to help her, Carrie wrung out linens from the sterilized water and handed them to the intrepid Mexicana.

"What is her name? Oh, I wish I could talk to her," Carrie said in sad frustration.

"It's Bright Leaf," Hawk replied.

"What was a child of eight or nine doing out there all alone!" Carrie was shaken. She had never seen such stoic endurance as the child displayed while Feliz cleansed the fierce claw gouges. Even while the rawest places were washed, she made no cry.

"She's six," Hawk replied. "Cheyenne are tall, even the children. She was with her older sister and got separated. Wandered off to follow a butterfly and got out of earshot."

"Are her people near here? Surely they wouldn't desert her!"

"No, not normally, but if nothing is found but the bear and her tracks, they might conclude Bright Leaf is dead. I'll have to check around and see which band she's from and then locate them. It may take a while."

"Well, she can't be moved for some time, anyway," Carrie said, wincing as Feliz applied an astringent poultice to the deep, angry gashes on the thin sturdy leg.

Hawk looked at Carrie, sensing her unspoken question. "I'll help you with Noah."

"He'll not throw a sick child out to die!" She vowed it fiercely to herself, not even realizing she spoke the words aloud. Then her green eyes softened as she looked at the tall, dark figure standing beside the bed. "Thank you, Hawk."

"She's one of the People. I could do no less, but you could have, Carrie. Perhaps I should be the one thanking you."

Over the next several days, Carrie stayed close to the house and helped Feliz tend to Bright Leaf. Once her initial awe and fear were dispelled, the child responded wholeheartedly to the warmth and kindness of the Mexican cook and the flame-haired young woman. Feliz knew a few simple words and phrases in Cheyenne and taught them to Carrie. The girl was as bright as her name and quickly picked up a similar vocabulary in English. The three of them communicated fairly well.

Hawk went in search of her band the next morning, figuring the more rapidly he returned her to her own people, the better things would be. Carrie did not need another incident to antagonize Noah. Even if he faced the old man down, Carrie's love for the child would be obvious. The second night, when he returned to the ranch after an unsuccessful search, he heard her halting attempts at Cheyenne and Bright Leaf's similar efforts in English. Hawk could see that Carrie would not suffer Noah's slurs against the child in silence.

Seeing him in the doorway, Bright Leaf beamed and began to speak rapidly in Cheyenne.

"What's she telling you?" Carrie was always amazed at how silently he could move. His presence took her by surprise, and she did not even think to say hello.

He replied to the child, then to her. "She asks how you captured a piece of the sun. Did it fall from the sky on the day of your birth?"

At Carrie's blank look, he strode effortlessly across the small room and picked up a lock of her hair for a brief second, then let it drop. "This. Fire like the sun in the morning sky."

The intensity of his gaze was as blazing as the sun itself, she thought as a flush stole up her cheeks. Nervously, she turned her attention to Bright Leaf. "It's just hair, like yours, only a different color. No magic." She took the curl Hawk had just released and proffered it to the girl, who touched it gingerly.

As he translated Carrie's words to Bright Leaf, Hawk thought to himself, *She expects to be burned; I already am.* Aloud he said, "She must be from a band that seldom goes south, where they'd encounter more whites. She's never seen red hair before."

"How long do you think it will take to locate her people?"

He shrugged, glad to move his thoughts to practical considerations. "Hard to say. I talked to my grandfather. He's sending out messengers to comb the hills for small isolated groups that left the summer camp early. They may be far away by now, as far east as Dakota. If they can't locate her family in a week or so, I'll take her to Iron Heart's band to spend the winter. She'll be well cared for."

Carrie sighed. "I suppose it's best, but I . . . that is, I rather like having a child here."

His face darkened. "Be realistic, Carrie. Noah will hardly let you adopt her! He expects his own children—white ones—to fill these rooms. No more Cheyenne." At her look of surprised hurt and even embarrassment, he relented. "Anyway, she's better off being all Cheyenne, growing up knowing only one way." Oddly, thoughts of Wind Song flashed into his mind, her clear green eyes so untroubled and calm. Her white blood was not the curse his was, causing him to want things he could never have.

"She needs to sleep. We can't take her back until she's stronger," Carrie replied, tucking the child in and planting a kiss on her forehead.

"We?" Hawk questioned, gently mocking.

Carrie flushed scarlet as she fled past him into the hall. "I can't just desert her. I want to know she's going to another woman who'll take good care of her."

"I know a woman in my grandfather's village who'll be willing to help. She has a twelve-year-old sister, and they'd be happy to care for her. They're both under Iron Heart's protection, and Bright Leaf would be, too."

Carrie felt a swift stab of some undefinable emotion. Who was this young woman under his grandfather's protection? "I would like to meet them," she said, daring him to explain more.

"Would you, really?" He said no more but smiled archly. Just then they were interrupted by the slamming of the front door and Noah's furious voice.

"Carrie!"

Despite herself, she flinched. "He's home, and someone's already told him about Bright Leaf."

"If Mathilda Thorndyke didn't break a leg running down the front steps with the news, I miss my guess." Grimly, Hawk started to walk toward the stairs.

Squaring her shoulders, Carrie quickly caught up with him.

They descended together. Seeing them, Noah snorted in disgust. "I might have known *you'd* be in on this, Hawk. I'm not running an orphanage for stray Cheyennes. Send her back to her people. You know she'd be happier with them."

Before he could reply, Carrie burst out, "I don't care if she's Crow! She's an injured child, and until she's well enough to travel, you can't move her!"

Noah blanched at her mention of Crow. However, he had grown used to her defiance, and felt he could deal with it quickly enough.

Hawk was another matter. "She's right, Noah. A six-year-old girl isn't exactly a threat, and she doesn't eat much. I'll take her to Iron Heart the first of the week." With that, he walked past his father and into the parlor to pour himself a whiskey before retiring for the night. He waited to see what the old man would do, but no further confrontation ensued. Judging by his bleak, defeated stance,

Noah's mission to Chicago must have been a failure, too. Hawk took a long pull on the whiskey and smiled in satisfaction. Then he heard a muffled exchange between Carrie and Noah before her footsteps retraced the stairs. His smile vanished.

That week was a misery of antagonism in the big house. Hawk seemed most impervious to it, as he was used to Noah's outbursts and Mrs. Thorndyke's hateful silence, but Carrie literally tiptoed through the days, not wanting Bright Leaf to know how upset she was. God forbid Hawk and Noah might come to blows while the child was in the house.

If Noah was unwilling to face down his son over the brief stay of one six-year-old Cheyenne, he was more than willing to subject Carrie to his sarcasm and cruelty for her part in the affair.

The very night of his return he questioned her about possible pregnancy, and she confessed that her courses had come once again. After his disappointment in Chicago and finding an Indian child in his house, this was the last straw. "I'll just have to make good my promise to you about bedding you more often. I'm afraid I've neglected my wife. Since I have to go away next week for a stockmen's association meeting in Helena, I'll make it up to you tonight."

However, after nearly two weeks on the road, with no comfortable sleep during the grueling train and coach travel home, Noah was exhausted. He began his usual swift taking of her, shedding his robe and climbing naked into her bed. He could feel her cool, stiff form lying still, willing herself to let him touch her. By now even her freshness and striking beauty had worn stale for Noah. What he wanted, needed, was an experienced woman to stimulate his tired flesh. Of course, a good girl like Carrie did not and should not ever know how to do that. Nevertheless, he was angry with her lack of response. God, how he detested her passivity! Duty. She was doing her duty, damn her! But he found himself unequal to the task of doing his.

As he ran his hands over her delicate breasts and down

her sleek legs, he could feel himself softening. A few times in whorehouses after he'd been drinking all night it had happened, even when he was younger, but that was different. Tonight he had only one drink after dinner and came to bed early. A sick fear began to gnaw at the pit of his stomach as he fumbled to stroke himself back to an erection. He knew Carrie must wonder what was wrong with him, and that galvanized his fright into fury. This was her fault, damn her! Cold, barren, willful bitch! She was as bad as Lola, only in different ways. With Lola, too, it had happened toward the end, but then he *had* been drinking heavily and blamed it on that—that and her spiteful comparisons between his performance and her first husband's. Despite knowing Carrie had no one else to compare him with, he was not reassured.

Finally, after he had lain still for several minutes, she worked up her courage and said, "Is—is something wrong? Are you all right?"

"Yes, something is wrong," he hissed at her, rolling over and grabbing her by the shoulders. "I'm all right, but you certainly leave much to be desired! Barren and cold to boot! I gave a penniless orphan a home, wealth, position. All I asked in return is that she give me a son. All you want to do is adopt filthy savages and lay woodenly in this bed!"

His snarling attack left her stunned and terrified, especially when he accompanied the verbal torrent by harshly clutching her arms and shaking her violently. Then he kissed her brutally, running his hands all over her body in rough, painful strokes, pulling, pinching, and rubbing. The abuse seemed to renew his sexual tension and he felt himself growing hard once more. Swiftly he clawed her thighs apart and thrust into her, spilling his seed in a few painful grunts. Immediately, he rolled off her and out of the bed, grabbing his robe and stalking from the room wordlessly.

In all their previous degrading and painful copulations, Carrie had at least been passively cooperative and he had seemed to enjoy her flesh, even if she could not respond in turn. He was her husband and she felt he had the right to her body. But tonight, this was truly rape. There was no other name for it. The earlier unintentional, even negligent brutality which he had inflicted on her paled in comparison to this. Her head ached from the way he had snapped her neck when he had shaken her. Wincing, she touched her abraded skin where he had scratched her with his nails and had rubbed so hard he actually had burned her, much as a rawhide rope might.

Why? Oh, why this? She did not begin to understand. Was she so clumsy and cold as he said? So undesirable? Then why did Hawk look at her the way he did? Put his hands on her and kiss her so feverishly? No! She could not allow herself to think of that. Least of all now. *If Noah is a rapist, then I am an adulteress, at least in my heart!* In pain and humiliation she sank down into the covers and sobbed brokenly for what she had just confessed to herself.

CHAPTER 11

Mercifully, Noah had to leave for Helena that Friday. The annual Montana Stock Growers Association meeting was too important to miss. For Carrie, his trip was a reprieve. If he had been inconsiderate and cold before, he had been truly brutal and sadistic the past four nights.

Hawk left for Iron Heart's village hoping to hear that Bright Leaf's parents had been found. He was not expected back until Noah was due to leave. In truth, rather than stay at the house and endure the crackling tension between Noah and Carrie, Hawk had wanted to escape. He hadn't felt this helpless since his mother had died. He knew Noah would not touch the child. He only wished that Noah could not touch the woman.

Saturday morning Carrie awoke after an undisturbed sleep. It was her first night in five that had been so, and she was grateful. Stretching, she sat up in bed and looked around. Judging by the angle of the light streaming in her window, it must be quite late. Swishing aside the covers, she leaped from the bed and grabbed a silk wrapper. In a minute she was in Bright Leaf's room. The girl walked haltingly from the window to the door, then stopped in midstride when she saw Carrie. Bright Leaf stretched her arms toward the flame-haired goddess who had befriended her. She limped quickly into Carrie's embrace and chattered joyously, obviously proud of her rapid recovery. Carrie, too, was happy for Bright Leaf's healing, but would be sorry to let her go.

As if echoing her thoughts, Hawk spoke from the doorway, "Looks as if she'll be ready to travel Monday."

Carrie gasped as she released the squirming child who ran into his welcoming embrace. Self-consciously, she stood up and tightened the meager protection of the thin silk across her breasts. Damn, if she had known he would return this early, she would never have left her room in such a state of undress!

As if sensing her discomfort, Hawk looked over the shoulder of the chattering child and scorched Carrie with his hot black gaze. He smiled at her pink cheeks and nervous gesture as she folded her arms across her breasts.

"Must you always sneak up on a person like a —" She stopped short.

He supplied, "Like a savage?" His voice was level, but his expression turned hard as she blushed in guilty admission of her reflex response.

Carrie raised her downcast countenance, looking straight into the midnight depths of his hypnotic eyes. "I'm sorry. I didn't mean it as a slur. It's just that you always seem to appear where I least expect you." *And your presence disturbs me in ways I do not want to admit.*

He relaxed and smiled, then said, "You mean places like the lake?" He was almost chuckling now, and she blushed again. The softening of his harshly chiseled features made a magical transformation, and Carrie was struck anew by how startingly handsome he was.

Just then Feliz padded up the stairs with Bright Leaf's tray. It was time for the midday meal. Excusing herself, Carrie rushed off to dress.

Beneath the baleful glare of Mathilda Thorndyke, Bright Leaf came downstairs for the first time that afternoon. Her leg had healed wonderfully under Feliz's careful ministrations, and she was able to walk with only a slight limp. Carrie took her through the spacious, beautiful parlor and dining room, allowing the child's natural curiosity free rein. After a few minutes of awe-filled staring, her six-year-old energy reasserted itself and she began to rub the satiny shine of the glossy oak table in the dining room, giggling at seeing her own reflection in its polished depths. Carrie picked up a precious cut-glass flower vase and let the child examine its glittering prisms. Bright Leaf ran her fingers over the diamondlike surfaces in amazement and smelled the spicy essence of the huge fall mums it held. She would have many wonders to tell her friends about when she returned home.

While Noah was away, Carrie and Bright Leaf ate in the kitchen with Feliz. Knowing where to find them, Hawk came straight from the corral with Kyle and headed there to tell Carrie that Bright Leaf must leave early the next morning.

She did not receive the news with good spirits. "Must she go so soon? Noah won't be back until the end of the week. We could—"

He interrupted her impatiently. "Look, I know you've grown fond of the child, but it will only be harder the longer you wait, both for you and her. She's very attached to you, too," he said, affectionately stroking the shiny black hair of the child as she sat cuddled up against Carrie on a kitchen bench.

He said a few words in Cheyenne to her, and her expression darkened. Questioningly, she turned her eyes to Carrie and clutched her hand tightly, murmuring in her halting English, "Carrie go," and motioning to herself.

"She wants ya ta make th' trip with her. I guess she's afeard o' goin' ta a big village where she won't know no one," Kyle said to Carrie.

Hawk scowled. "That's out of the question. They'll make her welcome and she'll be fine." He spoke again to the child, gently, and once more she clung to Carrie, but this time did not argue, only nodded in resignation.

Taking a deep breath, Carrie said, "If I go with her she'll feel much better, Hawk."

"You can't go," he replied in exasperation.

"Why not? I care for Bright Leaf; would your grandfather's people not welcome me because I'm white? Or is it because I'm Noah's wife?"

He shook his head impatiently. "No, they'd treat you

like royalty, I'm sure. But it's a hard four-hour ride there and another four back.''

"That's not far. I could easily make it there and back in a day," she said spiritedly, waiting for him to voice his real objection.

He looked levelly at her. "Do you seriously think you could keep Noah from finding out you went to a Cheyenne village?" *And rode back alone with me?* "He'd be furious with you."

She gave a sad little nervous laugh. "In case you hadn't noticed, I've never been able to please him anyway, so what difference can it make?"

Realizing this was shaping up into a duel of wills, Feliz left her tasks by the stove and picked up the child. Kyle, who had been busily stuffing sweet rolls in his mouth, followed her outside. "We will show the *muchacha* some of those big chrysanthemums that grow in the garden. She loves to smell them," the cook said airily.

With that they were gone, leaving Carrie sitting alone on the bench and Hawk draping his long-legged frame over a chair across the table from her.

"Now's not the time to push Noah further just to satisfy a girlish whim for adventure," he argued.

"Whim! Why, you insufferable—" She began to jump up, her eyes blazing at him. Then, dejectedly, she sat back down and took a deep breath. "Look, in spite of what you think, I haven't acted on childish whims for a long time. In fact, I had a remarkably unindulged adolescence. I just want Bright Leaf to be all right, to know I care enough about her not to desert her. When she's met your grandfather and the young woman who'll care for her until her family returns, then she'll accept my leaving her."

He looked at her earnest face, determined and full of genuine love for the little girl. "We'll leave at daybreak. Have Feliz pack some food."

As bright fiery orange slashed across the morning sky, casting its warm light on the rustling dry prairie grass, they set out. Bright Leaf rode with Carrie on Taffy Girl, her slight frame adding little to the horse's burden. After an hour or so, the steady plodding of hoofbeats lulled the still-weakened child asleep. Motioning for Carrie to hand her over, Hawk took the girl whose unconscious weight pressed against Carrie uncomfortably. Bright Leaf stirred, but did not awaken.

He held her effortlessly. Carrie thought they made a splendid picture, the delicate little girl and her fierce, tall protector. Hawk had been so gentle with the child. Although she had considered his complex personality many times, here was indeed a side to him she had never seen. Her reverie led her to ask, "Why did you become a gunman?" The minute she spoke the words, she wanted to call them back, fully expecting he'd turn on her once more, furious at her presumption.

He surprised her, however, smiling ironically and seeming to ponder the question for a suspenseful moment. Then he said, "Lots of reasons, I guess. Part accident. When I wandered down to the Nations as a kid, it was either learn to shoot or be shot. That's where I found out I was naturally fast. A drunk cowboy called me a half-breed in a bar and threw his drink in my face. I hauled off and socked him. When he reached for his gun, I reached for mine." He shrugged fatalistically. "I was seventeen."

She shuddered at the violence of frontier life and how it hardened everyone, especially the young. "You could've stayed east. You obviously had a great deal of formal education."

He snorted in disgust. "Yeah, I learned a lot, a lesson a day. Do you know where I first learned to fight? Not at my grandfather's village. At boarding school when I was ten. Cheyenne children are taught to cooperate, not brawl among themselves. But rich white schoolboys are just the opposite."

"They picked on you because of your Indian blood?" She knew the answer, and it saddened her.

"I don't have much use for most white men. Maybe that's really why I became a drifter and used my guns. No roots, no ties.'' He stared at her defiantly. "Maybe I like to kill whites.''

"But you have white friends," she said, undaunted by his provocative remark. "Kyle, Feliz, and Frank. There must be others.''

"Damn few," he said laconically.

"So, the whites were cruel. Did the Cheyenne accept your white blood?'' Once more she sensed the answer.

He sighed. "Not always. Actually I had to fight a few of my own cousins when I was growing up, too. Being Iron Heart's grandson, I'll always be welcome, but there are some who'd rather I didn't stay with the People. Maybe that's part of the reason I drift with Kyle so much. Men outside the law are men with no families, no prejudices. We understand each other.''

"Maybe it's also a way to get back at your father. I think he's afraid of you.''

Her perception no longer surprised him, but he found himself amazed that he was talking so openly with her. "Yeah, I guess if he ever feared anything or anyone, it's me. He spent my childhood trying to make me white, keeping me away from my mother's people as much as he could, shipping me east to school after she died. But it didn't work.''

"Or it only half worked," Carrie said gently, realizing the sundered world in which he had grown up. "Part of you is white, Hawk, whether you like it or not.'' She could still picture him elegantly attired in formal evening clothes, dancing so superbly that night of the ball in Miles City.

They rode in silence for a few minutes, but he did not attempt to argue her point. He had always known what he said was true. He belonged nowhere. Had he never wanted to choose, as Wind Song said? Or was the choice truly not his to make?

He changed the subject, wanting to understand her earlier life. "What about you? You grew up in one secure world, then came here where it's brutally different. Why?''

The way he asked the question indicated to her that he

no longer prejudged her to be the cheap fortune hunter he had once imagined. It was incredible that they could talk this way for the first time.

"I grew up in a split world, too—oh, of a different kind than yours. My parents loved me and pampered me, but they were killed when I was thirteen. My father's investments went bad, and he left me nothing. His brother took me in, grudgingly."

She went on to tell him of her nightmare years with Aunt Patience and Uncle Hiram and their spiteful daughters, describing incidents where her clothing, even her most treasured possessions, such as her porcelain doll and her mother's pearl necklace, were taken away in punishment.

"Aunt Patience couldn't have me sweep the sidewalk or drive the rig. The neighbors and servants would talk, but she found plenty of ways to keep me in my place. I scrubbed floors, waxed furniture, and washed dishes aplenty. I was also sent away from school. I hated that worst of all, for I did love to learn. Luckily, Uncle Hiram inherited my parents' library, one of the few things left when they died. I read and studied on my own after Miss Jefferson's expelled me."

"What did you do to get expelled?" He looked genuinely interested.

She cleared her throat nervously. "Well, you see there was Therese, my friend and schoolmate. She hated Charity, my eldest cousin, as much as I did, and Charity was inordinately terrified of insects. You know, things like big woolly caterpillars?" At his grin of dawning understanding, she went on. "We collected a whole nest of them from a big elm tree on the school grounds and smuggled them into her writing desk over lunch break one day. Then I took a stick and broke open the webbing so they began to crawl out—all over her books and writing utensils. When she opened the lid and reached inside—well, she lost her lunch."

"And you lost your place in school," he supplied with a chuckle.

Carrie joined him in the laugh. "Unfortunately, several

other girls had seen me climbing up that elm tree and descending with my prize. They tattled. The headmaster would have been inclined to let me off with a reprimand and some extra Latin conjugations for penance, but Aunt Patience took matters in her own hands. So much for girlish hijinks. It was *almost* worth it.'' She laughed again rather wistfully.

Hawk knew there was a great deal left unsaid about her unhappy youth. ''And your cousin Charity—was she by any chance a bland-looking, plain creature?'' Things were becoming clearer to him.

Carrie nodded. ''Stringy tan hair and a great fondness for Switzer's licorice and other confections. Charity's probably fat by now,'' she finished on a note of long-repressed spite.

He laughed. ''I can imagine what your competition did for her chances at every social gathering. Why didn't you marry some young swain and escape the Pattersons?'' He couldn't imagine her not having droves of offers, beautiful and bright as she was.

Her face drained of color when he said that, and she swallowed hard. ''I did marry someone and leave St. Louis.''

Hawk felt his chest tighten. He was not sure he wanted to hear what she was about to say, but sensed that she needed to tell him.

''I was engaged to Gerald Rawlins, my young swain as you called him. A medical student of good family but poor means. Charity had always fancied him. So, like everything else his darling wanted, Uncle Hiram bought Gerald for her. Rather an expensive acquisition, too,'' she added darkly, ''since Gerald planned to keep mistresses on the side after he married poor plain Charity for her money.''

Hawk could see the glaze of tears in her eyes now, but she fought them back and went on gamely. ''I was honored by being the first one he asked to fill that position—the same afternoon he explained to me that our engagement was off and he was going to marry Charity instead!''

Hawk winced. *The stupid bastard.* "So, you met Noah and decided to leave it all behind," he said gently.

Her lips broke into a false but dazzling smile. "Convenient, wasn't it, Noah arriving the same time Uncle Hiram made his offer to Gerald? When Noah asked my aunt and uncle about a suitable wife, you can't imagine how quickly they leaped at the chance to rid themselves of me."

"Oh, yes, I can," he said quietly.

"I refused, of course."

He looked startled when she said that. "Why? He must have been the answer to your prayers after what had just happened. Noah can be very charming when it suits him."

"Like his son," she shot back, wounded that he'd ever believe she willingly married Noah. "I was given a choice by Uncle Hiram—marry Noah or be turned out on the streets. Do you have any idea what it's like for a woman, alone, with no family and no money, not even any prospect of employment?" She laughed. "But the obvious one, of course." She blushed hotly. "I seriously considered trying to get a job as a tutor or even a factory girl, but I knew when my Aunt Patience got finished with my reputation, no one would hire me. So . . . they won, the three of them. In two days I was married and packed off on a steamer for St. Paul as Mrs. Noah Sinclair."

"I'm sorry, Carrie." He said it with genuine contrition, ashamed of his earlier misjudgment of her. "Did you still love Rawlins?" For some reason he felt a self-punishing need to know.

Suddenly, she felt horribly vulnerable. She had revealed so much to this man, a man about whom she had very ambivalent and distressing feelings. "Let's make a deal, Hawk. You don't pity me and I won't pity you. We neither of us had a very good time growing up or easy choices along the way. All right?"

He nodded, understanding her pride and admiring her for it. "Now who's building walls? You accused me of doing it, and you were right."

"I never told you—" She stopped short, remembering

that she had said those precise words to Frank not too long ago. "Frank told you."

He smiled. "I imagine just like he told you about me and Lola, and a whole lot of other things."

"Yes," she confessed. "I guess he did."

"I'll make *you* a deal. I won't be mad at Frank if you won't. Agreed?" His smile was beautiful, and she warmed to it instantly.

"Agreed."

Bright Leaf awakened and Carrie eagerly took the girl back on her horse for the next hour's ride. They stopped midway for a brief lunch.

Carrie marveled at the soft haze over the mountains, pale lavender in the distance. The vastness of the big sky was awesome, the autumn sun hot and dazzling. The rolling grasslands of the basin seemed to undulate into eternity. She stared up and around. "This land is so desolate, yet lovely. Do you ever get used to the distances, the size of everything?"

He laughed as he munched on a slice of Feliz's spicy roast pork. "Oh, you'll get used to the open spaces, at least in good weather. Just wait until a summer rain squall catches you unaware, or worse yet, a blue norther."

She had heard Frank and the hands describe the sudden blistering cold rain or snowstorms that often caused temperatures to drop fifty degrees in a matter of hours, turning warm summer into killing winter. "No, thanks," she said with a shudder. She alternately loved and hated this wild country.

When they arrived at Iron Heart's village, the noon sun was blazing. Carrie had not realized how large the Cheyenne encampment would be. Several hundred lodges stretched in a rough horseshoe shape, facing the east.

Women worked in the open, cleaning hides, pounding various concoctions with mauls in stone bowls and stirring pots over open fires. Men sat polishing arrowheads, sharpening knives and attending to other weapons. Small children raced about, playing with willow hoops and hitting skin-covered balls along the ground with wood sticks. Everyone seemed busy, except for a few old men who chatted together in small groups or sat solitary in the openings of lodges, observing the rich tapestry of Cheyenne life around them.

Carrie was nervous now as curious liquid brown eyes alighted on her and the unfamiliar Cheyenne child. It was not lost on them that she rode beside Iron Heart's grandson, who was now dressed in white man's garb. Soon word spread of Hunting Hawk's return with visitors. Everyone was polite, but Carrie felt she was on display. Despite the peacefulness of the villagers, it was not a comfortable sensation for her.

Without ever turning around on his big red horse, Hawk intuited her nervousness. "Just relax, Carrie. They only wonder who you are and why you're here with Bright Leaf."

"And with you?" she quipped back nervously.

He grunted and reined Redskin in beside a large lodge where a tall old man with dark gray hair stood. At once Carrie knew this must be Iron Heart. Something in the facial features and the bearing marked him and Hawk as kin.

"I welcome you, Hunting Hawk. You bring the little one. It is good. Wind Song and Sweet Rain have been summoned." His eyes turned to Carrie.

"Grandfather, this is Carrie Sinclair, the wife of He Who Walks in Sun. She has cared for Bright Leaf and did not want to give her up until another woman could win the child's trust."

The old man regarded the beautiful flame-haired woman who held tightly to the frightened child. She rode astride like a Cheyenne woman, and sat straight and proud. "She has courage and a good heart," he said in Cheyenne to Hawk. Then, in English, he addressed Carrie. "Welcome to the wife of He Who Walks in Sun. You have been kind to one of the People. For this I offer you thanks."

Surprised to hear such clear English from Iron Heart, Carrie glanced at Hawk even as she nodded at his grandfather. She replied, "You're welcome. Bright Leaf is a wonderful child. I was pleased to help her."

Hawk had dismounted and reached up for Bright Leaf,

who went uncertainly into his arms, glancing around at all the unfamiliar faces in the huge encampment. Just as Carrie swung down from Taffy Girl, a tall, striking-looking young woman stepped up to Iron Heart. He turned and spoke to her, gesturing to Bright Leaf. Were all the Cheyenne so tall? Carrie wondered peevishly, unused to being dwarfed by those around her. Then she noticed the woman's eyes, a vivid dark green, just like her own.

Warily, with Hawk standing between them, the two women looked one another over. Hawk continued holding Bright Leaf and spoke to Wind Song, then to the child, introducing them.

Realizing the little girl's uncertainties, Carrie reached over and took one small copper-colored hand in her own, speaking to Hawk as she did so. "Tell her I will always remember her. Maybe someday we will meet again. . . ." Her voice choked and she stopped, knowing an emotional scene would never be appreciated by these stoic people.

Hawk spoke to the child, translating Carrie's painful farewell and assuring her that Wind Song also would love her like a sister until her own mother and sisters returned to fetch her next summer or perhaps even sooner.

With one last clasp of Carrie's neck, the child went to Wind Song's open arms. As she carried Bright Leaf toward Sweet Rain, curiosity ate at Wind Song. Who was the white one with Hunting Hawk? Was she his woman? Perhaps the child could tell her. When she asked and had her reply, Wind Song smiled softly and hugged the girl affectionately.

Carrie watched the stately young woman walk away, regal as a queen. With a sudden wrench, a thought hit her. *Hawk could marry her.* Hoping he could not read her mind as he sometimes seemed to, she turned quickly, listening to what Iron Heart was saying to her.

"You are welcome to rest in my lodge through the heat of the day. Calf Woman has food and drink. I have some words to speak with my grandson." With no further ado, he motioned her inside the large tepee.

It was surprisingly light and spacious inside, since the bottom of the skin wall was rolled up in several places, admitting a gentle breeze. The direct heat of the sun was broken, making it cool, as Iron Heart had indicated.

A wizened old crone smiled at her uncertainly and set before her a bowl full of berries and a portion of what looked like roasted fish. A gourd of cool water accompanied the repast, which Carrie was surprised to find quite palatable. She lay back on what she could best describe as a chaise longue, a wicker-backed, fur-padded couch by the perimeter of the tepee.

Just as she finished the food, Iron Heart came in and gracefully sat down against one of the couches. In Cheyenne society men did not eat with women, but since she was done, it was time to talk with her. She was the wife of He Who Walks in Sun, once a brother, now a bitter foe. Yet this woman had shown great kindness to a helpless child. Iron Heart did not understand and desired to learn more. He had not been oblivious of the exchange between Wind Song and the fire-haired woman. They both wanted Hunting Hawk; of that he was certain. But this one was wed to his father. Such a thing was an unpardonable offense under the laws of the People or the *veho*. Despite this, Iron Heart was drawn to like Carrie. She was kind and had courage; she was accepting of other people's ways, a thing few of the *veho* could be.

"You are the wife of my sworn enemy, a man who has hurt my grandson, who hates the People. Why did you help Bright Leaf?"

Taken aback by his piercing black eyes, so like Hawk's, and by the unexpected and direct question, Carrie did not know what to reply, so she said simply, "I cannot help what Noah does. He is a twisted, bitter man. But I don't make war on injured children. My people are taught to love even their enemies. It is a basic part of our religion."

He grunted. "Most white men must not be religious, then."

She smiled sadly. "I suppose not. I can only speak for myself, not Noah, not others."

"It does not make sense to love your enemy. Better to understand him, maybe make him your friend. Then you no longer have to fear him."

She nodded at that unusual bit of logic. "I suppose it's another way of looking at the same thing. Where did you learn to speak our language so well? Did you go to school like your daughter?"

He smiled. "No. I visited your Great White Father when I was a young man, and I came home with many things in my heart. Your cities are great, your people as blades of grass on the prairies. We are few. I sent Laughing Woman to learn the ways of the whites. She came back here to teach me. Then I gave her to a man she loved. I hoped for gladness but reaped sorrow."

Wishing to console the old man, Carrie said softly, "But you still have Hawk. He's the good part of Noah, maybe the only good thing Noah's ever done."

He gazed at her measuringly for a moment. "You love him." He did not ask it, only said it. Carrie knew he meant Hawk, not Noah.

She sat frozen, riven by guilt and shame. She was married to Hawk's father. How, what could she reply? Surely it was not really true? A wild surge of pain welled up in her, and she struggled to subdue it.

"Do not answer. Your heart speaks for you, and it speaks in pain. Please listen. I want Hunting Hawk to come home to the People. He will not stay with his father. There is no place for him. He will only go off to die in the hot lands to the south. It almost happened once before. If he lives among the *veho*, they will kill him."

Suddenly Carrie understood. "You want him to marry that woman, the one with green eyes." Her heart felt leaden in her breast.

"She is of mixed blood, like him. She would be a good wife. You cannot be. As much freedom as the white men allow their women, I know they do not permit them two husbands." His humor was gentle, tinged with sadness for her.

Swallowing a lump in her throat, thinking of Noah and the bleak existence stretching before her, Carrie smiled weakly. "No, they do not. I know what you say is true about Hawk going back to the Nations. But I'm not so sure he can totally forget his white half. He lived much of his life in that world, too. Can he be all Cheyenne?''

The old man's face became shuttered as he battled with her logic. He had always known the division in his grandson's heart was wide and deep. "The only way to live is to choose one or the other, I think. His father will not give him the land he holds. It goes to your children.''

Carrie hung her head, saddened but unable to deny his statement. "I do not wish it so.''

His face softened. "Your heart is good. I know this. But what He Who Walks in Sun will do, we cannot change. Hawk will go south and search for death unless he chooses the way of the People. Here he will have a place.''

"But what can I do? I do not hold him. We—we are not . . .''

"Lovers," he supplied softly, nodding. "I did not think so—yet.''

Her head jerked up at that last word and her cheeks flamed. A heated denial came to her lips, then died. Could she be sure it would never happen? Did she wish that it would never happen?

"Only you know what you must do. Think about it. You will find a way to free him.'' With that he rose and was gone before she could speak again.

Carrie sat in mute misery for an undetermined amount of time, probably not long, but she was uncertain, so lost was she in her own and Hawk's pain.

Hawk entered the lodge. Looking at her pensive expression, he wondered what his grandfather had discussed with her. The old man seemed well satisfied with her and liked her because of the care she had given Bright Leaf. Iron Heart was a fair man. Being married to Noah Sinclair was no black mark against Carrie.

"If we're going to get back by dark, we'd better ride, Carrie," he said softly.

She whirled and gazed up at him like a startled fawn, her eyes huge and liquid. "Ooh! I didn't hear you come in! I guess I never do," she finished ruefully. Still preoccupied, she rose and followed him outside, where Iron Heart stood by their horses.

"Have a safe journey, Hunting Hawk. My heart is gladdened that the wooden road will not come to this place. The People thank you for this." Then he turned those searching black eyes toward Carrie when she had mounted up. "Farewell, Carrie Sinclair. Remember what we spoke of, and I will be grateful."

"I will remember," she said softly, promising nothing. Her green eyes held his black ones for a long, parting moment, each of them trying to read the other's thoughts, perhaps the future as well.

Hawk watched the exchange silently. If his grandfather had wanted him to know what he told Carrie, he would have said something. Perhaps she would tell him.

They rode in silence for a while after leaving the village. It was as if they were once again uneasy with one another, now that the unknowing chaperonage of Bright Leaf was left behind.

Hawk had explained to Iron Heart about the railroad route change to the north. It only delayed the inevitable. They both understood that, but at least now there was a reprieve.

The old man told him that several handsome offers had been made for Wind Song, among them one from Angry Wolf. The girl favored none of them. Still, she was seventeen summers old and ready for marriage. Hawk sighed, knowing the direction of the wily old matchmaker's thoughts. If he married Wind Song, he would have made his choice irrevocable, and he could not see his way clear to do that yet—if ever.

Almost unconsciously, Hawk's eyes strayed to Carrie, riding beside him, her lovely profile etched in sharp relief against the azure sky. She seemed as silently troubled as he was. He swore to himself, suddenly realizing what Iron Heart had discussed with her. Damn all meddling relatives!

As if in answer to his thoughts, Carrie looked across at him and said, "Now that you beat Noah and the railroad's not coming here, what are you going to do? It's a waste for you to be a drifter and hired gun. You could do so much with your life, Hawk."

He gazed at her hair trailing down her back like a river

of sun. What was she asking him? Telling him? He smiled sadly at her. "What do you think I should do, Firehair?"

The day was warm, made warmer by his eyes and the endearment he made of the nickname Firehair. "It's not for me to say. I just want . . . for you to be happy." Carrie realized this was not coming out at all the way it should. She struggled to go on. "I mean, if you stay at Circle S, you and Noah will just fight more. You have an education. You could go east, maybe get a job with the government, help the Cheyenne, all Indians."

He gave a sharp, bitter laugh. "The Indian Bureau is full of corrupt politicians and idealistic bunglers. Not a single red man. No, that's not for me. I've had a bellyfull of the east, enough of *veho* cities."

Her heart constricted. "You can't go back to the Nations. It's certain death."

"Maybe that's the answer," he said softly. "Maybe it's what Iron Heart told you I'd do, too." His shrewd glance spoke volumes, and she blushed in mortification.

"You don't deny it. Is he right?" She was getting in deeper and yet couldn't accept his fatalism. He must not throw his life away, but she could not bring herself to mention the beautiful Cheyenne woman, either.

He shrugged carelessly. "I don't know. Hell, I never think a week ahead, much less a year. I don't plan on going south now. Let it alone, Carrie. Neither you nor my grandfather can run my life." At her wounded, embarrassed look, he relented. "I'm sorry. I didn't intend to hurt you. You've grief enough of your own. All Noah can do is disinherit me. He's done a lot worse to you."

"But you're losing your birthright because of me—if I have . . ." she choked over "children," unable to say the word.

"You don't want his children, do you, Carrie?"

She shuddered, then took a deep breath and answered in a small voice. "No . . . I don't know. It's all mixed up. I loathe the thought of giving him another heir, but—but if I'm with child, he'll leave me alone." Then she reddened. Of all things to discuss with a man, any man, especially this one!

He felt a tightening in his chest, recalling all the crude sexual taunts he had hurled at her, the lewd accusations. "What he does to you, Carrie, it isn't the way it should be. If you'd married a man who cared for you, he'd make it good for you, too, not just for him."

She was so forlorn that it seemed impossible to stop unburdening herself. "It isn't just me—that I don't—like it. He doesn't either anymore. He said it was my fault. That I'm cold and clumsy. He only wants me to be pregnant. Then he can go to those women in Miles City. They know what to do...." Her voice trailed off in humiliated misery.

He swore. First in Cheyenne, then English. "That filthy, depraved old bastard!" Looking at her beautiful, guilt-riven face, he could have shot Noah Sinclair point-blank at that moment. "Carrie, don't believe him. It's not you—not your fault. If a man has to resort to whores and blames his wife for not responding to him, he's no kind of a man."

"Maybe if I could love him it would be better," she said brokenly.

"Love's a two-way street, Carrie. Did he ever try to love you?"

Recalling their "honeymoon" on the riverboat, she cringed, remembering Noah's sarcastic words on that subject. She shook her head mutely.

"My mother loved Noah Sinclair with her whole heart. He trampled on it!" His voice was laden with hate. "Don't—don't ever try to love him, Carrie! Even if you could, he'd only destroy you." He watched her lovely, expressive face, as a whole spectrum of emotions played across it.

"Thank you, Hawk. For understanding, for believing me." Her eyes were full of unshed tears. "For being my friend."

Friend! God, they both knew that was not the right word. He struggled against the urge to lead her beneath the canopy of cottonwoods by the riverbank and make love to her. He could teach her lush, unawakened body such fierce, sweet passion. He shifted uncomfortably in the saddle and swore again to himself. No, in that lay madness. He was a penniless, half-breed gunman. She was a married woman.

"He's an old man, Carrie. You're young and strong. Outlast him, don't let him beat you. Someday, some man will love you the way you deserve."

She looked straight ahead, and he could see her nod and swallow hard, fighting down the urge to weep.

They both knew Noah Sinclair was fifty-five years old and strong as an oak. He could easily live another twenty years.

CHAPTER 12

Noah swore as the coach hit another rut and jounced his aching backside for the thousandth time since leaving Helena three days ago. Tonight he would be home to a decent meal, a soft bed, and to Carrie. If the first two things appealed to him, the third one did not. Where had he gone wrong, he asked again in impotent anger. He had chosen a beautiful, docile young girl from a good family; she was to be his to mold. But her dutiful quiescence in bed at night infuriated him as much as her willful behavior during the day. Thank God a good enthusiastic whore in Helena had assuaged his fears about failing virility. He was as good as ever. Once he got his young wife with child, he would leave her bed for good, provided the child was a boy, of course. That miserable Indian brat would be gone, too. In spite of the choking dust, autumn heat, and bone-splintering ride, Noah's humor improved.

If all went according to plan, by this time next year when the railroad was through Miles City, he would own the K Bar land it ran across. Two could play Krueger's game. If Squires had been run off by Hawk and Kyle, no reason someone just like him couldn't be hired by Circle S. Yessiree, no reason at all. In fact, Noah had met such a man at the association meeting in Helena. Caleb Rider would sign on at Circle S in about a month.

Noah considered how Hawk and Hunnicut would react to his plans. Kyle had always been for hire, and Noah was sure he wouldn't give a damn if Circle S stole from Krueger. Hawk was another matter. If it came to an all-out range war for control of the eastern territory, the Cheyenne would suffer and that would bring Hawk down on him. Noah pondered how he would handle the situation. He would have to make it appear Krueger had begun the fight. He turned the situation over in his mind, considering various ideas. He had a month to work on it.

If Hawk was too clever for his own good and started to interfere, maybe it would be time to deal with him permanently. Ever since Hawk had come home from preparatory school as a callow seventeen-year-old and Lola first cast her lascivious eyes on him, Noah had truly hated his son.

He had always been uneasy around the dark, silent child who seemed so much more red than white. When all attempts to civilize him had failed and he had repeatedly run off to those murdering savages, Noah had washed his hands of the boy, hoping to sire another white son on Lola. To have her betray him as she did had been more than his monumental ego could withstand. If Lola had not been from a prominent Chicago family, he would have killed her instead of divorcing her. If Hawk had not fled to the Nations, Noah might have shot him as well. But the cunning, lighting-fast gunman who returned a year later was far too dangerous for that. Noah had been relieved when Frank convinced the youth to attend a prestigious eastern university for a couple of years.

Noah Sinclair, who had faced down wild Sioux, fought snarling wolves and ridden through blue northers, was afraid of his own son. Not that he had ever admitted it to himself, but the vile taste of fear lingered in the innermost recesses of his soul, eating at it like corrosive acid. Had the time finally come for a showdown? To kill Hawk would mean admitting his fear, because he would have to hire another gunman to do the deed in secret. Noah's musings skittered around the issue, unwilling to confront it just yet.

It was dusk when he made the last leg of his journey by horseback, arriving at the big house in time for the evening meal. He had sent word ahead of his arrival. Mrs. Thorndyke would have everything in order, that savage child would be gone, and Carrie had damn well better be dressed for dinner. Fleetingly he hoped Hawk was off somewhere with Hunnicut or Lowery. Noah did not want to face him across the table tonight.

Carrie sat at her vanity and fidgeted with her hair. She had heard Noah arrive over two hours ago, order a bath, and then dress for dinner, all without coming to her room to greet her. She did not go down to welcome him home either. Insidious, how subtly and quickly their hostility had set patterns. She was certain Mrs. Thorndyke had found a way to let him know his wife had ridden to Iron Heart's encampment with Hawk. Dinner would be another nightmare. Small wonder she had been losing weight for weeks. Every meal with Noah was an ordeal.

Carrie did not know if Hawk would be present or not. He had spent the past three days working with Frank. They rode out at sunup and often did not return until dark, so she had seen little of him. It was just as well, considering Mathilda Thorndyke's silent, feral-eyed curiosity since they had returned from the Cheyenne village. It was as if the hateful woman was just waiting to pounce. Carrie rubbed her pounding temples and forced herself to calm down. She had done nothing wrong. Neither had Hawk. Still, she could imagine the warped way the housekeeper had presented her story to Noah. Carrie's own painful confusion about her awakening feelings for his son added to her case of nerves.

You are not lovers—yet. Iron Heart's words returned to lash her with guilt. *Yet.* "No, never! It cannot be!" Almost in tears, she swore at her schoolgirl vapors. She was past the age for such weakness. Once again she turned her attentions to her toilette. Looking good might not appease Noah's wrath, but it would help her own self-confidence.

As she closed the door to her room and took a steadying breath before descending the stairs, Hawk called to her encouragingly, "Ready to face the wolf in his den?" As he walked down the hall from his room, he took in her carefully groomed appearance. She wore a deep emerald-green silk dress, austerely cut in straight, simple lines with a high jewel neckline and long sleeves. A magnificent rope of pearls was her only jewelry, reflecting the luster of the silk and the jade glow of her eyes. Her hair was piled high and pinned in a soft bouffant style that framed her face. The overall picture was one of poise and maturity as well as startling beauty.

She returned his appreciative stare, almost against her will. Dressed in dark blue homespun with a white shirt open at the collar, he looked both arrogantly handsome and irritatingly casual. Just what he intended, she thought wryly. Noah insisted on formal attire for dinner and would hate the open shirt and boldly winking silver medallion he always wore. No help for it, they would go to the parlor together, like two conspirators facing an execution. If only she could be as calm as Hawk.

The minute they entered the oak doorway to the parlor, Carrie flinched under Noah's intense, scowling stare. ''Courage, Firehair,'' Hawk whispered as he walked just behind her into the room.

For the first time Noah considered Carrie and Hawk as a couple. His son's tall, darkly sculpted form contrasted with her slim, fiery elegance. Could Mathilda Thorndyke's veiled obscenity be possible? Could they be lovers? Would Hawk seduce the chit just to spite him? At once he dismissed the idea impatiently. Impossible. Carrie hated sex and was not interested in any man that way. She was as different from Lola as day from night. His son's aversion to white women made the question more absurd. No, they just shared a ridiculous fondness for that brat of an Indian girl. Mathilda hated them both and was reading more into the situation than it warranted.

Nevertheless, he was still furious with Carrie. The impropriety of going alone with any man to an Indian village was horrifying—even more horrifying if that man was a half-breed. He vowed to make her sorry. Without even a hello after his long absence, he launched into his attack. ''While I was away, I have been given to understand you rode—astride—to an encampment of hostile

Cheyenne. Not only was it dangerous, it was appallingly improper. If word of it got out to my friends, they and their wives would ostracize you, Carrie." He was proud of the cold, deliberate tone of his voice.

"I took Carrie to meet Iron Heart and to give over Bright Leaf to him, Noah. You know damn well my grandfather wouldn't let any harm come to Carrie. *He* is a man of honor." Hawk's words were measured, with a veiled threat beneath them.

"I'm concerned with my wife's reputation! I do trust, Carrie, that you can speak for yourself?" He turned with wrath from his insolent son to her pale, beautiful face.

She looked him squarely in the eye and said, "What's the use, Noah? You've already judged me. I'm guilty as charged. I always am, whatever the crime. I wanted to assure Bright Leaf that she'd be well cared for until her family can be found. None of your splendid friends in Miles City need ever know."

Her calm speech made him angrier than Hawk's menacing pose. "Unless one of my hands tells one of Krueger's! I have a reputation to uphold in this territory. You go nowhere unchaperoned, ever again!"

"I guess Carrie and I aren't considered family, are we, Noah? I wonder, would I be a proper chaperone if I were white? Or she were twenty years older?" He left the taunting threat hanging in the air.

What in heaven's name is he doing, Carrie thought frantically, *trying to provoke a fight right here in the parlor?*

"If Lola couldn't remember her relationship to you when you were seventeen, I doubt you'll seriously consider Carrie your stepmother now!" There, it was out in the open, the festering jealousy of an old man. The minute he saw Hawk's eyes leap with predatory joy, Noah hated himself for revealing so much in front of them both.

Trying to soothe the situation, Carrie walked over to Noah and put her hand on his arm. "This is solving nothing. Hawk is your son and I am your wife. What happened with Lola Jameson is in the past. Nothing's to be served by dredging up ugly memories. I promise never to return to Iron Heart's village. Will that satisfy you, Noah?''

He fixed her with a baleful glare. ''Considering you'll never be genuinely sorry for any of your hoydenish actions, I'm sure it's no use to demand an apology. See that you keep your word, however.'' Catching sight of Mrs. Thorndyke in the doorway, he announced, ''It's time for dinner. Shall we?''

Hawk followed them toward the dining room, but this time instead of ignoring Mrs. Thorndyke's venomous presence as he usually did, he smiled coldly at her, affixing her with his hypnotic black eyes. Catching her shrinking shudder as he glided past her, he was gratified. *Bitch. Let her fear me.*

Hawk had debated about coming to dinner tonight. He could have easily eaten with Kyle and Frank or have gone into town for some diversion, but he knew he could not leave Carrie to face his father alone. Too late he realized that his taunt to Noah about his and Carrie's relationship was stupid. But Noah's possession of Carrie—his rights as a husband—were increasingly galling to Hawk and he let his temper best him. Baiting the old man would only bring more pain to her. The meager satisfaction he gained from exposing Noah's jealously and weakness was not worth it. He swore to curb his tongue through dinner.

It was not easy. Somehow, the three of them managed to complete the meal without coming to blows, although none could have said what they ate. By the time Feliz's famous chocolate cake came to the table, no one wanted it, despite its luscious richness and delectable taste. Carrie asked to be excused and went upstairs, to steel herself for another night with her husband.

Hawk and Noah adjourned to the parlor and both drank stiff brandies, with little conversation in the interim. It had all been said now. When Noah went upstairs, Hawk poured a generous whiskey, took one swallow, and then flung it out the open parlor window in disgust. Getting obliviously drunk would solve nothing. He slammed the empty glass on the sideboard and stalked out the door to take a walk. The night was warm for autumn and all the stars were out, creating a brilliant canopy of icy-white fire in the dark velvet sky.

Carrie lay quietly in her bed, arms at her sides, attempting to steady her breathing. She must remain calm. Like a wolf—Frank had told her Noah used to be a wolfer—her husband sensed fear in other people and preyed upon it. All her early encounters with him, beginning in St. Louis, were colored by her fear and his manipulation of it. Well, she was not that quaking green girl any longer.

She was a woman now. Of course, that was part of the problem. In the months—had it only been five?—that she had lived here, she had left the remnants of girlhood behind. But in becoming a woman, she began to feel a woman's needs, needs Noah could never fulfill, longings deep within her soul he could never touch. She knew Hawk could. Lying in her lonely, dread-filled bed, she confronted that which she had denied for so long. She loved Hawk Sinclair. When had it all begun? When Iron Heart spoke the actual words? That night at the ball when Hawk kissed her? The day at the lake when she could not tear her eyes from his splendid nakedness? Or did it go all the way back to their first meeting as antagonists in the parlor when she arrived at Circle S?

"Oh, Hawk, why did it have to be this way?" With a guilty start, she realized she had whispered the words aloud. As they echoed in the still, empty room, tears streamed down her cheeks in acid rivulets. She loved a man she could never again be near, never touch. Lord, she dare not allow another encounter like the one in the water, with their naked flesh melded together, or another devastating kiss like the first one they shared. But, oh, how her whole being, soul and body, cried out for him! She rolled over and buried her face in the pillow, muffling her sobs.

By the time Noah prepared himself for retiring and opened the door to Carrie's room, she had fallen into a restless, exhausted sleep. The covers were kicked off her slim frame and the delicate curves of her body were revealed in the bright moonlight streaming in the French doors. She wore a pale-white silk night rail trimmed with delicate dark-orange ribbons. The matching robe lay tossed across the bedside chair. Impatiently he threw his own brown robe over it and knelt naked on the side of the bed.

Without even bothering to awaken her first, he rolled her over roughly and pulled at the fastenings of her gown, tearing the stitches of the orange silk ribbons in the process.

She couldn't lie still another minute. Praying Noah was asleep in the next room, she bolted from her hateful bed and grabbed blindly for her robe. Donning it carelessly, she padded to the French doors and stepped outside. The fresh air was slightly cool and incredibly welcome after the stuffy confines of her room and the vile activity that had just taken place inside it.

Carrie traversed the length of the veranda, her hand trailing absently along the rough whitewashed banister as she looked out over the side yard where the flower gardens lay, reposing coolly in the moonlight. The tall chrysanthemums waved in invitation and she began to descend the stairs at the rear of the house. The yard was deserted but for the flowers, the lovely, placid flowers.

She walked across the damp grass to the edge of the chrysanthemum bed and bent down to pluck a big yellow blossom. Pressing its spicy fragrance to her face, she moved to the small iron bench in the center of the yard and sat beneath a stately pine tree. The moon reached ivory fingers through the lacy branches of the tree and bathed her with its light. For several minutes she sat, inhaling the balm of the flowers, thinking of nothing at all.

Then the dam burst and low, suppressed sobs wracked her slim shoulders. Once begun, they were unstoppable. Yellow petals scattered like eiderdown across her silk robe and the ground underneath her as she shredded the chrysanthemum in a frenzy of weeping.

'What's the matter with me! I have not cried this much since my parents died. All I do lately is wallow in self-pity.'' Her whispering voice cut through the still, silent night air while she fought unsuccessfully to regain control of her broken emotions. *Hawk, oh Hawk, help me. Please, help me.*

Hawk had walked briefly after dinner and then returned to the lonely solitude of his room. After an hour of feverish tossing, he had slipped on a pair of buckskin pants and padded outside for another attempt to cool off in the night air. Lord knew there would be no sleep. However, the quiet starry night offered him no peace, and he once more retraced his steps toward his room with leaden feet. Strange, he could have sworn he heard his name, softly called on the night air.

As he rounded the corner of the house near the back stairs, he saw Carrie silhouetted beside the pine tree. Her white silk robe and dark fiery hair gleamed in the moonlight. She looked so rapturously lovely, so delicate and vulnerable, sitting alone on the cold iron bench. Then he saw the convulsive shuddering of her whole body, and knew why she had called his name.

Carrie did not know he was beside her until he touched her softly, caressing the cascade of shining hair that tumbled from her shoulders down her back. Wordlessly, she raised her head and reached out for the comfort of his embrace as he sat next to her on the narrow bench.

As he held her securely in his arms, her sobbing stilled and she nestled against him, her hand clutching at the silver medallion nestled in the thick black mat of hair on his chest. Suddenly she realized he was clad only in soft leather pants. His scanty attire served to remind her of the thinness of her silk peignoir.

Nervously she looked up into his face, her hands still lightly clasped around the hard contours of his biceps. She composed herself. "I—I had to get out of that stifling room." She could see by the look in his eyes that he knew why, and it had nothing to do with a need for fresh air. Unable to meet his piercing black gaze, she looked over his shoulder at the night sky, spread with dazzling stars, like a spilled bucket of diamonds. "It's so beautiful, as if you could reach out and touch it, walk into its solitude and find peace."

"That's what the Cheyenne believe," he said, turning to look up at the brilliance of the Milky Way, pulling her along in his embrace as he shifted positions on the bench.

"They say after death each soul goes to find its rest up there by climbing the hanging road to the sky."

"If it takes death, maybe—"

"Shh. Never say it!" He interrupted her fiercely. "You're alive, lovely, aflame like the sun, not cold like the dead."

"My soul is dead, Hawk, or it soon will be."

"No. Don't let him win, Carrie. Don't—" He could not finish his admonition once he fastened his gaze on her face. When she looked up into his eyes, her own were jewel-bright in wonder and entreaty. His mouth touched hers. He could not stop himself from taking the kiss. Slowly, forcing himself to be gentle, he prolonged the tender joining, tasting the silky insides of her mouth, twining their tongues together, fusing their lips.

With ever-growing ardor, she returned his kiss, so fierce yet so sweet. Her soft little fingertips crept across his shoulders, then up his neck, to stroke the bristling whiskers on his jawline. Delicate and featherlight, her hands caressed the harsh angular planes of his face.

He growled softly and buried his face in her hair, clasping her against his pounding heart while his hands burned through the thin silk on her back and thigh.

Carrie arched against him, pressing her breasts to his bare chest, lacing her fingers together behind his neck and pulling his lips to hers once more. Some mindless well of primitive instinct seemed to guide her. And she wanted never to stop, or be stopped.

Finally, Hawk broke the magic of the kiss and pressed her face to his chest, holding her still in his arms. His breathing was as labored and wild as his heartbeat. He could feel the rise and fall of her firm young breasts and hear her gasp for air. Never in his sundered life had he been this torn, never had he wanted a woman this much, or known so certainly that he should not take her.

Carrie pressed her hands against him and raised her head so that she could look into his eyes. Her palms trembled on his chest and she swallowed hard, working up her courage to speak. He knew what she was going to say.

Her dilated bright-green eyes locked with his liquid black ones as she ran one trembling hand across his cheek and down his jaw. "Please, Hawk. Just once in my life, I want to be loved, not used." Timidly then, for the plea had taken all her courage, she lay her head back against his chest and was still.

If his conscience warred within him, it did not do so for long. Silently he rose, never letting go of her but taking her up into his arms and carrying her through the calm, silver beauty of the moonlight toward the back stairs and his isolated room. Noiselessly his bare feet trod the wooden risers and glided across the veranda to his door.

The room was large and cluttered, but Carrie did not notice as he carried her inside. He stopped to push the door shut with one foot, then padded silently to the big brass bed and gently placed her beside it. As her feet touched the floor, she held on to his shoulders and leaned against him, nervous and uncertain of what to do. His hands showed her as they roamed sensuously up and down her sides, gliding slowly up to cup her breasts, then downward to stroke her hips and back up, tracing the delicate curve of her spine. All the while, he rained soft, brushing kisses over her face, neck, and hair.

Carrie returned the kisses and let her hands trace the hard ridges of his biceps and shoulder muscles; then she ran her fingers through the dense black hair of his chest, pushing the heavy silver necklace out of the way. She could feel his heart pound as she circled her arms behind him and felt his back muscles tighten. Every inch of him was hard and sinuous, sleek and pleasing to touch.

Hawk reached up and gently untied the silk ribbons that held the thin robe together. With one smooth motion across her shoulders, he slid it from her arms and it dropped like a whisper at her feet. He stood back for a second, holding her at arm's length to feast his eyes on the slim curves revealed through one layer of sheerest white silk remaining on her body. Pale nipples hardened to sweet proud points thrust against the night rail. Reverently he reached for the ribbon that held the gathered neckline together and loosed it, freeing the ivory mounds.

He slid the top of the gown down to her waist, and she helped him, working her arms free of the restraints of the

garment. She wanted desperately to hold him once more.
Then she hesitated in a sudden thrill of sexual pride. His
eyes told her she was beautiful as they feasted on her bare
flesh. She stood still while he knelt, easing the gown over
her slim hips and letting it drop to the floor. Hawk let his
eyes travel up the length of her naked body, drinking in
each contour—her slim ankles and flared calves, the satiny
thighs, hips that rounded so perfectly and then narrowed
toward her tiny waist. Her breasts stood out in breathtaking relief from his vantage point below, their delicate
pointed shape accented by the angle at which he viewed
them.

As he rose slowly, he ran his hands up her long, slim
legs, over her hips, up to the hollows at the sides of her
waist. All the while he rained brushing kisses in their
wake. Then he cupped a breast in each hand and gently
hefted them while his thumbs worked the hardened nipples
in small tight circles. Once more his mouth followed his
hands, licking and suckling each breast in turn. She gasped
and writhed under his caresses, dizzy with both pleasure
and power. It was so wonderfully, beautifully different
with Hawk. He gave her pleasure while deriving joy by
touching, looking, anticipating what was to come.

Eagerly they embraced once more in a deepening kiss,
their hands stroking, arms enfolding. She could feel the
rough abrasion of his buckskin pants and pressure from the
bulge in the crotch as he thrust his hips into hers. Shyly,
she gloried in his need, even as she felt a gradually
building ache in her own belly, uncoiling slowly, spreading
through the core of her. She rubbed her palms against him,
wanting to melt into him. He let out a soft growl and
picked her up, depositing her on the big bed. Then, while
she watched, he stripped off the pants and stood over her
for a moment. Now it was Carrie's turn to look up at him.
How splendid he was, silhouetted in the moonlight, so
tall, lean, and powerful, like a bronzed savage god, naked
but for the gleaming silver around his neck. Darkness
obscured his features, but his eyes glowed like fiery coals
as he knelt on the bed and reached out to her.

Murmuring soft endearments in the Cheyenne tongue,

he held her gently to him and the heat of his skin spread its fire through her. She rubbed the length of her body against his, moaning and arching her back, reveling in the pleasure such contact with his hard flesh gave her. She could feel the probing of his erection as it pulsed between her legs, and she eagerly trapped it between her thighs and then squeezed them together. Hawk gasped in startled pleasure. He could not wait much longer. Carrie must surely be ready, too. Experimentally he slid his hand down her belly and over the tangle of fiery curls at her mound. She let out a whimper as he stroked the honey-drenched lips that opened hungrily to him.

"Oh, my Firehair, yes, now," he murmured as he rolled her on her back, kissing her neck and breasts while he spread her legs with one knee. Eagerly she complied, opening to him, arching up to meet his first slow, careful thrust. He slid into her full-length and then held still a moment, allowing her body time to adapt to his filling of it.

She had never experienced anything like this before. It was glorious, so smooth, wet, and delicious. She ached for more movement. Never with Noah had she been anything but dry and tight. Every stroke had been a painful misery. Now she found herself bucking and arching, desperate for Hawk to thrust. He began to oblige her, slowly at first, then gradually with increasing speed. When she cried out her pleasure, he silenced her with a devouring kiss. Fiercely she kissed him back, all the while wrapping her legs tightly around his hips and rising to meet every move he made.

I'm drowning, in a whirlpool of incredible, wonderful, beautiful . . . Her mind went blank as she buried her face against his neck and felt the orgasmic contractions radiate throughout her body, like a tidal wave of ecstasy. *I love you, Hawk, I love you.*

He felt her climax, realizing it was a new experience for her. It filled him with unspeakable pleasure to give her this gift. When he allowed his own body to join hers, after holding himself so carefully in check, he was amazed at his own feelings. The intensity of his release was like nothing he had ever felt before—searing, blinding. It left him as weak and shaken as she was.

They held one another in the still, starry night, panting and sweat-soaked, sated in body, yet aching in soul. He lightly kissed her brow, eyes, cheeks, lips, neck. Her hands were gentle in reply, softly memorizing every hard, sleek muscle, the tawny texture of his skin. She spread her fingers and ran them through the scratchy dense forest of his chest hair as his heart quieted its beat to a measured, even thud. The medallion was warm to her touch, heated by both their bodies.

Carefully he rolled off her and drew her to nestle alongside him. There were no words to be spoken. They lay locked in each other's arms, lost in a bittersweet mixture of joy and pain until exhaustion claimed them, then slept, bathed in the ivory embrace of the moonlight as it filtered through the open window.

After a couple of hours, Carrie woke. She stretched out her hand and ran it up and down his body, as if to reassure herself that he was really there and all the glory of their lovemaking had truly happened. With a pang, she knew all that she had missed, all she would never have known but for him, her splendid barbarian.

Unable to resist, sensing that this was her one night of love, she leaned over his face and looked at it. He was so young, so beautifully handsome, asleep in the soft dim light. Her fingertips traced the ridge of his brows, then her tongue traced the outline of his firm, sculpted lips. He awakened, tangling his hands in the welter of her long hair. He murmured something in Cheyenne that she did not understand and pulled her on top of him. Feeling his already hardened shaft, Carrie eagerly grasped it and guided it inside her as he held her hips securely in his hands. He lowered her face to meet his by pulling on her hair, then locked them in a slow, languorous kiss.

Carrie had never before been in command of sex, had never been able to set the pace as she could now. She began to raise and lower herself on his shaft, gasping in startled delight at the exquisite sensations they created together. She sped up, slowed down, wiggled and shifted while he lay back, his eyes riveted on her writhing, lovely body, his hands stroking her breasts and hips lightly. Like a wild Viking goddess she rode her dark lover, ever faster and harder. He responded, thrusting up to impale her in swift, sure surges. She stiffened and arched her back while he supported her weight by holding her waist. When he felt her convulsive shudders, he pulsed his seed deep within her at the same time.

Gently he lowered her to lay on top of him. As he stroked her back and held her, Hawk could feel the wetness of her tears on his chest. Silent sobs shook her body as she held tightly to him. He waited for her to speak, only running his hands slowly back and forth through her hair.

"Was I better off not knowing it can be like this? I don't ever want this night to end, Hawk. Hold me, just hold me." She did not dare speak the words aloud, but let her love for him flow out through her body as she melted into him.

With callused fingertips he traced the damp tracks of teardrops down her cheeks, gently drying them, crooning soft words in the liquid cadence of his Indian language.

The night hour grew late and the air was chilly as he reached down, trying not to awaken her, and pulled a coverlet over them. Carrie snuggled unconsciously back against his body. She was made to fit so perfectly there, he thought with a pang. Was she right? Would they both have been better off never knowing the joy of this night? Despite all the women he'd had over the years, Hawk had never known anyone like Carrie. What they shared was as new and beautiful to him as it was to her.

As the first pale pink streaks of light signaled false dawn, he lay awake and watched her. She was so lovely, so alive and fresh. The deep purple shadows were gone from beneath her eyes, now closed in sleep. The thick red brush lashes fanned over her cheeks and fluttered as she stirred, placing one slim golden hand across his chest possessively, grasping the medallion in her sleep.

He smiled sadly. *Yes, I guess you do own me, Firehair, body and soul.* Reaching up, he took her hand and placed a soft kiss inside the palm, causing her to awaken. As her eyes opened, her hand pressed against his lips, then moved to stroke his jawline and run through the thick black hair falling across his face.

"Good morning, Firehair. Almost time to take you back to your room," he whispered, steeling himself for the inevitable.

"Almost time," she said, drawing his head over to hers, seeming to ignore reality as she emphasized the first word.

As they kissed and rolled across the bed with arms and legs entwined, reality quickly receded. An urgency, a race against the sun, seemed to spur them to fierce abandon. No slow, languorous caresses now. They were greedy, almost rough in taking and giving, joining their flesh for one last desperate, glorious ride. Hawk looked down at her through passion-glazed black eyes as she writhed and bucked beneath him, her hair exploded like a fiery meteor across the pillows while her head tossed from side to side in ecstasy. When the deep crimson blotches began to stain her neck, breasts, and belly, he felt her orgasm and allowed himself a fierce, pounding climax.

Carrie watched him stiffen and felt his final hard thrusts as he joined her in surfeit. She kept her legs tightly locked around him, wanting never to free him.

Hawk dropped his long, sweat-soaked body down on top of hers, careful not to put all his weight on her slim frame. They both labored for breath in the cool morning air. When he gently rose, leaving her body, she felt an ache of loss so intense she wanted to sob aloud, but before she could move to grasp him, he was reaching back to her with a towel in his hand, snatched from the wash basin next to the bed.

Gently he dried her perspiration-slicked flesh, from her face to her breasts, down her belly and legs, even her feet. Carrie could have wept for the tenderness of his gesture. Then he handed her the gossamer silk night rail and robe, carelessly tossed at the side of the bed last night. While she donned the peignoir with trembling, clumsy fingers, he toweled off his own body quickly and slipped back into the buckskin pants.

They stood facing one another then, both uncertain of what to say, knowing what they must do. Wordlessly he reached up, pulled the heavy medallion from his neck, and lifted her mass of burnished hair. Then he placed it around her neck, tucking it securely between her breasts beneath the silk gown.

He did not need to say, "Let no one see it," for she knew that. "It belonged to my uncle, Gray Fox, and before that to his father, Iron Heart," he said simply.

Placing one hand on it, she pulled his hand to hers and covered it, locking them both over her heart and the necklace. "I will keep it always."

He picked her up then and carried her from the room. Silently, he walked down the long veranda to the far end, where the French door to her room stood barely ajar. It was getting light, and faint sounds could be heard emanating from the bunkhouse and corrals on the other side of the house, far down the hill. Noah's drapes were closed, and he slept yet. Soon everyone would be awakening.

Pushing open the door to her room, Hawk gently set her down in the doorway. When she reached one hand up in mute entreaty, he took it and kissed the palm quickly, then placed it back across her breast and turned away. Silent as ever, he vanished down the porch.

Seventy feet was seventy miles now. With a muffled sob, she turned numbly and entered her hated room, throwing herself across the bed to stare dry-eyed at the sunrise outside her window. Never before had she hated its fiery brilliance.

CHAPTER 13

Once inside his large, empty room, Hawk padded silently to the rumpled bed and looked down at it. After a moment's deliberation, he swore and yanked the twisted sheet up over it, as if burying the past night in one swift, angry gesture. He must leave. There was only madness in staying to watch Noah put his hands on her, to know each night that she must lay with her husband, to sneak bittersweet stolen moments with her like a criminal. No. That would lead only to destruction for them both.

Woodenly he began to throw a few simple items in his saddlebags. Now that he had given her his medallion, he owned little else that he valued, save his guns. He would need those where he was going.

For one fleeting moment he considered taking her with him, then rejected the idea. He cursed again as he dressed in the faint morning light, shaking his head and walking out of the room without a backward glance. He knew he would never see it again.

Colt and knife strapped to his hips, rifle slung over one shoulder and saddlebags over the other, he strode noiselessly toward the corral. He could hear the hands stirring and knew he must hurry. Before he saddled Redskin, he walked quickly to the north end of the main bunkhouse where Kyle slept. Most of the men were eating breakfast in the big cook shed next to the bunkhouse. Kyle often slept later and filched better fare from a softhearted Feliz at the big house. Today was no exception. He snored blissfully, hat over his face and bare feet sticking out from the bottom of a thin blanket. Hawk stood silently at the foot of the bed and looked down at his sleeping friend, a faint grin on his lips.

"Ya gonna stand there admirin' my toes fer a hour 'er whut?" It came out on the expelled breath of one snore, without missing a beat.

Hawk snorted. "I'm supposed to be the Indian no one can sneak up on. You sure you're not part Comanche?"

"Naw, jist all desirin' o' keepin' my skin whole. Whut ya up ta, Longlegs? 'Pears ta me yer fixin' to do yew some travelin'." Kyle sat up, assessing his friend's clothes, weapons, and troubled look. He slid from bed and grabbed a rumpled pair of pants from a hook on the wall next to his bunk, muttering to himself as he dressed hastily, "Least ya might do if yer plannin' ta slope off so sudden like is give a body a decent warnin' so's he kin get his gear stowed. Shit!" He hobbled around, yanking fiercely on one recalcitrant boot that refused to slide on until he collapsed on the bed.

"I'll saddle your horse," Hawk said as he strode out the back door to the corral.

"Don't suppose ya'd have time ta git a batch o' them sweet rolls from Feliz," he called out hopefully after his friend's retreating form. "Naw, course not." He swore a few inventive oaths and stomped the boot into submission on his foot.

They rode for about an hour in silence while Hawk looked straight ahead toward the south. Kyle studied his friend's bleak countenance and held his peace.

Finally he spoke. "'Pears we're headin' back ta th' Nations, less I miss my guess."

"Or Texas, maybe New Mexico Territory. I hear they have a dandy range war going on. Pay's tops for a gun." Hawk's voice was cool and noncommittal. "You decide."

"It finally happened, didn't it?" He waited, but Hawk made no reply.

"Yew 'n' Carrie—"

"Yes," Hawk snapped, "it happened, last night. Now

it's over and done with, and I'm too damn sorry to talk about it. All right?''

Feeling his friend's pain, Kyle knew, too, what Carrie must be feeling at that moment, what she would face alone now. ''Mebbe ya shouldn't o' left her behind, Longlegs. Noah's mean. If'n he ever found out—''

''He won't. It was just one time. That's why I left, before he did find out. You know I couldn't take her, Kyle.'' He sighed raggedly. ''Not that I didn't think of it. What kind of life would it be with a drifter like me, a man who lives every day one bullet from the grave? Only my life between her and a pack of animals who'd tear her apart if I were dead. Frank and Feliz love her. They'll watch over her. Anyway, she's my father's wife.'' He ground out those last words in finality, as if trying to put a seal on his emotions once and for all.

Kyle said in a stunned voice, ''Thet's th' first time I ever heerd ya call Noah yer pa!''

Darkly, Hawk said, ''That's the *only* thing keeping him alive.''

Carrie slept late that morning, trying to blot out the harsh reality of the day by reliving the incredibly beauty of the night. Finally, near noon, she forced herself to arise. *I have to face my life, face Noah tonight. Oh, God, how can I sit at the same table between him and Hawk?*

Her thoughts skittered frantically from facing Noah to facing Hawk. How could she looked at her love and not give away her feelings? She could not endure Noah's crude, selfish touch, never again, not now. What answer could there be? He would only free her if she were barren and he was far from satisfied on that score. She shuddered. The only answer seemed to be flight. She would talk to Hawk. He must know what to do. Lovingly she fingered the heavy silver medallion and then took it from her neck. She must find a safe place to hide it until she could wear it proudly, openly. Where could the snooping eyes of Mrs. Thorndyke not find it? Not her jewelry case, certainly, nor any bureau drawer. Just then, her foot touched a squeaky board beneath the thick braided rug on the floor. Quickly she knelt down and tossed the rug aside, then pried up the loose piece of wood using a heavy shoehorn from her dressing table. There was just enough room to slide the lovingly wrapped piece of jewelry between the loose plank and the flooring beneath it. She carefully replaced the plank, then pulled the rug over it and stood on top of her treasure. The squeak was even gone!

Too upset to eat, Carrie dressed for riding and went down to the corral after telling Estrella to inform Feliz that she was skipping lunch. When she approached the stable, her thoughts were still a jumble of confusion. Should she look for Hawk now or wait until tonight? Nervously she scanned the corral and was surprised to see Frank Lowery's lanky frame leaning against a post, talking casually to the mess cook, Turnips Benton.

The minute he caught sight of Carrie, Frank sent Turnips off and ambled toward her, the tension in his body belying his casual pose. He had been waiting all morning for her, with her little mare saddled and ready. Since Noah was off for the day, he knew Carrie would wear her split skirt and ride astride.

"Mornin'." His toothy smile was disarming.

Carrie forced a smile in return and then looked beyond him to Taffy. "You have her ready to ride. Sorry I'm so late. I overslept, I guess. Can you ride with me?" Her invitation was brightly given. She enjoyed Frank's easy company, but he seldom had free time to spend with her. It would be a rare treat if he could do so today.

"Yep, figgered I would, if'n ya wanted," he replied as he turned and gathered the reins of his sorrel and Taffy Girl, bringing them both from the corral.

They rode the opposite direction from that which Noah had taken. It was always a tacit understanding between them. After desultory small talk about the warm fall, roundup, and other topics, Carrie worked up her courage and asked casually, "Have you seen Kyle or Hawk today?"

"Fer a minute, this mornin' real early. They're gone, Carrie. Headed south."

She took a moment to digest what he said while the numb shock wore off. "You mean left for good—headed back to the Nations?'' Her voice was queerly high and unsteady.

Frank watched her anguish, and it tore at his vitals. Her hands clenched into fists as she sat rigidly on Taffy, staring straight ahead. He could see her swallow down tears. *Dammit, I shoulda' knowed.* He swore helplessly to himself. He had been watching the two of them since their first antagonistic encounters last spring. Perhaps it was inevitable, a beautiful young woman married to a bitter old man, meeting a fascinating loner like Hawk. He had sensed their attraction to one another almost from the start. They could have been so good for each other, but it just was not in the cards, he concluded sadly, thinking of Noah's fury if he ever even imagined the possibility. Frank prayed they had not progressed past the initial stage of falling in love. Maybe that was why Hawk decided to leave, before things got out of hand. Of course, he had left awfully suddenly. Frank swore again silently, then said, ''Mebbe it's better this way, honey. He couldn't stay. Ya know thet. Sometimes a quick stab heals better'n a slow tear.''

''I'll never heal, Frank. How can I, after—'' She stopped herself abruptly and seemed to cringe down on Taffy, then kicked the mare into a faster trot and took off.

Frank Lowery had his answer, and he did not like it.

Noah poured a stiff whiskey and quaffed it as he contemplated Hawk's unannounced departure. Frank had told him that his son and Hunnicut packed up and left at daybreak. Just like last time. No word, no warning. Infuriating, irresponsible savage! He was angry for the loss of two valuable guns that tipped the balance in his contest against Krueger, but at the same time he was relieved that the major obstacle between him and K Bar land was now removed. When Caleb Rider arrived, they could get down to work. He polished off the drink and placed the glass forcefully on the bar.

It was late, and his little wife awaited him upstairs. She had been pale and withdrawn at dinner tonight, almost listless. Lord, he was tired of her joyless, aggravating presence, mute and resigned one minute, willful and defiant the next. He must get her breeding. The more he considered that, and his woeful sexual performance in her bed of late, the more he decided he needed another drink. If only she could stimulate him like the women in Miles City he would be fine. He cursed and decided to forgo taking her tonight. There was plenty of time. Why punish himself?

For the next two days Carrie went through the motions of being alive, like a sleepwalker, pushing the dread of Noah's looming presence from her consciousness. Sooner or later he must come to her once more. Each night she lay awake, her eyes rigidly fixed on his door. When would it open? When would he come to defile the beautiful memories her body had imprinted on it?

By the time he did open that door, Carrie was so on edge with dread, she almost welcomed him. At least it would be over with and she would be back to the same deadening, degrading experience as before. In time she would forget what might have been. For the sake of her sanity, she must.

Noah came to her room late on the third night after Hawk had gone. She had been unable to sleep and was reading, her lamp still lit. He looked almost satanic in the shadows by the door as she reached over to douse the light. He stopped her with an abrupt command.

"Let it burn. Maybe if I can look at your delectable flesh, it may compensate for your coldness."

He strode over to her, pulled her from the bed, and roughly yanked the gown up over her head, tossing it across the floor. Then he stood back and stared at her.

I will not cringe or cover myself. I will show him no fear. She held her head high and stood tall, breasts thrusting proudly, long legs gleaming sleekly in the flickering light. Her green eyes were cold and unflinching as she returned his stare.

Angry at her passive defiance, he roughly pulled her to him for a bruising kiss, then changed his mind and pushed her abruptly back onto the bed. He quickly shed his robe, letting it drop heedlessly onto the floor, and moved over her on the bed. The minute his flesh made contact with hers, Carrie stiffened. How different he felt, flaccid and soft, not like—No! She must not compare, not think of Hawk. She forced her mind to go blank.

Eliciting no response from her after that first flash of defiance, Noah found himself wishing perversely that she might fight him—anything but this resigned passivity.

"What's this, so patient and dutiful? For a minute I thought you had some fire, wife!" He said the word like a curse. "Let's see if I can't stir you up just a bit." He ran his hands over her, tweaking her nipples cruelly and rubbing her soft flesh with greedy, hurting pressure.

She did not beg, did not even flinch. The degradations had gone on too long; it was too late to redeem anything from her travesty of a marriage.

When he could get no further resistance from her, Noah spread her legs and thrust into her. In a few quick, frantic movements, he was finished. He withdrew, got off the bed, and turned from her. Dousing the light with one hand, he reached for his fallen robe with the other. After wrapping it around his shoulders, he vanished through the door to his room. She heard the latch click shut.

Carrie lay still and tried to keep her mind a blank. Then, with a sudden rush, she leaped up and ran to the basin across the room where she was violently sick.

Noah was relieved by Hawk's sudden departure, but Mathilda Thorndyke was ambivalent in her reaction. Ever since Bright Leaf had come and gone, the woman had covertly watched the shifting relationship between Hawk and Carrie. Although they no longer taunted each other, nor fought, neither did they act like covert lovers. The housekeeper's hints to Mr. Noah about that had gone unheeded. He seemed to treat the idea like an absurd joke, but still she had kept her vigil, hoping to catch them in some incriminating act so that she could present the evidence to her employer. If so, that vicious savage and that crafty hoyden would be dealt justice! But now, he was gone before she could prove anything, which left Mathilda Thorndyke still at Carrie's mercy. At least the Indian was gone—and good riddance!

The housekeeper stewed and brooded as she went about the house inspecting the maids' work. As was her habit, she simply barged into Carrie's room without knocking. "Sorry, Mrs. Sinclair, I assumed you were out," she muttered. Carrie was holding the white silk peignoir she had worn the night she and Hawk had made love. She ran her hands over its softness, lost in her bittersweet memories.

"What's wrong?" Mrs. Thorndyke asked sharply. She snatched the gown from Carrie and said, "The orange ribbon that ties the neck is ripped off."

Carrie's cheeks flooded with mortification as she recalled how roughly Noah had torn the gown from her body. "I, er, must have forgotten to ask Feliz to restitch it. It was coming loose. It's probably somewhere around here. I'll look later on."

The housekeeper harumphed. "I'd take better care of such beautiful things if I was you. Think what this must have cost Mr. Noah."

Carrie sighed exasperatedly. 'If he paid for it, then I guess he can tear it off me if he wants to!" With that, she whirled and departed, leaving a beet-faced Mrs. Thorndyke standing agape in the middle of the room.

Hawk and Kyle drifted as far as the north fork of the Canadian River, through a nameless host of squalid settlements, bizarre mixtures of tents and prairie mud houses, smattered with grimy saloons where dusty cattlemen stopped on their way to the railheads in Kansas. Life was fast, cheap, and violent. It suited Hawk's mood. Outlaws from Wyoming to Texas, New York to California, fled to the isolated island of no-man's-land known in 1880 as the Indian Nations. No one tribe owned it, and no government, federal or local, kept order. It was not an organized territory as were Montana or Arizona, but a vague jurisdiction that was contested by Indian tribes, Texas cattlemen, Kansas farmers, and eastern railroad barons. A scant handful of U.S. marshals from Fort Smith in Arkansas were assigned the impossible task of keeping order in a wide open land without form or law. In one year alone, over sixty of them died for their trouble. In any given year

of the past decade, hundreds of thousands of Texas cattle
traversed the Nations' length to the railheads of Abilene,
Hayes, Ellsworth, and finally Dodge City in Kansas. Men
lived violently and died suddenly.

The farther south they rode, the quieter Hawk became,
seemingly fixed in his misery. Kyle, who had observed his
friend over several rough weeks, was finally moved to
speak.

"I got me a habit when I wuz a tad, Longlegs. Eatin'.
We be near outta cash money. Looks ta me we better git us
a job o' work. Right soon."

"You particular what?" Hawk looked at Hunnicut levelly.

"I 'spect yew ain't, thet's fer sure. Havin' a downright
dislike fer drovin' cows er any other hard work, I figger
we cud see if'n them whiskey runners down on Cashe
Creek need shotgun guards." He waited for a rise out of
Hawk.

And got one. "They sell to Cheyenne, Arapaho, even
Cherokee! I won't help that scum kill any of them with
rotgut. Let's head to Sill. Always something shaking
around there."

Kyle smiled, assured Hawk still felt a few things were
worth living for. He grunted. "Sill it is, then."

Fort Sill in 1880 was assigned the impossible task of
keeping order amidst the chaos of relocated Indians and
cattle-trail drivers, as well as controlling the depredations
of trespassing sodbusters and wandering outlaws. Often,
it was difficult to tell who was who in the cast of characters.
An army outpost, Sill attracted more than its share of camp
followers and hangers-on, red and white. If various post
commanders over the years looked the other way while
whiskey runners and whores peddled their wares, those
were the least of sins in the Nations, a place the manifest
destiny of civilization neatly bypassed on its headlong rush
to the Pacific.

Hawk and Kyle settled in at the garish frame building
that passed for a hotel and headed to the nearest saloon,
the only one actually made of wood, the others being tents
and mud houses. Despite its construction, it had little to

recommend it but rotgut whiskey and even less savory women.

One girl looked younger and less used than the rest. She had long, dark hair that was reasonably clean and huge chocolate-brown eyes. Perhaps it was the sad eyes that caused Hawk to forget her thickly rouged cheeks and carmine-coated mouth. She smiled in greeting, then, uninvited, sat down at the rickety table.

"Howdy. Yer strangers. I kin tell. Know all th' reg'lars. Shore is hot out fer fall. Buy me a drink?"

She looked at Hawk, who was reclining against the rough plank wall, his long legs stretched beneath the table, hat shading his face. He did not move, but Kyle responded.

"Shore thing, pretty lady." It had been a long time since Miles City and the cathouse there. He needed a woman and so did Hawk, but Hunnicut knew better than to get mixed up in his friend's business. He would simply take care of his own.

All the while they talked, Chelsey—that was the name she gave—watched the silent Hawk in fascination. *Niver seen it beat, th' way women fancy him,* the little man thought, half peeved, half amused. After a few minutes more, he left on the pretext of going outside to relieve himself. If she was so all-fired raring to snare Longlegs, let her have a shot at it. Maybe it might lighten his mood.

Straightening her yellow satin dress, which had seen better days, Chelsey looked the tall dark gunman up and down boldly. "Yew part Injun 'er somethin'?"

"Or something," he replied laconically. For the first time he pushed his hat to the back of his head and returned her perusal. For a whore, she wasn't bad. Young and reasonably clean, even a little pretty in a coarse, country sort of way. The eyes were the thing. Soon they would be dull and hard, but now they were still shiny, giving off a liquid glow.

"My grandma was Cherokee, 'er so my ma tole me one'st, afore I run off from th' hills o' Tennessee."

He smiled for the first time at her pronunciation of "Tennessee," with the accent on the first syllable. Her heart stopped. He was positively the most dazzlingly

handsome man she had ever seen. "I got me a feelin'
'bout me 'n' yew, sugar. Yessiree, I have."

Hawk awoke the next morning in a strange room, filled
with strewn articles of female clothing, stale cigarette
smoke, and greasy glasses with the odorous remains of
whiskey clinging to their sides. He raised his head and
immediately lay it back on the lumpy gray pillowcase. It
throbbed in an old familiar way that he had not experienced in months. *Damn! What was in that bottle last
night? Or was it more than one bottle?*

As he reached up to rub his aching temples, Chelsey
stirred and rolled over next to him, but did not awaken.
The harsh light of morning was not kind to her, especially
with her eyes closed. Into his memory flashed a fleeting
vision of Carrie's face softly touched by the first streaks of
dawn as he carried her back to her room. Swearing, he
forced the image aside and crawled from the bed. By the
time he had dressed and left Chelsey some money, he had
barely enough remaining with which to buy a meager
greasy breakfast. Kyle was right. They needed to go to
work.

A morning spent asking around the post netted them
several names of big cattle outfits looking for men to deal
with rustlers. Deciding to head to the Turkey Cross camp
the next day, they encountered an unexpected surprise. A
tall, well-dressed man of middle years came into the
saloon, where they sat discussing plans over warm beer.
His black broadcloth suit marked him as an eastern preach-
er, but his facial contours and smooth braids indicated that
he was an Indian.

Watching the sharp black eyes scan the room in shrewd
assessment, Hawk wondered what a man like him was
doing in a dive like this. Then he moved toward their
table. "Good afternoon, gentlemen. I am John Tall Oak.
You are Hawk Sinclair and Kyle Hunnicut?"

Hawk stood up and looked eye-to-eye with the tall
stranger as they shook hands. "Your name is well chosen." Few men were as tall as he.

Tall Oak laughed as he shook Hawk's hand. "I'm afraid
I didn't earn it. It's been our family surname for four

generations, although I'm told my great grandfather who lived in Georgia was even taller than I. I'm Cherokee, born and raised in this, the land of our exile.''

"Yes, one of the civilized Tribes," Hawk said smoothly.

"And you, I have heard, are Cheyenne," John Tall Oak replied.

"One of the *un*civilized tribes," Hawk shot back without rancor.

The Cherokee laughed as Kyle offered him a chair. "Whut 're ya doin' in this dive? 'Pears ta me yer used ta better."

"You know us." Hawk asked no question, only waited.

"Let's say I've heard of you. More to the point, Mr. Sinclair, I want to hire you and your friend to do a job for us."

"Us?" Kyle looked puzzled.

"I represent the tribal council of the Cherokee Nation. For quite a few years, since the trail drivers have been bringing Texas beef north, they've grazed them on the grasslands the great white father so generously allotted us, to the north of here. We've charged them for that privilege by the head, per season, until they fatten the cattle and move them to market. However, a few of the larger spreads have gotten together and decided they no longer like our prices."

"They're welchin' on th' deal," Kyle supplied.

Tall Oak nodded. "They say they have five thousand head in a graze. My men see three, four times as many. Maybe they can't count. Maybe they think we can't." He shrugged expressively, then when on. "The money adds up, as much as a hundred thousand per year in a good year. Of course," he said, watching Kyle's eye light up, "it must be divided among a whole nation of people scattered across this wilderness."

"I think we might talk a deal, Tall Oak," Hawk interjected.

So they went to work, visiting the camps where big herds were to be wintered, taking Cherokee police with them merely for an official look. Tough Texas range drovers knew of Kyle Hunnicut from a long time back.

The tall, dangerous-looking half-breed with him had already acquired a reputation in a land filled with gunmen. Mostly, they collected the due bills without mishap. On a few occasions they had to resort to force. Kyle had a nicked wrist and Hawk a shallow flesh wound in his left thigh. Their opponents didn't fare as well.

Months slipped by and winter came, cold and desolate. With enough cash to see them through, they settled down to enforced idleness, playing cards, drinking, and amusing themselves with women.

Chelsey had not forgotten her half-breed lover and welcomed him back, even giving him a pair of gold loops for his ears. She said the earrings had belonged to her grandfather. Hawk wore them, reopening the partially sealed holes in his ears for the first time in several years. His hair grew shaggy, down to his shoulders, and he wore buckskin leggings, moccasins, and all the gold and silver rings he'd brought from Montana, all his jewelry except Iron Heart's medallion.

Kyle watched the gradual transformation in him as the thin veneer of civilization slipped away. Hawk lost or won money at cards, he did not care which, and slept with Chelsey most nights. As the monotony of winter's inactivity wore on, he drank more than anything, beginning in the afternoons on many days.

On just such a day, Hawk sat in his usual place in the corner of the saloon, back to the wall, legs stretched indolently in front of him, sipping a whiskey. A tall, thickset man in his late teens or early twenties with short-cropped yellow hair and piercing blue eyes came in and walked up to the bar. His square face betrayed nothing as he ordered beer and sipped it, casting his eyes across the room. It was not crowded. A few off-duty troopers played cards at one table, two trail drovers sat at another with Gracie, an aging but obliging whore, and an old drummer ate a plate of congealed stew while standing at the bar.

The stranger finished the beer, then ordered another from Ben the barkeep. Chelsey arrived shortly after, beginning her evening turn before the dinner hour that night. He watched her with appreciation as she sauntered across the rough plank floor in her high-heeled satin slippers and rustling green taffeta dress. After she greeted several regular customers, she looked over toward Hawk, who pushed the hat back on his head and raised his empty glass. Noting the gesture, she came over and took the glass, heading to the bar to get him a refill.

"Hello, little bird. All bright green and pretty as a songbird. Can you sing?" The blond youth's voice was precise and pleasant, but held a smug, almost menacing quality that set her on edge. Chelsey had seen his kind in a dozen saloons between Tennessee and Texas. Young, crazy mean, and looking for a cheap thrill.

Smiling brightly, she moved past him to the bar. "Nope. 'Fraid not." With that she started to turn, but he caught her arm, causing the refilled drink to spill, sprinkling her dress with staining spots.

As she let out a sharp oath at the ruination of her best dress, one Hawk had bought her, the stranger laughed and grabbed her. "I'll buy you another drink, or dress, baby. Just come sit with me."

"I already have a customer, over there," she responded peevishly.

"That Injun? Where I come from, white women don't fuck with Injuns, and white saloons sure don't serve 'em whiskey."

The room became very still. Even the old drummer froze, his spoon suspended halfway between bowl and mouth. Then Chelsey let loose a volley of oaths and kicked him in the shin, jerking her arm free of his brutal grasp.

He struck her a stinging slap and began to grab her shoulder when Hawk's voice cut in. "I hate to interrupt, but it seems to me you owe me a whiskey and the lady a new dress. *Now*."

The young man turned incredulously to look at the hard, unshaven face of the half-breed. Although slimmer, Hawk was easily as tall as he. Blue and black eyes clashed. The eerily insane glow in the pale-blue eyes flashed up and down the buckskin-clad form with contempt.

"I don't buy breeds whiskey and I sure don't plan to pay the price of a dress to have the likes of her." He gestured to Chelsey offhandedly. As he waited to see what Hawk would do, the stranger's fair-complected face looked guileless.

"I don't drink with spiders, either. Just put the price of my drink on the bar and leave. I'll buy the lady a new dress." He reached over and put a hand possessively on Chelsey's shoulder, smiling evilly at the younger man.

"You're asking for a bullet, breed. You know that?" The feral gleam in the ice-blue eyes was anticipatory.

"How old are you, twenty maybe? Stupid age to die, kid." Hawk stood at ease, his anger beginning to abate as his sobriety returned.

With a snarled obscenity, the big blond went for his gun. Before he could get off a shot, Hawk put two .44 slugs in his chest. "Maybe you're right. It is a good day to die." With a few curses muttered in Cheyenne, he holstered his gun and turned toward the shivering girl crouched against the bar. "Now, refill that whiskey, Brown Eyes."

Just then, Kyle uncocked his gun and slipped it back into its resting place. He stood in the door. "Thought I heered a bit o' trouble. Nothin' ya couldn't handle, I see." He squatted down next to the body and pulled the face up for inspection. "Yep, he's daid. They git younger an' dumber ever' year. Yew know him?"

"Not that I recollect," Hawk said, rubbing his eyes and laying his head against the back of the wall as he sat down in his chair once more. "Just one more young asshole on the prod, trying to impress a woman and get a reputation." He took the drink Chelsey offered him and swallowed half of it in a fierce, burning slug.

"Soon be spring. We cud head ta Texas. Get us a good-payin' job o' work. A man needs fresh air 'n' a clean place ta clear th' cobwebs out, Longlegs. This here place's trouble fer us!"

Hawk snorted and finished the drink morosely. "Everywhere I go is trouble—or hadn't you noticed, Kyle?"

"Some men need a place ta belong," Kyle began uncertainly, his shrewd gray-blue eyes assessing his friend.

He had watched Hawk in several fights lately. The younger man seemed not to care if he lived or died. This life was killing him. He said so to Hawk.

"My grandfather told me the same thing last summer."

Knowing better than to bring up the festering wound of Carrie, Kyle stayed on a safer course. "Wal, 'pears ta me he's right. All's yew do is drink, kill time, 'n' shoot a occasional varmint. Sooner 'er later one'll do fer yew, Longlegs."

"What are you suggesting? I don't want to go to Texas, Kyle. I've already seen it. Just more men with guns, more card games and whiskey. Hell, what does it matter?" He took a pull on the whiskey glass and realized it was empty, then slammed it down in disgust.

Watching him, Kyle said softly, "Whut about yer grandpa's people? Would there be trouble there or would ya be welcome?"

Hawk shrugged. "Some of both, I expect. Maybe she was right. Maybe I do have to choose," he mused.

Kyle's eyes crinkled in curiosity. Who was "she"? Carrie? Or someone else—someone with Iron Heart's band?

For a couple of days Hawk brooded, realizing that he could not drift and drown himself in a vat of whiskey at trail's end each night. Dreams of Carrie continued to torture him. Only whiskey brought oblivion. Chelsey certainly did not. He could barely stand leaving her bed most mornings in a hung-over stupor of misery, unwilling to look at her painted face and none too clean body. In a few years she'd look like Gracie. In a few years he'd be dead.

"It is a good day to die," the old Cheyenne death chant said. Perhaps so, if one had a cause worth dying for— home, family, honor. What had he?

"I'm going back to the People. I made a bust of living white, I should at least try to live their way before I give up." Hawk's face looked grave, but for the first morning in months, his eyes were not bloodshot. He was freshly bathed and shaven, looking more like himself than he had since they left Circle S.

Kyle nodded. "Guess I'll be slopin' off ta Texas without yew, then."

Hawk smiled sadly. "If you'd ever learned Cheyenne, you'd make a hit with the women. You always like them tall."

Kyle chuckled. "Thet I do, Longlegs, but they're right pertic'lar 'bout bein' married 'n' all afore ya kin have any fun. I might jist git myself scalped fer my trouble. Sides, yew know I lived all my life in Texas 'n' kin scarce spit out a couple dozen words o' Spanish, much less learn Cheyenne. Shucks, I had a schoolmarm tell me one'st thet I couldn't talk English, neither. Friend, I'm plumb hopeless."

His eyes turned from merriment to graveness. They both knew they would most likely never meet again. Neither could express what he felt in words, but their eyes and handclasps communicated it.

"Take care of that tough Texas hide, you hear? I don't want you shot the first time you hire out alone."

"Don't yew go countin' coup on no bluebellies, neither!" Kyle snorted back.

CHAPTER 14

It took Hawk almost a week after arriving back in the Yellowstone country to locate the winter campground of Iron Heart's band. The country was invigorating. He let his eyes sweep the majestic high prairie, now awash with pristine snow gleaming diamond bright in the blinding sunshine. The snow had drifted high as a horse's head in many places, tossed about by the cruel plains wind that left other spots swept clean. It was as if a capricious housekeeper had plied her broom at random over the landscape. The mountains stood in faint lavender relief on the far horizon and the tangy scent of pine needles assailed his nostrils. A dense stand of hardy evergreen trees grew in the crevices of a nearby outcropping of rock. Now the pines' jagged outswept branches beckoned him with snow-laden arms. Hawk took a deep breath and watched a vapor cloud form in front of him as he expelled it. It was good to be home.

He had packed away his boots, cotton shirts, and other articles of *veho* clothing and rode into the village dressed in his best buckskins. He still wore the earrings Chelsey had given him, as well as several rings and a bracelet, all worked by Cheyenne craftsmen. His chest felt naked without the medallion. He knew his grandfather would wonder about its absence, but would not ask. The wise old man would wait for his grandson to tell him what he wished to impart.

Hawk was deep in thought as he wended his way past

the lodges, alternately sorry for his impulsive gesture in parting with the medallion, yet achingly glad to have given it to Carrie. On more than one occasion he considered that Noah might find it and realize its significance in her possession. No, Carrie knew better than to be so careless. The real problem was that it remained a link between them, however tenuous.

As if I need a tangible reminder. She is burned into my soul. Such morose considerations were quickly put aside as he stopped before Iron Heart's lodge and dismounted. Word of his approach had preceded him. The old man stood outside in the bitterly cold, bright March air and watched him.

After Hawk had greeted several old friends and relations who had congregated around the lodge, they embraced and entered the warm shelter. Considering it a great honor, one youth eagerly took Redskin to rub down and feed. Hawk adjusted his eyes to the dim interior after the bright glare of the sun on snow, and then turned as Iron Heart spoke.

"You have come home to stay." It was not a question. The old man took in his grandson's clothing, jewelry, and long hair. He grunted then, indicating Hawk should sit. "It will take more than beads and braids for you to be a part of the Cheyenne way."

"I know that. I have come to try. I do not know if I will succeed," Hawk said simply.

The old man smiled. "If you wish it, you will succeed."

As the weeks passed, it seemed that he would succeed. There was certainly no time to brood and no whiskey to drink. An abundance of both had brought him to grief in the south. Here he rose with the sun each morning and went hunting, often spending the better part of the daylight hours tracking antelope, elk, deer, and small game. They saw scant few buffalo. In the brief span of his twenty-six years, Hawk had witnessed the virtual extinction of a species. Soon, with the coming of the railroad into the north country, there would be none of the great shaggy beasts left at all.

Game was growing scarce, and workable firearms for hunting were also scarce. Hawk's guns, here as in the white world, were his fortune, but here they were used to provide sustenance for human beings, not destruction. He had spent much of his cash reserve before coming home to purchase several good Winchester rifles and a large quantity of ammunition, as well as a number of good, sharp hunting knives. He kept the remaining cash he had earned from John Tall Oak to use for whatever other utilitarian items he might need to buy from white traders in the uncertain future.

The life was harsh but clean and simple. Calf Woman tended the household chores for the old man and his young grandson. Hawk repaid her for cooking and sewing by providing her and her widowed sister with fresh game. On the long winter evenings, he sat and mended the more primitive weapons inherited from Iron Heart—tomahawks, bows, and arrows—as well as the religious gear worn in the summer ceremonies. His own buffalo-hide shield, with its blazing sun and hawk in flight painted on it, was worn and brittle with age. He made a new one and painted it under the critical guidance of his grandfather. They shared pipes of fragrant tobacco and often talked far into the night until their lodge fire burned to winking coals.

While Hawk settled into a routine he had not lived since adolescence, Wind Song waited and dreamed. She stood in the back of the crowd that had gathered to welcome him home, shyly holding herself aloof. There would be a time when it was right to speak with him, but this was not it.

As the weeks flew by, the bitter northers of late winter kept her confined to the camp, making an accidental encounter with Hawk nearly impossible. The harsh weather did not keep Angry Wolf from plaguing her, however. He came offering gifts—fresh game, soft pelts, even a new iron cookpot.

At one point, Sweet Rain teased her older sister mercilessly. "Why don't you want Angry Wolf for a husband? He would be a good one. He is brave and handsome." She paused to consider teasingly, "Of course, not so brave and handsome as the half-blood, Hunting Hawk."

"Be still!" Wind Song admonished the irritating child

while Bright Leaf sat quietly, stirring the stew pot over the fire. She had heard this conversation often before.

"Wind Song is right, Sweet Rain," her childishly high voice piped. "Hunting Hawk is the best choice. Someday I will marry him. Of course, I will be a second or third wife by the time I'm old enough," she finished sadly.

Wind Song whirled angrily between her two young tormentors. "The white men take only one wife! Have you learned nothing? If—when he marries, he will choose only one."

Sweet Rain giggled, but Bright Leaf's eyes became suddenly wistful in remembrance. "If that is so, if white men only love once, then he will wait for Carrie."

Wind Song paled. "She is his father's wife! Don't ever speak such an obscenity! He is Cheyenne now. He will marry here."

Sweet Rain laughed out loud. "If he is Cheyenne now, he may take two wives. Maybe me."

Wind Song grabbed a thick buffalo robe, wrapped it securely around herself, and stormed out of the tepee into the cold wind for some fresh air.

Standing Bear took Angry Wolf's suit seriously, feeling he was a good match for his eldest daughter, still unmarried at the scandalous age of seventeen. The old man's health worsened steadily, and despite the security Iron Heart's protection offered his family, Standing Bear desperately wanted Wind Song to accept Angry Wolf, who was a tribal leader and a skillful hunter. He would make a good provider. Standing Bear knew the reason his daughter refused all her suitors. Several times he had tried to speak of it to the girl, had tried to convince her that Hunting Hawk had gone to the *veho* for good. She had cajoled and pleaded to wait, half convincing the softhearted old man that she had a dream in which she was given to the half-blood. Since white blood flowed in her own veins, he had held his peace. Perhaps it was meant to be.

When Hawk returned to live among the people, Standing Bear waited patiently for him to make some indication of his intent. None was forthcoming for weeks. Finally the old man decided it was time to act. A break in the weather gave him a good opportunity to go hunting with a small group of men, among whom was the object of his daughter's desire.

When Hawk mounted up that morning, he found Standing Bear with the other riders. It was a short excursion, close to camp, but despite the ease of their agreed-upon mission, he felt grave misgivings about taking the ill, older man along. To voice such an opinion would cause Standing Bear to lose face, so Hawk held his peace.

After an hour of slow, careful stalking, Hawk sighted a small antelope. His shot brought it down cleanly, and Standing Bear was the first to arrive at his side, helping him tie it across Redskin's haunches for return to camp.

"This will make a beautiful shirt. I have some fine porcupine quills to trim it. Wind Song is very skilled as a shirtmaker. She could do this for you, since Calf Woman is not trained in that art."

Hawk smiled at the old man, alarmed at his frail wheezing yet amused at his transparent ruse to be a matchmaker. *So that's why he came along on this hunt. I should have known*, he thought to himself. Then he said aloud, "Is Wind Song yet unmarried? I expected Angry Wolf to win her hand by now."

"He tries, but she does not favor him," was the disconsolate reply.

Hawk knew this. Iron Heart had hinted as much often in the past weeks. Still Hawk shied away from any commitment. His troubled dreams were still filled with Carrie. *I cannot let her hold me in thrall for the rest of my life, if I am to have a life here*, he thought bitterly.

Part of the problem was his continued uncertainty about being Cheyenne. Did he want to live by their tribal, ritualized customs? He found much to admire in the People. They were honest, cooperative, possessed of a sense of humor, bound by a system of laws fairer than the white ones; their medical treatments were often more advanced than those of the whites. Yet he had existed on the periphery of this society for bits and pieces of his life and been away from it for years, years spent in eastern universities. He knew of a world far beyond the banks of the Yellowstone. He also held the image of a flame-haired woman close to his heart. She would not free him. Could he free himself?

His musings were interrupted by a call from White Owl. "We must make haste. See how the sky darkens?"

Hawk looked up from his task and realized the blue-black clouds rolling in indeed heralded another norther, the sudden terrible winter storms that decimated the high plains. White Owl and Big Elk quickly helped Hawk finish tying the antelope onto Redskin, and then took off for the village.

Its icy fingers slicing like blades of frozen steel, the norther struck with brutal force, cutting them to the quick. Big Elk, White Owl, and Hawk could have made it. Standing Bear could not.

After a scant half hour, the older man began to slide from his horse. Hawk caught him and attempted to hold his frail form on his mount. At once he could feel Standing Bear's frozen hands and arms. Even he and the other younger men were growing stiff with the cold. Realizing something must be done for Wind Song's father, Hawk signaled the other two men and quickly dispatched them to the village for a travois. He stopped near an outcrop of rock that provided some slight shelter from the wind. There he pulled Standing Bear off his horse and laid his shivering form down. Then he untied the freshly killed antelope and sliced it open with his knife. He managed to shove the old man's hands and feet into the warm carcass, then lay across it himself, providing what additional shelter he could.

"It is a good day to die, Hunting Hawk," the reedy voice rasped in his ear. Then he coughed furiously.

"White Owl and Big Elk will return with help soon. We are not far from camp. Do not speak of dying," he replied impatiently.

"I must speak what I know. I will die. You will live. Wind Song will live. Angry Wolf will live. She wants you for her husband, not him. For too long I let her rule me. Now it passes from my hands. I should have given her to Angry Wolf when I could. Now only the gods know what will happen to her.'' Gasping for breath as he lay on his side, he punctuated the long speech with frequent coughs.

Hawk swore to himself. Trapped. What was he to do? "I promise you I will speak with Wind Song when we return to the—" He stopped short as a convulsion shook the old man. Before Hawk could say anything more, he knew Standing Bear was dead.

When the rescue party arrived, Hawk had tied Standing Bear to his horse. The ride to the village was made with the wind keening a death chant of its own.

Wind Song and Sweet Rain followed Cheyenne mourning customs, cutting their arms and letting their hair hang unbound. A burial platform was erected in a staunch willow tree by the frozen riverbed. All of Standing Bear's most treasured possessions were placed on it with him: his pipe, hatchet, a fine hunting bow, and beaded quiver of arrows.

Hawk did not intrude on Wind Song's grief, although he did notice Angry Wolf attempt to speak to her several times in the following days. When he saw Angry Wolf heading for Wind Song's lodge the third day, Hawk intercepted him.

"You intrude on their mourning, Angry Wolf. It is not good to do this thing. Only wait a few weeks." He kept his voice level and civil, but could see the fierce, burning hatred radiating from the other's eyes.

"Go back to your white father. You do not belong here, Sin-clair," Angry Wolf said, scornfully drawing out Hawk's white surname.

"I would not quarrel with you, Angry Wolf. You violate the ways of the People, not mine." He stood before the lodge, daring his old nemesis to pass him.

Realizing that Hawk was right and the tribal elders would agree, Angry Wolf stalked off after grinding out, "We will see who wins her, white man. You are no fit husband!"

Hawk's own thoughts ran along that same course as he turned to leave, but just then a soft feminine voice called to him.

"Wait, Hunting Hawk! Come in and share our fire. It is cold outside." Wind Song's smile was winsome.

He nodded and entered. Bright Leaf and Sweet Rain sat in the far corner of the lodge, painstakingly scraping an antelope hide with sharp stone tools. He greeted them and squatted by the center fireplace, silently watching Wind Song as she poured hot broth into a gourd and offered it to him. Even in her sorrow she was lovely. Her hair was unbound, flowing down her back like a curtain of midnight satin. Slim copper arms showed through the skein of loose hair. Her strong, handsome face glowed by the firelight. The deep-green eyes haunted him. Jade, fathomless, like Carrie's eyes.

She broke his reverie. "Thank you for sending him away. I did not wish to speak with him again."

"I should not be here either," he said, smiling at her.

"But I asked you to enter," she countered. "Have you now chosen the way of the People, Hunting Hawk? Last summer I hoped you would."

He shook his head in confusion. "I honestly do not know, Wind Song. There is peace for me here. No violence, no whiskey, none of the evils that tainted my life among the whites."

"Then why do you hesitate to embrace this life and make it your own?" Her heart leaped at her own boldness. Both of them knew she meant more than her words indicated.

"I have only returned a few months. I cannot give an answer yet," he evaded.

Looking over at the two younger girls busily at work, apparently ignoring their conversation, Wind Song wanted to speak more, but dared not.

Hawk finished the broth and handed the gourd back to her. "Thank you for sharing the food and the warmth of your fire." He rose to leave.

She moved over and opened the heavy skin flap to let him out, then abruptly stepped into the freezing air after him. "I will speak plainly and quickly, Hunting Hawk. Now that my father is dead, several men have asked Iron Heart for me, among them Angry Wolf. I do not want any of them. I want you. But I will not wait forever. Choose your path, or else I must choose mine." With that astounding speech, she whirled and vanished into the lodge.

He grinned in spite of himself. A bold, forthright woman. She was truthful. If he would stay here, he must choose a wife. He needed a woman, and knew his own weaknesses enough to confess he could never live the celibate life of a Contrary. Hawk snorted at that, thinking of Medicine Shield, who was the only Contrary with Iron Heart's band, a maniacal loner who lived in a world of visions. The Contraries were those supposedly touched by the gods and called to live a life of religious taboos. They were chaste, reckless in battle, perverse in behavior to the point of responding to every request by doing and saying exactly the opposite of what they meant. Personally, Hawk felt they were touched by the madness of some dark spirit, not a god. He was grateful they were few among the People and only one lived with his band.

His band. When did he start thinking of himself as belonging? Could he dare hope to become a part of these people? He had never really fit into white society. Could he fit here, or must he end his days in the self-destructive world of outlaws and riffraff?

Always when he became introspective, thoughts of Carrie crept into his mind. Thus troubled in spirit, he walked slowly back to his grandfather's lodge.

Observing his grandson's pensive mien during their evening meal, Iron Heart lit a pipe and pondered. Should he tell Hawk the news he had heard from the white trader? If he had interpreted all of Hawk's medicine dream correctly so long ago, he might be defying the will of the gods. It was difficult to be sure. He only knew that he wanted his daughter's son to spend his days among the People. It was a good life, and Wind Song would be a good woman for him; she could cleanse him of all the sickness and hurt the *veho* had given him. He made his decision.

"This day I have news from Matthew Clinton," he began, inhaling on his pipe.

Hawk looked up absently. "That half-blood trader?

What's he doing here so early in the spring before the snow has gone?''

The old man shrugged. "He brought word of a thing that you may want to know. Concerning He Who Walks in Sun and your inheritance." Wisely, he chose not to mention Carrie by name yet.

The reaction was just as he expected, and he knew the reason, although it grieved him. Hawk's face became tense and his eyes darkened in pain. He had an inkling of what the old man was leading up to, and he did not want to hear it. "I have no inheritance with Noah. We both know it," he said tersely.

"Now that part of your life ends, my son. Soon your ties with him will be severed forever. Your father's wife is with child. It will be born in the summer." He spoke the words softly, knowing each one opened a stinging wound afresh. Yet it must be done. If a suppurating sore is not cleansed and cauterized, it will never heal.

Hawk did not speak, but only stared into the flickering firelight. *I knew this must happen someday.* Then why, why did his chest feel as if a vise were squeezing the breath of life from him? "I must think, alone, Grandfather." With that he rose and donned a heavy buffalo robe, then left the lodge to brave the howling anger of the night storm.

Hawk rode for several hours. The winds abated and the stars came out, icy diamonds on the black velvet cloth of night sky. The dry, still air was brittle with cold yet oddly comforting to him. The chill only sharpened his senses. When he returned to the lodge at dawn, he knew what he would do.

The old man was up, standing in the doorway, facing the east to watch the sun rise as he always did. Calf Woman was inside, busily preparing their first meal of the day. Hawk slid from Redskin's bare back with effortless grace and began to remove the headstall.

Watching his grandson tend to the great red beast, the old man sensed a new resolution in him. He waited.

"Do you think I should observe the proprieties and send Calf Woman to you with gifts for a bride-price?" He asked the question with the hint of a smile tugging at the corner of his mouth.

It was the custom for a suitor to officially request a maiden's hand in marriage by sending an older woman to act as emissary, bearing gifts to the girl's father, brother, or other male guardian.

Iron Heart smiled broadly. "I do not think it will be necessary, under the circumstances. We both know she wants you. I will tell her to start sewing her wedding garments. Building a lodge will take a while, but I am not without influence. New Moon is the most skilled tepee maker in our band. She will begin at once if I request it."

The marriage was set for one month hence, in the spring, when the last snows of winter should fade and the first touches of green appear in the fertile valleys of the Yellowstone.

CHAPTER 15

Caleb Rider was a lean, rangy man of medium height, loosely put together and casual in manner. Many men tended to underestimate him. Like a thousand other cowboys, his sandy hair and seamed face bore the stamp of dozens of harsh winters and blazing summers under the western sky. Only his flinty-gray eyes gave him away as a cunning, ruthless killer. He was wanted for horse stealing, cattle rustling, and several murders in Oregon and points east.

Noah had made discreet inquiries through other stockmen at the association meeting and then had his own sources check the man out thoroughly. He had a big job for Rider, and he wanted to be sure the man could handle it. There must be no amateur bungling such as Krueger's man Squires had done.

When Rider knocked on Frank Lowery's cabin door after supper that chilly November evening, he was laconic and noncommittal. Mr. Sinclair had offered him a job as a range detective at the association meeting in Helena. Frank sized him up shrewdly, noting the strapped-down gun, which was expensive and meticulously cared for. The foreman put Rider in the bunkhouse, giving him Hunnicut's old place. He didn't like the way things were shaping up, not at all. First Hawk and Kyle took off like scalded dogs, then Carrie grieved herself sick, now Noah hired this fish-eyed killer. Sighing, he vowed to keep a close eye on what occurred on the north range near Krueger's land.

It had been a month to the day since Hawk left. Carrie continued to lose weight and was listless and exhausted. She did not even make any pretense of standing up to Noah, praying nightly that he would not come to her. Then, if he did, she unresistingly submitted to whatever he wanted. What was the use in fighting? Her only salvation lay in conceiving his child. Then he might give her peace. She would raise Noah's son, but would try to make him like Hawk. *Hawk*. The thought of him still clawed at her, as she alternated between a sense of acute betrayal and a welling loneliness of desire that threatened to engulf her.

There was to be a Christmas dance in Miles City. All the big cattlemen, bankers, and other dignitaries would be there with their wives. One morning before he headed out with the new man, Rider, Noah informed Carrie that she must have a new gown to attend the gala. In compliance with his command, she set out with Frank early the next morning for a two-day stay in town. She dreaded the fittings at the dressmaker's.

"Lands sake, Mrs. Sinclair, you're getting thinner each time I fit you. I know that Mexican cook of your husband's can do better than to let you starve yourself." Elsie Grummond was as loquacious as she was skilled in dressmaking. Her flying fingers pinned, clipped, draped, and folded. By the time she was satisfied with the results, Carrie was exhausted.

When she left the shop with a stern admonition from Mrs. Grummond to eat dinner that night, she was too tired to focus her eyes. In her dazed state she was not watching where she was going and she stepped from the rough wooden planking of the steps onto the street. She collided with a tall, thickset man with dense, iron-gray hair. His large, expressive eyes were at first surprised, then amused as he supported her slim form, apologizing for the accident.

"My dear lady, a thousand pardons. So sorry I am that one so broad as I should injure one so slight and lovely as you." His speech was educated but foreign.

He was Karl Krueger, Noah's rival, the one who brought

Lola to the ball! Tired, shaken, and wanting only to forget that disastrous evening, Carrie rubbed her temples and moved away from his solicitous hands. "That's quite all right. I'm afraid I wasn't looking where I was going."

He raked her fiery hair and slim, elegant body with a rapacious stare. A very handsome young woman. No wonder Noah was glad to be shut of Lola! "You are too gracious, Mrs. Sinclair. I am—"

"Karl Krueger of the K Bar Ranch, I know. We were introduced at the ball here in early fall," she replied breathlessly, nervous over the predatory way he was looking at her. Were all these cattle kings as ruthless and unappealing as Noah? "If you will excuse me, I have to meet Mr. Lowery for supper at the hotel, and I'm already frightfully late."

"I shall look forward to our next encounter, my enchanting flame." His smile was gracious, but his eyes looked at her as if she were a ten-course banquet and he a starving giant.

As he watched her retreating form, Krueger considered how very much he would enjoy stealing her away from his old enemy. He had considered taking Lola before she married Ernst, but then had rejected the idea, because Noah no longer valued her. However, this one, so young and dazzling with that unusual coloring and those jade eyes, yes, she would be a most delectable way to crush Noah Sinclair's vanity. A deep, rumbling chuckle welled up from his massive chest.

A month later Carrie sat disconsolately staring at a plate of *huevos rancheros*, soft fried eggs swimming in spicy red sauce. The breakfast, one of Feliz's specialties, Carrie had loved from the first time she tasted the dish. Despite her loss of appetite when dining with Noah, she used to make up for it in the mornings with a hearty breakfast. When Hawk left two months ago, she was so depressed that her eating suffered even more. Then, prompted by the dressmaker's advice last month, she tried to eat. Nothing seemed to agree with her lately, especially breakfast.

"What's the matter, *chica*, not hungry again?" Feliz's

voice was laced with concern. She had spent the past several weeks baking and cooking special dishes, all in the feckless hope of enticing the wan young woman before her to eat.

Suddenly, after she had forced a forkful of the rich eggs into her mouth, Carrie bolted for the washbasin.

Quickly Feliz came over and supported her weight while she leaned against the counter and heaved painfully. Wetting a clean cloth, Feliz bathed Carrie's brow until the unnatural flush retreated, then helped her to a chair. "I will brew some herbal tea. It will settle your stomach."

"I don't know what's come over me lately. Hot and cold, shaky, queasy, tired all the time." Carrie sighed, unconsciously rubbing her tender breasts with one hand to ease a twinge she had from leaning over the sink.

Feliz watched Carrie as she methodically brewed the tea. Then, sitting down with her, she made her young charge drink the pale concoction and eat a piece of plain dry bread. "You are tired and do not want to eat, yet your clothes grow tight here." She indicated the straining buttons on Carrie's blouse.

Self-consciously, Carrie looked down at the unbecoming gap in her blouse and sighed. "I can just hear Mrs. Grummond now. First take it in, then let it out! Honestly, I wish I'd just feel better."

Hesitantly, for Feliz was not at all sure how Carrie would accept the idea, she asked, "Do you think you might be with child? How long since your last time of bleeding?"

Carrie sat as if struck by lightning. Could it be! Incensed that she did not conceive, Noah had hounded her about her periods. But last month about that time he had been so busy with his new stock detective, he had scarcely talked to her. Now, when he entered her room late at night, he bedded her in grim silence and mercifully it was over quickly. Both of them had been too preoccupied to think about pregnancy.

In reply to Feliz's query she said, "I missed last month." Calculating in her mind, she couldn't believe her lethargic depression over Hawk's desertion had caused her to overlook something so obvious. Feliz's next question cut into her thoughts, scattering them.

"When was your last time before that?"

"About two weeks before . . ." she started to say, before Hawk left. *Before Hawk made love to me.* Could it be? She would be almost three months along then.

Feliz watched the varying play of emotions cross Carrie's lovely, pale face. "Before what, niña?"

Carrie shook herself. "I mean, I missed two times, I guess. Oh, Feliz do you really think it's true? The nausea, the weight gain, the missed courses."

"Do you want it to be true, Carrie?" Feliz's lined brown face was a study in kindly concern.

"Yes, oh, yes." Really, she did want it to be. Even though it was Noah's child, it would mean that he would leave her alone. If she gave him a son, he would probably never put his hands on her again. That would be reward enough. But what if—against all likelihood—it was Hawk's child? The thought at first thrilled her. Then she reconsidered. If so, would it look like him, bear the unmistakable stamp of Cheyenne blood? Noah would kill her, and probably the child, too.

"What is wrong, Carrie?" Feliz watched Carrie clutch at her heart and grow pale.

Looking up at her friend's face, Carrie sat mute while Feliz clucked over her. *I can tell no one such a secret, not even Feliz.* Besides, it was a very thin chance that the baby would be her love's.

Perhaps the child would resemble her, with red hair and green eyes. Then Noah would never know he had been betrayed. However, she would not know who the father was either. But if the baby was dark with black hair and eyes, everyone would be shocked. Even though she knew it spelled disaster, Carrie hugged the idea to her heart. She desperately wanted this baby to be Hawk's.

Hawk, where are you? Come home to me.

Carrie sat at the dining-room table across from Noah. The magnificent emerald necklace and earrings she wore lay ice cold against her skin, a gift from her delighted

husband when she told him of her pregnancy. It was
March, and she was showing quite a bit, making her feel
uncomfortable dressed formally for dinner. However, Noah
insisted, just as he insisted she have a dozen elaborate
high-waisted gowns sewn by Mrs. Grummond and that she
wear the expensive jewels tonight.

She felt suffocated despite the cold. Winter held the
landscape outside in its snowy thrall, but the room seemed
unaccountably warm. *Guilt. That's why I'm always so
uncomfortable around him now.* At least he had mercifully
abandoned her bed once Dr. Lark confirmed her quickening.
Recalling the doctor's degrading examination, she shuddered
in revulsion. He had even acted surprised that she was
with child, after he himself had pronounced her physically
sound, Carrie thought in disgust.

"Something wrong, my dear? Is it too cold in here? I'll
have Feliz bring you some hot tea." Now that she had
done her duty and was breeding, Noah was all solicitude,
lavishing unwanted gifts on her and treating her with
unusual concern.

The only thing Carrie wanted from him was that he
never put his hands on her again. *Please, God, let it be a
boy.* It was her nightly litany. She suppressed the question
of the child's paternity since nothing could change the
outcome of her pregnancy. After so many nights with
Noah and only one with Hawk, it was most likely that the
baby was her husband's. It would be a yellow-haired,
fair-complected Sinclair. *But what if it is Cheyenne?* The
thought terrified yet tantalized her. She wanted it to be born
of love and joy, not of hate and ugliness. There was no
answer. Carrie lived from day to day, waiting.

Noah came around the table and pulled out her chair.
Awkwardly she rose. At nearly six months, she was not
overly big, but she felt exceedingly self-conscious in Noah's
proprietary presence. *The hypocrite.* She grew to hate his
solicitude more than she had his sneers.

"I'm very tired, Noah. If you don't mind, I'll take my
tea with Feliz and then retire for the night." She could not
bear another evening in the parlor with him drinking and
brooding while he schemed with that hateful gunman

Caleb Rider. She felt "range detective" was just a euphe-
mism for their late-evening visitor. Carrie hated his veiled,
lascivious eyes. There was also the matter of their business
dealings. They spoke of cattle sales, of moving stock to
the east and selling it quickly. She understood little of
Circle S operations, but it sounded suspicious to her, as if
they were handling stolen livestock. But that surely must
be absurd.

Noah nodded in irritation at her request to be excused,
but said nothing. Humor the chit. Soon she would have his
heir, a son worthy of the Sinclair name. Scowling at her
fondness for socializing with servants, he bade her good
night. "For all she can't abide Mrs. Thorndyke, she sure is
fond of that greaser cook," he muttered in vexation, then
swore and went into the parlor to await Caleb. The hell
with his wife and her idiosyncrasies.

Every time Caleb Rider came up to the big house, he
concealed his awe behind a facade of nonchalance. He had
never seen anything like the gleaming furniture and crystal, the gold and silver appointments, the thick carpets,
and French wallpaper. Damnation, the old man had money!

Then there was the matter of his wife. Succulent piece
of womanflesh. Of course, swelled up now, she had
temporarily lost her appeal, but Rider remembered how
her tall, slim form had looked when he first met her last
winter. Shame, a beautiful young woman married to such
an old geezer. But then, all the more reason for her to
appreciate Caleb Rider when he decided to make a move
on her. He could wait.

"Whiskey or brandy?" Noah inquired almost genially.

"Whiskey," Rider replied. Looking around to be certain
they were alone, he said, "I got that small herd out of the
basin and sold them yesterday. Neat profit."

"Next time, we'll go after bigger fish. I understand Herr
Krueger has brought some fine-blooded breeding stock
from Oregon, at least a dozen stud bulls. Ought to be
worth a bundle if your contacts on K Bar can get them
away." Noah looked at Rider as he handed him the glass.

Rider accepted it and took a sip, then said, "We may
have us a problem, boss."

Noah looked up, his face wary now. "What?"

"Your foreman, Lowery, he's been doing some snooping, I think. Caught him up by Krueger's property line, looking over the mixed herds there, where I cut all the K Bar stock out last month after that storm."

"So you think he's suspicious?" Noah's eyes were cold. He and Frank Lowery went back a lot of years. The man was a top ramrod. He was also a shrewd son of a bitch who just might create some really serious trouble. Noah swore. Damn the fool! He had always known that his foreman had been in love with Marah. Why Frank stayed on after she died, he never understood, but until now he had been glad of it. However, if Frank tried to expose Noah Sinclair as a rustler, he would die for his trouble.

Frank Lowery let out a sharp volley of oaths as he stood up and brushed the dust from the knee of his pants. Clear sign, all right. There was no doubt about it. That sharpie range detective—Frank snorted in disgust at the title—was stealing Karl Krueger blind. At least one hundred head of prime K Bar stock had been taken off this range in the past couple of days, run in with Circle S cattle and driven east, probably to meet with some Dakota buyer who wasn't particular about previous ownership and who quickly drove them to the railhead for sale.

Frank had followed Rider's comings and goings for over a month now and knew his horse's prints. No doubt about who led the strange riders to the herd and helped them drive it off. These tracks were damning evidence. Caleb was guilty, but was he working for himself or for Noah? Much as Frank would have liked to believe otherwise for Carrie's sake, he strongly suspected Noah had ordered the thievery. Too many times this spring he had watched his employer ride out with the gunman. Noah had not been present at this operation, but doubtless he knew about it.

As he mounted and headed slowly back toward Circle S, the old foreman mulled over what he should do. Lay a trap for Rider and catch him red-handed? If he did that, Rider might implicate his boss and then Carrie would face the humiliation of seeing the father of her unborn child hang for rustling. Much as she might be better off with Noah dead, that was not the way to handle it! Circle S was her child's inheritance, and Frank would not jeopardize it. He wished Noah would show as much concern. If Sinclair continued this war with Krueger, one of them would destroy the other. He cursed roundly. If innocent people weren't their victims, they could fight to the death for all he cared and the devil take all the cattle and land in Montana Territory.

Lowery thought back over the years he had worked for Noah Sinclair. The man had more than any one human ever deserved—a fabulously successful ranch, a position of prestige and power in the territory. Most importantly of all, he had been gifted with two lovely, spirited wives, a splendid son, and another child on the way. Why was nothing ever enough for some men?

Grimly, he decided he would confront Noah as soon as he had enough evidence. If nothing else, he would blackmail the son of a bitch into stopping this madness.

As Frank crossed the stream, swollen with melted snow, he decided to stop for a cooling drink. It was an unseasonably warm May, and he was thirsty. Born in the dry country southwest of Texas, Frank had always loved the sweet abundant water of Montana. He drank deeply and wiped his mouth with the back of his hand. Ah, it was so good. It was the last sensation he ever felt. The rifle slug hit him cleanly in the back of the head, killing him instantly and propelling his lanky body face downward in the clean, rushing waters, now pink with his blood.

Hank Allen found Frank the next afternoon, far over on a deserted stretch of the northeastern range adjoining Krueger's place. Noah stormed and swore vengeance, laying the blame on K Bar men. Of course, Krueger denied it and nothing could be proven.

Carrie grieved as if her own father had died. Kyle and Hawk were gone, and now Frank; only Feliz remained as her friend in this hostile wilderness.

Living with gnawing guilt and fear about the baby's paternity, Carrie had been ill and depressed during the whole of her pregnancy. Dr. Lark had assured her last week that she had only another six weeks to go. She was huge now. Walking was tiring, and when as she lay down to rest, the baby moved and kept her awake, she could hardly wait until her child was born.

Considering her rounded belly, she thought to herself, *Despite my guilt and even the fear of what Noah would do, I want you to be his, not my husband's. Am I really so wantonly wicked?* She shook her head sadly. Realizing it was far more likely to be Noah's child, she vowed to love the baby anyway, regardless of how much she had grown to hate and mistrust the father.

Frank's death had thrown her into bleak depression, and Mrs. Thorndyke's hovering malevolence continued to cast a pall over the house. Carrie had finally concluded the old woman was deranged, imagining herself to be mistress of Circle S all the years since she had been hired as a housekeeper. If Mrs. Thorndyke wasn't so mean-spirited and filled with hate, Carrie would actually have felt pity for the woman who counted the silverware as conscientiously as if it were her own. She had accepted the news of Carrie's pregnancy resentfully and watched with stiffly repressed jealousy as the young woman's belly grew. The child cemented Carrie's position at Circle S. No matter how Carrie and Noah hated one another, if she gave him a white son, the boy would inherit everything and Carrie would live out her days as mistress of the Sinclair empire.

Carrie sat in the flower garden, on the very bench where Hawk had found her weeping that night. Since the weather had become pleasant, she had come there every afternoon to watch the spring flowers grow and to feel in some small way close to her lost love. She had never again gone into his old room. It would have been too painful and certainly would have aroused suspicions if she had been found there.

Until yesterday the room had been closed up without having been cleaned. Noah had announced at dinner last night that it would make a good room for the nurse he planned to hire for his son. Today Mrs. Thorndyke was in there sorting through Hawk's things, directing the maids in their task of scrubbing years' worth of dust and neglect.

Carrie's heart ached as she thought of Hawk's things being thrown away, displaced as carelessly as he had been. Circle S should belong to Noah's firstborn, and here she was, the very instrument of his disinheritance. How sadly ironic. Her pensive spell was shattered by Mrs. Thorndyke's clipped nasal voice.

"Mr. Noah wants to see you in his study, right now." The feral gleam in her eyes brightened them from their usual stone-gray flatness to an almost whitish-silver shine. Her whole face radiated triumphant hate. She stood over Carrie as if restraining an impulse to pounce and disembowel her prey.

Realizing the hateful woman was waiting until she did as ordered, Carrie got up. The hair on the back of her neck prickled in warning. What was going on to make the housekeeper so agitated and gloating? Why did Noah want to see her in midafternoon?

Slowly, feet dragging, she walked toward the house with a terrible foreboding filling her breast. Mrs. Thorndyke followed her like a shadow. When Carrie reached the door to Noah's office, she turned to dismiss her jailor, but something in the woman's facial expression stopped her. Stepping inside, she simply shut the door in the housekeeper's face.

"You wanted to see me, Noah?" Her voice was level and calm despite her strong sense of unease.

When he turned from the window and faced her, she gasped and took a step back, trapped against the door. Using it to steady herself, she met his piercing stare. His face was not triumphant like Mrs. Thorndyke's, but furious in cold, murderous rage. Carrie had lived with Noah's moods long enough to recognize that.

He took several steps across the room until he stood at arm's length from her. "Yes, my darling wife. I have something to show you." He paused, then reached in his pocket and pulled out a soiled length of ribbon. Loose, fluffy bits of dust clung to its satiny length. It had once been bright orange. "Recognize this?" His voice was almost silky.

She reached for it almost involuntarily, baffled. "Yes,

it's off my white silk night rail. I never found it. You tore it—Oh! Last fall . . .'' Her voice trailed away as a dawning horror began to choke her throat. "Where—''

"Where did I find it? I didn't. Mrs. Thorndyke did—under Hawk's bed!" Each word cracked like a whiplash in the hot, still room. His eyes riveted her to the door like barbed arrows. "Care to hazard any guesses as to how it got there? Let's see, it must have been eight or nine months ago, somewhere around the time you conceived that.'' He suddenly placed one hand on her belly, pressing until he could feel the baby kick.

Carrie thought her knees would surely buckle when he removed his clawlike fingers. Her thoughts whirled in a maelstrom of frantic confusion. "But how? I don't know! *You* tore it loose.''

How vividly that ugly memory stuck with her after all this time, right alongside the beautiful memory of how gently Hawk had taken the gown from her later that same night. Her cheeks flooded with incriminating crimson as she stood mute and frozen.

"I may have torn it loose, but my son,'' he spat the word like an oath, "seems to have pulled it free. No doubt as he bared these for his pleasure!" With that he grasped her breasts in his hands and cruelly pinched the nipples, grinding her swollen breasts against her ribs until she gasped in breathless pain.

"Don't, please, don't hurt the baby, Noah!" The plea was torn from her.

He jerked his hands away as if she were a leper. "The baby, yes! *Whose* baby seems to be the question. Well, whose is it? Am I to be a father or grandfather? Or do you even know!"

As she struggled to regain her breath, Carrie choked out, "It must be yours, Noah. After all the times, surely it is. I was only with him one night, just one—''

He hit her then, so hard she saw an explosion of red and yellow light behind her eyes and the room began to grow dim. She could hear his voice, raised from its low, cold pitch to full-blown screaming rage now. "So, you expect me to thank you for only cuckolding me one time! You filthy slut! What is it about women and that goddamned stinking savage! You, so cold and prim, so innocent, as different from Lola as day from night, and still you went to him! Was it really only one night, or were there others? Why the hell should I believe you!''

''Because it's true,'' she ground out, struggling to stay on her feet and clear her spinning head. God, if she fell, he might turn on her like a wolf on a downed deer, tearing her limb from limb! ''That's why he left the next morning. We both knew it could go no further. We never intended for it to happen.''

As he stared into her clear green eyes, full of fear, yet also hinting at a resolute, growing strength, he began to regain some semblance of control over his raging emotions. Yes, she was probably telling him the truth. She had never been good at hiding her feelings or dissembling. More likely the child was his.

He took a long breath. ''We'll just have to wait and see, won't we, dear wife?'' His eyes were calm and calculating. He had a position to consider in the territory. After his fiasco with Lola, he would not have another wayward wife. ''Yes, I'll know when the child is born if it's Indian or not. If it's mine, and a boy, I'll allow you to live here, with proper guardianship, of course. If it's a girl, I'll get you breeding again.'' He paused and reached out to stroke her face, which was beginning to swell and discolor from his blow. ''But, oh my dear, if the little bastard is a filthy redskin I will personally kill you both. You have my word on it!''

CHAPTER 16

Wind Song awoke to the sound of spring birds. The sun was bright, but the breeze brisk and cool, for the last of the snows were only now leaving the valley. It was a glorious day—their wedding day. Her elkskin dress, tanned soft as butter, trimmed with elaborate rows of gleaming elkteeth, lay before her. Lovingly, she ran her fingers over its rich folds. She had already sent her wedding gift to Hawk, a magnificent shirt of antelope hide, painstakingly worked with porcupine quills.

Eagerly she awaited Sweet Rain and Calf Woman, who were to assist her in the ritual preparations for her wedding night. First she would go to the women's sweat lodge, then bathe in the icy stream. Her hair would be freshly washed and perfumed and she would be dressed in her finery. The Cheyenne had no marriage ceremony as such. The relatives of the bride simply carried her to her bridegroom on a new blanket, depositing her at the door of their new lodge. Iron Heart would stand in place of her father, imparting his unspoken blessing on their union this night. She knew the day would seem endless.

Hawk, too, thought of the night to come as he dove into the breathtakingly cold water. Over and over he told himself he was doing the right thing. Every time he saw Angry Wolf and felt his silent hate, he knew Wind Song was well rid of the cruel warrior. *But you don't love her.* His conscience would not leave him in peace. He rationalized

233

his answer as he had thousands of times before in the past
five weeks. He would learn to love her. They would share
a life together, children; he would belong. Lord knew,
Wind Song loved enough for both of them. Secure in
that fact, he let the old arguments die and busily began
drying himself.

That night, when he stepped out of their new lodge to
watch the bevy of giggling women and girls leave Wind
Song in front of him, he was aware of Iron Heart's smiling
benediction. The tall old man stood beside his adopted
daughter, beaming as she looked up into Hawk's eyes. Her
face was alight with love. Hawk reached down and took
her hands in his, pulling her up to stand in front of him.
He embraced her, and they were considered from hence-
forth husband and wife.

The feasting, dancing, and celebrating lasted far into the
night. Hawk and Wind Song did not stay long, but soon
departed for the privacy of their lodge. Once inside, he
turned to her and stood looking at her startling beauty. In
the softly flickering light from the firepit, her coppery skin
glowed in warm, flawless perfection. Her high cheekbones
and slanted brows gave her face a strong, austere appearance, but her lovely, curving smile softened the effect. He
took one long, gleaming braid in his fingers and felt its
sleek weight. Raising it to his lips, he kissed it. Looking
deeply into her eyes, he could see her soul laid bare. Did
his own eyes reveal as much?

Wind Song felt shy now, eager to please her new
husband but uncertain of what to do. Several of the older
women of the village had taken her aside and instructed
her in the basics of sex. She was to do as he asked, but
doubts assailed her. He had lived among the whites, and
she was sure he had lain with many white women. Did
they act differently? Please him more than she could? She
smiled at his tender gesture with her hair.

Hawk sensed her nervousness. He knew she had never
been with a man and was unsure of what he would do to
her. He could only surmise what those old women had
told her, probably only the most rote mechanical aspects of
consummating a marriage. A great warmth stole over him

as he gazed at her dusky loveliness. For all his women, white or red, she was his first virgin.

Taking a plump braid in each hand, he drew her close to him. Then he put one arm around her back and took her chin in his free hand, tipping her face up to meet his eyes. Slowly, he lowered his lips and kissed her, a light brushing motion, meant to reassure and warm her. He let his lips travel across her cheek, over her ear to nibble on one earlobe, then trail soft, wet kisses down her neck.

Offering her face and neck joyously to his mouth, Wind Song leaned toward him. Tentatively she placed her hands on his shoulders. As his embrace tightened, drawing her snugly against him, she naturally wrapped her arms around his neck, straining closer and closer.

Hawk murmured her name, then slowly drew her down to the luxurious pile of buffalo robes and rich pelts that would be their bridal bed. "Loose your hair. I want to feel it in my hands," he whispered hoarsely, caressing her face with one hand while gazing into her eyes.

Kneeling next to him, she complied, unplaiting first one, then the other braid. Her mass of midnight hair was dense and shiny, falling straight and long to her waist. When it was all free, she shook her head and tossed it back, facing him proudly.

"You are very beautiful," he said softly, burying his face and hands in her hair, clasping her to him as they knelt on the bed. He kissed her once more, this time using his tongue to trace delicate patterns on her lips until she parted them in a gasp of wonder. He emitted a barely audible groan and slipped his tongue into her mouth.

As he teased and caressed her soft inner cheeks, tongue, and teeth, Wind Song found herself clinging to him, opening her mouth freely, wanting more of these incredible sensations. Her hand moved from his shoulder, where she could feel his muscles flex as he held her, to steal down to his chest. Ever since the first time she had seen him, she had wanted to feel that exotic mat of black curly hair growing there.

His shirt was open. She stroked the hard, furry surface

and was startled to feel the pounding of his heart. It matched her own, which was thrumming a furious beat.

Hawk intensified the kiss and felt her response. Gradually he broke the joining of the kiss to unfasten her dress. As he unlaced the elaborate ties, he whispered, "The dress is beautiful, but I know what it hides is even more beautiful." When he freed the last laces, he reached inside and lightly touched the dark brown tip of one proudly upthrust young breast. The nipple instantly hardened.

Wind Song let out a soft, startled gasp at the electric pleasure it gave her. When he used both hands to cup and fondle her breasts, she became dizzy with the wild new sensations he was evoking. Her own hands kneaded frantic patterns across his chest, fingers busily weaving in and out of its black hairy covering.

"Raise your arms and let me take this off." He held the heavy dress in his hands.

Obediently she complied, helping him free her hair when it became entangled in the laces. She knelt before him, clad only in soft leggings and moccasins now. His eyes glowed with frank admiration as he swept them across her straight shoulders, high-pointed breasts, and long, narrow waist.

"Lay back, love." Carefully he lay her onto the mound of pelts, then caressed down her sides with both hands. His fingertips glided over her sleek hips, slim and shapely, then down to begin unfastening her leggings. As he unlaced, he stroked and petted her silky flesh, until finally she lay naked before him.

"Do I please you?" Her voice was hesitant as she lay so vulnerable, watching his eyes travel up and down her body.

"Yes, Wind Song, yes, you please me," he replied hoarsely.

In a few swift motions he slipped his heavy leather shirt and pants from his body and kicked away his moccasins. Wind Song watched his lean, hard muscles ripple as he shed his clothing. She wanted to touch every inch of his body, to feel the sinewy, hairy texture of him.

Before her eyes could drink their fill, he rolled down

beside her and took her gently in his arms. His hands seemed to be everywhere, stroking, caressing, petting her back, flanks, buttocks, breasts, belly. All the while he kissed her feverishly, drawing her hesitant tongue from her mouth into his to explore and delight them both.

After a lengthy period of mutual caressing and exploration, he slowly but firmly took one of her hands and guided it downward to grasp his hard, pulsing sex. In complete trust, she allowed him to guide her, stroking up and down until he arched and gasped in ecstatic need. He released her busy hand and placed his own between her legs to test her readiness. There was little need, for she was slippery, wet and open. Her legs spread eagerly, instinctively, to welcome him. Slowly he rolled her on her back and raised himself above her.

Exerting iron control, he slowly began to push inside her eagerly welcoming flesh. Meeting resistance, he paused and kissed her with searing intensity, running one hand along her side, up and over her breast, then back down her thigh. Gradually he increased the even, gentle pressure of his shaft, waiting for any signals that he was hurting her.

Wind Song only knew she wanted him close to her, wanted some unknown, desperate hunger appeased. She arched and bucked, causing him to break her maidenhead and slide inside her in one swift, clean thrust. She gasped at the stab of pain, small and quickly gone. He was buried deep within her now, and it began to feel wonderful.

Hawk took several deep breaths, desperate not to rush and spill his seed before he could bring her to pleasure with him. She seemed eager for his caresses, not at all in pain after that one small gasp. Very slowly he thrust up and down, then repeated the motion until she joined in the natural rhythm. He murmured soft, indistinct love words, urging her on, kissing her eyes, temples, mouth, and neck as he stroked in increasingly hard thrusts, faster and surer.

Wind Song held on to him in mindless pleasure, until she felt a swift contracting that blinded her with its unexpected ecstasy. As it widened out in scorching ripples, she cried his name and held fiercely to him, feeling him stiffen and swell, gasping in the same startled awe.

He covered her with his body, protectively, realizing for the first time what this meant. He was her husband, her lover, her provider. He must dedicate himself to her alone for the rest of his life. Smiling, he kissed his bride lightly on the tip of her nose and rolled to his back, drawing her to lay beside him.

She did not want him to leave her flesh, and felt empty when he withdrew. But snuggled securely against his side, she found a perfect niche in the curve of his shoulder as he put his arm around her. He pulled a thick, soft buffalo robe across them and kissed her lips gently, saying, "Sleep, sweet wife."

Wind Song awoke at the first filtering light of dawn. Feeling Hawk's warm, hard body beside her, she snuggled closer to him, reveling in the glorious memories of the preceding night. Slowly, so as not to awaken him, she turned and raised her head, propping it up with one hand as she lay on her side. Looking down on his sleeping face, she studied it carefully. The black bristle of whiskers had magically sprouted across his jaw once more. Gingerly, she reached up and stroked them, recalling that first time in the woods when she had spied on him as he shaved.

Suddenly he reached up and caught her caressing, curious fingers in his hand. As his eyes opened to look into her startled face, he smiled and said, "Does my beard displease you? It's part of my white half. I cannot change it."

Wind Song leaned over and planted a lingering kiss on his mouth, then brushed her lips back and forth across his bristling whiskers in light, teasing motions. Breathlessly she said, "There is nothing about you that does not please me, my husband."

"Is that so," he replied, rolling up and over her, swooping down to continue their kiss in a more serious fashion.

It was finally spring in the Yellowstone country, and Iron Heart's band was preparing to move from its winter camp grounds to the site where the summer gathering of Cheyenne bands would once more take place.

The Elk Warrior Society was in charge of the move to summer camp. Within the loose confederation of northern Cheyenne bands, there were three such societies, the Crazy Dogs, the Foxes, and the Elks. Most young men joined one of the groups at puberty and thus received their training as fighters and hunters. The societies organized the communal hunts, conducted the moves from camp to camp, and organized the defense when villages were attacked.

Hawk had not lived with Iron Heart's band long enough as a youth to be initiated into any of the societies. His grandfather was one of the few ruling chiefs who had not chosen to join a society. A wise leader and brave fighter could be selected as a chief without belonging to such a fraternity. Being a natural loner, Hawk was just as happy to follow his grandfather's way regarding the societies. He had no illusion that he could become a chief; his mixed blood and a childhood and youth spent mostly away from the tribe would prevent it. However, as he did not wish to lead, this did not trouble him.

He did resent Angry Wolf's authoritarian behavior, however. Angry Wolf was the leader of the Elk Warrior Society and was taking full advantage of his position to show off before the group. When Hawk wed Wind Song, Angry Wolf had lost considerable face, since everyone knew he had offered for her and been refused. He brooded and waited for his chance at revenge.

Within a month of the marriage, he could see all was not going well between the newlyweds. Hawk became more reserved and brooding, frequently going off to hunt alone for several days at a time. Wind Song went about her chores in subdued silence.

The rift had begun over a foolish woman's matter. Little Bright Leaf was always chattering about her time with the *veho*. One day Angry Wolf overheard her telling Sweet Rain that the fire-haired wife of He Who Walks In Sun did not wish to be married to the old man. The child also observed how splendid Hunting Hawk and Carrie looked together and how they had laughed and talked in the white man's language when she was with them. When Carrie's husband died—for he seemed very old to a seven-year-old girl—Carrie could come to live with the People and be Hawk's second wife. That was sufficient to start Angry Wolf thinking.

He approached Wind Song the next day and mentioned the child's prattle, tauntingly inquiring if she would mind sharing her half-blooded husband with another woman who was all white. She vehemently denied the possibility that Hawk would take his father's wife. It was indecent. But Angry Wolf could tell his barb had struck home. She had already been listening to the child and to other talk about the mysterious flaming one whose exotic beauty had stirred such a furor when she had come to the village last summer. The seeds had been planted. Angry Wolf watched while they grew.

Wind Song was confused and melancholy. Before Hawk returned to live with the People, she already knew about Carrie. Bright Leaf had talked about little else, always singing the praises of her beautiful white friend and linking her to Hawk in the innocent manner of a child. But when she began to fantasize about Carrie's being Hawk's wife, Wind Song was devastated.

She had been lost from the first moment she had seen him, fascinated by his handsome foreignness, then in love with his strength, humor, and intelligence. She had always heard white men took only one wife. If Hawk chose her, would he be true to the *veho* way, or follow the Cheyenne custom? She loved him so desperately and had begun to dream of finding her singular love returned. Now she could not bear the thought of sharing him, or worse yet if his white soul so dictated, losing him altogether to the firehaired one.

Last fall he had come to live with the People, full of some nameless hurt that had driven him away from his father's place. He had not sought her out as she had so fervently prayed for, but had kept to himself until her father's death and her own bold words to him this spring. Did he love his father's wife? She, Wind Song, was his wife, yet Hawk had never told her that he loved her. Even before Angry Wolf's jeering insinuations, Wind Song had harbored secret doubts.

One day she awakened to hear him tossing in his sleep, crying out indistinct words in the white tongue. Most she could not understand, but a few she knew—the names of Carrie and Noah! The next morning she worked up her courage to speak some of what was burning in her heart.

"Do white men love their women more than Cheyenne?"

He was shaving, a morning ritual he performed in the confines of their lodge, not wanting everyone to observe this necessity brought about by his white heredity. Slowing the deft strokes of the razor, he replied, "What makes you ask that?"

"My father had two wives, my mother and her sister. He was always kind to them, but when they died, well, I just never thought he was nearly as saddened as he was when my brother died. I—I just wondered what you had observed in their world."

Thinking of Noah and how he treated his wives, Hawk grimaced. "I think it depends on the man, Wind Song. Some Cheyenne love their wives and daughters. Some white men don't. Love is love, red or white."

"I do not think so. If a white man may take only one wife, he must value her . . . differently." She floundered for a way to direct her questions without being so obvious. *Do you love me, Hunting Hawk?*

He smiled despite the sadness in his eyes. "Is that why you married me, Wind Song? For my white half?"

Taking a deep breath, she said, "I love you because you are Hawk. No other reason. If half of you is white, half is Cheyenne. I love all of you."

"But you're afraid I'll take a second wife like your father did?" He wiped his face free of soap and stepped over to take her in his arms. "Don't be. I will have no other wife."

"No Cheyenne wife," she said, stung despite his assurances because he still had not told her he loved her.

"What is that supposed to mean?" His face became shuttered.

"Nothing," she murmured quickly, realizing she could not bear to hear the truth. She held on to him tightly, kissing his neck and rubbing her face on his hairy chest. Even as they embraced, they both knew what lay unspoken between them.

As the weeks passed, Hawk busied himself hunting, often staying away overnight. When he slept by their hearth, sharing her bed, Wind Song often heard his nightmares. Sometimes he would awaken and reach out to her for solace in the darkness. Other times she would stop his cries with her mouth, willing him to forget the past and the white woman who called to him.

One day when Hawk was away, after Angry Wolf's hateful words to her, Wind Song sought out Iron Heart in his lodge. With a leaden heart, the shrewd old man listened to her, knowing what she was leading up to with her carefully chosen words. She had the right to know the truth, he finally concluded sadly.

"You must be patient and hold your love for him strongly, Wind Song. In time he will grow to love you, too. He has much to learn of love and belonging. All his life has been spent being pulled in two directions at once."

She swallowed, nervously fingering the long fringes of her tunic sleeve. "He is still pulled to them, to *her*."

They both knew who the "her" was. He sighed and puffed on his pipe as he considered what to tell her. "Be secure in knowing this. She is lost to him forever. Not only is she wife to his own father, but now she carries the father's child."

Wind Song's head flew up. "Does Hawk know this?"

"I told him. It was a hard thing to accept, but in time he will know his bond to her is forever broken. You must give him unconditional love. Do not let outsiders come between you; not Angry Wolf, not even the harmless words of a child."

With tears in her eyes, Wind Song nodded. He was wise, knowing the doubts that assailed her from so many quarters. "I will never stop loving him, Grandfather. Do not fear."

Through the summer, Wind Song used every opportunity to draw Hawk to her for making love. She offered her body. She knew it pleased him and fulfilled his male needs, and she prayed he would quickly plant his seed in her. If they had a child, he would sooner forget Carrie Sinclair.

Then one night in the midst of fierce, wild passion, as he spilled himself deeply inside his wife's body, he cried out Carrie's name. The instant it happened he knew what he had done.

For months he had tried to block Carrie from his mind, but found, perversely, as the time for her travail neared he thought more and more about her being delivered of Noah's child. The surcease he found in Wind Song's embrace was sweet but fleeting. He took her often, feverishly spending his frustration in passion, only to have Carrie's tear-ravaged face haunt him afterward. Now he had done that which he dreaded above all else.

He looked down at his wife's stricken face. Her huge green eyes were dark with pain and unshed tears. Gently he withdrew from her and rolled over onto his back. After a minute, he reached over and stroked her cheek. She flinched and turned her eyes away.

"You look into my eyes and you see hers. You caress my body and you feel hers." Her words were spoken rapidly in a soft, low voice, thick with tears.

He lay still, his thoughts in turmoil, his spirit crushed with guilt and remorse.

"Did—did you ever lay with her?" There, it was spoken. She had to know.

"One night," came the dreaded answer. "Since our marriage I have touched no other woman," he added softly, defensively.

With rising anger, she replied, "I would understand if you went to the harlot's lodge outside our village when I am in the moon hut. That is a man's physical need only, but your very faithfulness mocks me. I have your body, but she has your soul!"

"Wind Song, I am sorry. I have never meant to hurt you," he said helplessly, watching the crystalline tears stream down her cheeks. "You asked me once if I would

ever take a second wife. I said no. I meant it then and I
mean it now, but maybe I am more Cheyenne than white.''
He continued stroking her cheek, drying the trail of her
tears with his fingertips.

She turned her face to him once more, a puzzled
expression shadowing it. ''What do you mean?''

''I will not lie to you. I fell in love with my father's
wife. Maybe part of me will always love her. I do not
know. But she is forbidden to me. I need love, a woman of
my own. You have given me the treasure of your heart. I
will not cast it away. I will learn to love you, Wind Song.
Perhaps I already love two women, as is the Cheyenne
way. But you are my only wife. This I swear to you.''

She turned swiftly into his waiting arms, sheltered,
comforted, crying. ''I will make you love me, Hawk. This
I swear to you!''

CHAPTER
17

Carrie lived in hellish misery during the weeks following her confrontation with Noah. Mrs. Thorndyke, the only other person who knew the scandalous secret, hovered like a miasmic fog, filling the house with her spite. Carrie became a virtual prisoner. Noah ordered the housekeeper to bring her meals to her room, allowing her one brief spell of exercise each afternoon when he accompanied her on a walk through the garden. Other than that, she was confined to the house and watched by the housekeeper every waking moment. Each night a cowboy guarded the French doors to her room. Noah told them Carrie, fretful and imaginative as her confinement neared, was worried a thief would try to break in.

To avoid suspicion and scandal, Carrie was allowed to visit with Feliz and her daughter, Estrella, but that was the extent of her freedom. *He is afraid I'll run off, in my condition*, she thought to herself in hysterical amazement. As if she had anywhere to go. Numbly, she waited.

Carrie thought of confiding in Feliz, but decided it would only add to her burdens uselessly. She was as powerless in the household as Carrie. Now that Frank was dead and Hawk and Kyle gone, no one could challenge Noah and his angel of wrath, Mrs. Thorndyke.

The doctor, Feliz and Estrella would be present when the child was born. Surely Noah could not hope to silence them all, even if the child was Cheyenne. No, he would throw her out, destitute and disgraced, but he could not possibly carry out his threat to kill her and her child. Praying this was true, she spent the last weeks of her pregnancy caged up in the ranch house, desperate in fear and loneliness.

Oh, Hawk, why did you leave me? I would have gone anywhere with you.

In mid July since Carrie showed no signs of being ready to deliver, Noah decided to go to Miles City on an overnight business trip. She felt more at ease, even if Mrs. Thorndyke and her guards did not relent in their vigil.

With a good thick steak and six shots of whiskey under his belt, Noah felt better than he had in a long time. Now he lay back on the red velvet of Charlene's bed watching her undress. She was Clancey's fanciest whore, and Clancey's was the best house in town. What a piece! Her long yellow hair hung in curls across her large, heavy breasts. Her round hips were soft and white, inviting his hands to pinch and squeeze the marshmallowy flesh. She posed and pouted, playing her striptease for all it was worth, tantalizing him as he enjoyed the show. He knew what she would do next.

She sauntered boldly to the bed and began stroking his partially erect shaft. She scolded, teasingly, "Too much likker makes ole Jack here a bad boy. I'm just gonna have ta punish him." She lowered her thick, reddened lips and opened her mouth to envelope him.

Noah relaxed, then tensed as she began her skilled ministrations. Finally, as the whiskey wore off, he impatiently grabbed her and rolled her on her back, pulling the interfering remnants of his clothes from his body. Then he straddled her and plunged into the dark nest of curls, panting heavily with his exertions. Damn, it felt good to be in control. He had not done it this way in quite a while, but he was not so old yet he couldn't if he wanted to!

In midthrust, a sharp, tearing pain grabbed his chest, then another, in rhythmic, agonizing contractions, more regular than the ancient exercise he was performing. His skin grew suddenly wet and cold, and his arms felt numb. He was dizzy, so dizzy, and he heard Charlene's voice as if from a great distance. "You look funny, Noah, plumb peeked. Here, let me up."

"No, damn her!" The words rasped from his throat, ripped out on his last expelled breath. "I've got to— know—I . . ."

The sheriff rode out the next morning very early to break the news to the widow. He considered how best to tell the pretty young missus, her being pregnant and all. Word of the old cattle baron's demise in Charlene Creely's bed was already all over Miles City, and Sheriff Woods knew sooner or later she would hear the truth. Cowardly, he decided it would not be from him. As gently as he could, he told her that her husband had suffered a heart attack and had died instantly. Doc Lark had confirmed it.

Rather than the hysteria he expected, given her condition and all, the young widow simply asked, dry-eyed and calmly, where and how they had found him. After squirming for several seconds, Sheriff Woods coughed and said Mr. Sinclair had been upstairs in Clancey's place when he died. He reddened as soon as the words were out. Surely even a lady like this must know what kind of place Clancey ran.

Carrie did. But she also knew immense, triumphant relief. He was dead and her child was safe! She was safe. Thank God! It might be blasphemy to be grateful for her husband's death, but she could not stop the inadvertent silent prayer of thanks from escaping heavenward. It was ironic that Noah had died with one of his whores. Call her a whore for having one night of love with a man, would he? After all his nights at Clancey's and other places like it from Helena to Chicago, Carrie felt a tremendous satisfaction in knowing that the reputation he was always so concerned with had been ruined by his own actions, not hers.

However, as she was soon to find, there was a double standard for morality. Her lack of grief at his funeral shocked people. Indeed, her stoic dignity at the graveside service made tongues wag in the town. They were willing to forgive a man his little peccadilloes with Clancey's girls, especially considering his wife was so far along in her pregnancy. But for the young widow to be dry-eyed, calm, and radiantly beautiful, that was unnatural, sinful, wrong.

It was only the beginning of her conflict with the town. The day after the funeral, Carrie went to Jebediah Cooper's office and demanded the will be read. She had to know if Noah had done anything to jeopardize her position at Circle S or her child's birthright. In her heart of hearts, she wanted Noah's attorney to tell her that the ranch still went to Hawk. But that was not to be. Shortly after bringing her to Montana, Noah had had a new will drawn up. Everything went to her and her children. He had not changed it since learning of her relationship with his son. He did not plan to die, and doubtless intended to act only if the baby was not his, an unlikely event from all standpoints.

As the prim old lawyer read through the maze of legal jargon, translating to her as he moved along, Carrie could feel his disapproval. Here she was, widowed less than three days, brazenly sitting dry-eyed in his office. It was far too soon to read the will. Everything, of course, went to her. What was she afraid of? Surely not that Noah would have left anything to that half-breed son of his. Jebediah Cooper's sense of propriety was offended. The way he sat ramrod-straight in his chair and even the precise hold his fingers had on the legal document bespoke disdain. Upon finishing, he looked over his steel-rimmed spectacles and affixed her with his cold blue eyes. "I trust everything is quite clear? You and your child are sole heirs of Circle S and all Noah's holdings."

Carrie was not surprised that Hawk had been completely disinherited, not even that Frank Lowery had been omitted after all his years of faithful service. But even the fanatically loyal Mrs. Thorndyke was not given a dime. Noah had never rewarded those who served him, unless they were likely to provide him with a white heir, she thought with a trace of black humor.

"Since my husband left no provisions for those who worked for him many years, I wish to do so myself. Please have a five-thousand-dollar stipend drawn up for Mrs. Thorndyke and another for Feliz Mendoza. Oh, yes, please don't let anyone know I've added in these bequests, Mr. Cooper.''

"Ten thousand dollars is a lot of money, Mrs. Sinclair. But then, you are a very rich young woman now. I daresay you can be as generous as you like," he added piously.

As Carrie turned to leave, she paused for a moment and could not resist adding, "You will understand, I trust, if I decline to give a stipend to Charlene Creely?" *Or, on second thought, perhaps I should!* She swept out as gracefully as her enceinte condition permitted, leaving the emaciated old man agape with indignation.

When Carrie called Mrs. Thorndyke into the study the next morning to tell her of the inheritance, she had not expected gratitude, but the woman flew into such a rage, it took her aback nonetheless.

"After all my years here, running this house, putting up with that insolent savage and that Jameson tramp, this is my reward, a paltry five thousand dollars! You did this, you and that old man Cooper! How did you get him to change the will? Entice him like you did Noah or that Indian?"

"I did nothing to change the will. Mr. Cooper is quite impervious to my charms, I assure you, Mathilda," Carrie said dryly with more than a touch of asperity in her voice.

"You did! Mr. Noah would have provided for me, not you, you harlot! He knew you for what you are—"

"What I am," Carrie cut her off sharply, "is Noah Sinclair's widow. My child will inherit Circle S!" Carrie had already begun to think of the baby as hers alone, now that Noah was dead.

"It's not fair! He should have married me!" Mrs. Thorndyke fairly shrieked, then unexpectedly burst into tears, her bony fingers clutching the arms of the wooden chair on which she sat. "When that Indian died, he brought that tramp here, her with her fancy airs and flashy looks. I should have been his wife! I would have given him good, decent white children. She didn't, and you won't either. You never loved him, never, any of you. . . ." She subsided into wracking hiccups.

Shaken by the unforeseen revelation, Carrie stood up.

"No, Mathilda, I didn't love him. He forced me into a marriage I never wanted, but he didn't love me, either. I don't think Noah *could* love anyone," she added gently.

Mathilda Thorndyke sat rigidly straight on the chair, her face a hideous distortion as she cried, making no attempt to staunch the flow of self-pitying tears. She did not even hear Carrie's words or see her leave the room to fetch Feliz.

"Put her to bed and see if you can get her to drink something to make her sleep. When she's rational again, I'll have to dismiss her, I fear. I hadn't planned to fire her, but I think she's too unstable to keep on. The bequest should enable her to live in modest comfort."

"Yes, Carrie, I think you are right. That one is loco." Feliz tapped her head and shivered. "I will get a good, strong dose of sleeping powder."

"Thank you, my friend. I don't know how I'd survive if it weren't for you. Lord, I am tired this morning! I— Ooh!" Carrie whitened and doubled over in the midst of rubbing her temples with her fingers. Clutching her belly, she swayed toward a kitchen chair.

"Señora!" Feliz reverted to formality in her fright. "What is wrong? Is it the baby?" She rushed over and helped Carrie sit down.

"No, Dr. Lark said almost two more weeks. It can't be yet."

The older woman scoffed. "Pah! Men doctors. What do they know? A few days one way or the other, quien sabe?" She helped Carrie stand and said in a firm, no-nonsense voice. "Now it is you who will go to bed. I will send for the doctor at once."

Carrie managed the stairs and changed into her night-dress under Feliz's clucking ministrations. After the rotund Mexicana dispatched a hand to town for the doctor, Carrie's contractions began in earnest. At first they were widely spaced, allowing her time to think. Feliz, assuring her that moving would speed the delivery, supported her as they walked around the room. She considered names as she walked. Noah had already chosen Abel, for his long-dead brother. She had not been consulted. Because having a daughter meant submitting to his bestiality again, she had not wanted to think of girls' names, but had finally decided upon Naomi, for her mother. She never mentioned it to Noah, feeling sure he would be furious to even consider the prospect of a girl child.

Now, however, she could choose a son's name, also, if indeed the child was a boy. Of course, there was always the slim chance that it would not be Noah's child at all. That thought pleased her greatly, but she suppressed it, feeling certain she could not bear the disappointment if it proved to be wrong. "No matter if you are Noah's, I will love you and raise you to be a good, loving person. I swear it."

Feliz heard Carrie's whispered words. Just then another contraction came, and the cook held her hand until it passed. She felt such intense sorrow for this beautiful young woman, forced to endure Noah's attentions and now to go through the rigors of childbirth with no memories of joy and love to sustain her. *I only hope you can love the child of that devil-man.*

Mrs. Thorndyke sat forgotten in the study, wondering what was going on. Hearing all the commotion in the house, she finally brought herself under control and went into the hall, where she spied Estrella scurrying upstairs. Upon being told of the impending birth, she went to her room to wait. *Now we'll just see if it comes out white or red!*

By the time Dr. Lark arrived in late afternoon, Carrie's contractions were very close together. Sweat-soaked in the July heat, she dutifully followed Feliz's instructions, kneeling on the bed, panting, relaxing her body to flow with the contractions, not fighting them. It helped.

Overhearing Feliz speak to Carrie as he came in the door, the fat man frowned and set down his bag forcefully on the bedside table. "All right," he made a dismissing motion to the cook, "we've had enough of this superstitious nonsense. Get her to lie down and leave. I'll call you when you are needed."

Carrie's contraction was over, and she looked gratefully at her friend, who was lovingly sponging her face and neck with a cool cloth. "Please, doctor, I want her to stay. She won't be in the way." Now that she was lying on her back, the pain seemed greater.

He harrumphed noisily as he opened his bag. "Just see to it that you listen to me and not that gibberish," he said pompously.

Carrie looked past him and winked at Feliz, who grinned and said, "I will fetch more clean water and linens. I think you will need them soon." With that she vanished out the door.

"How on earth would she know when this child will be born?" he said peevishly.

Carrie couldn't suppress a grin as she said, "Maybe because she's had four of her own?"

As Feliz had predicted, the final stage of the delivery was imminent. The Mexicana held Carrie's hands and spoke soothingly to her while Estrella scurried about, fetching things for Dr. Lark. A few final stabbing contractions, and through her haze of burning pain and exhaustion, Carrie heard the lusty wail of a baby.

"Well, *Mrs*. Sinclair, you have a son," the doctor said brusquely. His voice was cold and sarcastic. "I'll finish this delivery, but never again ask me to come to this place of iniquity!" With that he handed the squalling bundle to Feliz after tying off the cord and turning his attention back to Carrie.

"Let me see him, please, oh please, Feliz!" Carrie panted as the final contractions expelled the afterbirth.

Feliz held the infant, staring down at its tiny face in awe. "Hawk has not been disinherited after all," she breathed as she wiped away the birth cream. A fierce surge of exultation swept over her, reminding her of the dark Yaqui gods her ancestors had worshipped in Mexico long ago. *It is justice*. Now so much made sense: Noah's black rage, his confining Carrie to her room the past month, Mrs. Thorndyke's renewed spite, and Carrie's fearful case of nerves the whole duration of her pregnancy. Gently she placed the squirming infant in his mother's arms.

Before she saw him, she knew. Ignoring Dr. Lark's

shocked, indignant show of self-righteous temper, Carrie looked at her son, her lover's son. His thick black hair was straight, his cheekbones set high, even in his infant's face. The brilliant coal-black eyes and coppery skin unmistakably proclaimed him Cheyenne.

As her fingertips caressed his tiny face and head, tears began to stream down her cheeks. "Oh, thank God, thank God," she breathed aloud as relief and joy flooded over her.

Proudly, she looked up at Feliz, facing what she knew should be her shame. What she felt instead was joy, pure mindless joy. Would her friend understand or condemn her as the doctor had? Instantly she knew, and it gladdened her heart.

"He is a beautiful baby, Carrie." Feliz's eyes glowed. "He looks just like his father did. I know. I was there when he was born."

"He is an Indian, and most obviously not your husband's! I shall, of course, report this to Attorney Cooper." With that, Lark snapped his case shut and started to leave the room.

Feliz's voice stopped him. "You cannot deny he is a Sinclair, can you, doctor?" His florid face mottled even more darkly at her temerity.

"It really won't matter what you tell Cooper," Carrie said. "The terms of my husband's will are very explicit—I and *my* child inherit. When he wrote the will, it never occurred to Noah that it wouldn't be his."

Just then Mrs. Thorndyke burst in the room, bridling in rage. "I knew it! This brazen slut, carrying on with that filthy savage! It's indecent, a sin, a black nasty sin!" She advanced on the bed, one bony finger shaking in front of her.

Feliz's considerable bulk blocked her progress, and then Carrie cut in with a voice of quiet authority that belied her exhausted state. "Your services at Circle S are terminated, Mathilda. I think the good doctor here will be happy to give you a ride away from this place of iniquity, won't you, Phineas?"

Too livid to speak, Lark grabbed Mrs. Thorndyke's arm and practically marched to the door.

Daybreak the next morning found Carrie propped up in bed, nursing her infant son while Estrella fussed with the sheets and Feliz set up an elaborate and hearty breakfast on the bedside table. As the baby nursed, his tiny fingers clasped and unclasped over the gleaming silver medallion that lay between his mother's breasts. Immediately after her delivery, Carrie had had Feliz pry up the loose floorboards beneath the rug and retrieve the beloved talisman from its hiding place. With fingers trembling in love and exhausted happiness, she had placed the medallion once more where it belonged, as surely as she belonged to the man who had given it to her.

When Feliz had finished laying out the ridiculous quantity of food, she said, "What are you going to name him, Carrie?"

Carrie's eyes took on a faraway look as she recalled a dream from her childhood. It had been a recurrent nightmare to her until now; now she understood the wolf and the hawk. "I shall call him Peregrine. Perry for short."

Thinking of the fierce predatory breed of migratory hawks, Feliz nodded in approval.

Looking down at Perry, Carrie added a brief prayer. *If only we can bring the wanderer back to see his son, little one, if only . . .*

In the weeks that followed, Carrie was to learn a series of bitter lessons about running a large ranch as a woman alone, especially a woman fallen under the stigma of consorting with an Indian and bearing a half-breed child. Few people in town remembered Noah's infidelities or cared. He had not been loved, but he had been a rich, powerful white man who had tried to live down the shame of his youthful and ill-advised marriage to a Cheyenne woman. His luck with white wives had served him no better, they sadly clucked.

Mrs. Thorndyke, now living in town and working at Cummins's General Store, fanned the fires of lurid gossip. She told any and all who would listen—and most did—that Carrie and Hawk had carried on openly and brazenly, breaking poor Mr. Noah's heart. She was a gold-digging whore who only entrapped him for his wealth. In an area where fear and hatred of all red people was rampant and fighting between hostiles and the army still a reality, it was easy for the discharged housekeeper to win an avid audience for her lies.

The hands at the ranch were ambivalent in their feelings. Most had heartily disliked Noah and his high-handed, brutal way, but he had been their boss and a white man. They had also admired his beautiful and spirited young wife, but to have her caught in such blatant unfaithfulness violated every rule they held sacred for decent women, especially since her sin was with Noah's Cheyenne son. Most of them had viewed Hawk as an enigma, a distant, overeducated, fearfully dangerous half-breed gunman. Whether they liked him and Carrie or not, or even hated Noah, the fact remained that white women simply did not lay with red men. That was the code of the West. Few men were brave enough to stand against this prejudice.

Frank Lowery would have been one to do so. Everyone knew he favored Hawk and had been at Circle S since the boy was born. But Lowery was dead. And since the vacuum created by Noah's death, leadership at the ranch had gravitated to Caleb Rider by dint of his close association with Noah and his reputation as a gunman. Caleb did not like Indians any more than Noah did.

Despite the heat, trouble with the hands, and even Caleb Rider's studied insolence, Carrie felt radiant. She checked her appearance in the mirror across the floor of the big room she now occupied. The day after Perry's birth, she had Feliz and Estrella move all her things into Hawk's old room at the rear of the house. It held beautiful memories, whereas her own room held ugly ones. It was large and, once cleaned out, surprisingly airy. She would do some simple redecorating one day. For now, it was convenient to the kitchen downstairs, where she spent most of her time.

She checked her figure critically in the mirror. A month after Perry's birth she could scarcely believe how well her shape was returning. Secretly, she had harbored fears about gaining weight, especially since Feliz insisted she

eat so much and her appetite was voracious. Nursing
mothers need extra nourishment, admonished the old cook.
"Well, so far, she's right," Carrie said to her reflection,
adjusting the bodice on her green batiste dress. It was the
coolest thing she owned. Cut with loose sleeves, a soft,
full skirt, and low, rounded neckline, it was both casual
and comfortable, yet flattering to her dark green eyes and
flaming hair. Reaching for a green ribbon, she tied it
carelessly around her hair at the back of her neck, allowing
the riot of tumbling curls to fall to her waist. Not fancy,
but no company was coming.

She sighed as she headed downstairs to help Feliz with
the baking. Perry was asleep next door in the coolest room
in the house, with Estrella hovering over him. Carrie had
seen little of anyone else since Mrs. Thorndyke and Dr.
Lark had stormed out a month ago. She had gone to town,
to be sure no one could contest her claim to Circle S.
Attorney Cooper had stiffly replied that her assumptions
regarding the will were correct. His eyes had been icy in
disdain, as if she were a leper. Numbly leaving his
office, she went over to Cummins's General Store to buy
some supplies for Feliz. If Cooper had been aloof, Cyrus
Cummins was downright rude. Even more surprising was
his daughter's reaction. Kitty Cummins, her wedding date
set with her fat, nearsighted banker, had obviously forgotten her earlier infatuation with Hawk. She called Carrie an
Indian-loving adulteress! Remembering the scathing comments of the vicious-tongued girl, Carrie decided she was
probably just jealous.

However, though Carrie could laugh off Kitty Cummins,
she could not ignore her total social ostracism. Mrs.
Grummond had informed her she did not need "that kind
of money" and would no longer sew for her. Several other
ranchers' wives who had been friendly, even motherly
before, stepped across the street rather than have their
skirts contaminated by "Hawk Sinclair's squaw." Even
Reverend Becker had told her to take the savage's child
back to his people, that he would not baptize an Indian
child conceived in sin!

"Well, damn them all, bigoted self-righteous prigs,"

she said defiantly. But life would be lonely without a single caller from town. Even worse was Cy Cummins's threats to stop doing business with Circle S. Of course, as long as she paid the bill, Circle S business was far too lucrative for him to give up. He still needed "that kind of money."

As long as she could pay, she was all right; but with so many hands wandering off and Caleb Rider in charge, Carrie was fearful about holding on to her son's birthright.

With these weighty thoughts preying on her mind, she went down to the kitchen only to have Feliz inform her Karl Krueger was waiting to see her in the parlor. Unnerved at the unexpected turn of events, Carrie smoothed her hair and wished fervently that she had worn a more formal dress that warm day. Too late to go back up and change. *Whatever could that leering old pirate want?* she thought nervously.

As he waited for Carrie to appear, Krueger paced across the wide parlor floor. It galled him to come to Noah Sinclair's house, even more to deal with his half-breed son's mistress. Nevertheless, he was a practical man. He wanted clear title to all the Circle S lands, and one way or another he would get them.

How would he handle her? All things considered, it was hardly appropriate to offer condolences on Noah's demise. He could scarcely congratulate her on the birth of her son, either! He swore in German and resumed his pacing. Just then he heard soft footfalls on the carpet.

Krueger looked just as she remembered him, tall and somewhat overweight, with massive bones and hard brooding eyes that seemed to skewer people as if they were insects. She did not like him.

"Good morning, Mr. Krueger. What may I do for you?" Her voice was cautious and puzzled.

"Good day to you, Frau Sinclair. I trust you are well?" He walked over and reached for her hand before she was aware of his intent. Raising it to his lips, he planted a kiss on it, his hypnotic eyes never leaving her face. God, she was even more striking than he remembered! The Sinclair

men had good taste in women. Too bad they tended to
share them a bit more than was customary!

"Surely you didn't ride all this way to inquire about my
health." Withdrawing her hand and steeling herself to
show none of the revulsion he aroused in her, Carrie faced
him with a challenging look in her eyes.

He put up his hands in a gesture of mock surrender.
"You are right. I admire a forthright woman, so I will be a
forthright man." He put on his most disarming smile.
"You are a widow, alone with an infant to raise, an
easterner in a wild uncivilized land. You cannot possibly
hope to hold Circle S together, especially now that Frank
Lowery is dead. Even if he were alive . . ." He shrugged
in an expressive doubt. "I propose to buy the ranch from
you. I'll make all the arrangements with Attorney Cooper
so you need not even concern yourself with such complex
affairs."

She let him talk, kicking herself for not anticipating his
move. "Complex affairs," indeed! As if she were so
stupid she could not read a legal document. *I'm surprised
he thinks I'm smart enough to sign my name.* Smiling
chillingly, Carrie said, "If I may be so unseemly bold as to
ask, what exactly were you prepared to offer for Circle S
and all its livestock?"

Something in her tone of voice set his teeth on edge and
warned him. Had he handled her wrong? He swore silently.
"But of course, I did not mean to insult you, Frau
Sinclair. How does fifty thousand sound?"

And you didn't mean to insult me, huh? "I realize that
you think it should sound like a lot of money to a penniless
St. Louis orphan, Herr Krueger," his eyebrows went up as
she paused, confirming to her that he had checked on her
background, "but the cattle alone are worth more than
that, not to mention the horses, buildings, and land.
Anyway," she paced over to the window and looked out at
the big open sky, "it doesn't matter how much you offer,
the answer's the same. No. This ranch is my son's birthright. I mean to keep it for him."

Krueger's face became shuttered as he marshaled every
ounce of self-control he had. The nerve of the chit!

Married off by her own family, without a dime, now saddled with a half-breed's bastard, no one to run this place, and she threw his money back at him! "I would not be so hasty, my dear," he ground out. "You cannot get men to take orders from a woman, especially an eastern woman. Who will be your foreman? I've heard rumors that most of the hands are not working now. Some have already left your employ. Even your domestic staff has deserted you."

"If you're referring to Mrs. Thorndyke, I fired her. If some of the men want to quit, I'll hire new ones and I'll get a ramrod. I don't think my being an easterner should be any greater obstacle than your being a foreigner, Herr Krueger. What do you think?" She stood, head cocked to one side, exuding confidence.

"I think you are still a woman, young and vulnerable . . . and foolish," he taunted, growing impatient with the charade.

"Evelyn Henderson is a woman also, and she manages to run Lazy H quite well. Even Noah remarked on that. I may be new to this territory, but I think you'll find me a very quick learner. I've had to be. Now, if you would like some coffee or a mid-morning luncheon, I'll be glad to have Feliz—"

"That will not be necessary," he interrupted. "You will live to regret your actions, my dear, I assure you." With that he turned to storm out of the room.

Before he got to the door, Carrie's voice caught up with him. "Ironic, those were my late husband's exact words, Herr Krueger."

CHAPTER
18

Still fuming inwardly at Carrie's audacity, Krueger approached his foreman, Reuben Cade. "Did you get to talk to Rider while I was inside?"

Cade smiled, revealing several missing teeth. "Yep. Reckon I did. Rider wuz real interested. He don't cotton to workin' fer a woman, leastways one who's let a Injun in her britches."

Krueger snorted. "She is no lady of quality, that is for certain, but there is something there—beauty, fire—she would make a good mistress, I'm thinking. Once she loses Circle S, who knows?" He shrugged as Cade laughed. "When we meet Rider at the north fork at sundown tomorrow we will discuss terms for his contribution to the demise of Circle S."

Carrie felt drained after her show of bravado with Krueger. Of course that shark would come after Circle S with Noah and Frank both gone. If only Hawk were here, Krueger would never dare, she thought furiously, swinging her skirts as she whirled and stomped back to the kitchen. Well, she would just have to learn how to manage a ranch, that was all. If Evelyn Henderson could do it, so could Carrie Sinclair.

The following weeks proved that her resolve was more easily made than kept. Hands continued to do slipshod work, and a slow, steady trickle drifted off after collecting their pay, searching for more secure jobs where the boss was not a female. Stock started to disappear also. While Hawk and Kyle were here, losses were small. When Caleb Rider came, it seemed that the herds had grown greater than ever. Carrie had some suspicions about Noah and Caleb stealing from K Bar, but that was irrelevant now. For the past month it was the Circle S herds that were shrinking. She knew nothing of how Krueger fared against rustlers, nor cared. Her passion, her obsession, became holding Circle S for Perry.

You hold on to the land in hopes of bringing him back. Brushing the nagging dream away, Carrie walked to the corral early one hot September morning. Nervously, she scanned the clusters of hands saddling up for their day's work, heading out to various sections of the vast Circle S land. She needed to speak with her interim foreman, Caleb Rider. Two more hands quit yesterday. Circle S was down seven men at present count, and she had no luck in town recruiting any replacements.

Rider watched her cross the busy corral and once more was taken with her extraordinary beauty. The split riding skirts she wore hugged her slim hips and rounded buttocks, and the loose cotton shirt revealed her full breasts, swollen from nursing an infant. He felt a stab of desire jolt through him once more and muttered under his breath, "Maybe it's time to make my move. Yeah, I reckon it is." With that he flicked a cigarette away and sauntered toward her, circling around to surprise her from behind.

"You lookin' for me, Boss Lady?" The way he said the title was insinuating and insulting. He could feel her stiffen, and it pleased his male predatory instinct.

"Yes, Mr. Rider, I was. Hank Allen and Jim Snow quit yesterday. We simply need more men. No one in town was interested. Surely a man like you has some contacts, someone who'd be interested in earning good money. I'll pay top dollar."

"While you still have it, you mean," he said, watching her reaction.

"What do you mean, 'while I have it'?" she shot back, feeling distinctly uneasy.

He smiled placatingly. "Now, don't go gettin' your back up. 'Course, your eyes do get a pretty dark green when you're mad. All I meant was if you keep tryin' to run things yourself, the men will just keep leavin' till you're flat broke. Men won't work for a woman."

Ignoring his compliment and annoyingly personal manner, she retorted, "Evelyn Henderson runs her place very directly, and she has no shortage of men willing to work for her."

"Evelyn Henderson was born on the Lazy H. Anyhow, she's never had your, er, other problems to contend with. People hereabouts hate Indians," he said bluntly.

So, it was out in the open. Looking levelly at him, she replied, "Some of the men may have hated Hawk, but they all followed his orders. If he were here now—"

He cut her off. "But he isn't. You need a man, Carrie, a man to run this place. Someone who'll stand up to Krueger and whip all these bitchers in line so they work for Circle S."

Prickling warnings shot up and down her spine as she looked at Rider's icy-blue eyes and pale, cruel face. God, just like Noah, even the stringy yellow hair. "Just what are you proposing, *Mr.* Rider?" She stressed his title, pointedly ignoring his use of her given name.

"You know what I'm proposin', and you know I'm right. I can handle the men for you, bring in any guns we need, but if I do, pretty redhead, I want somethin' in return. Hell, you could do a lot worse than marryin' me. Come to think on it, you already have—twice." He leered at his own cleverness.

It took every ounce of her willpower not to slap the filthy smirk off his face. She must not infuriate him or show him how revolting she found his proposal. For now, he was her only slim link to keeping the remaining men drawing Circle S pay. Taking a deep breath, she said, "Well, that's hardly a conventional proposal of marriage, or a very kind one. You're right, though, I do need someone to run the place. But my husband's only been dead a couple of months and—"

"If you're hoping the half-breed'll come back, think

again. He took off like a scalded dog. Probably dead drunk in some dive in the Nations, or just plain dead. You'll never see him again," he finished coldly.

She flinched at the certainty of his statement, half afraid he was right. "What you say is probably true, but I was forced to marry once without love. I won't do it again, no matter what the price."

His face darkened as he heard the finality in her voice and saw the stubborn set of her chin. Damn the little whore! "The price will be Circle S, Boss Lady. You'll lose it. I'm a patient man, to a point. Think it over. . . .'' With that he sauntered off, planning his next meeting with Krueger. The number of head he delivered would go up. He would give Carrie a month or so to come around while he continued to make money rustling Circle S cattle.

It was a golden-warm fall, with fleecy white clouds whipping briskly across the deep azure of the sky. Heavy late-summer rain had made the rolling swells of buffalo grass sweet and green. Cattle fattened and ranchers prepared for winter, rounding up and cutting out prime beef for shipment to market before the winter storms descended in paralyzing finality, freezing the cattle kingdom in limbo until spring.

In the midst of the fall roundups, Carrie worked as hard as any of her men, the inadequate handful remaining. She rode from section to section, checking actual tallies against Noah's records. The real count always came up short. Some of the hands were cavalier about it, figuring a woman incapable of even being able to read the ledgers, some were evasive as if hiding something, and a few were afraid. Afraid of what or whom? Carrie pondered the frustrating puzzle, wondering if Krueger was now stealing from Circle S as Noah had stolen from K Bar. Was that why Frank had been killed? Had he found out something about the missing cattle?

She sat in the study late one evening, poring over the books for the hundredth time, the questions still whirling around in her head. Just then, Feliz came in with a cup of herb tea.

"You will never get to sleep if you worry so. Here, drink this. It will soothe you so you can rest."

Carrie smiled and took the tea. "If I don't worry, I'll have plenty of time to rest. We all will. We'll be off Circle S, Feliz. We're losing cattle at a terrible rate and I think Krueger may be behind it, but I can't prove anything. None of this makes sense. Frank may have thought K Bar men were the rustlers, but Krueger wouldn't have bothered to kill him. Noah had already accused Krueger publicly. I think Noah was a thief, God help him, but he's dead and the rustling goes on, only now our cattle, not K Bar's, are the ones missing. And several of my men are acting afraid of something, and they won't tell me what." She sipped the tea and rubbed her eyes, squeezing the bridge of her nose with her fingertips.

"If you ask me, they are afraid of Señor Rider," Feliz said darkly.

Warily Carrie said, "What makes you think that?"

"Why be afraid of rustlers who work on the outside? As you say, why would K Bar men kill Frank? No. I think someone works from here, telling those who steal where and when it is easiest to do. I have watched the men, how they act around Caleb Rider. I think Señor Rider is a traitor who has stolen from both sides."

"If Frank found out that Rider was stealing from K Bar—Oh, my God, do you think Noah . . . ?" Carrie couldn't finish the sentence. Then her eyes hardened, like polished green glass. "If Rider killed Frank, it was to cover up for Noah's involvement. Or maybe Noah did it himself. I've honestly come to believe he was capable of anything," she said with a shiver, recalling his cold-blooded threat to kill her and Perry.

"If Señor Rider stole K Bar cattle then, he steals ours now. I would bet my best iron skillet on that," Feliz said emphatically.

Carrie nodded. "Yes, he's switched sides. His kind always finds that easy, and it would explain why our men act so nervous around him. Oh, damn, Feliz! What can I do? If I fire him, I drive him to Krueger openly. It could start a range war. And without a foreman, the men who are left will quit in a minute, I'm sure of that.''

Feliz stood up and walked around the cluttered desk. Gently she massaged the younger woman's thin, tense shoulders. ''Is it not better to face a snake from the front than have him lunge and bite your unprepared back?''

Carrie knew it was her only course of action. Having him live at Circle S and post the men's work schedules was tantamount to quartering the wolf in the sheep pens. ''I'll go into town and see that worthless Sheriff Woods. I can show him my records and tell him I think Rider's involved. I doubt it will spur him to action, but at least I'll go on record accusing Rider. Maybe he'll leave Circle S without more trouble. I can try posting a notice for a new foreman again at Cummins's store, too.'' Her voice was tired but steady.

The sheriff's office was a rickety frame structure with a dilapidated front porch and grimy windows. As she entered the door, Carrie could smell stale cigar smoke and musty bedding. The place was layered in dust and clutter. Wrinkling her nose, she looked around for Sheriff Woods. A noise in the rear of the building drew her eyes to the back door. Behind its rather flimsy-looking wooden construction lay a couple of cramped, filthy cells, usually inhabited by local drunks. The door to the privy was also in the back room. Hearing the outside door latch click, she called out, ''Is anyone here?''

Woods, a short, squat man of middle years and rumpled appearance, shoved open the door to the front office. Looking surprised, he said, ''Miz Sinclair, whut're yew doin' here so early?'' It was nearly noon.

''Good morning, Sheriff. I have a matter of importance to discuss with you.'' She plunked her ledgers down on his desk, wincing as a cloud of dust floated up and enveloped them. ''In these are the tallies for Circle S cattle, going back several years. Over this summer and fall, I've had a marked decrease in herd numbers.'' She flipped open a page, waiting for him to offer her the courtesy of a chair.

He stood still, putting his hands truculently into his belt instead. Rolling onto the balls of his feet, he seemed to thrust his overample belly out even farther. Affixing her with a now baleful glare, he said, "Whaddya want me ta look at yer bookkeepin' fer? Ain't nothin' ta me. Outside my jurisdiction anyways."

Carrie took a calming breath and smiled her most blinding smile at him. "Well, Sheriff, I had hoped you would at least make note of the fact that I've lost cattle and that I think Caleb Rider is responsible. Yesterday I followed him to the east range, where I watched from a distance while he talked to several strangers. They rode off and he came home. This morning I checked cattle on the east range and I'm down fifty head!"

His eyes shifted nervously. Rider was a mean gunman, and the sheriff wasn't about to get himself shot over the likes of this Indian-loving tramp, nosiree. "Why not git yer Injun kid's daddy ta run Rider off? 'Pears ta me he's th' one's got th' stake out there, not me."

Carrie did not even flinch at the unexpected insult. She was growing accustomed to such. "I'm not surprised you won't take action, Sheriff. I imagined you'd be terrified of Caleb Rider. The only thing that does surprise me is that you have the courage to insult a lone woman to her face!"

By the time she arrived at Cummins's store, Carrie had her temper back under control. She had also reached a decision. If no one else would help her, she would act by herself. As she wended her way past crates and barrels in the clutter of the overstocked store, she withdrew her supply list, mentally making several additions to it.

Cy Cummins saw her crossing the crowded emporium and scowled. There had been no love lost between him and Noah Sinclair, but he had outright hated Noah's dangerous son. His Kitty had been much too fond of that killer. Now to have the half-breed's mistress come in as owner of Circle S, lording it over her betters, well, it galled him to do business with her.

"Good day, Mr. Cummins. I have a list of supplies here, and I need some technical advice." Carrie kept her voice brisk and impersonal. The old storekeeper had already made his feelings toward her quite plain.

His lips pursed and his eyelids drooped, giving his

rotund face a strange buddahlike appearance. "You figgering to pay your bill while you're at it, Mrs. Sinclair? You owe me for last month yet."

Why, the punctilious bastard! "You certainly know when you have a monopoly, don't you, Mr. Cummins? I hadn't planned to go to the bank today, but I can, if you think between now and the first of the month I'll sell Circle S and abscond owing you." Her scorn was withering.

His mouth whitened and he nodded. "I'll wait till the first, no later." He took the list from her hand and gave it to his gaping clerk to fill.

When he turned away, her voice interrupted him. "I need another thing, not on the list. A small-caliber handgun and some ammunition."

The next morning Carrie went down to the corral to find Rider. As she approached the melee, she could smell leather and horseflesh, hear swearing and singing, see a kaleidoscope of black, brown, and red horses. Men pulled on bridles, strapped cinches, and calmed skittering animals with rough endearments. Suddenly, as she looked up at the brilliant orange fingers of sunrise climbing over the stable roof, she realized how much a part of her all this had become. She loved the ranch, the land, the life. For better or worse, there would be no going back to St. Louis. Her future was in Montana now.

"I'm looking for Caleb Rider, Joe. Have you seen him?" She called out over the noise to one young hand, who doffed his hat and smiled. A few of them were loyal, despite her fall from grace, she thought ruefully.

Joe Plimpton replied, "Yes'm. He went back to Frank's—I mean, his cabin. Goin' over some papers, he said."

Thanking Joe, Carrie turned and strode determinedly toward the small log structure down behind the bunkhouse. It was a plain, clean little building set next to a stand of scrub pines. Frank had built it himself, Carrie thought with a pang. How she had hated giving it over to Caleb Rider. Well, now Caleb would be leaving.

Before she could knock, the door swung open and a smiling Rider lounged against the sash, making a grand gesture of ushering her into the front room. Careful to avoid touching him, she stepped inside and turned to face his Cheshire-cat countenance. Sneakthief and bushwhacker!

Rider walked over to the kitchen table and motioned for her to have a chair. When she refused with a shake of her head, he picked up a big granite pot from the stove and poured himself a mug of thick, black coffee.

"What can I do for you, Carrie?" His very tone of voice was an intimate insinuation.

"Pack," she said in a crisp, clear voice. "You're fired. I want you off Circle S by sundown."

Choking, he sprayed coffee all across the table, then put the scalding cup down and wiped his chin. "Where the hell do you get off firin' me?"

"Where the hell do you get off stealing my cattle?" She stood with her back to the door, giving him as wide a berth as possible in the small room.

His face went from surprised anger to ugly menace. "Mighty dangerous words if you can't back them up, darlin'." He made no attempt to draw his gun, but began to walk toward her, like a puma ready to pounce.

Quickly she brought her right arm up from where it had been hidden in the folds of her riding skirt. In her hand was a Sharps thirty-six caliber pistol, cocked and pointed squarely at Rider's midsection. "From this range, I don't need to be a good shot, Caleb, just a determined one."

He scoffed. "You couldn't shoot a man." But he did not move.

"You could. That's why I'm taking no chances." Carrie's gun did not waver.

"As I keep reminding you, baby, you're not a man. Now, put that thing down before it goes off." His voice was growing more confident now in anger and impatience.

"Oh, it'll go off all right, I figure between your third button and your belt buckle. Frank once told me how long it takes a gut-shot man to die." Carrie's voice was as cold as ice now.

"I'd give me a listen ta th' lady, mister. I purely would." The sound of his Colt being cocked was as unmistakable as Kyle Hunnicut's drawl. He stood in the door behind her. Grinning broadly, he said, "I think she'll shoot."

Carrie was simultaneously amazed and overjoyed, yet she could not take her eyes off Rider. "How long have you been here, Kyle?"

"Long enough ta figger ya kin handle th' likes o' this 'un. I'm jist backup. Seems like thet's become my habit with yew Sinclairs." Then, turning his full attention to the immobilized Caleb Rider, the little Texan said, "Take th' gunbelt off real easy, 'n' git packin' yer gear."

After another breathless moment, Rider complied, swearing virulently all the while.

By the time Kyle saw Rider off Circle S and came up to the big house, Carrie and Feliz had an enormous breakfast ready for him, including his favorite sweet rolls.

When he came in the door, Carrie fairly flew across the kitchen and gave him an exuberant bear hug. "You sweet, wonderful Texan, you! How did you get here? Where have you been? You're the most beautiful sight I've seen all year, trail dust and all!"

The homely little banty guffawed and lapped up her affectionate compliments, then threw up his hands at her questions. "Jist wait up a minute 'n' I'll tell ya everythin'. Feliz, how's my gal? Still th' sweetest roll maker west o' th' Mississip?"

"Yes, Kyle, and yes, I have a batch in the warming pan right now. How one man can eat so much and stay so skinny, I'll never know. It is not just." Shaking her head, she returned to the stove and began to serve up the meal.

Kyle ate as he talked of his journey, dreading Carrie's inevitable questions about Hawk.

"What made you decide to come back?" Her earnest green eyes asked more. *Why did you come back alone?*

"I wuz workin' on the XIT down Texas way fer a spell. Got plumb homesick fer some fresh Montana air."

"So you came just in time for winter," Carrie said dryly.

He chuckled, then grew earnest and looked her straight in the eye. "Hawk 'n' me, we split up over six months ago. I mosied south 'n' he went ta join his mama's people.

He wuz drinkin' somethin' fierce 'n' grievin', Carrie. I reckon he thought it wuz better ta be a sober Cheyenne than a drunk white-eyes.''

Carrie's face registered shock, then a haunted fearfulness. "He—he's with Iron Heart's band? They can't be far, Kyle.'' Her eyes held an unasked question for him.

"I'll try ta find him afore th' snow flies. I know me a couple o' traders who kin track fly sign through cracked pepper. Reckon a man oughtta know he's got a fine youngun'.''

Carrie felt the heat steal into her face for the first time in months. She was used to the cruelty and rudeness of people, but the little gunman's gallant kindness touched her deeply. "How did you know about Perry? You knew Noah died?''

He nodded, biting off a generous hunk of a sweet roll. "Yup. I got ta worryin' bout yew 'n' him. He could be right mean when he put his mind ta it, which wuz most o' th' time. Anyways, like I said, I wuz plumb tired o' Texas heat, so I started north. Didn't clear Wyomin' Territory afore I heerd th' old man's dead, 'n' Frank, too. Sorry 'bout Frank.''

"And that Noah's wife had a red baby by his Cheyenne son?'' Carrie softly supplied the rest for him.

Now it was Kyle's turn to blush. "Figgered ya might cud use some help. I knowed Krueger'd be on ya like a coyote on a broke-leg dog.''

"Yes. We've lost nearly half our stock since July!'' Carrie told him all she knew about Frank's murder, the rustling, Krueger's offer to buy Circle S, and Rider's highly suspicious moves. Finally, after they had spent the better part of the morning talking, she fixed him with a cool green-eyed gaze and said bluntly, "Well, Kyle, do I have a new foreman? I know I couldn't find a better man to run Circle S.''

He grinned crookedly. "Mighty proud ya feel thet way, Carrie. 'Course, yew 'n' me both know who'd be better ta run Circle S 'n' anyone. I'll track him down fer ya. Till then, yew got yew a ramrod.''

They spent the following weeks busily getting prepared

for the onslaught of Montana winter. Kyle sent for several men he had known down in Texas, men who knew cattle and guns. Slowly, as winter descended, an equilibrium of sorts began to return to Circle S. The men who stayed on easily accepted Hunnicut's leadership. The new recruits were a hard-bitten, silent lot who did their job effectively. With Rider gone and pairs of armed men regularly patrolling the herds, the rustling slowed to a trickle. Circle S had been given a reprieve. By the time the snow flew, moving any number of cattle was totally impractical. Kyle and Carrie settled down to wait for spring.

It was to be a long, cold winter. The first thing Kyle did after he organized the hands was to go in search of a Frenchman named Le Beau, a trader among the Sioux and Cheyenne. If anyone could find Hawk Sinclair, he could. Whether or not he could find him before the high country became snowbound was uncertain. Hunnicut located Le Beau at an outpost near the Dakota border and received his promise to search out Iron Heart's grandson. Not wanting to raise Carrie's hopes too soon, Kyle warned her it might be summer before Hawk came home. It never occurred to either one of them that he would not return. They settled down to their routine around the ranch and waited.

If Carrie was bothered by her status as a pariah in town, she did not reveal it to Kyle. He watched her crisp, impersonal manner of dealing with the local merchants when they went to town for supplies. If she missed having Mrs. Grummond sew her clothes, she seemed pleased with Feliz's efforts instead. When women crossed the street rather than talk to her, Carrie walked on by, head held high, as if they were invisible in their scurrying haste to avoid her. To show her contempt for them all, she even wore her split riding skirts and took Perry with her on her visits to the bank and post office. She had become the scandal of Miles City, and rather than attempting to live it down, she seemed to take a willful delight in fanning the flames of gossip.

But for all her defiance and bravado, Carrie was lonely, and Kyle knew it. She had no women friends except for Feliz. Most men treated her with rudimentary politeness, but looked at her with lustful speculation when she turned away. After all, she had lain with a half-breed. That made her fair game, at least for their fantasies. Kyle knew he and the Mexicana were the only people on earth Carrie trusted. For a beautiful young woman of scarcely twenty years, it was not an easy or good life. He prayed for word about Hawk. Then, when it finally came in the icy blasts of early November, he wished he had not heard.

Blackie Le Beau spat a wad of brownish tobacco juice and wiped his greasy chin with the back of his buckskin sleeve. Not by nature an overly fastidious man, the little Texan still found the trader's habits and odor hard to endure.

"Yew heerd 'bout Hawk, Blackie?" Kyle knew the filthy little Frenchman wanted his payment before he would say anything. He also knew the trader would not have sent word to him unless he had some definite news to report.

"Oui. I know where he ees and who ees weeth heem." He waited, his shrewd black eyes assessing how the Texan would take the news.

Kyle shrugged, hefting a small pouch of coins, then threw it at the wiry man whose grimy little paw caught it deftly. "Now, where's Hawk?"

Le Beau shifted uneasily on his mule, scratching some straying vermin that had wandered too far afield and become isolated on his arm. "You weel not like eet, monsieur. Zee half-blood Hunting Hawk remains weeth hees grandpere's band, high een zee mountains to zee west." He paused. "He can be reached, eef you weesh eet, monsieur."

Kyle became suddenly uneasy. What didn't the Frenchman want to tell him? "Yeah, I reckon I do 'weesh eet.' Why 'n tarnation wouldn't I?"

"You look for heem, not for yourself, but for zee woman, hees father's wife?" he inquired haltingly. At Kyle's silent nod, he continued. "Perhaps you weel not want to tell her thees, but zee half-blood, he ees married— to a Cheyenne woman, since last spring. She ees enceinte, weeth child. The bebe ees to come weeth zee new year." He looked over at Kyle, unsure of what the gunman would do. Le Beau knew about Noah's wife and her half-breed baby. He could easily guess why her foreman searched for the child's father now that Noah was dead.

Kyle sat rooted to his saddle, freezing in the gusting prairie wind. How could he face Carrie with this? It would break her heart. He swore to himself, furious with Hawk, with the town, Krueger, everyone who conspired to make her unhappy. Taking a deep breath, he said, "Hawk know 'bout his son? Thet his pa's dead?''

The wizened face became sympathetic. It was rotten luck, and he was sorry for them all. "No. When you asked me to find heem, I had not been to Iron Heart's camp seence last weenter. When I find them last month, I deed not theenk you would weesh me to say anything."

Kyle nodded. It was better that way. No point in either of them knowing about the other. Hawk couldn't claim his son now, and she for sure couldn't marry him. If she knew about the Cheyenne woman, it would break her heart. If he knew about Perry, it would break his.

Bidding the Frenchman farewell, Kyle started back toward Circle S. Usually after a hard day's ride in the blustering winter cold, he could not wait to see Feliz's warm kitchen. Tonight it did not beckon him. What would he tell Carrie?

The drums were beating low and steadily. A keening chant spread its eerie pall across the clearing. The village was still as death. It was filled with death, over half the people dead or dying. It always happened this way, ever since the white traders first started to come among the People, Iron Heart thought sadly. Even when they came in peace they always brought death—measles, diptheria, cholera, smallpox. Feverish wasting diseases that infested the body and drove the breath from it, all brought by white men.

Looking about the deserted camp, the old man thought sadly, *They will win, not with guns and bullets or even with wooden roads and iron horses. Only this will defeat the People.*

His sad reverie was interrupted by the pounding of hooves. Hawk leaped off Redskin's back, kicking dirt and

pebbles from the frozen ground and scattering them into
the fire. "Where is she?" His face was pale and drawn,
his black eyes glowing in anguish.

The old man answered, "White Buffalo is with her, in
there." White Buffalo was a medicine man, a skilled
healer when the enemy was a broken bone, an aching
tooth, even a snakebite or bear clawing. However, for the
spotted throat of the white man, diptheria, there was
nothing he could do.

Seizing the flap of the lodge, Hawk pulled it open
roughly and slipped inside. It was warm, too warm, fetidly
cloying with death. Shedding his heavy furs, he watched
as the old healer chanted over the woman lying on the
pallet. She was flushed and laboring to breathe. Silently he
waited until the medicine man had finished. When White
Buffalo rose, Hawk crossed the small space and knelt
beside his wife. He had seen by the sad, hollow expression
on White Buffalo's face that he could do no more.

Gently Hawk took her dry, hot hands in his own, still
cold from the outdoors and his long ride through the night.
He had been gone for two weeks, hunting in the mountains
to the south.

Winter had come early, promising to be bitter and long.
Game was scarce, even in this isolated region of jagged
mountains and rushing streams. Before the full brunt of
winter struck, Hawk had gone hunting to get them as much
meat as possible. He knew he must provide for Iron Heart,
Sweet Rain, Bright Leaf, and now more importantly for
Wind Song and his unborn child.

As he rode toward camp, travois-laden with two big elk
and a deer, he was met by the dread news. An epidemic of
the spotted throat had broken out. Many were stricken,
among them his wife.

He looked at her strong, lovely face, its chiseled profile
illuminated by the flickering firelight as she lay with her
head turned toward the flames. She was burning up with
fever, and her eyes were closed.

Stroking her hands, he spoke in a low, urgent voice. She
must hear him. "Wind Song, I have returned. Can you

hear me?'' His voice almost broke. He could not let her die!

As she moaned and turned her head, he reached to caress her cheek. Her eyes opened and focused with difficulty on his beloved face. They glowed with fever and also with the sudden joy of seeing him once more before she must make her journey across the hanging road to the sky.

"I knew you would come," she rasped out. It hurt so to speak, but she must, while there was time.

"Shh . . ." he soothed her, "I am here now. I will never leave you, Wind Song."

She smiled sadly and said, "It is I who must leave you, Hunting Hawk, much as I do not wish it. Especially now." One hand slipped down to hold her mounded belly, full of their child. Her face was filled with anguish for the loss of the child above all.

He shook his head in denial, willing the nearness of death away. "You will not leave me. I will not permit it," he said fiercely.

Wind Song put one slim hand on his hard chest, gently rebuking him. "The Spirits do not always listen to our wishes, my husband. We cannot go against their will. I had hoped above all else to give you this child, a man-child. Then I might take her place in your heart. But it is not meant to be."

"No!" The cry was torn from him. "No, there is no one but you in my heart. You are my wife. I will not let you die!"

She reached up, stretching her long, slim arms to wrap around his neck as he knelt over her, clasping her to him and holding her feverish body. Wind Song buried her face against his neck as the fiery, wracking pain suffocated her once more. Yet she was glad to be in his arms one last time.

Her voice was muffled when she spoke again, breathless and low. "You must not grieve too much, beloved. Things happen as they must. You will return to the world of white men someday, to her. I think I always knew that. Still, it

was worth the pain to have loved you." She coughed,
gasping for air as her swollen throat closed.

He held her silently, shaken by grief and guilt, denying
all she said, still unable to forget the white woman who
came between them even in death. His heart felt crushed
by the burden. "Please, do not leave me, beloved wife.
Wind Song . . . ?"

He held her for several moments more, then gently laid
her still form back on the furs of their bed. The swollen
mound of her belly seemed even larger now, so lifeless and
yet accusing. He lay his head on it and wept. There would
be no children, no joy, no belonging.

Slowly, fighting for breath and strength, he began the
death chant, mourning for all that might have been, should
have been in her young life, snuffed out so cruelly by a
disease of the white man. It was not only one death but
two, hers and the child she so desperately wanted to give
him. How much better the *veho*'s pestilence killed than his
bullets. It was not the first time Hawk cursed his white
blood, but never before had he hated all white people and
himself as much as he did at that moment.

It was spring at last. The snow melted and clear water
burbled its way down the rocky ravines, billowing into the
rivers and lakes. Willows sported pale lime-colored fuzz
on branches that whispered in the wind, promising lush,
verdant greenery soon. The sky was azure and cloudless,
the wind still gusting, but with a hint of sun-kissed
warmth. Soon.

At last free from snow's fetters, cattle, thin and sluggish
after their winter struggle for sustenance, were gamboling
in anticipation of fresh grass. New calves bawled for their
mothers and walked on shaky legs across the rolling
prairie.

Carrie sat on Taffy Girl, looking over a herd of prime
beef that had survived the winter. Things were looking up
at last. Despite a bitter winter, spring was early and most
of the cattle had pulled through. The calf crop would be
good, despite the smaller herd. The hands were out in

work crews, beginning to get organized for a mammoth spring roundup.

When would Hawk come home? All through her lonely winter vigil, the thought had been with her incessantly. Ever since last fall, Kyle had been vague and evasive about receiving word of him. First he said it would take weeks to locate Iron Heart's band. Then he predicted it could not be done until the snow was clear. Now with even the high country opening up, Carrie could not understand why no one had found such a large encampment. Surely Hawk must be there. The thought that he did not wish to return to her nagged at the back of her consciousness, but she refused to acknowledge it. Of course, if it were so, it would explain the little Texan's nervous avoidance of her questions about Hawk. No. The Frenchman must not have found their band yet. Hawk was alive and well. She knew it, feeling sure if anything had happened to him she would know.

Clasping the silver medallion at her breast with her hand, she felt its warmth against her beating heart. He would come home. Soon.

CHAPTER 19

"Peregrine. Ain't thet some kinda bird, er somethin'?" Kyle studied the wiggling boy seated on his mother's lap in the big kitchen.

Carrie flushed slightly. Strange that she should still feel shy about her relationship with Hawk around his best friend. "Yes, Kyle, it's a migratory falcon."

"A Hawk, 'n other words?"

"Yes, a predatory hawk."

"A huntin' hawk." He nodded shrewdly, then reached over and tickled Perry's tummy.

The little boy giggled and grabbed Hunnicut's fingers. He would be a striking man one day. That much was already apparent from the thick, dark hair and glowing black eyes. Even the child's cheekbones and jawline, undefined as yet, gave promise of looking like his sire's.

Carrie shoved her coffee cup away and hefted the boy as she stood up, stretching from the cramped position she had been sitting in while holding the fidgety handful. "I think I need some exercise, Kyle. I'll take Perry with me and ride over toward the river."

Grabbing several rolls off the heaping platter Feliz had placed before him, Kyle followed Carrie out of the kitchen, munching as he went. "Yew be careful," he admonished her, knowing from long experience that it did no good to demand she take an armed escort along. Always an independent loner, Carrie had become even more restless with the arrival of spring. "They's been hostiles seen over west aways. Sioux, even some Cheyenne bucks with 'em, stirrin' up grief. Yew don't need ta cross th' river with thet young'un.''

Carrie turned, adjusting Perry on her hip, and replied with a sunny smile, "Don't fret, Kyle, I just need to do some thinking. I'll be back by late afternoon."

He shook his head at her retreating form, waving at the bright-eyed boy who watched him over his mother's shoulder.

It was a hot day in early June, dry and still, with the sun moving in a blinding arc across the pale-blue heavens. Nearly a year had passed since Noah's death and Perry's birth. Carrie felt the bonds linking her to Hawk and his child drawing tighter. It had grown increasingly difficult for her to wait in this endless limbo, especially with the breaking of spring and then summer. Why didn't he come home?

Carrie needed this time alone to think through her ambivalent feelings about Hawk and his long-overdue reappearance in her life. Of late she had been troubled by dreams. One was the old familiar one about the hawk that had plagued her since childhood; others were about Hawk and Lola Jameson, Noah and herself, all blurred together in confusing, chaotic images. If truth were told, she was still uncertain about her feelings for Hawk Sinclair.

Looking down at the sleeping child in front of her, Carrie felt a tremendous rush of unconditional love. But did she love the father that way also? No, it was not that simple. The past year had left deep, bitter scars. A great deal of the pain she had lived with was because of Hawk. She had learned to withstand the bigotry and sneers of the town, but did she accept his desertion which had left her to face them alone? Why had he gone to Iron Heart's village, so near Circle S, without stopping to find out about her and learn he had a son? *Why doesn't he come home now?*

Lonely, hurting and frightened by the enormity of her responsibility for Circle S, Carrie let her thoughts drift back over the past two years to when she had come west as a green girl, naively hoping to establish a loving relationship with Noah Sinclair. Now she scoffed at her immaturity and inability to read people. In his entire life Noah had never had a loving relationship with a living soul!

Just then, Perry awakened and began to babble in his melodic child's voice. He was hot and thirsty, letting her know his needs in no uncertain terms. When she reached for the canteen, Carrie noticed how far she had ridden, much farther than she intended or than Kyle would have approved. She had crossed the river several hours ago and was on the southwestern border of the farthest section of Circle S. She sighed in exasperation at her own absent-mindedness, a defect that sorely plagued her lately.

As she turned Taffy and began to retrace her path home, her progress was watched with great interest. Scouting Horse and Little Otter, two Sioux warriors on a raiding party, had watched her aimless meandering for nearly an hour, uncertain of whether or not they should take her captive. When she abruptly wheeled her tan mare around, Little Otter spoke.

"See, the daughter of the sun returns from whence she came. Let her depart in peace with her child. We do not make war on women and children."

His younger companion scoffed. "She is white and therefore our enemy. Her flame hair would make a scalp with very strong magic. The child would be given to one of our women who mourns the loss of her own, killed by white men."

Just then the rest of the war party, mostly Sioux with a smattering of Cheyenne, came riding up. They had followed the tracks of Carrie's horse and those of her silent pursuers. In the lead and fast becoming one of the most vocal and belligerent of the young raiders was the Cheyenne Angry Wolf. He and a handful of other braves from Iron Heart's band had left their peaceful people to join the hostile Sioux of northern Montana. Retreating into Canada and the high country to the east, the Sioux had not yet bowed to the inevitable loss of their hunting lands or their freedom. They were still at war against the white man.

Their belligerence perfectly suited Angry Wolf's sentiments. Always a surly and embittered man, he had found his disappointments during the past several years more than he could endure. He, a leader of the prestigious Elk Warrior Society, had not been selected to sit on the tribal council of the People. That insult would not soon be lived down. He refused to admit that his arrogant and contentious disposition had anything to do with the elders' decision. There was also the matter of the half-blood who had come to live among the People. Angry Wolf had hated Hunting Hawk since they were boys; then Iron Heart's grandson took Wind Song in marriage. Angry Wolf could never forgive Hawk for stealing what he considered his property.

The sporadic raids against white settlers and Crow satisfied his desire for excitement and vengeance. Now he reined in his swift black mount and looked down to where Spotted Horse gestured. Below them, riding along the stream's edge, was a lone white woman, mounted on a good horse, carrying a small child. He listened absently to the exchange between the Sioux and Cheyenne braves while he watched the woman. Something about her and her horse stirred memories from the past. He had seen her before. The buckskin horse was decidedly familiar, and when Little Otter called her daughter of the sun, he caught sight of her fiery hair and remembered.

It was her! The one who had come to his village two years ago with Hawk! Some in the band had gossiped, saying she was really Hawk's woman. He himself had tried to convince Wing Song of that.

And here she was with a child, riding right into his hands. Overhearing Spotted Horse's prattling about a magic scalp, Angry Wolf cut in abruptly, "She is too valuable to be killed! Look at her beauty and long, strong limbs. She will make some warrior a splendid slave! I, Angry Wolf, lay claim to her!"

With that, he kicked his big black in the flanks and began a rapid descent down the loose, rocky trail that led to the stream floor. Several of the other younger braves who were admirers of the seasoned veteran quickly followed after him.

Carrie heard the thunder of horses and clatter of loose

rocks spewn forth by their slashing hooves. Quickly looking over her shoulder, she saw three Indians riding toward her from the top of the cliff. She did not know what tribe they were, but it was a foregone conclusion that they were not friendly! Leaning over Taffy's neck, she spurred her forward into a furious, ground-devouring gallop. Perry began to cry, held in a crushing position in front of Carrie on the racing horse.

"Oh, dear God! Why didn't I listen to Kyle? How could I have been so stupid!" Muttering under her breath as she raced helped to quell her panic so she could concentrate on guiding her horse. However, it was a losing proposition. The Indian horses were larger and fresher than hers, and the riders more skillful.

Carrie felt the force of an iron-hard arm curling around her, sweeping her and Perry clutched in her arms from Taffy Girl's back. She and her son were held tightly against the savage's side until he brought his rapidly galloping pony to a rough stop and then dumped them onto the ground. He slid after them, quickly reaching down to grasp her arm and drag her to a standing position.

As she struggled to stand up and then to calm a wailing baby, she could feel the heat of her captor's gaze on her, boldly surveying her body from head to foot. He was very tall; indeed, they all were. Half a dozen other savages, all armed to the teeth, quickly caught up and surrounded them, jumping from horseback to survey the prize. They spoke rapidly in their language, laughing and talking. The tall, cruel-looking man who had pulled her off Taffy was gesturing to her hair and making obviously lewd comments to his companions.

As she shivered in terror, Carrie crooned to Perry, desperately trying to force herself to be calm. She must use her wits and try to save her son. Then she noticed that the Indians' attention had shifted from her to Perry. Several of them were looking at him closely and talking animatedly among themselves. Of course! They recognized his red ancestry. She looked closely at the men, noting their facial features, the patterns of their clothing, the adornments on their weapons. Several of them were Cheyenne, including her captor! She was sure she recognized the clothing designs and even the tall, handsomely chiseled facial planes. If only they would be able to understand her. Slowly she reached inside her shirt and pulled out Hawk's medallion.

Angry Wolf was filled with an all-consuming rage as they rode steadily toward Iron Heart's camp with the flame-haired woman and the boy she claimed was Hunting Hawk's son. If only she had not possessed the medal Iron Heart brought from the White Fathers in the east! When she showed it and claimed to be Hawk's woman, his two companions recognized it, as did he. They were not in the village the day she visited as he had been, but they had both grown up with Hawk. White Arrow even knew enough English to understand her tale. Angry Wolf's furious bombast failed to swerve them from their course; they felt honor-bound to take her to Iron Heart. After all, did she not wear the great chief's sacred medal? Was the manchild not of Cheyenne blood? Angry Wolf's arguments to the contrary did not sway them. Short of killing his friends, he had no choice but to take her to Iron Heart, who would decide her fate and that of the child.

He cursed the child. Looking at the boy, he could see the old women of the village had gossiped truthfully. He was Hawk's son, all right. A fierce anger burned in him that the child would escape his vengeance, but the woman must not. There was a good chance the chief would allow him to keep her, Angry Wolf consoled himself. Ever since Wind Song had died and with her Iron Heart's hopes for a great-grandchild, the old man had been bitter against the *veho* and their diseases. Now he would welcome his great-grandson, but he would not want the white woman in his lodge. At least, Angry Wolf convinced himself this would be so.

The daughter of the sun would be his white slave! When Hawk returned from his long journey taking Bright Leaf to her parents, he would be too late. Angry Wolf would have bedded her and she would belong to him. Satisfied that his plans had only been postponed, not thwarted, he became calm, watching her with hot, hungry eyes as she rode next to him.

Carrie marveled that she had been successful in convincing them to take her to Iron Heart's encampment. Thank God they recognized the medallion. Two of the men had argued with her captor, prevailing over him. One even spoke halting English and said he was a friend of Hawk's.

Looking over at Angry Wolf, she shuddered. Even his eyes on her made her skin crawl. His hands on her would be a horror beyond imagining. She did not recognize him from her brief visit to the encampment, nor know he was Hawk's longtime rival and deadly foe. Nevertheless, she could feel more than simple lust emanating from him as he watched her. He was demented, wanting to inflict pain. She said a silent prayer for Iron Heart's sense of justice and prayed Hawk would be there when they arrived.

They rode until almost dark. Then the Sioux left, and the Cheyenne led her into a narrow ravine through which a clear stream meandered. After following its twisting course for several hundred yards, they rounded a bend and came upon a wide, grassy valley; in its center was the encampment. It did not seem as large as it had two summers ago. Perhaps it was only the difference in the site that made it appear smaller.

Carrie scanned the faces of the people who stood impassively as she was led into the center of the horseshoe configuration of tepees. Trying desperately to maintain her dignity, for she knew the Cheyenne respected courage, she sat straight and tall on Taffy, holding Perry securely in front of her. All the while she continued to look in vain for Hawk.

The village was much as she remembered, a summer camp with men sharpening knives, fletching arrows, and cleaning rifles while women stirred steaming pots over open fires, pounded fruit with dried meat in stone mortars, and tanned hides stretched on broad frames across the ground. A motley assortment of small children who were playing with balls and sticks now stopped to stare in wonder at the *veho* woman with the strange and wondrous hair. One small girl with luminous brown eyes clutched a doll to her thin chest and regarded Perry with shy curiosity. She resembled Bright Leaf, Carrie thought with a sudden pang. Was the child still in the camp? Suddenly Carrie felt less afraid, eager to confront Iron Heart and show him his great-grandson.

By the time the war party reached Iron Heart's lodge, word had already spread like wildfire through the village. However, the chief did not come out to greet them. Angry Wolf, White Arrow, and Owl Man dismounted.

Carrie waited expectantly, but the buffalo-hide flap of the lodge did not open. Taking the initiative, she grasped Perry firmly and dismounted, then marched toward the opening of the big lodge. Angry Wolf stepped quickly in her way and grasped her cruelly by one arm, saying something in Cheyenne that was obviously a harsh reprimand. He then stepped inside the tepee and dragged her roughly behind him. Almost losing her balance as she stooped to enter while holding Perry, she quickly righted herself and stood proudly, letting her eyes adjust to the gloom.

Iron Heart sat near the center of the large circular interior. He looked older, sadder and subdued, Carrie thought. Then the chief motioned for Angry Wolf to speak. After a brief exchange in which the old man interrupted with a number of questions, the two other Cheyenne were called.

Carrie stood in the center of the group of men, uncertain if she should say anything. Angry Wolf no longer held on to her, but his very presence next to her was threat enough; he seemed to think he owned her. She knew it was customary for women to remain silent in any serious deliberation such as this, but she did not understand what they were saying and desperately wanted to present her side. Surely Iron Heart would recognize his own flesh and blood!

She fixed her attention on the old man as he conversed with the three warriors. Not once did he look at Perry. Her heart sank. Then he abruptly dismissed them all and motioned for her to stay. With a snarled oath, Angry Wolf turned and stalked out of the lodge with the other two behind him.

"Sit, Carrie Sinclair." It was his first acknowledgment of her existence. As she knelt on the thick cushion of pelts where he indicated, she watched him study Perry. The boy stared with huge, glowing black eyes at the wizened face before him. After several seconds of mutual perusal, the chief spoke again with a grunt of acceptance. "He is the son of Hunting Hawk. There can be no doubt of it."

"Where is Hawk?" Carrie could wait no longer to speak.

"Where is your husband?" His words were measured but nonetheless accusing.

She was shocked; then realization swept over her. No one here knew! "Noah died a year ago, before Perry was born."

"But not before he was conceived," came the gentle rebuke. His eyes suddenly seemed weary, defeated and hurt.

Her face flamed red as her hair under Iron Heart's intense scrutiny. Never with any of the priggish townspeople or even with Kyle had she felt this discomfort. Collecting herself, Carrie looked him squarely in the eye. "I make no apologies. I was forced against my will to marry a man who was a cruel, vindictive animal." She paused and took a swallow for courage. "Hawk and I lived under his roof. We were thrown together repeatedly, until we couldn't resist any longer. After one night with me, Hawk's sense of honor compelled him to leave. I loved him, and when Perry was born I was overjoyed that he was Hawk's son, not Noah's." She stopped and looked from Iron Heart to Perry, a glow of intense love and pride infusing her face.

"He gave you that?" The old man gestured to the medallion hanging proudly between her breasts.

"Yes. After—after we spent that one night together, he placed it around my neck. I knew how much he valued it because he always wore it." She unconsciously stroked its intricate, gleaming surface. "Then he left. I haven't seen him in a year and a half. Is he here?" Her heart was in her throat now.

Iron Heart sighed. He should have known he could not go against the will of the Powers. This was ordained, even if it boded ill for his grandson and the young woman who sat so proudly before him. "He has lived with the People through two snows. You will find him much changed, I fear. We are all of us much changed. Many have died from the spotted throat—what you call diptheria."

"Bright Leaf," Carrie cut in abruptly. "She's all right?"

He nodded. "That is why Hunting Hawk is not in the village. He is taking her to her parents. This spring we finally received word of them. There will be much rejoicing in their camp," he said wistfully.

"When will he return?" She could not keep the anticipation out of her voice.

Iron Heart fixed her with a penetrating stare, both a rebuke and a warning in his manner. "It will be several days. There are many things to consider before he returns."

Something in his voice sent a ripple of apprehension through her. "What did you mean when you said he is much changed?"

"He has been married," he said levelly.

Carrie sat riveted to the ground. If she had been hit full in the heart with a sledge hammer, it could not have hurt more. Married! He left her alone to face Noah's killing wrath, deserted her to bear his son and live down all the censure, and then he married another!

Her face betrayed her anguish and her anger to Iron Heart. He watched her stroke the hair on her exhausted son's head as he lay sleeping on the pallet. She had reason to be hurt, he supposed, but then, so did Wind Song, so did he. "His wife is dead. Killed by the spotted throat, she and her unborn child."

Carrie's eyes were huge and dark green as she fixed them on him, eloquent with pain. "It was Wind Song, wasn't it?" She already knew.

He nodded. "Hunting Hawk blames all whites for their deaths, even himself. Maybe most of all himself," he said sadly, thinking of the bleak desolation that still enwrapped Hawk, even six months later.

"What will happen now, Iron Heart? Will he want his

son?'' *Will he want me?* She sat very still, pondering all that had happened. Could she forgive what she perceived as a betrayal? Did she still love him?

The old man's next words shocked her. ''I must confer with the other chiefs. Angry Wolf is a powerful man in our band, and he has claimed you. You belong to no man now, not He Who Walks in Sun, not Hunting Hawk. Many in our band want to join with our Sioux brothers and take up arms against the *veho*. Angry Wolf is their leader. If the elders do not deal fairly with him, it may lead many more young warriors to sing their wolf songs and go to war. I would not have this.''

''But you cannot give me to that horrible man! Keeping a white captive would bring the army down on you for certain!'' She was really terrified now. ''What of your great-grandson? Angry Wolf doesn't want him. I fear he'd kill my son!''

''As to holding a captive, we move like the wind deep in the mountains and leave no trails across the wide plains. No bluecoats would ever know you were here or see you if we wished to hide you. No one will harm the boy. He is of my blood and I will protect him, but I can make no promises about you.'' He stood up and began to walk toward the opening of the lodge. ''I will send women with food and water. Rest and refresh yourself. It will take several days to decide.'' *And may Hunting Hawk return by then,* he prayed silently.

Carrie sat alone, hugging herself in disbelief and numbness. What would happen to her and Perry? Shortly, two older women came in bearing bowls of fruit and stew, and a flask of water. They spoke no English and did not seem inclined to be friendly, so Carrie simply indicated her thanks and settled back to feed Perry and eat to keep up her own strength. She knew she would need all her wits about her for the ordeal to come.

Gradually as her panic subsided, it was replaced by a low, simmering anger. She and her child were trapped in a hell not of their making. Of course, she felt horribly guilty for her careless wandering that had brought Angry Wolf and his cohorts down upon them, but it was certainly not her fault that an epidemic had decimated the village! Or that Wind Song was dead. She still felt mortified and furious remembering Iron Heart's accusing words, *Where is your husband?* The world and all its rules were made by men, red or white!

All through the next day Carrie waited, confined to another lodge where she and her son had been taken. She shared it with Calf Woman. The old woman was not unkind. In fact, she brought Perry a rawhide ball and a string of brightly colored beads to play with and watched his bright, alert movements with obvious delight. Toward the boy's mother, however, she showed no emotion at all, neither hostility nor friendliness. They waited.

Early the following morning Carrie was disturbed from her toilette by a great commotion outside. She had just finished washing her face and combing her hair with a bone comb given to her by Calf Woman when the furor erupted. Male voices speaking stridently in Cheyenne were calling across the clearing in front of the lodge. Then Calf Woman entered and motioned for her to bring Perry and follow her. Forcing herself to remain calm, she took a deep breath and scooped up the boy.

The brilliant morning sunlight blinded her for a moment. Then she saw him, standing directly in her line of vision, almost twenty feet away. Hawk. At least, he had once been Hawk Sinclair. Now he was Hunting Hawk, grandson of Iron Heart, a Cheyenne warrior. He was almost naked in the heat of the morning, dressed only in breechclout and moccasins with that same evil-looking knife strapped to his waistband. His sinuously muscled body glistened with perspiration, running in rivulets through the thick black hair of his chest, for he had ridden hard to get to the encampment. His hair was quite long now, plaited into two gleaming braids, woven through with rawhide thongs and feathers. Copper armbands gleamed on his hard biceps and a matching necklace lay suspended against his chest. Large copper earrings completed the barbaric adornment. He needed a shave, a task he rarely neglected. His face was shuttered and expressionless, very Indianlike to Carrie. What was he thinking?

Hawk slowly walked over to her, his eyes shifting from her face to consider the boy. If he was surprised, he concealed it, or perhaps he just did not care that he had a son, she thought bleakly. Her heart lodged in her throat and she found herself unable to speak, desperately wanting him to say something in English, to prove to her that he was still Hawk, not some alien, savage stranger.

"What is his name?" He finally broke the silence between them as they stood face to face. He put out his hand and gently touched the boy's black shiny hair.

"Peregrine . . . Perry," she managed to choke out.

He smiled enigmatically. "A name that means something. Good." Then he turned and walked over to where Iron Heart and Angry Wolf stood. The old man motioned them inside his lodge, and they vanished behind the tent flap.

"She is mine. I claim the right of her capture. She is my slave." Angry Wolf's voice was loud and carried far as he intended it should.

"You cannot have her. She is the mother of my son, Angry Wolf." Hawk's voice was quiet. Dreading what might come, fearing what he might have to do, he looked at Iron Heart.

"The council has debated long and thoroughly, Angry Wolf," Iron Heart began. "The woman is well known among the whites. Her firehair would be too difficult to conceal if she were your slave. It would bring soldiers to our camp, death to everyone here. We must send her back unharmed, her and her son."

Angry Wolf's face grew rigid and darkened as his fury rose. When Iron Heart had finished speaking, he lashed out, gesturing to Hawk. "It is because of him! He is your grandson and she lay with him, giving him that child when they had no right! He has no claim on her under our law. She has a white husband!"

"He Who Walks in Sun is dead." The old man said the words with finality, ignoring Angry Wolf's tirade and looking at Hawk as he spoke. Hawk's face still showed no emotion, but the old man heard him release a tightly held hiss of breath at the startling news. "The council has spoken, Angry Wolf. You cannot have the woman." The chief watched his grandson stand poised; Hawk waited to see what the infuriated warrior would do next.

Angry Wolf whirled and vanished through the opening of the tepee. As he strode toward Carrie, he said loudly, for all to hear, "I will not give my captive to a half-blooded adulterer!" He challenged Hawk openly as a gasp of horrified indignation went up around the large circle of people gathered to witness the spectacle.

Carrie almost dropped Perry as Angry Wolf yanked her to him. She began to fight him then, kicking at his bare shins with her booted feet, but before she could do any damage, he struck her a savage blow across the face. As he raised his hand to hit her again, Hawk's body smashed into his, forcing him to release his vicious hold on Carrie.

They tumbled to the ground at her feet, rolling and thrashing in the dust as she clutched Perry and jumped out of their way. With a snarled oath, Angry Wolf rolled to his feet and drew his knife. Hawk did the same. The circle of men around them widened. No one moved to stop them, for indeed everyone, even Iron Heart, knew it could not be done.

The two men circled one another, right, then left, then right again, like two mountain lions, each poised and ready to spring. Angry Wolf feinted high with his blade, then lunged low, but Hawk parried his thrusts with uncanny accuracy. For several minutes the stalemate continued as they alternately attacked and retreated. Carrie let out a muffled gasp when Angry Wolf's knife slashed a bloody furrow across Hawk's forearm. Just as quickly Hawk opened up Angry Wolf's chest with a long gash, narrowly missing his throat and knocking him to the hard-packed earth. Soon they were both covered with a murky film of sweat, dust, and blood as they rolled on the ground until Angry Wolf came up on top. Hawk held his foe's knife hand in a deathlock, struggling desperately to keep it from his throat.

Angry Wolf's face grimaced in an ugly caricature of a smile. "Now you die and I get your flame-haired woman to replace Wind Song, white man!"

Just then Hawk gave a twisting roll and caught his leg around Angry Wolf's. The leverage pulled him over and they rolled again in a blur of flashing steel and dust. This time Hawk came up on top when they stopped, halfway across the clearing.''

"You have always coveted what was not yours, Angry Wolf. Now you pay for your greed!" Hawk's knife inched its way closer to his enemy's bare throat.

With a desperate surge, Angry Wolf broke free at the last moment as Hawk's knife plunged down to slash his shoulder. He twisted free of Hawk's grasp and they separated once more.

Carrie stood isolated at one end of the circular clearing. The majority of the Cheyenne onlookers gave her a wide berth. She shielded Perry's eyes from the bloody carnage taking place, fearful he would be scarred for life if he witnessed this butchery.

Hawk bided his time, circling like his namesake in predatory arcs, back and forth, taunting and infuriating Angry Wolf into making a move. Angry Wolf lunged and missed, but as he was propelled forward into the open space where Hawk had stood a split second earlier, he felt Hawk grasp his right forearm, yanking him around while raising his knife hand harmlessly into midair. In a blur Hawk's own blade came up, slashing Angry Wolf's throat deeply. After a few thrashing movements Angry Wolf lay still. Hawk stood staring at his dead foe for several minutes, then sheathed his knife and looked up at Carrie. Her ashen face spoke volumes as she stood clutching the boy to her. Hawk turned wordlessly and strode over to Iron Heart.

The old man's face was gray with anguish. Looking into his eyes, Hawk felt as if Angry Wolf's knife had twisted in his own heart. God, anything but this! Yet he knew the law and knew what his grandfather must do.

"You have shed Cheyenne blood," the chief intoned. As if lending moral support to the old man, several other of the tribal elders gathered around him.

"I understand," Hawk said simply, facing them. "The penalty for killing another Cheyenne is banishment for

four years. I will take the white woman and child and go.''
With a parting look at his grandfather, he walked dejectedly
toward his lodge to retrieve the relics of his white life, a
life to which he did not wish to return, not this way.
Perhaps not at all.

Carrie did not know what to expect when Hawk stalked
off and Iron Heart came toward her. His face was drawn
and his words flat. ''Hawk Sinclair has made his choice.
He will take you and the boy to your home. Wait in the
lodge until he comes for you.'' With that he turned and
walked away. She did not understand what had just transpired, but she did know that it was unnatural for Iron
Heart to refer to his grandson by his white name. Uncertainly she went inside and sat down. The keening death
chant over Angry Wolf's body had already begun. She
gritted her teeth and waited.

It did not take Hawk long to change into a pair of denim
pants and a white shirt. He strapped on the Colt .44 and
resheathed his knife in the heavy leather belt. Gathering up
his few possessions, he let out a bitter laugh. When he had
left Circle S it had been the same. He owned nothing that
could not fit in a pair of saddlebags. He probably never
would.

When he pulled back the buffalo-hide flap and stepped
into the lodge where Carrie sat with his son, Hawk moved
noiselessly and reached for the boy. His silent entrance on
moccasined feet took her by surprise, and she gasped in
shock as one of his braids brushed her cheek. Flinching
back, she clutched the fussing child to her.

''No! I'll carry him.'' Her voice came out sharper than
she intended. The gruesome fight and then the horrible
wailing death chant had finally succeeded in breaking her
iron reserve of calm. She had eaten and slept little in three
days and was teetering on the edge of hysteria.

''Don't be foolish. You're exhausted and shaky.'' With
no more debate, he scooped the boy from her arms and
turned to carry him outside.

Furiously she whirled on him, lunging at his back with a
fierce maternal cry dredged up from the depths of her soul.
''You can't take him! Let me have my son! He's mine.

Damn you, you filthy savage! Let me—'' She was sobbing
and flailing by this time, and Perry responded with his own
cry of fright.

Hawk stood very still, with his son on one arm, holding
her away from him with the other. He released her shoulder when she stopped short.

My God, what have I just said? One look at the set lines
of his face made her realize the enormity of what she had
done. "Hawk, I'm sorry. I didn't mean—''

He cut her off by turning sharply on his heel to leave
with Perry, saying, "Get your gear. I have Taffy saddled
outside. Mount up, or I'll leave you behind!''

Grabbing her hat and gloves, she quickly followed him
out. By now Perry had stopped fussing and seemed well
content to sit in front of his father on the big red horse.
With the bright eyes of childhood he eagerly looked
around the village as they rode away. Hawk never looked
back.

CHAPTER 20

Hawk stared straight ahead and held Redskin at a steady, ground-eating pace. Carrie was afraid to speak, alternately ashamed of her hysterical outburst, then angry with him for his brutal actions and bloodthirsty appearance. Even in a white man's shirt and pants, he looked savage with his long braids, barbaric jewelry, and arsenal of weapons.

Hawk's emotions were in turmoil as well. When he had arrived in response to the cryptic message from Iron Heart, he did not expect to see Carrie there, much less with a child. One look at Perry's face was all it took to know the boy was his son. Against all odds, the one thing that he had never considered had happened. The child was his, not Noah's. He had cursed himself for a fool, feeling overjoyed, guilty, and angry with her for endangering herself and the boy at Angry Wolf's hands. Then he had realized how she had looked at him, the uncertainty, fright, even revulsion in her eyes as she had taken in his Cheyenne appearance. All he had really seemed to her in white man's garb was an exotic version of a *veho*. Now she had seen him as he was, as a Cheyenne, and she did not like it. *A filthy savage.*

The hurt festered along with the guilt. He had just killed a man, one of the People. He should have let the elders stop Angry Wolf. They had already decided he could not have Carrie. But Hawk could not bear to see him put his hands on her and flew at him in a rage of possessive jealousy. Perversely, he blamed her for being there, for wandering off so far alone and getting captured. Then he looked across at her and saw his medallion. She wore it proudly, and he cursed himself for the sudden surge of desire that seized him. He had many things to ponder.

As they rode silently through the hot morning air, they were both wrapped in misery and did not hear the approaching horse until the rider was almost upon them. Hawk recognized the wiry little frame of Kyle Hunnicut as soon as he whirled in the saddle and caught sight of the Texan.

"Longlegs, yew son of a bitch!" Kyle was relieved and overjoyed, pulling up to reach over and thump his old friend heartily on the back. "I tracked her 'n' th' boy there, but couldn't git near 'nough ta git 'em out. Been watching' nigh onta three days on th' other side o' th' camp. Shore glad ya come along when ya did. Yew all right, Carrie?" He shifted his gaze from Hawk to Carrie, confused as to what had been said between them. He noted the careful and possessive way Hawk held his son. One thing had been settled, at least.

Carrie nodded, still numb from her ordeal and the turmoil of confronting Hawk. "I'm fine, Kyle."

She didn't look fine, but he held his peace. What a pickle this was turning out to be, he swore to himself. The tension between Hawk and Carrie quickly transmitted itself to the Texan who rode toward Circle S with them, the silence broken only by desultory conversation in which Hawk related how Carrie and the boy were captured and how he freed her.

Kyle swore, realizing what it meant. Long ago Hawk had told him enough about Cheyenne law for him to realize that his friend had been banished from the only place where he had ever felt he belonged. And he had left a wife behind. Did Carrie know about her? Surely her child had been born by now. What would Hawk do? He needed to talk with Hawk alone after they arrived at Circle S.

"I can't go back, Kyle." Hawk's voice was weary as he sat in Frank Lowery's cabin that night, sharing a drink with his friend. Since the departure of Rider, the small cottage had become Hunnicut's place.

There had been no chance for them to talk until now. Feliz had fussed endlessly over Hawk's wounds, all superficial but encrusted with dried blood. She had insisted on a hot bath, poultices, and pounds of ointment. Then there had been supper and all the arrangements to be made about sleeping quarters. Hawk firmly told Feliz that he would stay in his mother's cabin, not return to the big house. Carrie had moved her things and Perry's into the room he used to occupy. He could scarcely sleep there now, much less occupy Noah's old room.

Hawk knew he must learn from Kyle the details of what had happened in his absence. They sat at the table in Frank's old kitchen and hefted two glasses of whiskey.

"Ain't yew got a reason ta go back, Hawk? Mebbe two o' 'em now?" Kyle's eyes were shrewdly assessing, knowing his friend would tell him in his own good time.

"Wind Song died last winter, Kyle. Diptheria. Our child died with her. Even after my four years of exile are over there'll be nothing left for me in my grandfather's village. I've betrayed him and all the People. I can imagine what he thought when he saw Carrie with my son." He gave a self-deprecating laugh. "You know, it's ironic. When I took her there with Bright Leaf, the old women gossiped about us, saying that we were lovers, betraying her husband, my father. Their suspicions were vindicated with proof positive, weren't they?"

"Don't appear ta me yore bein' fair ta Carrie 'er yerself, Longlegs."

Hawk rubbed his hand over his eyes and made a dismissing gesture. "Tell me what's happened while I was gone. When did you come back?"

They talked late into the night about Frank's murder, Noah's death, Caleb Rider and Karl Krueger's collusion, the precarious state of Circle S's finances, all the things that needed to be settled, except the most basic one—the relationship between Hawk and Carrie. That, Kyle hoped would work itself out.

Carrie lay in bed late that night, exhausted but unable to

sleep. She had sat at the big kitchen table earlier in the evening and studied him covertly as he ate. *Was I watching to see if some residual savagery would linger in his table manners?* She scoffed angrily to herself as the confusion and hurt washed over her once again. He was half red Indian. She had always known that, but somehow she had never really considered what it implied until she saw him bronzed and naked, locked in a bloody death struggle with another savage. A part of him *was* savage, had always been, would always be.

She tossed and pounded her pillow, realizing that her reaction was only one of initial shock. Buried deeper lay the memory of Wind Song—Wind Song and her unborn child, Hawk's child, too. *While I carried Perry, he lay with his Cheyenne wife, giving her a baby.* Tears stung her eyes. Could she forgive him?

Yes. Carrie knew she still loved him, savage or not, faithful or not, but he was so cold, so accusing, as if he blamed her for the death of that vile man who had captured her. Her pride had been dealt a bitter blow. He had loved his Cheyenne wife and valued the life he had with her and her people more than he valued Carrie Sinclair. That was obvious. But what of Perry? The boy had a right to a father even if she was too proud to demand the right to a husband. Tomorrow she would simply ask him outright what he planned to do. A small voice taunted her: *If he's tied to his son, he's tied to you as well. Isn't that what you want?*

She punched the pillow another fierce blow and rolled over. "Damn if I'll beg him to marry me! He can just stay in Marah's house, and welcome to it!"

Carrie brought her cup of scalding black coffee from the stove to the table. It was barely light, but knowing Hawk's predilection for rising with the sun she decided to wait for him in the kitchen. He would have to take his meals here, at least until he stocked his cabin with supplies. Knowing Feliz's reaction if he tried to get out of eating her cooking, he would probably continue having supper with them regardless. She and Kyle had taken to eating with Feliz in the big, comfortable kitchen. Since Noah had died, the dining room had not been used. Carrie was not interested in using it now. Better to keep things simple and informal.

Her chaotic thoughts were interrupted as the back door swung open and Hawk entered as silently as ever. He had shaved and changed his shirt, but otherwise looked as barbaric as he had yesterday, with his earrings and long braids.

Looking at him over the rim of her cup, she blew on its steaming surface. "Get your hair cut, or one of Krueger's men'll shoot you for a Sioux raider."

He threw her a cynical smirk as he poured some coffee. When he tasted it, he grimaced and said, "Feliz didn't make this coffee."

"I did," she dared him.

"It's lousy. Too strong," he replied levelly.

"Kyle and I like it that way," she shot back.

"You didn't get up this early just to make rotten coffee or drum up business for the barber. You have something to say to me, Carrie?" He straddled a kitchen chair, leaning his chin on its backrest. As he sipped his coffee, he stared into space, giving her time to collect her thoughts and speak her piece.

She took a deep, steadying breath and plunged in. "I suppose Kyle's told you about our trouble with K Bar."

"Yes."

Damn him, he wasn't going to make it any easier for her! "Well, are you staying? Circle S belongs to you."

He continued staring, then sighed and said, "That's not what the law says, and you know it. It's yours—yours and Perry's."

"And Perry is your son," she persisted, goaded to unreasonable anger by this hardheaded man.

"Yes, I'm staying, Carrie. At least for now, to see this through with Krueger." He looked at her wearily, sorry things had to be this way.

Carrie misinterpreted his dejection as disgust with her, the feeling of being entrapped by the accident of Perry's birth.

"Fine. Settle it with Kyle about who runs what. I expect he'll want you to take charge." She set the cup down with more force than she intended and rose. Stopping midway in her retreat from the kitchen, she said, "After all, you *are* the Sinclair around here now."

That morning Hawk and Kyle made plans for a fall roundup, posted the work assignments for all the hands, and agreed to hire several more men who were good with guns. If Krueger planned a range war, Circle S would be well prepared to stand him off. The men accepted Hawk's return as natural. He was Noah's son and certainly capable of running the place. If they were curious or uncomfortable about his scandalous relationship with Noah's widow, they kept it to themselves. All were relived not to be working for a female who was an easterner at that.

Two weeks later the first warning of possible new trouble with Krueger materialized. Kyle rode in with a body tied across the saddle of a strange horse.

"Yew ever seen him 'er thet bronc afore?" Kyle swung down from his horse, tossing a careless glance back at his prize.

Hawk strode over and raised the head of the dead man by the hair. After a careful inspection he let it drop. He circled the buckskin gelding and checked its shoes. "Don't recognize the man, but I remember the horse—at least I've seen his track before. On the north range last week, when fifty head were missing." He looked at Kyle's shrewd, assessing gaze. "You shoot him?" It scarcely needed to be asked.

Kyle nodded. "Come up on 'em red-handed, but afore I cud do more'n draw, they's shootin' an' jumpin' like a sack o' Mexicali beans. Two others got away. This varmint warn't so lucky."

"Well, we figured the winter's truce with Krueger would end sooner or later. Guess it's overdue at that," Hawk said, wondering what the crafty German's next move would be.

"But Karl, aren't you glad to see me?" Lola pouted prettily, posing by the enormous carved oak mantel in Krueger's study. Her lavender silk dress was as cool and fresh as a spring sunrise, carefully chosen to complement her pale hair and blue eyes. She had spent the last of Ernst's money on this elaborate wardrobe. Now she must play her role with utmost care.

Krueger looked over her artfully curled blond hair and reddened lips. She was beginning to get hard-looking, but then, she was pushing forty, he considered philosophically. "You hardly look the part of a bereaved widow, Liebchen."

Lola shrugged and swished over to him, her silk skirts rustling seductively. "Karl, darling, you know Ernst and I had an understanding. He wanted a young, beautiful wife and—"

"You wanted his title and his fortune. Pity you were cheated of both," he supplied nastily. "Since he died without issue, I am now Baron von Krueger. My poor brother also died in virtual penury."

At her intake of breath and shocked facial expression, the big man laughed. "Who do you think he came to for loans, my dear, when the family estates in Germany were milked of all they had to give? My elder brother was a good match for you in profligacy, dear Lola."

Lola shrugged, a careless, sophisticated gesture that she had cultivated to conceal her temper. "Well, it was quite an unhappy surprise to me, Karl, to learn that my husband, the baron, held an empty title. It seems I chose the wrong brother . . . the first time," she purred seductively as she looped her arms around Krueger's neck.

He stood still, seeming to evaluate her blatant offer momentarily. Then he shook with laughter, the sound rumbling from his barrel chest.

"What's the matter?" she spat at him in fury, withdrawing her arms and standing back to glare at him with icy blue eyes.

"I have been turning the matter of marriage over in my mind here of late, Liebchen, but not to a penniless fortune hunter. I do not share my brother's bad judgment in matters financial—or amatory."

She squelched the overwhelming urge to slap him soundly and smiled archly instead. "If not me, darling, on whom would you consider bestowing the honor of becoming Baroness von Krueger?"

A fleeting look of distaste crossed his saturnine features but quickly vanished. "Another of Noah Sinclair's women, my dear. The present owner of Circle S. You would have done well to outlast him as Carrie did. Now she is a rich woman and you are once more impoverished."

Lola was completely taken aback by his statement. "You'd marry her, after all the scandal, with her Indian brat in tow?" She was frankly incredulous.

His face darkened and he turned sharply, striding over to the liquor cabinet in the opposite corner of the large room. As he poured himself a shot of schnapps, he spoke measuredly. "I would not normally consider lowering myself to take the leavings of a savage, regardless of how beautiful she might be." He paused and sipped the fiery liquor. "However, I am a practical man. I want Circle S. With all the southern range in my control, I will run eastern Montana and drive out all the small cattlemen, dirt farmers, even the Indians. I will be the power broker when Montana becomes a state." His eyes took on an intense, dark gleam. "I shall be a real baron, not just the holder of a bankrupt European title!"

Lola considered his speech and then said carefully, "What makes you so sure Carrie Sinclair will fall in with your plans? She's had a child by Hawk. Maybe she'll marry him now that he's come home." Making a comparison between the big, corpulent German and the lean, handsome half-breed, Lola had no doubt whom she'd choose were she Carrie Sinclair!

He brushed that aside. "He has been living in a separate house. He runs the ranch for her, but she has not married him. From all reports I have received, they seem to be polite strangers these days. Perhaps her ostracism by the whole community has finally made her see the folly of involvement with a penniless gunman, much less one with the added stigma of being a half-breed! No, she will never marry him, and no respectable man in the territory will marry her unless she once more gains social acceptance."

"And you plan to revive her fallen reputation," Lola supplied with a cynical laugh. "Don't count on too much gratitude, Karl. You may just have to think of another way to get Circle S.''

It promised to be a very interesting fall in this godforsaken wilderness after all, she thought to herself, settling down on the plum velvet sofa to sample some of Karl's schnapps. Very interesting indeed.

It was time to get a haircut, Hawk decided that morning as he considered the hot, cumbersome braids hanging down on his bare chest. He nicked himself shaving and swore absently. The long hair had been like a badge of defiance, to soothe his hurt pride and fierce anger when he first returned. But what the hell was he proving by continuing to dress like a Cheyenne? And to whom? He threw down the towel after wiping the remnants of soap from his face. He would ride into town this afternoon.

Miles City had changed somewhat since the coming of the railroad. A few new faces were scattered among the old familiar ones. Jeb Brighton had sold his livery stable to a young Swede named Magnusson and the bank had several new clerks. Business was booming. Cattle prices were high back east and the easy access to rails made rapid delivery of livestock a reality for the ranchers.

As he rode by Cummins' Emporium, Hawk noticed the fancy new title and sign hanging on the wooden facade of the big old store. Idly he thought of Kitty, then dismissed her from his mind. He would get a bath and haircut, then head to Clancey's for a much-needed release. He thought back over the better part of a year's celibacy, now amazed at his lack of interest in women.

When Wind Song died, he was so numbed by guilt and grief he had no desire for months afterward. But when Carrie came back into his life, his feelings quickly changed. The air at Circle S was charged with sexual tension every time he encountered her. Damn her *veho* soul to hell!

If the citizens of Miles City were not exactly overjoyed to have Noah Sinclair's half-breed son return, everyone knew better than to cross him openly. His shocking liaison with his father's wife gave the town gossips plenty to talk about. They sniped behind his back, and Hawk certainly

provided ample grist for their mills, alleviating the bore-
dom on many a long, hot summer afternoon.

No one contributed more to keeping the fires of scandal
blazing than Mathilda Thorndyke. She had settled in town
after having been discharged from Circle S and now
worked at Cummins' Emporium and resided at Mrs.
Crump's boardinghouse. Her nest egg was safely deposited
in the local bank. Since her arrival she had devoted her life
to making sure every last soul in the eastern territory heard
the sinful tale of adultery that surrounded Carrie Sinclair.

Hawk saw her standing on the wooden porch of the
newspaper office. "Probably going to take out an ad
denouncing me as a heathen killer and despoiler of white
women," he smirked bitterly. Then, unable to resist, he
swung Redskin over toward her and paused to tip his hat
insolently. "Good day, Mathilda. You look in the bloom of
health, like you just strangled a litter of newborn kittens."
When she gasped and jumped back, almost falling over a
bench next to the plate-glass window, he laughed and
kneed his big red horse on toward the barber shop down
the street.

Lola Jameson took in the exchange between Hawk and
the Thorndyke crone from her vantage point inside the
bank. She had come to town today to check on her meager
resources and make discreet inquiries about Hawk and
Carrie. Lola did not believe they could continue to live at
the same ranch and not resume their earlier relationship.
Krueger was a fool, hoping to win the Sinclair girl. Lola
had decided to take a gamble and wait it out as her
brother-in-law's houseguest. She was desperate. Her money was running low, and she must find a husband soon.

Karl was her perfect answer—titled, rich, and worldly.
They could appreciate each other and overlook one another's flaws. If only she could make him see how stupid it
was to pursue Carrie Sinclair. Her eyes narrowed as she
thought of her rival. Lola had wanted revenge on the
acid-tongued redhead ever since their encounter at the ball
two years ago in Miles City.

As she watched Hawk, Lola felt the same old hungry
compulsion seize her. What was it about dangerous men

that had always drawn her to them? Her reputation was in shreds back east despite her marriage to a titled European. During her years with Ernst, she had flitted from one scandalous amour to another, earning the censure of eastern society. Now she felt that yearning stir her again, made doubly strong by the unattainable status of her quarry. Hawk had resisted her blandishments since he was a youth, but Lola loved a challenge. Taking what was Carrie Sinclair's would sweeten the bargain even more.

Wetting her red lips with the tip of her tongue, she stepped out of the bank just when she saw him leave the barbershop. Her timing had never been better as she stepped onto the walk at the exact moment he looked out to cross the street. They narrowly missed colliding, and she reached one silk-gloved hand out to steady herself on his arm.

"Why, Hawk Sinclair! I heard you had come home." She scanned his freshly barbered black hair, now cut crisply above his shirt collar. One inky lock fell across his high forehead as he reached down to extricate himself from her grasp. "Still sinfully handsome, and so aloof, darling. I've heard all sorts of the most delicious gossip about you since I came to visit Karl. You have heard my poor, dear Ernst died this spring? *I'm* a widow, *too*." She emphasized the first and last words of the sentence overmuch.

He scoffed. "I can see how much you mourn poor, dear Ernst's passing." His black eyes took in her elegant red suit with its matching feathered hat. Her overblown curves were displayed so no man could miss their blatant invitation.

"Don't be cross, darling. After all, you can scarcely throw stones now, can you? If I'm willing to overlook your rather obvious lapse with Carrie Sinclair, you should be willing to overlook my past indiscretions." She saw him stiffen and quickly went on, "Besides, I have some news you'd be very interested in hearing. It concerns Karl and your redheaded light o' love."

"Whatever Carrie has to do with Krueger is her own business. I just run Circle S, that's it." His eyes were shuttered, his voice carefully controlled.

"Even if Karl is at your ranch right now, having lunch

with her, inviting her to a special party next month? Aren't you the least bit curious about why he's willing to negotiate her re-entrance into polite society?'' She could tell she had his attention now.

Hawk slid her hand on his arm and they began to stroll up the street. ''Suppose you just let me in on Karl's plans, Lola.''

''But why on earth invite me to such an elegant social occasion, Baron von Krueger? You must realize all the right people in the area will decline to attend if they know a harlot like me will be there.'' Carrie was frankly baffled by Krueger's unexpected visit and oily, effusive European charm.

He smiled. ''Please, my dear young woman, do not distress yourself. I realize that you have been ostracized since last summer. If I may speak bluntly, your reputation will continue to be in shreds as long as that gunman lives on this ranch with you and you are not married.''

She smirked archly. ''I scarcely think my stock would go up in town if I married him at this late date!''

''But of course not! I did not mean to imply you should ever marry the barbarian who took advantage of you. I merely meant that you need the protection of someone whose influence and respectability are above reproach.''

''Such as yourself? Why sponsor a fallen woman like me?'' Could he possibly have the gall to think she'd marry him and hand Circle S over to him just to regain her reputation!

''Would you not like to—how do you Americans put it?—thumb your nose at all those snobbish women? How long has it been since you have dressed up in a beautiful gown or waltzed with a man? Would it not be a pleasure to be admired by all the gentlemen? You are a very beautiful woman, Carrie Sinclair.'' His hooded eyes shone with lust as he spoke.

Carrie repressed a shudder of revulsion. His manner reminded her so much of Noah. The naked ruthlessness of him, the enormous bald nerve. He wanted her ranch and would do anything to get it. Well, two could play his dangerous game of intrigue. It might be interesting to see the palatial mansion he had built on K Bar land. And, yes, she would love to flaunt herself in front of every hypocritical, psalm-singing man and woman in the territory! Accepting Krueger's invitation would infuriate Hawk and possibly make him jealous as well. "I accept, Baron." As he bowed and kissed her hand, she smiled wickedly.

"You can't seriously consider going to a party at K Bar!" Hawk glared at Carrie across the parlor as he paced back and forth in agitation.

"Why not? Surely you don't think I'm so naive and gullible that I'll fall in his arms and hand Circle S to him, signed and sealed for some marriage lines?" She stood squarely in front of him now, hands on her hips, glaring right back.

"Then why go at all?" His look was both cynical and accusing.

"You wouldn't understand," she replied bleakly, thinking of all those women in town who crossed the street to avoid contamination from her skirts, and the men like Cy Cummins with his insolent demand for cash payments on all Circle S supplies.

"Lola told me exactly what that old badger is up to. I just hope you're not stupid enough to fall for some hand kissing and a Continental accent, Firehair."

Her head shot up and she flinched, not only for the insult of his patronizing, but also because he used that old endearment. It had been so long since he'd called her Firehair. "You're a fine one to talk, listening to anything that sluttish Lola Jameson says. Her husband's scarcely cold in his grave and she's on the prowl for a replacement!"

He laughed harshly as he poured himself a generous predinner whiskey. "I'll hardly fall for Lola's charms after all these years. Anyway, she's not after a gunman without a cent in the bank. She wants Krueger. Let her have him."

"I won't argue that they don't deserve one another," she said darkly, "but I'm going to the baron's little party. You never know what I might find out about Caleb Rider and the rustling."

He scowled. "They're both dangerous men. You're getting in deep water, Carrie. If you won't stay clear of Krueger, I'll just have to invite myself along as your escort."

She almost smiled, but caught herself, suppressing the surge of triumph. "Suit yourself. It's a formal affair," she replied levelly.

"I still have dress clothes," he said defensively, irked at her flat acceptance of his offer.

Remembering how he had looked the night of the ball in that elegant black suit, she felt the heat stealing into her cheeks and turned to excuse herself abruptly.

He cursed silently, certain she was mortified at the prospect of attending the baron's party with a half-breed.

CHAPTER 21

Carrie took special pains dressing for Krueger's party. She found after living so long in riding skirts and boots that it was a genuine pleasure to try different gowns and hairstyles, to primp and pamper herself. That was the real reason for her elation, she told herself repeatedly, not that she would be beautiful for the man who was escorting her. She finally decided on a gown she had never worn, part of the elaborate trousseau Noah had bought for her. It was a deep honey-colored silk, trimmed with bronze-gold lace across the shoulders, so elegantly and simply cut that it did not look dated. She had not liked it when she first tried it on because of the color, but now with her golden suntanned skin it was exceedingly flattering. Her fiery hair was set off beautifully by the honey color as well. The low neckline emphasized the swell of her breasts, grown larger since Perry's birth.

Running her fingers idly across the four inches of lace at the neckline, she inspected her appearance in the mirror. Her long, slim waist seemed emphasized by the clinging layers of silk that fell away below it. Yes, the dress was quite perfect, bringing out amber flecks in her dark-green eyes. Estrella styled her hair with two long, soft curls on one side and then piled the rest high on her head in a rich, gleaming welter. A few wispy tendrils curled softly at her ears. She wore a thin, gold-filigree necklace set with an amber pendant nestling between her breasts, and matching amber earrings. Inspecting herself critically in the mirror, she decided she looked elegant in an understated yet sensuous way. *I hope Lola Jameson wears scarlet satin and pounds of diamonds!*

Clutching her shawl and reticule, Carrie anxiously went downstairs. She knew Hawk was waiting in the parlor. Thinking of the parties she had attended in St. Louis, she had to laugh at the recurrence of schoolgirl nerves. *I'm a grown, twenty-year-old woman with a child,* she reminded herself.

For once it was she who caught him unawares as she silently stood in the open door of the parlor. He had his back turned, gazing out the window, lost in contemplation. He looked splendid, just as she remembered from that long-ago evening at the hotel in Miles City, wearing that same perfectly tailored black broadcloth suit. The snowy-white shirtfront contrasted with his coppery skin and blueblack hair. One elegantly booted foot was on the windowsill as he leaned his arm casually across his knee and stared into space. She could see his face in profile as she moved soundlessly over the thick carpet. He looked for all the world like a sleek, dark panther poised to spring, powerful and dangerous even in repose.

Carrie felt the trembling begin to build deep inside her as she drank in his compelling maleness. It had been a year and a half since the night he had lain with her, the first and only time she had ever felt love and passion. Now she felt a wanton, shameful stab of desire that left her hollow and shaky. *I want him and he looks on me only as an encumbrance, a guilty reminder of things he would rather forget.*

Proudly she raised her chin and forced back the gathering tears. She would never let him see her as a supplicant again. One time she had asked for his love. Never again.

Suddenly Hawk sensed her presence and turned to stare at the fiery golden vision before him. The faint essence of wildflowers tantalized his nostrils as he gazed on her. God in heaven, she was beautiful! Lest he lose control of his tightly reined emotions and reveal his naked lust to her, he assumed the old familiar pose of casual arrogance, raking her beauty with glowing black eyes. "You'll dazzle all the men, especially Krueger."

She smiled chillingly. "I suppose that's your version of a compliment. Shall we go?"

Karl Krueger had built K Bar's big house to approximate the baronial splendor he had left behind in his native Germany. No expense had been spared in its construction. It was made of stone, three stories tall with high, vaulted ceilings, gaudy even in an era of ostentation and vulgar displays of wealth. The grand ballroom was indeed splendid with imported French crystal chandeliers, gleaming parquet floors, and ivory stucco walls. An elaborate black walnut trestle table intricately carved with gargoyles sat along one wall, groaning with all manner of food: iced fresh oysters on the half shell, huge slabs of roast beef, new potatoes in delicate parsley sauce, and even a huge fountain of champagne. Whiskey was available for the hard-drinking men in the crowd.

Hawk was one of them. He stood to one side of the room, sipping a whiskey while he watched Carrie fend off amorous advances from several besotted cattlemen. She looked like an amber jewel, warm and golden and tantalizing. *I might as well rescue her from those drunks before Krueger gets his hooks into her creamy flesh,* he thought angrily as he strode across the floor, denying to himself that he simply wanted to dance with her.

Without even the courtesy of a request, he caught her up in his arms to the tempo of the music, sweeping her away from two adoring ranchers whose jaws dropped in surprise and chagrin at being so rudely deprived of their prey.

"You could have at least asked for the dance," she spat as soon as she could catch her breath.

"You might have declined, Firehair." His low, breathy murmur left her prey to that familiar weakness. Damn him, why could he do this to her? After the betrayal of Gerald Rawlins and the brutality of Noah Sinclair, she should know better than to ever again bare her heart and soul to a man. She held herself stiffly in his arms, rigid in anger and fear, willing to die rather than let him see her weakness, her want.

Hawk could sense her guarded, wooden manner. It cut him to his soul, although he could not say what he had expected when he so precipitously seized her for the dance. So, she was embarrassed to be seen dancing with her savage lover, was she? His face hardened into a cruel, barbaric mask. "Since you obviously detest my touch, *Mrs.* Sinclair, I'll leave you to your host's Continental charm." With that he whirled her to the edge of the dance floor, nodded curtly, and stalked off.

Karl Krueger watched them dancing—both tall and slim, he so dark, she so fiery. Every eye in the ballroom was covertly on them, and Krueger was livid. When she had arrived on that elegantly dressed savage's arm he was taken completely by surprise. Surprise was immediately replaced by fury, although he hid it beneath a mask of Teutonic politeness.

When Hawk deserted her so abruptly, Krueger moved to her side, observing the transparent hunger in her eyes as she watched Hawk stalk across the crowded room. "You should not wear your heart on your sleeve, Liebchen," he scolded gently.

Caught in such a blatant revelation, Carrie gasped and then attempted to disguise her feelings. She pasted a brittle smile on her lips that did not reach to her emerald eyes, and said to the baron, "I'll recover, Karl. We American women are incredibly resilient."

He nodded approvingly. "I am glad to hear it. Champagne?"

At her nod of acquiescence, he ushered her toward the huge crystal fountain with its circle of ice swans. With a slight nod he had a servant draw two goblets of the bubbling wine and handed one glass to her. "To your beauty, Carrie, the loveliest woman in the territory."

She bestowed a brilliant smile on him. The flattery and attention of an attractive and powerful man was balm to her spirit, never more so than when she saw Lola placing one possessive hand on Hawk's arm. The voluptuous blond was dressed in ice-blue silk and looked cool and sophisticated.

"Darling, you are wickedly handsome tonight." She

reached up and grazed his cheek with her lips, then wet them again with a flick of her tongue.

He looked down at her. *Persistent bitch.* Then he caught sight of Carrie dancing with Krueger and smiling at him. Just how far would Lola go? Hawk decided to find out. He owed himself some divertisement tonight, all things considered. He pulled her to him, then swung them into the waltz.

He was holding her much more closely than propriety allowed, but if she didn't care, neither did he. After a few passes across the polished width of the floor, they neared a set of leaded glass doors leading to the garden. "Let's cool off, Lola."

She swished her skirts in front of him and glided into the night with a seductive chuckle. "If you insist, although I don't think we'll be cooler alone in the dark. . . ."

Krueger watched Carrie's reaction to Hawk and Lola. The besotted young fool. Superbly beautiful, poised, educated, she could have the world, and what does she languish for—a savage! Tightening his grip on her waist, he said, "Your lover is as fickle as my dear Lola. Why do you waste your passion on that gunman?" His heavy, dark brows arched up, giving his face a satanic caste.

She laughed, but it sounded forced, even to her own ears. "I'm learning the rules the hard way, I suppose, Baron."

When he had asked her to dance, she felt compelled to do so, if for no better reason than to show Hawk and Lola that she and Krueger could get on famously without them.

"If you held yourself so stiffly in his arms, it is no wonder he deserted you for Lola's voluptuous charms, Liebchen."

Her eyes betrayed a flicker of pain, but then she forced herself to relax, concentrating on the music, the champagne, the glittering elegant room and all its people. She would enjoy herself if it killed her!

He led her to the edge of the crowd, past several frankly admiring men and the veiled hostility of their wives, then ushered her down a thickly carpeted hallway. "Where are you taking me?"

"Are you afraid to come with me?" He dared her, pausing in the middle of the long, darkened corridor. The walls were paneled in rich walnut, and ornate brass sconces were recessed every few feet, set with flickering candles giving off uncertain light.

The champagne was going to her head. *Hawk, where are you? You said you'd protect me.* "No, Baron, I'm not afraid. Lead on."

He ushered her into his study at the end of the hall. It was a large, dark room, imbued with an aura of mystery and brooding, like its owner. He motioned for her to have a seat on an opulent sofa of purple velvet while he walked to the liquor cabinet across the room. "More champagne? There is a special bottle chilled right here." Without waiting for her to reply, he expertly removed the cork and poured two glasses.

Carrie was becoming increasingly nervous, and regretted her decision to come with him into his lair. The massive walnut desk in the center of the room was strewn with ledgers, legal documents, and newspapers. Baron von Krueger was obviously a very busy man. She itched to know what his private correspondence and pay vouchers might tell her about his designs on Circle S, and especially about his new foreman, Caleb Rider.

He handed her the stem crystal and clinked their glasses together in a silent toast. Over the rim he watched her as she sipped resignedly at the bubbling liquid. "Regretting your decision?" He arched one brow in that characteristic way, unnerving her. Could he read minds at times?

"Yes, a bit. When I arrived with Hawk I'm sure enough tongues wagged. Now I disappear with you. I'm afraid my reputation's beyond redemption." She attempted to keep a light quality in her voice.

"Only if you care what the petty bourgeoise women around here say. Ignore them."

"Easily enough said, but wasn't it you who asked me if I missed social occasions—dressing up and going dancing? Tonight I found I do miss these things."

"And other things." His voice held a magnetic, suggestive quality as he stood beside the small sofa she was seated on. "So foolish, Carrie. First you marry a man three times your age, then take an Indian for a lover. A woman of your beauty, your fire, needs a man worthy of her."

"A man like you, Baron?" Her voice had a ring of challenge in it that kept him at bay, at least for a moment.

"Yes, exactly like me. I'm forty-two years old, wealthy, from a noble lineage, not unattractive to women. You could do far worse. You *have* done far worse."

Before she could reply he pulled her up and into an embrace, his brooding, hooded gray-blue eyes locked with hers. "You are like a Valkyrie, with long legs and flaming hair." With that he grabbed the cluster of curls on one golden shoulder and pulled her head back for a devouring kiss.

She let him kiss her out of perverse curiosity, both to see what he would do and to gauge her own reaction. In truth, he was an attractive man, considered by many women to be the most eligible bachelor in the territory. Yet to her he was simply a different incarnation of Noah: cold, ruthless, vindictive. He continued grinding his mouth over hers until she felt suffocated. *What ever possessed me to let it go this far?* she thought frantically, breaking free of his bruising embrace at last.

He watched her straighten her dress and fuss with the welter of curls now fallen about her shoulders. *Cold bitch!* "Why do you play with me, Liebchen? Surely you know I can be a very lethal opponent. I play to win."

"I know," she said levelly, looking him boldly in the eye, her composure regained in the heat of anger. "And winner takes the prize—Circle S. You don't want me, Karl. You just can't see any other way to get my ranch."

"Oh, there are other ways, just not so pleasant," he said silkily.

"I don't find it pleasant being used, either." Her voice was crackling with anger now.

"You had been much used before I ever touched you, I believe. Your half-breed's bastard is proof of that!" All pretense at civility was dropped now. She actually dared to reject him and moon over a savage!

Carrie struck him hard in pure reflex. "Bastards are made, not born, Baron! Don't smear my son with your slime!"

He rubbed the reddening mark on his jaw and looked at her critically. "I once considered making you my mistress. Now I find even that casual a liaison distasteful."

They stood glaring at one another, both of them furious and flushed. It was at that precise moment Hawk opened the door and stepped inside.

Taking in Carrie's disheveled appearance and the angry red mark on Krueger's face, he could guess what had just transpired between them. A slow smile spread across his face, not reaching the black depths of his eyes. Disgust and fury warred within his breast. "I thought to rescue the *lady* in distress, but I should have realized you could take care of yourself, Firehair." Without taking his eyes off her, he addressed himself to Krueger. "She only gives in when she wants to, Baron."

The blatant implication of what he said pierced her heart, causing her to emit a wounded gasp that she quickly covered up by turning to the livid German. "I regret spoiling your party, Karl. We both should have realized it's better to have an honest truce than a feigned friendship." Not waiting for him to react, she swept out of the room without looking at Hawk.

The two men stared at one another in undisguised hatred now. "I am through playing games, red mongrel," Krueger ground out in a low, vibrating voice. "When I finish with you and your fire-haired whore, you will not own a square foot of this territory."

Hawk's face remained impassive but for the clenching of his jaw muscles. Wordlessly he advanced on Krueger, who realized his vulnerability, alone and unarmed with this lean, powerful barbarian. He took a few steps backward, saying nothing, hoping to reach the bellpull in the corner and summon help.

Just as Krueger's large, meaty hand grasped the cord and yanked, Hawk grabbed his starched shirtfront. One blow quickly landed in the baron's soft belly, and he doubled over. Sinclair pulled Krueger upright and delivered a punishing blow to his face. Nose and jaw both cracked with sickening force before he let the German's inert form slide to the carpeted floor and turned to stride from the room.

When Hawk caught up to her, Carrie was already out front waiting for a stablehand to bring the rig around. "Planning to leave without me? I'm not going to be very hospitably treated when Krueger wakes up. Let's just hope his pride will keep him from sending his gunmen after us!" Grabbing her elbow, he propelled her toward the stableyard as she tripped and struggled to pick up the wispy layers of her long silk skirts.

When he handed her into the rig, he could see the evidence of dried tears on her cheeks, but forced down the wave of tenderness they engendered.

She said nothing, and they rode through the starry night in hostile silence. The crackling sexual tension radiated between them like summer lightning. Scarcely had the carriage slowed in front of the Circle S big house than Carrie bolted out of it, ripping the golden dress in her haste. Too weary after the hours of riding to get down and saddle up Redskin, Hawk just slapped the reins and turned the rig toward his cabin and a good long drink.

He awakened the following morning with a foul hangover and rolled across the wide bed to free himself from the sticky encumbrance of the sheets. Lord, it was hot! Kicking off the offending covers, he sat up, swinging his feet to the floor in one jerky, angry motion. After holding his head in his hands for several moments to assure himself it would not come off his shoulders, he stood up.

As he rummaged about the cluttered bedroom, thoughts of the preceding evening came crowding back, doing little to lighten his humor. He had been ready to kill Carrie and that pig of a German. Damn her for being so beautiful. Damn himself for wanting her. Didn't he have any more pride than Lola Jameson?

He scowled, remembering how Lola had thrown herself at him, and how he had actually encouraged her in the dark seclusion of the garden. Finally her cloying kisses and busy, exploring fingers had begun to repel rather than arouse him. He actually believed that she would have undressed them both and impaled herself on him right there on the ground! The sour taste of self-loathing had filled his throat when he had broken her feverish grasp on him and had begun to straighten his clothes, urging her to do the same with a scathing rebuke. What a night! He rubbed his eyes and tried to forget the whole sordid mess.

"Damn place is a sty," he swore, searching through a pile of wrinkled clothes for a clean shirt. Marah's once immaculate, shrinelike cabin was now thoroughly lived in. A thick film of dust marred the gleaming perfection of the floor and randomly thrown articles of clothing were deposited across it and over the furniture. Unemptied ashtrays gave off the sour odor of long-dead cigarillos and pipe ashes. Tin plates and cookpots, caked with the residue of overcooked beans and fried beef, sat in careless stacks on the table.

Tucking shirttails into his breeches, Hawk padded over to the big granite coffeepot and swished the mold-encrusted grounds around inside its sinister depths. Swearing in disgust, he abandoned the idea of making coffee. It was too hot anyway.

What he needed was an invigorating early-morning swim before he went to work. He toyed briefly with the idea of picking up Perry and taking the boy with him, something he had been doing often in the past weeks. The prospect of facing Carrie made him abandon the impulse almost immediately. After last night, he would be hard put not to place his hands around that slim golden throat and squeeze.

He was outside before he remembered Redskin was at the big house and he had the two carriage horses unhitched and grazing in the small, fenced pasture near the cabin. No help for it, he would have to hitch up the team and drive the rig back to retrieve his bay.

By the time he neared the small lake, memories of his encounter with Carrie in its cooling depths came back to stir emotions he did not want to contemplate. "I hope the water's ice cold," he muttered under his breath, leaping off Redskin. Quickly he stripped off his shirt, breeches, and moccasins. Just as he tossed them across the saddle, he heard a splash from the other end of the crescent-shaped pool. Silently he walked across the grass, cutting through the bushes and alders to peer at the peace disturber in his private domain.

It was Carrie, gloriously naked, slicing cleanly through the pale greenish depths of the lake with fast, sure strokes. The sun caught her mane of water-darkened hair and set it afire, while warming the honey-colored flesh of arms and shoulders. Then she turned over, eyes closed, and began to float on her back, revealing two magnificent breasts in glossy wet perfection. He felt himself go hot, then cold all at once, trembling in desire and anger.

Before he could think or stop himself, he burst from the cover of the foliage to dive off a jagged rock that overhung the pool. He surfaced near where she had been floating. Now she was round-eyed with terror—until she recognized him. Then a furious flash of anger overcame her fright. She floundered in the water, gasping for breath to yell at him.

He beat her to it. "What the hell are you doing out here, all alone with no protection, sunning mother naked?" His voice fairly thundered. "Any wandering gunman could leap in here and attack you!"

"One just did," she spat disdainfully, shrugging free of his grip and kicking away.

The gesture of rejection infuriated him even more; he was already near the brink of irrationality. "Damn, Krueger was right. You are a fire-haired whore, teasing just like Lola. The only difference between you is that she delivers and you don't!"

At the mention of Lola, Carrie bristled, losing the caution that might have tempered her rising fury. "You dare castigate me after you spent last night pawing one another in front of the whole assembly!"

"Unlike you and the baron, who sneaked off in private for your little tryst!" He moved so quickly through the water she could scarcely turn to make a stroke before he was on her.

"Let me go!" She thrashed, sending water in stinging droplets every direction. The more her water-slicked flesh touched his, the more insistent he became, pulling her against him and propelling them nearer the shallow, grassy bank at the opposite side of the lake.

As soon as his feet touched the bottom, he stood, taking her in his arms and carrying her out of the water. For several seconds she was too stunned by the feel of his hard, hairy chest and torso pressed so intimately against her sensitive breasts and thighs to fight him. Then he knelt and tossed her on the soft grass, falling down beside her to grasp her flying skein of wet hair in his hands. When she saw the open lust in his eyes and realized his mouth was rapidly descending on hers for a savage kiss, she tried once more to break away. It was too late.

The moment he felt those long, sleek arms and legs entwine with his and the hardened nipples of her breasts brush across his chest, he knew he was lost, unable to stop what was happening as he subdued her and carried her to the shore. Now as he tasted Carrie's lips and tangled his hands in her hair, he knew why no other woman would ever again satisfy him. He loved her and he hated her.

Carrie was frightened by his intense desire, the lust and anger she could feel emanating from him as he forced her lips open in the kiss. He had no right to be angry at her after the spectacle he and Lola had put on last night! Fury warred with desire under the insistent pressure of his hard, warm lips and body on her soft, pliant flesh.

If he had gone slower, murmured a few words of endearment, been gentler, she would have melted into him. But he did not. Driven by his own desperate need, he kissed her with bruising force while his hands slid possessively down her waist and hips, back up to her breasts, then trespassed below to the fiery curls between her legs. His long, muscular legs held her with brute strength, stilling her thrashing as he felt the silky contours of her body once more.

When he raised up from kissing her and began to spread her legs, she caught her breath and cried, "No, Hawk, please don't—" The rest of her plea died in her throat as she looked into his implacable face. His eyes were glazed in passion, his lips parted in a feral grimace. He looked like a throwback to some ancient savage warchief of the Cheyenne.

Then he plunged into her in one long, hard thrust. Rather than being dry and painful as she thought it would be, as experience with Noah had taught her to expect, it was smooth and good. Instinctively she felt herself arching up to meet him. Then, ashamed of her wanton surrender, she bit her lower lip and tried to lay passively under his sensuous assault. It was the water—that was the explanation! If he had not caught her swimming, she would never have been so ready to receive him.

Her concentration on martyrdom was broken when he suddenly slowed his thrusts and cupped her face in his hands for another kiss. He tasted the blood from her bitten lip and ran his tongue softly, insinuatingly around it, then centered his mouth on hers for a searing, penetrating kiss. She could not hold back the little whimper that accompanied her return of his caresses, nor stop her hands from eagerly sliding up and down his back as she clasped him fiercely.

He let out a low triumphant growl as he felt her respond. As if to brand her his for all time, he deepened the kiss and prolonged the exquisite, slow thrusts into her body until he could hold back no longer. He moved faster, more frantically, and she moved with him. In a mutual frenzy of desperate hunger they rode to the crest, then spiraled back down into blackness after the explosions of light had blinded them like bursting meteors.

They lay locked together in the grass, panting and sweat-soaked, shocked at the intensity of the need each had revealed to the other. Feeling the sun beating down on his back with summer insistence, Hawk rolled off Carrie and up to his feet in one swift movement. Before she could gather her scattered wits he reached down, grasped one slim wrist to pull her up beside him, then waded into the water.

"It's hot. We both need to cool off." With those terse, uninflected words, he dove in and began to swim briskly toward the center of the lake.

Nothing could have more literally or figuratively dashed

cold water in her face. Carrie followed him into the depths
of the blue-green pool, simply to cover her nakedness. She
felt used and painfully vulnerable. Cursing herself for her
body's shameful betrayal, she swore at him even more
virulently for the brutal way he forced her to acquiesce. He
took every last vestige of pride from her and then calmly
swam away as if it meant nothing to him.

By the time she had crossed the pool to where her
clothes were laid out, she was trembling in hurt and anger.
With shaking hands and tear-blurred eyes, she groped
clumsily for her shirt and began to dress. What a stupid
impulse, to come here alone for a swim. After the last
time he had accosted her in these waters, she should have
known it might happen again! *Or did you know and hope?*
She shook her head in denial and swore.

Carrie was still struggling with her belt when he came
up behind her, clad in a half-buttoned blue shirt tucked
carelessly into tight tan breeches. His moccasined feet
made no sound on the soft earth, and she gasped in surprise
when she turned and saw him standing a scant three feet
away. His face looked bleak and sad, almost wistful, if she
had taken the time to read it.

"We need to talk, Carrie, about what just happened,
about everything."

"As to what just happened," she bit off furiously,
"there's little to say. I was a fool to come here alone
where you could rape me!"

He winced as if she had struck him, part of him
realizing in outraged anger that she had enjoyed the culmi-
nation of the act as much as he. Nevertheless, another part
of him knew he had forced her at the onset. His guilt
lashed him, and his undiminished desire for her goaded
him to speak in cruelly taunting tones. "Why, you lying
little bitch! I always thought a raped woman was terrified,
stiff and cold—*dry* when an attacker had his way with her.
You clung to me, moved with me, cried out your pleasure
to me! I'll be damned if that's rape!" He turned in disgust
to leave, but her next words froze him.

"You're just like Noah! You take what you want and
then leave!" She crumpled to the ground now, sobbing in

betrayed misery. "Just like that horrible dream I keep having over and over. I used to believe Noah was the wolf and the hawk that fought him was my rescuer, but I was mistaken. You're as much a predator as he was, damn you, damn you!" She knelt on the soft grass, her long, tangled masses of flaming hair covering her face as she wept into her hands.

Hawk was stunned by her unwitting revelation. The dream—she shared his medicine dream! If only he could talk to his grandfather. What did it mean? She was a white woman, born far from his home. He had scorned her and hurt her terribly, perhaps destroyed the fragile bond that had brought them together across cultures and miles.

He wanted to take her in his arms and soothe her with gentle words and kisses, to tell her he loved her, had always loved only her. But he sensed her abject rejection if he touched her now. They both needed time to sort out so many painful things. Softly he said, "I'm sorry, Firehair." Then he mounted Redskin and rode away.

CHAPTER 22

Hawk rode out in search of Kyle that afternoon and found him on the east range where stock losses had been heaviest lately. Both men knew the thief was Rider, working for Krueger. It was only a matter of time until they captured one of his men alive and got the truth from him. After last night and Krueger's open declaration of war, Hawk wanted Hunnicut to be prepared. He told him of the German's threat without mentioning what had led up to it.

When he arrived at his cabin that evening, he was bone-weary. All he wanted was to fall in bed and sleep. Feliz had reluctantly sent some cold food with him when he declined supper at the big house. He carried the sack she had given him into the cabin and lit a lamp over the kitchen table.

Then he saw it, lying in a carefully cleared space on the oiled wooden planks of the table. The medallion. Its intricate, wrought-silver design winked in the flickering light and a note lay beside it. Unwillingly he unfolded the note from the envelope and read:

Hawk:
    After all that has happened between us, I thought you would prefer to have this returned.

Carrie

He crumpled the message into a tiny ball, pressing it between his palms in pained, furious anger, then threw it with all his might into a corner of the room, where it was lost amid the clutter. Slowly he picked up the medallion and placed it around his neck. It was all he had of the old life now.

"Caleb, you are too transparent." Lola tapped Rider sharply on the shoulder when she caught him staring intently out of the window of Cummins' Emporium at Carrie Sinclair. The tall, lovely redhead was dismounting from her horse in front of the bank. Rider turned with a snarl and grabbed Lola's gloved hand.

"Don't play with me, *Mrs.* Krueger," he said nastily, ignoring her title.

Swallowing her revulsion at the crude gunman's manners, she bestowed a dazzling smile on him instead. "Don't get testy with me, Caleb. I've been considering some things that might be of, er . . . mutual benefit to us." Seeing his cold gray eyes measure her, she resumed her speech. "You want Carrie Sinclair. So does Karl. If you get rid of Karl, you get her. Of course, to do that, you'll have to eliminate her guardian angel, too." She looked outside at Kyle Hunnicut, who followed in Carrie's shadow. "Could you manage that, hmmm, Caleb?"

He assessed the scheming woman in front of him. "What would all this gain you, Lola? You never do anything for nothing. And don't lie to me," he grabbed her hand roughly, "I know you want Hawk Sinclair. But he's got no money, while Krueger has K Bar. Why choose a penniless half-breed?" He smiled a cold, oily grimace that set her teeth on edge.

"Who says I can't have both, Caleb?" His head swiveled in interest now. She laughed a low, throaty chuckle and said, "If you dispose of darling Karl and that odious little Texan, I inherit K Bar and you can have your redhead. When we control all the cattle lands in eastern Montana, Hawk Sinclair will crawl to me!" Her voice became hard, breaking in anger as she recalled his scathing rejection of her the night of Krueger's gala.

Turn from Lola Jameson, would he? Walk away as if she were some common trollop! If Karl wouldn't marry her, well, he need not. She had brooded all week after the debacle of the ball and finally it came to her in a blindingly simple revelation— Karl had no living relations and had written no will. If he died, she was his sole heir! It was so obvious she berated herself for not thinking of it sooner.

Rider's eyes grew hard and measuring as he watched the triumphant display of emotions across her face. "You mean if the new baron dies, you inherit? Well, I'll be damned. . . ."

Hawk spent the week doing some hard riding and even harder thinking. He was up at daybreak each morning, checking stock, preparing for the upcoming roundup. All the while he rode to isolated line shacks, along deserted cow trails, he mulled over his tortured and confusing relationship with Carrie.

He still could not accept the fact that she had shared his medicine dream. Did she first experience it twelve years ago when it came to him in that sweat lodge? She would have been only a small child. He longed to ask her, to share with her the mystic memories of that long-ago time. But he could not bring himself to approach her after the grievous wrong he had done her, falling on her and forcing her to couple with him, then scorning her when her warm woman's body responded to his need. Why did love always seem to end in hurt and anger for them?

The guilty shade of Noah's memory hovered over them too. She was his father's wife. Why had the Powers brought her from afar to share his dream with him? Why did he love her despite so many reasons he should have loved Wind Song? He had betrayed his wife, and that memory was bitterest of all.

But Wind Song and his Cheyenne child were dead, and Carrie and his white son were alive. Whenever he thought of Peregrine Sinclair, Hawk's mood lightened. The boy was bright and good-natured, growing every day to look more like him. From the first time he saw his son and carried him back to Circle S, Hawk had felt the bond between them grow stronger. Sensing their kinship, Perry always went eagerly into his father's arms, giggling and holding tightly when they galloped across the plains.

While Carrie was occupied with household matters, Hawk frequently picked him up early in the morning at Feliz's kitchen. He and the boy would watch the hands catch their broncs and saddle them. When everyone else was at work, Hawk would take Perry with him on part of his morning rounds, sometimes stopping at a branding fire to watch the men burn the Circle S brand into the hips of unmarked calves. Occasionally he took his son swimming at the lake, pushing aside the bittersweet memories of Carrie while he and Perry splashed and cavorted in the warm water.

Hawk was hopelessly trapped. He loved his son and could not leave him. Yet he could no longer bear living in such close proximity to Carrie, knowing that what had happened last week would happen again. To claim his son he must marry her, but she had made it clear she despised him. No matter that her body responded to his, her mind, her civilized white instincts, rejected him. And in truth, a hurt defensive part of his mind still rejected her as well. There seemed to be no answer.

Carrie existed in the same hell as Hawk, living out each day around him, unable to exchange more than minimal courtesies and discuss the essentials of running Circle S. Frequently she had Kyle act as intermediary. Hawk cooked his own meals at the cabin as often as Feliz would permit, sparing them both the poignant torture of sitting at the big kitchen table with their son between them.

Carrie watched Hawk and Perry grow closer over the course of summer's end. As the affection between them grew, it tore at her. Was there no chance they could ever be a real family? She feared losing her son to his father. Hawk loved the boy so much. Might he take Perry and vanish south to the Nations or return to the Cheyenne? Her imagination ran wild at times, but she knew she could never forbid him to see his son. That, at least, was his right and Perry's right, too.

"A boy should have a father," Feliz said one afternoon as she observed Carrie, who was gazing out the window at the approaching Redskin, who was carrying two riders, one tall and the other tiny.

Carrie sighed and said, "He has a father who spends lots of time with him. More time than I get with my own child here lately."

"And whose fault is that?" The old cook continued paring vegetables at the table, keenly aware of how hungrily Carrie's gaze fixed itself on the scene unfolding in the side yard by the pump.

It was a dry September. The roundup crews gathering cattle to ship to market stirred up thick yellow dust everywhere they worked. Everyone who rode into the camps came away coated with it. Hawk and Perry were no exceptions. Not wanting to take the child into Feliz's immaculate kitchen in such a filthy state, he went to the big pump by the well and stripped the chubby little boy.

Perry liked this new game, giggling and wriggling as his father pulled off the last hot, sticky garments, all the while tickling his toes and belly. Then Hawk stripped off his own shirt and scooped the boy up, holding him under the pump while a gush of cool water sluiced over them.

It felt wonderful! Perry splashed and squealed in delight, soaking Hawk, who was trying desperately to wash the slippery bundle. Agile for a child scarcely over a year old, Perry quickly succeeded in making a mud wallow around the pump and getting an astounding amount of the sticky stuff on them both.

Hesitantly, with considerable prodding from Feliz, Carrie finally approached them with a small washtub, soap, and towels. They did not see her or hear her approach until she was directly beside them and liberally splashed with muddy water herself. Kneeling alongside the pump, heedless of the bright blue skirt she wore, Carrie pushed the empty tub under the spigot. Just then Hawk looked up as he caught the patch of blue from the corner of his eye.

"Fill this with clean water and let's see if between us we can't get the little one clean at least." A smile tugged at the corners of her mouth now and she forgot her earlier shyness as Perry tangled his gooey fingers in her hair. She laughed out loud and hefted the child into the tub as Hawk worked the pump.

Hawk thought he'd never heard a lovelier sound than her laughter. Had he ever heard her really laugh before? He watched as she squatted gracefully in the mire, ignoring the clots of slime with which Perry had decorated her hair, vigorously working a sudsy lather all over the small copper body.

"Stand by for a rinse," he called out. She leaned back, holding Perry securely by one arm as the clean water cascaded over his head and shoulders. When his mother reached over with a fluffy towel and bundled him up in it, lifting him away from the pump, the child realized the game was over. He was clean and being dried! Well, this was no longer fun. He wailed in protest and thrashed two sturdy arms free of the towel to reach toward the waterfall, which had now mysteriously stopped running.

"Time for dinner, young man," Carrie said, giving one teary cheek a nuzzle and carrying him around toward the kitchen door.

"You better let Feliz take him inside and dress him, or he'll just get filthy again." Hawk's eyes were merry as his gaze traveled from her head to her feet. The outside of the towel was already liberally smeared with mud from her skirt, and one sticky lock of long, red hair was oozing droplets of yellow slime onto her arm as she held the wiggling boy.

Feliz hurried from the kitchen clucking at the sight the three of them made. She observed the merriment in both black and green eyes as she whisked her young charge away, leaving his parents standing in disarray in the yard.

Suddenly self-conscious, Carrie was aware she was staring at Hawk's bare, mud-spattered chest. Her own blouse clung like a semitransparent skin to her breasts and arms, revealing a great deal to his eyes. They looked one another in the face, and all the laughter of a moment ago fled.

Then he reached over, taking her by surprise, and grasped her hand gently, tugging her back toward the pump. "Lean over," he commanded gruffly, and she obeyed. He guided her head beneath the pump and doused her with cool water, rinsing the worst of the mud from her hair, arms, and upper body. "Now your feet," he directed when she stood up, squeezing the excess water from her hair. She obeyed, presenting first one foot, then the other to him as he pulled off the sodden slippers, tossing them into the nearby grass. She stood obediently with stockinged feet beneath the pump, filthy skirt hiked up to her knees while he once more worked the pump handle vigorously.

When she was dripping and free of the worst of the dirt, he reached over and scooped her up, quickly swinging her across the muddy ground to dry grass near the kitchen door. With a disarming smile, he set her down and said, "Now ask Feliz for another towel so you don't drip all over her clean floors." With that he turned back to the pump and kicked off his moccasins. She tried not to notice the way the water seemed to hug and caress the lean, corded muscles of his arms and torso as it ran down his back. Her thoughts were interrupted by Feliz, who offered her a towel with a worldly wise smile and then vanished inside once more. Wanting to flee after the cook, Carrie called out with a suddenly dry throat, "Do you want a towel?"

He shook his head, letting an explosion of diamond-bright droplets fly from his thick black hair. Combing long, copper fingers through it, he pushed the raven locks off his forehead. "Redskin's ridden through lots of rainstorms worse than this." He grinned, turning to pick up the muddy moccasins. Quickly he rinsed them off under the pump and replaced them on his feet.

Carrie stood there, lamely running the towel over her dripping hair and clothes while he walked toward the big bay and swung into the saddle. "Will you be back for dinner tonight?"

He smiled once more, melting her into the warm September earth. "If I can get the rest of this mud off me by then, yes."

An uncertain truce was called after that day. Hawk ate all his evening meals in the big kitchen with Carrie and their son, Kyle, and Feliz. They discussed the mundane affairs of ranch life, stock breeding, plans for shipping various herds to market before the snows. Kyle reminisced about their wild days in the Nations, occasionally drawing out Hawk, who described an amusing or exciting tale for the small group. Feliz recalled memories of Hawk's childhood. At ease in the company of the Texan and the Mexicana, Hawk and Carrie laughed and joked, but whenever they were thrown together alone, both seemed to withdraw into their protective shells, he aloof and shuttered, she stiff and formal. It was as if each was afraid to make the first move. Feliz fussed and Kyle swore while summer faded to autumn.

"Got me a real interestin' piece o' news, Longlegs." Kyle spat a wad of tobacco and grinned at his tall companion as he dismounted in front of the corral. He had just come from Miles City, where he and Carrie had gone for supplies.

"You hear something in town?" Hawk strolled alongside the banty-legged Texan as he led his horse into the stable and began to unsaddle him.

"Seems our friend th' baron went 'n' got hisself shot." His shrewd blue-gray eyes looked at Hawk measuringly. "Jist a graze, worse luck. He wuz ridin' in thet fancy gig o' his'n, comin' in from town, on a real deserted piece o' th' trail. Rifle shot tuk a piece outta his shoulder, but if his wheel hadn't a' hit a rock an' throwed him ta th' side o' th' rig, it'd a been plumb center."

Hawk whistled. "Some fancy shooting. Like the kind that killed Frank."

"Thet's whut I'm thinkin'," Kyle murmured. "Same kinda rifle, Remington 44.40. Caleb Rider carries one on his saddle.'' He continued rubbing down his horse, waiting for his friend to reply.

Hawk shrugged. "So do half the cattlemen in the territory. So did Noah."

"Yeah, but Noah's daid, 'n' th' rest o' 'em cain't shoot a gnat off'n a toad's ass neither."

"Who stands to gain if Krueger's dead? Looks to me like we're the best suspects. Rider's out of a job if the baron dies. Doesn't make sense unless—" Hawk stopped suddenly.

"Whut'r yew thinkin'?" Kyle threw the rubdown towel across the stall post and gave the horse an affectionate swat.

"Is my dear onetime stepmother still the baron's houseguest?"

Kyle snorted in disgust. "Yep, thet vain little bitch's still swishin' her fancy tail 'round town. She gits so much pleasure lookin' at her own shadow, cloudy day'd sure sour her outlook on life." He looked at Hawk expectantly.

"Krueger have any kin you ever heard of besides that brother who just died?"

The Texan scratched his matted red hair beneath the greasy rim of his Stetson. "Not that I heerd—say, yew don't mean *her*?"

Hawk nodded. "She's his sister-in-law. Might be possible. I sure believe she could twist Rider around her finger. Lola's damn clever, especially where money's involved."

Hunnicut let out a whoop. "Whooee! All we got ta do is sit back 'n' let them varmints do fer each other!"

"I don't like it, Kyle. That's too neat and simple. Circle S will be dragged into it one way or the other, I'm afraid." Recalling Lola's vindictiveness when he had scorned her the night of Krueger's party, Hawk felt distinctly uneasy. He knew what she was capable of.

" 'Pears ta me we'd better split up this here job o' work. I'll jist keep me a real close eye on ole Caleb. Yew kin tend ta thet devil woman." Kyle nodded as if it were settled.

"Thanks," Hawk said wryly.

* * *

Karl Krueger was in no mood to waste time. His shoulder ached abominably and he was tired and rattled. If he hadn't been thrown to the side of the carriage . . . He swore again, thinking of how near a miss it had been. But who? Someone at Circle S would surely top the long list of his enemies. But bushwhacking simply wasn't Sinclair's style, not the Texan's, for that matter. Still, they were his enemies and he must get to the bottom of this quickly. Strike before they struck again.

He sat behind the big walnut desk in his study, propped uncomfortably in the overstuffed leather chair. With a painful grunt he pulled the bell and summoned the butler. "Get me Caleb Rider at once."

At that precise moment Caleb was in his cabin—in the midst of an ugly confrontation. Lola stood in the doorway, glaring at him with the fires of hell in her icy blue eyes.

"I told you it's stupid to come here," he rasped. "What if the baron sees you? Or one of them backstabbing foreigners who work for him?"

She dismissed that with one disdainful swish of her skirts. "Forget servants! Why, after all the delays while you engaged in petty thievery, did you botch the job?"

He bristled. "Petty thievery—you're a fool! We've taken over five thousand head from Circle S since spring! Anyway, I told you, I only do a job when the time is right. It was just a piece of rotten luck that I missed. I won't the next time."

"When will that be, in the spring?" Her sarcasm was laced with barely leashed anger.

"You just leave it to me, lady," he ground out.

She snorted and spat a startling anglo-saxon vulgarity at him. "If I do, we'll both die of old age and so will Karl!"

As usual, Carrie came to town that Friday to pick up supplies. After her hands had loaded the wagon, she paid Cy Cummins while the crackling hostility between them mounted. Lord, she was sick of the priggish bigots in this place! Just as she emerged from the door of the emporium, she almost collided with Lola Jameson. *Wonderful*, she thought, *what a perfect ending to a great morning*.

Stiffly Lola nodded. "I don't make a habit of running other people's errands, but Mrs. Grummond is the only dressmaker in town, so I decided I had better humor her or she'll never finish my new fall gowns. Here!" With that brusque, peevish announcement, she thrust a note into Carrie's hand and stalked across the street.

Baffled and irritated at the surly attitude shared by visitors and locals alike, Carrie looked down at the flowery script. "What does that hateful old harridan want now, after telling me she didn't need my kind of money?" She ripped the envelope open and read:

My Dear Mrs. Sinclair:
   In clearing my inventory, I found two rather expensive items that your late husband purchased for you before his death, a jade green satin ball gown and a chocolate-brown velvet evening cape. Since they were paid for in advance, I feel morally obliged to give them to you.
   Please meet me at my shop when you finish at Mr. Cummins'.

                              Emma Grummond

" 'Morally obliged' indeed! The old witch couldn't find anyone else tall enough to fit them or who could afford to pay for alterations!" Carrie debated the desirability of another wearying confrontation in town, but the gown and cape sounded luscious. Why let that old bat chop a foot off them, let the seams out, and resell them to Mrs. Cummins?

She wondered why Noah had ordered such a lavish surprise, then recalled how he had solicitously showered her with gifts while he thought she was pregnant with his child. Doubtless it was part of her reward for being such a good brood mare! With a determined stride, she changed course, heading down the street to Mrs. Grummond's shop.

"I don't like this, Lola," Caleb whispered as he paced back and forth in Mrs. Grummond's rear parlor.

"The old biddy's gone to Wyoming Territory to visit her

sister. No one saw you force the lock on the door. Just relax and listen for your true love,'' she scoffed.

"What makes you so sure she'll come? What if she's heard the dressmaker's out of town?'' His hard face was creased with worry. Caleb Rider didn't like intrigue.

"No woman could resist those clothes made up in her best colors. Anyway, she's so ostracized in town no one would tell her the time of day unless she paid them. She doesn't know Emma's gone. She'll be here.'' Lola sounded confident, but she was nervous. This had to work. And if it did—how beautifully simple a solution to everything. She fairly purred when she heard the front door open.

"Mrs. Grummond? I'm here for the gown and cape.'' Carrie noticed the dust covers on the reception-room furniture, and a prickle of unease came over her. Just then a muffled female voice called her to the back room. As she stepped through the linen curtain into the hall, steel-hard fingers grasped her from the side, lifting her off her feet. When she began to scream, a thick cloth emitting a sickening sweet odor was jammed across her face, into her mouth.

After a minute's furious struggle, everything went black and she collapsed. Caleb scooped her up, marveling at her slim, long-legged loveliness. For all her height, she weighed surprisingly little. He could smell the faint essence of wildflowers over the ether.

"Quit mooning over that slut and let's get out of here,'' Lola hissed. "Has she got the gun? Good! Town gossip says she never goes anywhere without it anymore. Sure you didn't have something to do with that, Caleb?'' She laughed as his face darkened in remembrance of the time she had pulled the Sharps pistol on him and ordered him off Circle S.

"All right, let's get her over to the hotel and into that room to wait for Krueger.'' He cursed himself again for a fool, listening to Lola's wild schemes. Still, it just might work. He wanted revenge on Carrie, on Kyle, on her half-breed lover, too. Yessir, it just might work at that.

They wrapped Carrie's unconscious body in a thick piece of carpet. Then Caleb slung her over his shoulder and carefully followed Lola from the back of the dress shop to the waiting wagon. It took them nearly a quarter hour to get inside the Excelsior Hotel without being seen. With Lola in the lead, checking the corridor and stairs, they made their way undetected to the back room Rider had reserved in Krueger's name the previous evening. He deposited Carrie on the bed and began to strip her unconscious form with obvious relish.

"Leave her underwear on, Caleb," Lola said sharply, half afraid he was becoming so carried away he would rape the unconscious woman right before her eyes and ruin the precisely timed scheme she had so meticulously worked out. "You can have your fill of her later." She checked the delicate gold watch pinned to her bosom. "Karl should be finished with his meeting at the bank any time now, so get over there and grab him. You remember what you're supposed to say?"

He got up from the bed with evident reluctance, his eyes still fastened lasciviously on Carrie's bare flesh. "Hell, yes, we've rehearsed it a dozen times," he swore testily.

Karl Krueger was in a good mood despite the recent attempt on his life. The new expansion he planned had been well received at the bank and the covert profits from Circle S cattle sales were on the rise again. When Hunnicut and Sinclair got too nosy, he would simply have Rider deal with them as they had tried to deal with him.

He was crossing the street from the bank, heading toward his rig, when the sinewy form of Rider materialized and hailed him. Krueger responded. "What is it, Caleb?"

Rider's normally guarded, humorless face was creased with a broad carnal grin. "You got a lady waiting to meet you, real private like, boss."

Krueger looked blank. "What are you talking about?"

"My old boss lady is waiting for you in room sixteen at the Excelsior. She told me to ask you real nice." His expression was leering and suggestive. "You never can figure women, Baron. I bet she and her Injun loverboy had a fight. Might be your chance to move in on Circle S." He shrugged and waited for Krueger's reaction, his palms sweating despite his calm outward demeanor. Damn, much simpler to face a man down in an open fight than this twisty stuff!

Krueger's face scowled for several seconds, then a malevolent grin replaced the frown. "So, she is a change-able little cat once more. This time my terms will not be so generous. Come, guard the door."

Lola checked Carrie's gun one more time. She could scarcely wait to see the look on Karl Krueger's haughty face before she shot him. Scorn her for this piece of red-haired fluff, would he!

Carrie moaned and moved one hand faintly across the bed. Carefully Lola pulled open an eyelid, gauging how close to consciousness she was. Lola did not want to give her any more of the drug for fear of having her uncon-scious when the sheriff found them. Still, Carrie must remain under until Karl was dead and she and Rider were clear of the scene. Her long and checkered career had enabled Lola to pick up all sorts of useful information, carefully filed for future reference. The administration of drugs was only one of her talents. She was also a crack shot.

When Krueger knocked discreetly on the door, she smiled. Perfect. In a breathy whisper she called, "Come in."

When he opened the door and stepped inside the dimly lit hotel room, Krueger could see Carrie's partially nude form laying sprawled across the bed. Why did she seem to be asleep? He was rather unnerved at her boldness, but then realized she must be planning to use her body to get what she wanted. Without taking his eyes off the woman on the bed, he closed the door.

Suddenly he heard the unmistakable click of a pistol hammer being cocked. He whirled to confront Lola's cold blue eyes, glowing malevolently in the semidarkness.

"Don't move and don't bother to call for Caleb. He's right here. Disarm him, darling." She held the deadly Sharps pistol levelly on the big German as Rider slipped in the door and quickly pulled Krueger's derringer from his inside pocket.

Krueger fixed Rider with a measuring gaze and said icily, "What is the meaning of this? Surely you are not so stupid, my friend, as to throw your lot in with this woman?"

"Looks that way, don't it, Baron?" Rider smiled coldly. Damn the uppity foreigner! He wished he could stay and watch the show. With that he left, whistling as he closed the door behind him. Yes, it seemed as if Lola's plan was coming off without a hitch. Quickly he descended the back stairs and waited for the shot that would be his signal to head for the sheriff's office.

"Now, my dear baron, you were too greedy to marry a penniless fortune hunter—you wanted Circle S and that bitch. Well, you are going to lose." Lola's voice was almost hysterical, yet the gun never wavered.

Krueger was sweating profusely. Great rivers of sour water ran down his arms and back. Nevertheless, he kept the implacable facade in place, staring at the venomous woman holding the pistol. "You cannot succeed with this amateurish plan; and even if you did, what would you possibly gain by it—nothing more than seeing your beautiful young rival hanged. Give this up, Liebchen."

The offhand reference to her age and the empty endearment were all she needed to set her off. She heard Carrie begin to stir, and she fired point blank, twice. "Good-bye, Baron von Krueger. Too bad such an illustrious family name has to die out. But then, I plan to live a long time. . . ."

Carrie felt nauseous. What had she eaten for breakfast? God, could she be pregnant again? The dim light in the room hurt her eyes, and everything was spinning. Then two loud crashes jarred her into full consciousness. She sat up with a start, but then began to black out again and fell back against the pillows. Something heavy and cold was thrust against her side. She rolled over and tried once more to clear her head. It was chilly in this place. What place? Where was she?

Slowly Carrie sat up and looked around, focusing her eyes on a strange, expensively furnished room. She was clad only in a thin chemise and pantalets, shivering with cold. Then she saw the large crumpled mound of Krueger's body, seeping its lifeblood into the thick, dark-blue carpet. She screamed and collapsed once more in a sickeningly dizzy wave.

The cell was cold and filthy, sour with the stench of tobacco and urine. Carrie huddled against the hard wooden bench on one wall, fearful of even touching the vermin-infested cot across the floor. Still disoriented and in shock, she reviewed the nightmarish day that was only now coming to a close.

After Sheriff Woods locked her up, she had pleaded for him to send word of this monstrous conspiracy to the ranch, but he only gave an ugly laugh and told her the news about her whoring and murdering would travel fast enough! Kyle was out on the eastern range for several days, keeping careful tabs on the rustling that had erupted recently. Hawk had ridden off three days earlier on some unnamed mission of his own. Lord only knew when he would return. Feliz would be frantic by now, and Perry—she almost broke down thinking of her son. *Please come home, Hawk. Please.*

What had happened? Over and over she tried to make sense out of the bizarre series of events beginning with Lola's obviously forged note that entrapped her at Grummond's dress shop. Lola must have killed Karl with her gun, but, of course, the note had vanished and no one believed her. She rubbed her head in sick disbelief, realizing the whole town had already tried her and found her guilty.

As if on cue, the embodiment of every hostile hypocrite in Miles City was ushered into the rear of the jail by the sheriff. Mathilda Thorndyke swished stiffly to the bars of Carrie's cell and glared in. "Well, I had to see you get your comeuppance, you filthy harlot! Not bad enough you drive a fine man like Mr. Noah to his death, now you go and kill Baron von Krueger in cold blood. Luring a man to a hotel room for a cheap tryst. Your kind should stick to trash like that half-breed!" Her face was contorted in purplish rage. Even her present triumph was insufficient to overcome the insidious cancer of jealousy. She had wanted to be Mrs. Sinclair, to own Circle S. Now she never would.

Holding her chin high and spine stiffly erect, Carrie stood and walked over to the small window on the opposite wall, turning her back on the raving old crone.

"Don't you try to ignore me, missy! Sheriff told me, judge's coming tomorrow. You're gonna hang. Hang for murder! Hang!"

CHAPTER 23

It had been a long but worthwhile ride to Helena and back. Hawk pushed hard for home, thinking about the expression on Lola Jameson Krueger's face when he told her the news he had gone to such lengths to secure in the capital. He chuckled. If she was the one behind the potshots at Krueger, this should take the wind out of her sails, and he would bet his best rifle she was guilty as sin. Hopefully he could avert a range war if he could confront Lola and the baron together, making the German see that his real enemy was his conniving sister-in-law, not Circle S and Carrie.

Carrie. Every time he thought of her, he felt the same old ache begin. What should he do? He had asked himself the question a thousand times in the past months, especially since the bitter incident at the lake when he had once more lost himself in her sweet, silken flesh. Then after giving in and joining him, she had turned on him like a tigress. She owned Circle S, free and clear. Kyle would run it for her. She didn't need him anymore. He should leave.

But he knew he could not. "I won't leave my son. I've lost my mother, my grandfather, Wind Song, all my ties with the only people I loved, the only place I belonged. I won't lose Perry!" Even as he said it to himself, Hawk knew it was only a part of the truth. He loved Carrie too—quicksilver, aloof white woman. Ever since they had

washed Perry at the pump that day, he had sensed a
warming in her. Now they shared meals and talked of the
ranch, joked with Kyle and Feliz, played with their son. If
he asked her to marry him, would she turn on him and call
him a filthy savage again? Could he bear another rejection?
Could he stand to live at Circle S with her day in and day
out, wanting her but unable to reach out?

"What I need is a good, live-in whore," he ground out.
If only things were that simple.

She is your father's wife. He could still hear Iron
Heart's ringing words. He could see the bitter disappointment in the old man's face when Hawk left the village for
the last time. The ghosts of the past did not free him any
more than his Firehair. He swore, and kicked Redskin into
a gallop.

"Evenin', Sheriff." Caleb Rider smiled lazily as he
sauntered into the small, cluttered office. "I want to see the
prisoner."

Sheriff Woods looked dumbly at Rider. What did he
want with that dangerous hellion at this late hour? It was
after midnight. The woman had killed his boss in cold
blood. "Yew ain't gonna try nothin' like shootin' her, are
ya?" He looked nervously at the sinister figure of the
gunman. As if he'd try to stop Caleb Rider!

Rider laughed. "Never think of it, Woods. Believe me,
it's the last thing on my mind!"

Shrugging, the fat man reached for the cell key and
turned his back on Rider to pull the latch to the small cell
block. It was a mortal error. With one swift, silent slash,
Caleb Rider cut Wood's throat and shoved the body into a
corner behind the rusty potbellied stove. He lay heaped on
top of the wood pile, no neater than any of the other
broken, filthy things that filled the depressing little room.

Taking the cell key, Rider slipped into the dark recess
beyond the door. When he unlocked the cell, Carrie
awakened, rubbing her eyes, trying to see in the dim
moonlight filtering in from the small window. It was
nearly midnight, but she had slept little on the cold, filthy

mattress, half sitting up to keep her hair from its putrid covers.

"Who is it? Hawk!" The breathless, hopeful quality in her voice infuriated the gunman. He reached over to grab her before she recognized him.

Placing one thin, strong hand around her throat, he said, "Wrong, your ladyship. Don't make a sound or I'll snap this pretty, soft little neck. You're coming with me. That'll beat hanging, won't it?" He jeered as he shoved her toward the back door of the jail.

"I'd rather take my chances with a rope," she hissed at him.

His grip tightened ominously on her neck and on the arm he held twisted behind her back, but he did nothing more. "Open the door and..." he paused, flicking a wicked-looking blade up to her throat after he had freed her throbbing arm, "if you even think about screaming, you'll be dead meat just like the sheriff back there." The knife gleamed evilly in the moonlight as he propelled her toward a sturdy brown gelding waiting patiently in the alley.

Without warning, he struck her a sharp, hard blow on the back of the head with his gun handle. As she collapsed silently, he dumped her unceremoniously across the saddle and tied her unconscious form down.

"Not as neat at Lola's knockout drops, but it'll serve till I get you where I want you." He swung up on his roan and pulled the gelding behind him, riding into the darkness.

Kyle Hunnicut nearly broke his neck getting from Circle S into Miles City that night. When he arrived home that afternoon he had found Feliz nearly hysterical, saying Carrie had ridden to town with two hands for supplies that morning. The men had brought the loaded wagon back. Carrie had sent them ahead and said she would catch up later. She never arrived. When the men went in search of her, they came back to the ranch with an incredible tale. Carrie was being held by the sheriff for the murder of Karl von Krueger!

The ride to town was dangerous as the moon dipped

capriciously in and out of dense banks of fall clouds.
Several times Kyle lost the road and his horse stumbled in
the darkness. He arrived around one o'clock in the morning to find the town asleep. Not knowing where else to
begin, he went to Sheriff Woods's office. Maybe the old
buzzard slept with his drunks. He must get Carrie out of
that hole.

When no one answered the knock, the Texan almost
headed for the nearest cheap rooming house, thinking it
the most likely place to find Bert Woods. Then he saw
through the office window that a dim kerosene lantern was
flickering on the desk. Woods must be about. He turned
the doorknob and opened it, stepping cautiously inside.
Gut instinct told him things were not right.

The blood from the fat sheriff's throat had begun to
congeal in a long, thin river that ran from the woodpile,
beneath the desk, and into the center of the filthy plank
floor. Few people ever thought there was so much blood in
one human body. Kyle knew it was so, and also knew
Bertram Woods was quite dead.

It took him only three strides to cross the floor to the
cells, desperately afraid of what he would find there. He
almost passed out with relief. Thank God, the cell was
empty, its door standing ajar! At least someone had taken
her alive. But who? Where?

Kyle Hunnicut was almost as good a tracker as his
young half-breed companion, who had taught him. By the
first dim light of dawn he had made some headway
because of that skill—and a bit of luck. One of the horses
at the rear of the jail had left familiar tracks—the distinc-
tive mark of Caleb Rider's big roan. The Texan knew who
had Carrie, but it did little to console him as he trailed
them through the night, cursing the fool's errand that had
taken Hawk to the capital.

Hawk was unshaven, dusty and tired, but determined to
face down Lola and Krueger before he returned to Circle
S. It was about nine o'clock, Lola's late-rising breakfast
hour, if he recalled her habits. With any luck the baron
might be home as well.

As he rode, he speculated about whether Kyle had been able to nail Rider and his cattle-thieving companions yet. Hunnicut had shown him a base camp located in the eastern foothills, only a few days' drive from the Dakota railhead. Neat operation. Hawk hoped they could spring the trap soon. With Rider and Lola gone, perhaps the baron could be made to see reason. He was a lot like Noah, however, and that thought made Hawk's hopes dim. No, it might come to a range war yet, he considered grimly.

As he approached the garish rockpile Krueger called a house, Hawk noticed how still everything seemed down at the corrals. No one seemed to be working in midmorning. Odd. As he swung down from Redskin, reflex habit made him place one hand over his Colt. After that punch in his fat gut, the baron would likely not be in a hospitable mood.

Looking once more around the eerie, deserted yard, Hawk sprinted up the wide stone steps to the big double doors. The knocker was a gargoyle that Hawk had always thought a particularly appropriate decoration for Karl von Krueger.

The horse-faced German maid who answered the door looked at him as if he were dressed in breechclout and full war paint. Her blunt, doughy face grew even more floury and her pale eyes bugged from their sockets. "You! You dare come here, now!" The thickly accented English was emitted in a strangled voice.

Impatiently, he shoved her aside and stepped into the vast stone-floored foyer. His booted footsteps echoed on the cold, hard surface as he crossed to the big curving staircase that led to the second floor. A butler was coming down the stairs. Maybe he could raise someone.

"I want to see the baron and Baroness von Krueger immediately," he said, affixing the haughty servant with his most intimidating Cheyenne stare.

"That would be most difficult, Mr. Sinclair," the English butler said coldly, "considering his lordship is dead. I assume you have been away. I'll ask the dowager baroness if she wishes to see you. Please wait."

Hawk had no intention of waiting in the hall and went into the sitting room, where he helped himself to the baron's fine stock of liquor. Grimly, he mulled over the news. Damn the bitch, she had killed him, and from the look of things, gotten clean away with it. Lola Jameson, as Hawk had well learned from experience, was a very dangerous enemy.

"Well, darling, you've just heard the news, I understand. You look beastly. Where have you been?" Lola wore a pale-gray satin dressing robe, her concession to mourning for Karl. It clung sleekly to her breasts and hips and was draped open in front to reveal a gauzy silver gown beneath. She closed the heavy walnut door behind her. "Depressingly dark room," she said, looking around her at the purple drapes and wood paneling with distaste. "I'll have it done in pale blue, I think." She tapped her cheek with a long fingernail as she glided across to him, smirking in self-satisfaction.

"Don't start redecorating too soon, Lola. You shouldn't have killed your meal ticket, no matter how disagreeable a bastard he was." After setting the empty glass carelessly on the cabinet top, Hawk leaned against a leather wingback chair.

"I'll do whatever I want!" She smiled witheringly at Hawk. "And to think, darling, you could have shared all this with me."

"There's nothing to share, Lola. I just came back from Helena. Krueger didn't trust Mr. Cooper. He kept all his legal papers with his attorneys in the capital."

"He didn't write a will. I asked him," she spat contemptuously.

Hawk smiled. "That's right. But I went to Helena to check on just what does happen when a man like Karl von Krueger dies without a will in this territory. Very interesting point of law. It seems his estate will be turned over to a court-appointed trustee in Helena until they find out just who in the Krueger family is left alive back in Germany. It might take years." He shrugged. "But even if they finally come up with no one, you will lose. Kin by marriage only inherit when they're spouses, Lola. Karl's estate will go to the court for tax liquidation if no long-lost cousins turn up in the fatherland.''

Lola stood stock-still, her eyes widening and her pulse racing as Hawk's words sunk in. He must be lying. Surely he was fabricating the whole thing. Her fingers clenched around the edge of a carved walnut chair, which now served to hold her upright.

Relentlessly, as if to forestall her questions, Hawk withdrew an envelope from his coat pocket. ''I had Mr. Thrimble write this for your edification. It's simple enough, but I thought Krueger'd be here to elucidate the fine details for you. My mistake,'' he finished grimly and started to leave her in frozen misery as she held the papers in a talonlike grip, staring sightlessly at them.

He had the heavy door open and was about to step out when her voice stopped him instantly. ''Carrie is in jail for Karl's murder. She shot him with that pistol of hers. The sheriff found them together in a room at the Excelsior. She was undressed and he was dead!'' The venomous triumph in her voice grew more unmistakable with each word she hurled at him.

He stared at her with a shuttered expression on his face, watching her hate radiate like a tangible thing across the space between them. ''You're lying, Lola.''

''Just go to Circle S and ask Feliz!'' Her look of smug assurance left no doubt that Carrie was indeed in jail.

''Somehow, Lola, you arranged this. You killed Krueger. I know you thought you'd inherit K Bar. Now it looks as if you went to a lot of trouble for nothing. Kyle and I will straighten this out. No one's keeping Carrie in that filthy jail!''

As he spoke she glared at him, all her sense of triumph evaporating. She would not get Karl's wealth; she would not even be revenged on that redheaded bitch; Hawk didn't even believe her lies. Quivering with rage, she screamed at him, ''She's not in that filthy jail anymore! Caleb's got her! That's right, Caleb broke her out last night and carried her off to his rustler friend's hideout. He always wanted her, but she was too high and mighty for him—like you were too good for me. Well, we'll just see now who gets the satisfaction, won't we! He and those filthy gunmen will tear her apart by the time they're through with her!''

By the time he grabbed her she was laughing and crying all at once in bubbling hysteria. "Where, Lola—where has he taken her? Tell me or I swear I'll use every torture my Sioux friends ever devised on you!" He slapped her several times to still her insane laughter, then shook her until her neck cracked and her teeth chattered.

Grinding her jaws together, she said, "I don't know, damn you! He and Karl worked out their dirty little deals about stealing your stupid cows. He just wanted her and took her. If you beat me to death, I can't tell you!'' Another maniacal laugh surfaced as she hung like a rag doll in his harsh grip.

Swearing, he threw her roughly against the large leather chair in the corner and whirled, leaving the room with lightning speed.

Lola lay draped across the chair, her hair tangled around her shoulders, her robe torn and askew. Dumbly she looked at the floor where the legal papers Hawk had given her lay. No inheritance. No money or power. Nothing. She considered the future, growing older in poverty, she who had been a Chicago Jameson, the darling of the debutantes, a baroness, now a nobody who Hawk Sinclair would see charged with kidnapping, even murder. Slowly and unsteadily she stood up and walked over to the liquor cabinet, where she poured herself a very generous glass of whiskey, slugging it down with unaccustomed speed. Then she poured another.

Kyle had been gaining ground on Rider for several hours. A horse carrying double always slowed a man down, even if the passenger weighed as little as Carrie. Kyle had found her gelding wandering lame after stumbling in a gopher hole near the trail. The deeper prints of Rider's own mount told the tale as clearly as a road map.

As far as the canny Texan could tell, Rider was taking Carrie to his rendezvous point with the rustlers, on the northern end of K Bar land, near the Dakota border. It was close to the railroad line, an easy drive with stolen cattle to the railhead. Kyle's past weeks of careful tracking and surveillance had allowed him and Hawk to locate the thieves' hideout. They had been in the process of laying an elaborate trap, waiting for reinforcements to arrive from the Nations before they finished the deadly game with Krueger and his foreman.

Now, with Krueger dead, the whole plan had blown up in their faces. Perhaps something could be salvaged, but first Kyle must rescue Carrie unharmed. Just thinking of what Caleb Rider and his cohorts were capable of made his blood run cold!

It was a desperate gamble, but if he took off hell-bent, no longer bothering with the painstaking chore of trailing, he could overtake Rider before he got to his friends. Of course, if he were wrong and Rider wasn't headed there, he risked losing their trail entirely. The Texan swore. Never in his life had a hunch been so much of a risk. He thought of Carrie surrounded by half a dozen leering criminals, and spurred his horse into a furious gallop.

Carrie was groggy from the blow to her head. The right side of her scalp throbbed wickedly and her whole body was a mass of scratches and bruises. She had been bouncing against Rider's unyielding body for hours.

Dark had given way to the faint warming glow of sunrise when her horse stumbled and threw her. Her hands had been tied in front of her, and it was fortunate she had not broken an arm or even her neck. Rider had sworn vilely as he stopped and dragged her dazed, aching body off the rocky earth. The horse had to be abandoned, and he carried her in front of him, squeezed in loathsome proximity to his body. It slowed their progress considerably, and Carrie began to gather enough of her wits by midmorning to hope this piece of luck might give Hawk and Kyle time to catch them.

Finally, Caleb pulled his tiring horse off the trail by an outcropping of rocks. Carrie was disoriented, but it seemed to her he had doubled back for the past quarter hour or so. Why?

As if in answer to her silent question, he dismounted,

quickly dragging her bound form with him. He shoved her roughly to a thick, grassy mound of earth behind a large rock. Looming over Carrie like an incarnation from hell, he began to untie his neckerchief. Before she could cry out, he knelt and gagged her cruelly with the large cotton scarf. Then he took a length of rope and tied her booted feet securely, binding them to her wrists as well—hogtying her tightly. She lay on the ground, glaring up at him with fierce hate in her eyes. Living with Noah had taught her a great deal about intimidation. *God, don't let me give way now.*

"Think I'll just leave you here to contemplate the pleasures of tonight when we reach a nice cozy bed at the shack. I don't want to chance any unexpected visitors. I'd swear I've heard someone back a ways. You'll stay put now while I check it out."

Rider pulled his rifle from its saddle holster and walked over to the steep, rocky cliff that hid them from the road. With considerable agility he began to climb through the brushy crevices. When he crested the natural lookout point and scanned the trail below, a quick scowl spread across his face. A dim speck on the horizon was gradually increasing in size. When Rider could make out who the horseman was, the squinty frown was replaced by an evil smile.

"Payback time, you scrawny little son of a bitch! I get your lady boss there and you get a slug." He sighted his rifle and waited as the fast-moving horse galloped closer.

Kyle was certain he would overtake them within an hour at the outside. He had just decided to slow down and check to see if any of Rider's pals were nearby when the shot cracked from the rockpile to his left, knocking him off his terrified horse. As the animal bolted away, Hunnicut rolled across the dusty ground, his eyes searching for cover as he scrambled to regain his footing. Fortunately the area was brushy, with a twisting, dried-up creek bed off the trail to his right. He half rolled, half fell into it. He could not be certain where the shot had come from, but assumed it was across the road. Leave it to Rider to take the high ground.

He was no novice when it came to gunshot wounds, and

the Texan knew this was a bad one. As he checked his Colt, he listened for another rifle report. None came. "Yew come to me, Caleb boy. Yew jist do thet," he whispered to himself as he poked a sweat-soaked scarf against the widening red stain on his chest.

Carrie lay on the hard earth, struggling with her bonds, listening to the report of Rider's rifle. One shot. God, was it Hawk or Kyle? She squeezed her eyes shut and prayed Rider had missed, then continued to roll herself awkwardly off the grass to the nearby rocks. If she could only get a sharp piece of stone to saw her bonds! Caleb did not return. That was a good sign. He must have missed his shot. Frantically she searched the ground for something against which to rub the ropes. Her wrists were bloody and raw and the cord binding them to the ropes on her ankles was pulled tight, making it impossible for her to stand or even roll without pain. Despite nearly dislocating both shoulders, she made three more turns and reached a jagged outcrop of rock.

Caleb Rider swore as he saw the curled figure of the Texan vanish into the brushy streambed. The impact of his shot had knocked him most of the way, but long experience at killing made Rider sure that his prey wasn't dead. He had rolled that last turn on his own. Still, it had been a hit, and it would be only a matter of time until he bled to death. Hunnicut had come alone, but never one to leave matters to chance, Rider scanned the horizon for possible backup. Should he risk staying to finish the Texan or grab the woman and take off? He wanted to see Kyle Hunnicut die. Slowly he climbed down the side of the hill. If he circled to the east where the trail dipped, he could come back down the creek bed and nail his quarry from behind. As badly shot as he must be, not even that tough little rooster would be doing much moving.

Ten minutes ticked off slowly as Rider circled and Kyle bled. He was sweating profusely and growing lightheaded. Soon he'd pass out, maybe for good. How to draw Rider?

"Always figgered yew fer a sidewinder, Caleb. Bushwhackin' 'stead o' facin' a man down." He took a breath. Yelling was taking more energy than he had in reserve.

"Yew shoot Frank like thet? Yer a yeller dog coward, Rider!"

Just then the faint scuffling noise of a boot dislodging a small rock sounded in the still noon heat. Kyle turned painfully as Rider rounded the curved trail of the stream bed. Both men shot simultaneously. Both missed. The Texan's hands were shaking and weak from loss of blood. The bushwhacker was caught by surprise that the gore-covered man could still move so quickly. They took cover in the tangled undergrowth.

"You'll bleed to death real quick in this heat, Hunnicut. All I have to do is wait."

"Mebbe. But till I do, yew cain't cross thet road ta git yer hoss 'er Carrie, kin ya?"

"Maybe I don't have Carrie. Ever consider that, runt?" He edged through the grass, trying to pinpoint exactly where his adversary was hidden. With the rifle he had a decided advantage.

"Yew got 'er, right 'nough, jist th' way yew'd have ta git any woman, bound 'n' gagged," Kyle taunted.

Rider swore and lunged out of the bushes, crashing toward the sound of the drawling voice. "Time to finish this," he yelled as he sighted on the crouched form of the wounded man, propped up against the side of a rock. It was a bad tactical blunder. He had to aim the rifle, awkward in the close confines of the narrow creek bed. Before he could do so Kyle got off one shot, which knocked Rider backward as it slammed into his left arm. The killer scrambled for cover when he hit the ground.

Hunnicut swore as he pitched forward. "Purely meant thet bullet ta hit center." Then everything went black.

Hawk heard the shots. He had left K Bar to take a desperate gamble, guessing, as Hunnicut did, that Rider would head for his border hideout with Carrie. He had no time to backtrack to town in hopes of picking up a trail. Now as he pushed his exhausted bay nearer, he feared what he would find. Had Rider had a run-in with some of his fellow rustlers, or had Carrie somehow gotten hold of a gun? Either way he didn't like the direction of his thoughts as he came upon the sharp outcropping of rocks on the hillock overlooking the dry stream bed.

Catching the glint of a gun barrel, he slid off Redskin with practiced ease, rolling quickly into some thick dry bush with his rifle in his hand. A bullet glanced off the rock over his head, causing the soft shale to flake, showering him with fine particles. Rider was across the trail in the gully, but where was Carrie? Who else had exchanged shots with Rider?

The killer answered his unspoken question. "That little bastard you ride with is dead, half-breed. You're next. Think of me and your woman, all cozy in my cabin tonight—after I kill you."

So it had been Kyle. Hawk could see what a natural place this was for an ambush. Hunnicut would have, too, if he had not been so intent on galloping after Carrie. Of course, he had been doing the same thing himself. If Kyle hadn't stopped Rider first, he, not his friend, might be the one dead now. Quickly Hawk slipped off his boots and dropped the rifle noiselessly to the ground. Never in all his years with the Cheyenne had Hunting Hawk stalked his prey with such single-minded concentration, forcing his grief for Kyle and his fear for Carrie out of his mind.

After almost half an hour, Caleb Rider began to sweat. It was as if the rivers of perspiration rolling off him took his bravado along with them. He had been under fire many times in his life, faced uneven odds and deadly killers. And he had always walked away from death. But after Hunnicut got off that last lucky shot and then pitched face forward, Rider had been shaken. Not by the bullet, for the wound in his arm was slight and had already stopped bleeding. He had taken far worse punishment in the past, but no sooner had he recovered his rifle and seen the still form of the Texan lying in the dust than Redskin's pounding hoofbeats foretold Sinclair's arrival.

Some gut instinct told Rider that Sinclair would come. That was what unnerved him, the premonition and the fact that his adversary was fighting on his terms, in close quarters on rough terrain that could hide a dozen armed men. His own perfect ambush site now became an insidious trap. Carrie and his horse were across a wide-open space in the rocks beyond. Why didn't that damned savage make his move? Since he had vanished in the brush, dropping from his horse as if he knew Rider had a bead on him, Hawk had not made a sound. Was he still over there waiting? Or was he coming after his prey?

Now Rider's adversary was not a wounded, weakening man, but a deadly alert killer, a savage. Terror clawed at his guts, but Rider forced it down, tasting the sour bile in his throat as he swallowed.

Hawk could hear the faint sounds Rider made from his crouched hiding place. No matter how quiet a *veho* tried to be, he could never truly succeed. He recalled Iron Heart's words to him as a youth. *White men disturb the spirits of the earth. Listen, and you will hear their complaint.* Grimly he moved closer. When he caught sight of Rider's boot heel, sticking out from behind the rock where he was squatted, Hawk stopped and knelt. Then he took a small stone and tossed it between them. It landed with a loud thunk in the dust, causing Rider to whirl at the sudden noise behind him and fire wildly. It also led him to abandon his cover as he stood up, his eyes frantically searching for the source of the noise. By the time he saw Sinclair, it was too late. He had no time to draw a bead on his target, and his bullet only grazed Hawk's shoulder. Hawk's shot found its mark, dead center. He was only six yards away, and the impact carried Rider's body back into the rocks, sprawling his broken corpse grotesquely over them. Hawk approached cautiously to make sure Caleb was dead. Then he heard the moan, faint and low, coming from around the bend of the narrow stream bed. Kicking at Rider's body and satisfied that he would never kill again, Hawk rushed toward the sound.

"Kyle!" He spied Hunnicut in the dust, a widening stain of red across his upper body. Carefully he turned the small man over, laying him flat and checking for a heartbeat. He barely found it. "Tough old rooster, don't you go and die on me now," he said as he frantically tore off his own shirt and wadded it against the hole in Kyle's chest. In answer to his friend's words, the Texan's eyes opened in

an unsteady flutter. "I missed, but yew didn't, I reckon."
His voice was as faint as his pulse. "Leave me be 'n' find
Carrie," he attempted to command, but only succeeded in
croaking.

Carrie had spent the past half hour in frantic exertion,
rubbing her bloody wrists and arms against a rough piece
of rock, all the while listening to the sounds of the ensuing
fight. Forcing down her tears when she heard Rider's
claim to have killed Kyle, she persevered.

Hawk found her just as she finally broke the last of the
bonds off her wrists and was fumbling with the ones on her
ankles. When he cut her free and pulled her up, her
numbed legs gave way. She collapsed against him. "Where's
Kyle? Oh, Hawk, is he—"

"He's not dead yet, but it's bad. If I put you on Rider's
horse, can you hold on?"

She nodded. "Yes. Just get back to Kyle. I'll manage.
We've got to get him to a doctor!"

CHAPTER
24

The nightmarish ride to Miles City took until well past dark. Carrie clung stubbornly to Rider's horse, dizzy and aching but desperate in her determination not to further slow their progress by passing out. Hawk held Kyle in his arms, torn between a desire to urge Redskin to gallop and the need for a gentler pace lest the Texan start to bleed once more. Hawk had stopped the hemorrhage with some herbal concoction he gathered near the dry creek bed, bandaging the wound with his own shirt. Both he and Carrie prayed the crude remedy would work.

Phineas Lark was less than overjoyed to see the bedraggled trio—the bare-chested half-breed soaked in Kyle's blood, the gravely wounded Texas gunman, and the scarlet woman who was now wanted for murder. After seeing a light in the doctor's front parlor, Hawk had kicked open the door to Lark's private residence. By the time the irate, pompous physician came puffing up to them, Hawk was already depositing his burden on a table in Lark's home examining room.

If Lark had even fleetingly considered ordering Sinclair to take his stricken friend elsewhere, one look into those savage black eyes choked his indignation in his throat. Wordlessly he went to work, peeling away Kyle's soaked clothing and the makeshift bandage Hawk had made from his own shirt. He removed the grass poultice, muttering something beneath his breath, but seemed surprised that the bleeding was now so slight. While he dug the slug out, disinfected the wound, and sewed up the torn flesh, Hawk assisted him calmly. Carrie collapsed in a chair, fighting to remain conscious as her head injury and exhaustion took their toll.

After he had finished with Kyle, Lark looked up at Hawk and spoke somewhat hesitantly, uneasy now that his technical skills no longer put him in command of the situation. "He's lost a lot of blood and his collarbone's fractured badly. Frankly, I'm amazed he's still alive, but after surviving this long, well, he might make it. Incredibly tough man."

"How soon can we move him?" Despite the flood of relief the doctor's words brought him, Hawk's face was impassive.

"If he doesn't bleed during the night and his temperature is stable, I'd say he could be transported as far as a comfortable bed in the Excelsior in a couple of days."

Both men's attention was drawn to Carrie then as she slowly stood up and said, "You're sure he'll be all right? Thank God. . . ." Her voice was faint, and the dark smudges beneath her eyes made her pale face seem even more deathly.

Lark noticed the bloody raw abrasions on her wrists and the torn, disheveled state of her clothing, but he did not offer to treat her injuries until Hawk ordered him. "She's had a bad knock on the head. Take care of her."

Remembering the disdainful way the doctor had announced his refusal ever to treat her again after Perry was born, Carrie shook her head stubbornly. "No, no, Hawk. All I need is a bath and some sleep. Just so Kyle's all right."

"Shouldn't you be more worried about the marshal?" Dr. Lark looked at the tall half-breed out of the corner of his eye as soon as his retort was made to her.

"First some medical attention and rest, then we'll settle with the law. What's this about a marshal?" Hawk pinned Lark with his obsidian gaze.

"Sheriff Woods was found dead this morning, and she was missing. The mayor sent to Helena for a federal marshal to investigate,'' Lark said defensively, suddenly beginning to sweat as the realization struck him that he was standing next to a murderess and her accomplice.

Hawk scoffed. ''Don't worry, Doctor. We're hardly going to run off after coming all this way back.''

They left Dr. Lark's house and rode along the deserted streets to the hotel. Both of them were exhausted, and now that the crisis with Kyle seemed over, their spent emotions left them silent. The Excelsior clerk almost collapsed behind the desk in gape-jawed amazement when Hawk walked in with the town's infamous jailbreaker. However, he was even more easily quelled than Lark, quickly giving Hawk two room keys and agreeing to send up hot water and some first-aid supplies.

Before he availed himself of the luxury of a bath, Hawk quickly took the horses to the livery stable. By the time he returned to the hotel and cleaned up, Carrie had refreshed herself with a long soak and was quietly sitting at the table in her room, struggling with the salve and bandages for her wrists. She felt as if no part of her body was free of scratches, bruises, or lumps, but the wounds to her spirit were the worst.

Hawk entered her room after knocking. Carrie looked so wan and vulnerable that it grabbed at his heart. More gruffly than he intended, he said, ''I don't know why you didn't let Lark do that for you. Here, let me.''

''I could scarcely take a bath with bandaged arms,'' she replied in overly sweet reasonableness, some of her old fire evident in the tone of her voice now.

As he picked up the jar of salve, he grunted and began to apply it to the slim, fine-boned wrists. Seeing the way she had struggled against the cruel ropes and the damage they had done, he was struck with renewed fury at Lola and Rider, and, irrationally, at Carrie, too. ''How the hell did you get yourself into this mess anyway?''

He felt her stiffen as he wrapped a wrist with the clean linen. ''Do you think I had a tryst with Krueger and shot him in a jealous rage? That's what Woods said.''

Hawk snorted in obvious disbelief and kept on bandaging. ''No, but if you hadn't tangled with that damn

German in the first place, you wouldn't have fallen into Lola and Rider's hands so neatly, that's for damn sure!''

Just like him always to blame her for everything! "So generous of you to think I didn't shoot Krueger, at least," she snapped, wrenching her wrist away as soon as he tied the bandage. His touch still made her tremble, and now her response was intensified by anger and exhaustion.

He sat back on the wooden chair and rubbed his eyes. "I ordered that wet-eared clerk to send a meal up here. Now, tell me everything that happened while I was gone."

Carrie calmed down and went over the past two days of harrowing events. He interrupted with questions several times and rose abruptly to leave when he was satisfied with all the facts.

"I'm going to check on Kyle. Eat when the food comes and get some sleep. That's a nasty knot on your head."

Why did everything he said sound so damn accusatory to her ears? Wasn't he relieved at all that she was alive, or did he really harbor a faint suspicion that she had been involved with Krueger? Carrie's head and heart ached.

Just then the waiter bringing the food knocked. Hawk let him in and departed, too preoccupied to even say good night.

Hawk was deep in thought as he walked the streets to Dr. Lark's residence. Part of his mind turned over the problems of how to extricate Carrie from what appeared to be a carefully designed frame-up. Yet nagging right alongside practical considerations was the same old feeling that he had always experienced around her. He could still smell the faint whisper of wildflowers and feel the silky warmth of her pale, golden skin. He cursed his weakness and forced himself to plan for tomorrow. First he must send word of what had happened to Feliz at Circle S, then convince the local authorities, such as they were, that Carrie could be trusted to stay in Miles City while he went after the real killer of Karl von Krueger. He was sure Lola was at the bottom of it, and he would drag her in to confess if he had to peel the skin off her rottenly voluptuous body an inch at a time.

As it turned out, Sioux persuasion was neither possible

nor necessary. Lola Jameson Krueger was dead by her own hand. She had spent the previous day drinking, locked in Krueger's study, screaming and smashing things. Finally, in an alcoholic stupor she had placed one of Karl's fine German dueling pistols to her head and pulled the trigger.

Worthington Ashmore, playing his role of proper and professional English butler to the hilt, came to town, asking to speak to the authorities. He informed the astounded mayor and other dignitaries that he and the baron's German maid had information regarding their employer's murder.

Ashmore had been the one to unlock the study door and find Mrs. Krueger's body the preceding evening. With both his employers now dead, the butler decided it was no longer a breach of professional ethics to explain what he knew and to compel Frau Kaufmann, who had acted as Lola's maid, to do the same.

Both butler and maid, excellently trained European house servants, were simply regarded as part of the furnishings by the imperious baron and his sister-in-law. Krueger had been somewhat cautious, but Lola was not. Ashmore told of several loud arguments between them about marriage, her dire financial straits, even the baron's involvement with Caleb Rider in the rustling. However, the crucial testimony came from the sobbing maid, who explained in her broken English what she had overheard the baroness and the foreman plot. She knew only fragmented details about the timing for luring Carrie to the dressmaker's, drugging her, and leaving her to awaken in the room at the Excelsior, but it was enough.

When Hawk told the mayor how he and Hunnicut had rescued Carrie from Rider and she showed them her raw, blistered arms and the lump on her head, no one could dispute her innocence. After the whole bizarre tale had been pieced together, all charges against her were dropped.

The notoriety was another matter. Carrie had been the subject of scandal for bearing a half-breed's child while married to her lover's father. Now she further fueled the fires by staying in the same hotel room with the infamous gunman, Kyle Hunnicut, nursing him tirelessly while her Cheyenne lover went back to run their son's ranch.

Imagine, involved in a love triangle with Baron von Krueger and Lola Jameson, framed for murder, abducted and heaven knew *what else* by Caleb Rider! And now she continued to flout decency by sleeping in the same room with that Texas riffraff. Mathilda Thorndyke had so much to be indignant about that she could scarcely contain herself. She would see Carrie Sinclair run out of town with tar and feathers if it was the last thing she ever did!

Hawk busied himself at the ranch, doing the work of two men, covering for Kyle and carrying out all their plans for the big fall roundup and shipment of cattle to the railhead. With Krueger and Rider dead, the remnants of their gunmen and rustlers disbanded; thievery dropped abruptly to an all-time low. Still, there was a great deal of work to occupy the ramrod of Circle S. If he did not own the vast ranch, Hawk ran it nonetheless. Occasionally, when he had time to consider, he wondered how Noah would have reacted to seeing him in charge, or, for that matter, how the old man would have felt about a boy with Cheyenne blood inheriting Circle S. The irony of that amused him.

When his thoughts turned to Perry, Hawk felt alternately warm and anguished. He loved his son deeply, yet realized the boy would grow up in a white man's world, a world where the son could learn to adapt, but where the father did not belong. *No more than I belong with his mother.*

Carrie spent those weeks in Miles City caring for Kyle, whose return from near death was accounted almost a miracle by Dr. Lark. In three days' time he was moved from Lark's residence to the Excelsior. The physician and Carrie were glad to be quit of one another. Every few days, Feliz came into town. Then Carrie would return to Circle S and spoil her son for a brief interlude. She almost never saw Hawk. Once in a while when he could spare a few hours he would ride to town to visit with his recuperating friend.

After about a month, the doctor finally agreed that the gutsy little Texan was strong enough to be safely transported back to Circle S for the remainder of his convalescence. When the whole Circle S entourage departed, the town lost its liveliest entertainment. Mathilda Thorndyke attempted to keep the juicy gossip alive, speculating about a new, even more heinous triangle between Carrie, Kyle, and Hawk, but townfolk were tired of Circle S gossip—much more interesting was the murder of an honest-to-God baron by his own brother's wife.

As Kyle Hunnicut grew stronger he noticed the continued estrangement between Hawk and Carrie. The day Hawk brought the big flatbed supply wagon to town to take him home, Kyle watched his tall friend's cool manner. For her part, Carrie was guarded and nervous whenever Hawk approached. The sexual tension fairly radiated from both of them, yet neither would do anything to resolve the dilemma.

At first when Hawk returned from the Cheyenne, Kyle had been content to let things sort themselves out, especially after having found that his friend's wife was dead and that he planned to stay on at Circle S. But that had been last July and this was nearly October. All they seemed to do was antagonize one another. One morning he asked Feliz about it as she brought up his breakfast.

"Whut yew figger's eatin' them two?" He bit off a hunk of a sweet roll and downed it with a slug of aromatic black coffee.

He did not need to say more to the intuitive Mexicana. She knew what he meant. "Pride. Jealousy. Pain. Both have been hurt. Neither one wants to have the other turn away."

"Wal, it shore cain't go on this away," Kyle said disgustedly. "They got them a young'un ta think 'bout— not ta mention all thet aggervation, jist rubbin' next ta one another. Ain't nat'r'l."

"That is part of the trouble, I think," Feliz said, remembering last August when Carrie had come in wet from a swim, flushed in agitation. She was sure that Hawk, too, had gone to the lake that morning.

"Yew mean they been—" He spluttered to a halt, oddly indignant after what he had known went on two years earlier. Now they could get married! They *should* get married!

Feliz nodded shrewdly. "Not often, maybe only once, but, quien sabe? They cannot live so near and share the love of a child without sparks flying. Then the force that draws them to desire one another makes them angry and afraid, all at the same time."

"We gotta do somethin'. I'm gonna have me a lil' talk with thet long-legged Injun."

"It is not only him, Kyle. She has caused him much pain, cut deep into his pride."

Kyle only looked at her, waiting for her to continue.

"It was last summer," she said. "He had not been back long, a week maybe. He went to town and returned very late and very drunk. So drunk he let Redskin carry him to the big house instead of his madre's place. I was awake and heard him in the kitchen, trying to make coffee." Her eyes lit with fleeting mirth at the memory of the tall man caught like a small boy in some forbidden act. "I sobered him up with coffee and food, but not before he told me more than he would have otherwise about what happened at the village where they held Carrie."

"I know 'bout th' banishment fer th' fight. Leavin' his grandpa thet way wuz tough."

"That was only part of it, not the worst. After the fight—Dios, it must have been terrible—Carrie was frightened and said a terrible thing to him. A thing she did not mean, I know. She called him a filthy savage and tried to stop him from carrying Perry on their ride back."

Kyle whistled low. "An' him with all thet hard-shelled Injun pride, all th' years o' growin' up 'round his pa 'n' th' good white folks hereabouts 'n' back east . . ."

"Yes, all their cruelty he shut out, but not hers. He loves her, Kyle."

He scratched his head. "Yep, 'n' she loves him, too. I knowed thet afore he ever come back last summer. Pair o' damblasted fools, thet's whut we got us, Feliz!"

With that they made a silent pact to prod the recalcitrant lovers. Carrie brought Kyle's dinner that evening after being out riding with Perry through the warm autumn afternoon.

Ignoring the steaming plate of stew, crisp hot bread, and luscious apple pie, he fixed her with his most stern east-Texas poker face and bade her sit down. Guessing what he was going to bring up, she did so with great trepidation, hovering on the edge of a large wingback chair next to the bed. Her green eyes were haunted and sad.

"I'm gonna speak my piece 'n' I reckon yew ain't gonna like it, but damnit, Carrie, it needs ta be brung out in th' open." When she let out a long, whistling sigh of acquiescence, he went on. "Yew 'n' Hawk should git hitched. Noah's dead now, 'n' yew got thet boy ta think o'. 'Sides, neither one o' yew kin fool me. Yew always loved one another."

"He's got peculiar ways of showing his love, Kyle. Running out, leaving me to Noah's mercy, then marrying a Cheyenne woman."

Impatiently he ignored her anger. "Thet don't make sense if'n ya think on it, honey. First off, his wife's dead, same as Noah. Whether er not he cared fer her more 'n' yew did th' ole man, it don't change nothin' now. Yew got a fine son who needs his ma 'n' pa both. Anyways, it's plumb foolish ta talk 'bout him runnin' out on yew. I went with him thet mornin', 'n' I seen how bad he hurt."

"Then why did he leave me here?" Her voice was choked with anguish. "Noah threatened to kill me and Perry, too. He would have if he'd lived to see him born!"

"No way Hawk cud o' knowed thet. I bet yew didn't even dare hope Perry'd be his'n, not th' ole man's." Her guilty flush told him the truth of that. "Think, gal. Hawk wuz a gunman, out'n a cent ta his name. He only had him two choices back then. Goin' back ta his ma's folks er headin' ta th' Nations. Onliest thing between a woman like yew bein' tore apart by a dozen killers down there woulda been his gun. Life fer a man like thet's cheap. I oughta know, Carrie. I'm one, too. He couldn't take yew with him. Even Noah wuz a better risk'n thet."

"Oh, Kyle, it's so much more complicated than you know. We've both done things, said things. . . . Maybe he wants me, but he doesn't love me, not like he loved his wife. He wants to keep his son, not me.''

"All th' more reason fer ya ta fight fer him. Shit, th' Cheyenne's dead 'n' yer alive. Not much better odds'n thet! Yew said yerself he wants ya. With all yew got ta gain, I think yew kin make him love yew all over agin—if'n he ever quit—which I purely disbelieve.''

"Oh, my friend, I know you mean well, honestly, I do, but—''

He cut her off. "No buts. He gave up more'n yew know ta git yew 'n' th' boy outta thet camp. When a Cheyenne kills another Cheyenne, no matter why 'er how, it's th' most terriblest thing he kin do. By their law, he's banished fer at least four years. Then, if'n th' council agrees, mebbe they'll let him back in.'' He paused to see how she was taking this.

Her eyes were widened in shock. So that was why he was so angry with her—not because he cared about that brute he killed. His own grandfather had banished him from the only home he had, and it was her fault! "I didn't know that. He never told me,'' she whispered brokenly.

"Mebbe yew wasn't 'xactly in a listenin' mood then,'' Kyle said gently.

The tears, held back so long, flowed freely now. "You're right. I do love him so terribly. Nothing else matters but that. I'll just have to think of some way to convince him I'm worth all the grief I've caused him.''

She raised crystalline green eyes to look proudly into Kyle's crinkled, blue-gray ones.

"That's my gal talkin'. Sensible, finally.''

For the next several days Carrie mulled over what Kyle had told her. She had plenty of time to think without distraction since Hawk was with the roundup crews, spending nights out on the prairie where the cattle were gathered and tallied. Soon he would go to Chicago for several weeks. Last summer he and Kyle had decided the best price could be obtained by contacting the big slaughter-houses in that rail center. Circle S herds were large enough now to interest the meat packers in such a direct arrangement.

Carrie had a lot to do before he left to close the deal. Her first move entailed a visit to Jebediah Cooper. Despite her aversion to the self-righteous old man, she was forced to do business with him since he was the only lawyer in town.

"Mr. Cooper, what would happen to Circle S if I were to die tomorrow?" She sat calmly in the cluttered, stuffy little second-story office, ignoring his thinly veiled rudeness and patronizing airs.

"Why on earth ask such a thing? You're not in poor health, I trust?" His thin, sallow face bore the marks of a born hypochondriac.

"No. I just want to take precautions in case of an accident," she said impatiently.

"Well, a guardian would have to be appointed to run the ranch for your son." He stopped uncertainly.

Her calm green eyes looked at him steadily.

He shuffled papers on his cluttered desk. "Mr. Sinclair had relatives back east, also related to you. Your aunt and uncle, I believe."

"Noah also had a son and Perry has a father. Let's quit beating around the bush, Mr. Cooper. I know Hawk has no legal right in this matter, but he does have moral ones. I will never let Hiram and Patience Patterson get their greedy claws into my child or steal his inheritance!"

The gaping look of outrage on his face told Carrie what he thought of Hawk Sinclair's moral rights and morals—hers, too, for that matter. "What do you propose, Mrs. Sinclair?" His voice was grave and laced with sarcasm.

She told him in precise detail. Then, just as she was preparing to leave, a knock sounded and Mr. Cooper opened the door to admit an elegantly dressed man with blond hair and brooding dark-blue eyes. He was of medium height, solidly built, and rather young, sporting a neatly trimmed goatee, doubtless grown to make him look older. Carrie guessed him to be no more than twenty-two or twenty-three and was certain of his nationality the minute he began to speak. He was German.

"Ah, Herr Cooper. I am so glad to find you here, and this must be the beautiful Frau Sinclair." His eyes lit with obvious appreciation as he swept them over her flaming hair, then down her tailored tan wool suit to her gleaming brown slippers. He did not miss a curve in his lightning perusal, but the youthful admiration he exhibited made it most inoffensive. "Please, allow me to present myself. Baron Wolfgang von Krueger, at your service." He bowed formally and kissed her hand in a grand Continental gesture.

Carrie would have found the posturing amusing if she were not so taken aback by the name. "*Another* Baron von Krueger," she almost squeaked.

He flashed a dazzling boyish smile. "I am afraid so, although so recently have I acquired the title that I am not yet used to being addressed by it."

"Baron Wolfgang von Krueger is the heir to K Bar Ranch and has just arrived in Miles City to see about its disposition," Cooper put in pompously.

"Then you are related to Karl and Ernst Krueger?" Carrie could see no resemblance at all and was pleased by that.

"Distantly. I am the grandson of their aunt Katerina." He smiled.

"Second cousins, once removed," Mr. Cooper said in his precise, irritating manner.

Ignoring the attorney, Carrie asked, "Just what are your plans for the ranch? You scarcely look the part of a cattle baron, Baron." She dimpled, and his response to her smile reminded her of how long it had been since she felt young and truly happy.

"I think I shall sell if I can get my price. Or I may hire an overseer—a ramrod I believe you call him, to run the place in my absence. Now that I meet my competitor, I favor the latter course. Then I might have an excuse for return visits, ya?"

An idea was forming in Carrie's mind. Taking the young baron by the arm, she ushered him adroitly out the door with her, nodding a curt farewell to Mr. Cooper. "Would you be so kind as to have dinner at Circle S with me tomorrow night, Baron? My foreman is recovering from a grave injury and cannot ride to town yet. He and my business manager and I want to discuss your plans for K Bar. I promise our cook Feliz will outdo herself.''

There was no doubt he would accept. Barely acknowledging Mr. Cooper's good day, he strolled down the rickety side steps of the law office to the street. "Then it is seven tomorrow night! *Ach*, I look forward!''

CHAPTER 25

"What the hell is this? Why leave it in my cabin?" Hawk slammed the paper down on the big desk in the study, where Carrie sat working on ledgers.

"I couldn't very well leave it for you on this desk, since you refuse to work in the office. I had Juan put it where you'd find it first thing when you came in this evening." She looked defensive at his anger and also somewhat hurt.

"And why do I need a power of attorney for Circle S?"

"In case you forgot, you're going to Chicago Monday to sell cattle. This will certainly expedite matters," she said angrily now as he was leaning his tall body over the desk, glaring at her in a most unsettling way.

"I don't need a general power of attorney for that. The ranch is yours, Carrie. I'm only making a business arrangement in your behalf," he said with that cold, shuttered pride she had come to recognize. "I know my place, and it's at my mother's cabin, not here at the big house. What other little legal surprises did you arrange while you were in town this morning?"

With a sigh she realized just how difficult this was going to be. Damn all men and their idiotic pride! Thank heaven she had not told him about the will she had Mr. Cooper draw up, which made him Perry's guardian and trustee of Circle S.

"As a matter of fact, I invited the new owner of K Bar to dinner tonight. Just wait until you meet him," she added with a wicked glint in her eyes. If she couldn't reason with him, maybe she could make him jealous!

As he dressed for dinner that night, Hawk's thoughts were not exactly ones of jealousy, but of hurt and anger. She needed him to run the ranch, at least until Kyle was recovered, even then to negotiate in places like Chicago where Hunnicut would never venture. All that power of attorney meant was an indirect sort of bribe, feeling him out to see if he would assume the responsibilities of a business partner. However, his pride held him aloof. Noah never intended that he have Circle S. So be it. But another voice niggled, *Noah never intended that your son inherit either, but he will.* Ignoring that and all the guilt and confusion that roiled in his soul, he dressed for their first formal dinner in the dining room since Noah had died. Quite an occasion. He didn't think he wanted to meet the new baron.

In honor of reopening the dining room and having a guest, Carrie took particular pains with her appearance. If the young baron was shocked or disgusted with her past history, he did not show it, even though she knew Attorney Cooper and the townspeople had given him an earful before he had ever met her. He was young and attractive, not at all like his ruthless cousin Karl. She would flirt discreetly and enjoy herself. If Hawk was upset, let him do something about it!

When she went downstairs, her choice of costume was obviously appreciated. Kyle was shuffling nervously from foot to foot, uncomfortable in a suit and tie, when he looked up and saw her.

"Lordy, yew are a sight," he breathed in awe.

It was true. She was dressed in black peau de soie, a dark contrast of inky gown and her flame-bright hair. The gown had a severe straight skirt and fitted long sleeves. The neckline was a sharply narrowed mandarin style, slit deeply with just a hint of creamy flesh revealed in the opening. A mass of luminous pearls lay over the high neckline, seeming to hold it barely closed over her high breasts. Except for her deep-green eyes and fiery red hair, the severity of black and white was unrelieved.

"What are you doing standing here, Kyle Hunnicut? You've only been allowed downstairs for meals for a week. You are going to sit down right now." With that stern scolding, she took his arm and ushered him into the parlor. In her high-heeled black slippers she was several inches taller than he, indeed a Valkyrie as Karl had said.

Wolfgang von Krueger was quite punctual. Estrella ushered him into the parlor precisely at seven. Carrie made introductions to Kyle and they shared a drink. If Kyle had any awareness of her plan to make Hawk jealous, he did not indicate it, but seemed genuinely fascinated by the friendly, ingenuous charm of their young guest, who regaled them with colorful sketches about growing up in a German castle.

Hawk arrived late, dressed in a deep cordovan leather jacket and pants with contrasting snowy-white shirt and gleaming cordovan boots. He wore a number of silver and gemstone rings, and the silver medallion nestled snugly against his chest, revealed by the open shirtfront. All in all, he presented a picture of barbaric elegance, exotic yet strangely in tune with the land, unlike the young blond baron in his traditional black evening attire.

As she made introductions, Carrie knew sparks would fly. Wolfgang must know this was her Cheyenne lover, the father of her son. Hawk could see this was a young, wealthy, and attractive man of obvious charm and culture.

"Wolfgang is considering selling K Bar, Hawk. Do you think we might be able to muster the capital to buy it?" Her untutored innocence was disarming to the German, maddening to Hawk.

"We'd have to talk to Asa Fordham at the bank, Carrie. I'm not sure," he said in a noncommittal tone of voice, his eyes never leaving the glistening blond head, which was turned attentively to the flaming red one.

Kyle coughed and said, "I'd figger it'd take another fifty hands ta even consider runnin' th' two spreads together." He scratched his chin as if interested.

Hawk glared at him while Carrie and Wolfgang exchanged smiles.

Why, thet crafty little cat. Kyle chuckled to himself,

taking in the tableau before him with evident relish. *She jist might git us all o' eastern Montana an' thet boy's pa back in th' bargain!*

Feliz presented a marvelous dinner of roasted pheasant and apple dressing, crisp dry white wine, and freshly turned walnut ice cream for dessert. As they ate, they talked about the cattle business, Montana's prospects for statehood, even Karl's shocking death.

Throughout the meal, the undercurrents were not lost on the clever young baron whose youthfulness and blond good looks belied his native shrewdness. He watched the byplay between the tall, handsome half-breed and the beautiful redhead, reluctantly concluding that any suit he might press was probably lost at the onset. After Carrie rose and excused herself to tuck her son in bed, Wolfgang turned to Hawk. "You do not go with her? Forgive me, but I know he is your son, too."

Hawk looked levelly at the young man, measuring him carefully. "I'll see Perry in the morning," was all he said, indicating the subject was to be dropped. The German drew his own conclusions.

By the time the evening was over, Wolfgang had agreed to meet with Carrie and Attorney Cooper the following week to discuss a possible sale of K Bar. Failing that, Circle S might lease the operation and run it for the baron for a percentage of the profits. Either way, it was a coup to Carrie. No more threat of range war, no more rustling. She was inordinately pleased when she walked the young baron to the front door.

He kissed her hand with ardent abandon. "I shall look forward to next week. Will you have luncheon with me at the hotel—without the dried-up Herr Cooper, of course?" His eyes twinkled.

Her laughing acceptance carried across to the corral, where Hawk was mounting Redskin. He kneed the big bay and took off with a noisy flourish, kicking up pebbles and dirt in his anger and haste.

"He does not sleep in the big house?" Wolfgang's eyes watched Hawk disappear into the night.

"No. Nor in my bed, contrary to what you have doubtless heard in town," she said quietly.

"Then he is a fool." Wolfgang grinned and reached one finger to tilt her chin for a light, brushing kiss on her lips. "Yes, a very great fool, for you obviously love him."

She shook her head ruefully. "Your cousin Karl told me not to wear my heart on my sleeve. I believe those were his words."

"And now your Indian is angry, jealous, ya? I do not think, beautiful lady, that I would much like to have him for an enemy." Despite his words, his look was more amused and wistful than fearful.

"You will return to your enchanted castles and forests, leaving me to deal with my Indian. I am sorry to have involved you in our troubles, even briefly," she said in solemn apology.

He took her hands and kissed each one in turn. "I am not sorry, not sorry at all, Carrie. And I will one day return. If you are not attached by then, I shall do more than kiss your lovely hands!"

Hawk did not come to the kitchen for breakfast the next morning. At dinner that evening he was quiet and uncommunicative, only answering the questions directed at him.

"Yew think we ought ta go fer th' baron's price 'n' buy K Bar?" Kyle looked at Hawk's austere face and tried to draw him out.

"Depends. Fordham won't go much over a hundred and fifty thousand, even with a prosperous Circle S as collateral. It's up to the German and Carrie to make a deal." The very way he accented the words spoke volumes. "If you'll excuse me, I have to catch a train in the morning." With that he rose and left the room.

"Arrogant, self-righteous, pridefully blind . . . Indian!" She threw her napkin on the table and jumped up. "Good night, Kyle, Feliz."

As Feliz cleaned up the supper dishes, Kyle sat scratching his head. "Now, whut do yew think we should try next?"

"Quien sabe? Maybe when he comes back from his trip Hawk will have cooled off and come to his senses."

* * *

The trip to Chicago had been profitable, very profitable. Hawk relaxed in the plush traveling car, leaning back against the velvet seat cushions to inhale the expensive cigar he had just lit. The countryside rolled by outside, bringing him nearer to Montana with each mile. He had been gone for over two weeks and had secured top dollar for the cattle brought to market that fall as well as a contract to make regular deliveries the following year. He wondered bleakly about what had transpired between Carrie and Krueger while he had been gone.

"Why do you frown, querido?" Carlotta slithered into the seat beside him and draped herself conspicuously over him. Her voluptuous charms were well defined in the red taffeta dress she wore. Ignoring the envious glances of several women who watched her caress the mysteriously handsome cattleman's face, Lottie kissed him teasingly. Several men leered openly at the sight of an expensively dressed man obviously traveling with his mistress. Lucky devil.

Hawk was not so sure. He had picked up the pretty tart in a brothel in Chicago. She was departing the establishment after a loud and rather explicit verbal exchange with the madame over her choosiness in customers.

Carlotta Hernandez was from Florida, an expatriate Spanish Creole from the finest society family, she assured a dubious Hawk. She was striking-looking, with black sloe eyes, glossy midnight hair, and pouting ruby lips. Her petite figure was enhanced by round, full breasts, a tiny waist, and magnificently curvy hips. He had spent several inventive and diverting nights in bed with her at his hotel, fully intending to pay her off and send her on her way when he returned to Montana.

After months of unrelieved sexual tension, living so close to Carrie yet not touching her, Hawk had promised himself a holiday in Chicago. He had been sure Carrie was back in Montana being wined and dined with Continental charm. She was with the kind of man she belonged with and he was with the kind of woman he belonged with. So why was he so damned unhappy? He swore to himself while he watched Lottie's expressive features as she stared out the train window at the countryside rushing past them. She was really a child, for all her worldly experience in bed: pouty, gleeful, given to unexpected flashes of temper and artful wheedling. He had found that out when he tried to pay her off the morning he left Chicago.

After several days of enjoying the handsome Yankee's money and skills in bed, Lottie had no intention of letting so attractive a prize slip through her fingers. He ran a great *estanza* out west and was of an exotic mixed-blood ancestry, all of which intrigued her greatly. When he offered her a generous payment for time spent with him, she wept and clung to him, professing undying love, swearing to him that she left Madame Lou's place only to be with him, a story that they both knew to be blatantly untrue. When tears failed, she railed and threw things, calling him a gringo pig. Finally, when he subdued her destructive tantrum, she turned soft and seductive, preying on his physical needs once more. When even that failed, she resorted to cool business sense, asking him if there were any good houses in the towns of Montana, places that might appreciate her talents.

There she had him. Hawk could just see Kyle Hunnicut's eyes light up if he found a woman like Carlotta Hernandez in the parlor of Clancey's Place the next time he came to town. Against his better judgment he agreed to take her with him to Miles City and introduce her to Clancey. After all, he could give her top references for the job!

He had not wired his arrival date, so was spared the accusing looks of Kyle and Feliz, who would likely have met him at the train station. They still harbored romantic notions about him and Carrie. He doubted that she would have come to meet him even if he had wired. Anyway, the baron was probably keeping her quite busy these days. Kyle had wired his hotel in Chicago, indicating that Circle S was likely going to take over management of K Bar for a percentage of profits. The final details awaited his approval when he returned home. Bleakly he thought of all the meetings and plans Carrie had made with Krueger while he was away.

Shrugging, he helped Lottie off the train onto the uneven plank platform at the station. They were dusty and grimy from their long train ride, and he was eager to ensconce her at Clancey's and head for home and a long, hot bath.

Lottie soothed the wrinkles of her dress and patted her sooty hands disconsolately. "It is so bare, so open, querido. The town is so small."

He smiled sardonically down at her. "I warned you it would be like this, if you recall. This isn't Chicago. But Clancey's Place is pretty posh inside. Just think of all the business opportunities, Lottie. The West is the new home of free enterprise. Men'll be lining up for you, some of them rich cattle barons."

"Like you?" Her eyes caressed his face heatedly.

"I'm just a working cowhand, Lottie. I don't own a ranch," he said darkly, taking her arm and propelling her toward Clancey's.

Carrie put the napkin daintily to her lips and sighed. "Wolf, that was a wonderful meal, but I'm afraid I'm gaining weight from all these luncheon meetings." She looked around the Excelsior dining room at all the other cattlemen and townfolk who were carefully avoiding her eyes. *They pretend I'm invisible.*

Wolfgang Krueger smiled at her and arose to pull out her chair. "If you are fishing for compliments on your lovely figure, you already know, Liebchen, how much I admire it."

When she stood up, she looked him squarely in the eye. He was perhaps an inch taller than she, but no more. Still they made a striking couple, he muscular and elegant with his blond good looks and European charm, she willowy and graceful with her flaming hair and sun-kissed complexion.

Talk around town had not escaped her ears. In point of fact, with Mathilda Thorndyke stirring it up, it was impossible not to know that everyone thought she had abandoned her shocking liaison with Hawk and taken up with the baron. Why, she might actually get the fool to marry her and take her off to some foreign land to escape her shame. The injustice of her becoming a baroness rankled a great many more folks than just poor old Mathilda, not to mention the fact that if she left Montana, the juiciest source of scandal in a generation would be removed from their midst. Unthinkable!

It was unthinkable to Carrie as well, despite the fact that she liked Wolf and enjoyed his company. He was like the charming kid brother she had always wished for as a child but never had. Even though he was three years her senior, she felt much older than he. She liked him, but she was not in love with him and never could be.

As they walked from the hotel dining room, laughing and talking, Carrie's thoughts were drawn to Hawk. Often in the past two weeks she had wondered how he was doing with their cattle sale, when he would return, and how he had spent his free time in the large, wicked city.

As if in answer to that very question, she happened to glance across the street and see him, obviously travel stained and tired, in the company of a woman who could best be described as flashy. *No, make that vulgar and cheap,* she amended to herself. Vulgar, cheap, and very, very pretty!

Feeling her grip on his arm stiffen, Wolf followed her stricken gaze to see Hawk and Lottie entering Clancey's Place. The dark-haired beauty was clinging to him in artless abandon, obviously one of the creatures who inhabited the bordello. What a fool the man was, the German thought, but said noncommittally, "I see your business manager has returned home."

Hawk quickly placed Lottie in Clancey's best room and left her as she wailed, begging him to return soon. Clancey was delighted to have such a comely addition to his staff and distracted the girl by telling her about all the rich cattlemen who frequented the place. He did not elaborate on the far larger crop of impoverished cowpunchers.

Hawk decided the bank drafts he was carrying were an even higher priority than the much-longed-for bath, so he headed toward Miles City Savings to deposit them, preoccupied about his upcoming meeting with Carrie tonight. He was to see her far sooner than he anticipated, almost colliding with her and Wolfgang von Krueger in the bank door as he was entering and they were departing.

Simple but cool pleasantries were exchanged between Hawk and the baron. Hawk noted Carrie's guarded expression, which by now he knew was her attempt to hide pain or anger.

"Hello, Carrie. I just got off the train and thought these should go into the account before I headed for the ranch." He showed her the drafts.

As she quickly scanned the figures, she said, "You did even better than we'd hoped, Hawk. I'll deposit them, if you like. After such a long, arduous journey, I'm sure you need all the rest you can get." There was a barbed malice behind the sweet words that he could not miss. "Oh, I've invited Wolf for dinner tonight. We'll discuss final terms for our operation of K Bar."

"Until tonight, Herr Sinclair." The young German nodded politely and turned to escort Carrie back into the bank with a proprietary air.

With ground-eating strides, Hawk went to the livery stable to rent a horse for his ride to Circle S. God forbid he should intrude on their privacy by riding with Carrie and "Wolf" in their rig!

The one bright spot in his homecoming would be giving Perry the present he had brought from Chicago. First he went to his cabin to bathe, shave, and dress for dinner, deciding the hell with European nobility. Comfortable western clothes were in order. He had suffered enough in suits, ties, and tight shoes. If he wasn't grand enough for the dining room, he would eat with Feliz and Estrella in the kitchen. Riding up to the big house, he went to the kitchen door where he knew Feliz would be, likely with Perry playing on the floor nearby while she cooked tonight's feast.

"Hawk! It is you at last! Bienvenido!" Tossing a large wooden spoon carelessly into a pot, she embraced him. Despite her considerable bulk, he lifted her off the ground and gave her a return squeeze.

"Feliz, love of my life, I could smell good things cooking all the way down the road. Where's—"

Before he could say anything more, he spied his son, toddling toward him on uncertain feet. "Pa-pa! Pa-pa!" The squeal was repeated over again as Perry was scooped up and swung high in the air by his tall father.

Hawk looked incredulously at Feliz, then back at the giggling boy.

"We have been practicing while you were gone. He almost said it many times in the past month or two, but now he has it mastered." Feliz's face fairly beamed as she gazed up at the handsome pair. She could see the emotions in Hawk's eyes that he tried so hard to erase from his face. *Always the Indian in him tries to hide his feelings.*

"I have a present for you, Perry. All the way from back east." He had brought a small wooden horse on rockers, sturdy and quite realistically carved, just the size for the long-legged youngster. Seating the boy on it, he showed him how to hold on and make it rock to and fro. Soon squeals of delighted laughter echoed through the backyard, where they had adjourned to play while Feliz oversaw dinner and watched from the kitchen windows.

Carrie had arrived at the house several hours earlier and had gone upstairs for a nap, pleading a headache. A certain petite brunette had more to do with her malaise than any headache, but she would never admit it. She rose and began to dress for dinner, deciding if sophisticated elegance did not turn Hawk's head, she would try it his way. She selected a simple apricot silk shirt, clinging and open at the throat, along with a soft burnt-orange wool skirt and delicate high-heeled brown boots. She brushed her hair down and caught it simply at the back of her neck with an orange ribbon the same shade as the skirt. No jewelry; she would be a plain, unadorned western woman. It might be a good way to let Wolf see her, too, she decided, realizing guiltily that he was growing increasingly attached to her in a most unbrotherly fashion.

When she came downstairs, she could see his rig pulling up in front of the drive and went out to greet him. No sooner had they exchanged pleasantries and begun to ascend the front steps than deep baritone laughter and high-pitched squeals sounded from the backyard. Curiously they walked around the side of the house, past the path to the rose garden, to the source of the noise.

Carrie stood frozen, watching Hawk and Perry as the boy held on to the wooden horse for dear life, fairly flying back and forth. Hawk knelt protectively, guarding against the small rider's becoming unseated and urging him on at the same time. Unaware of the spectators, Hawk laughed and talked to Perry, who responded with gleeful cries of "Pa-pa" again and again.

"You belong with them, Liebchen. Why do you deny it?" Wolf said the words softly and reluctantly, but the truth of the situation was written all over her face.

Brightening in false cheerfulness, Carrie smiled at him. "I can't belong where I'm not wanted, Wolf." Quickly she turned and hailed her son, running over to plant a kiss on his chubby cheek and to inspect his new treasure.

Hawk stood up then and greeted von Krueger politely. The restrained gesture was returned by the German, and the tone of the evening was set. Kyle was working late and would not be joining them for dinner, Carrie explained, exasperated by the way he was jeopardizing his recovery with overwork.

This dinner was even more of an ordeal than the one prior to Hawk's trip. Without the easygoing banter of the Texan to smooth over tense spots, the two men were both fiercely guarded in their conversation. Awash in misery, Carrie did little to alleviate the situation. All her foolish schemes for using Wolf to make Hawk jealous had been abandoned. She liked the young baron too much to lead him on, and it was useless anyway. Over and over during the meal, she gazed at Hawk, dressed in a linen shirt, open at the throat with thick black hair curling out onto the stark white shirtfront. The silver medallion winked at her from its luxurious resting place, taunting her. She could just see that strumpet in the red dress running greedy little fingers across that hard, hairy chest, playing with the medallion— her medallion! *No, you gave it back to him.*

The three of them agreed on the leasing operation of K Bar for a trial period of one year. Wolf let it be known he would return to check on his property during the ensuing year. The message left a great deal unspoken between them.

Hawk was swift to read much more into the young German's words than the baron intended. It seemed to him that Wolf was assuring Carrie that he would be there if she needed him, if she changed her mind about Sinclair. Hawk saw only that a perfect husband for Carrie had materialized from the far reaches of Europe. Krueger was wealthy, cultured, and attractive, young and genuinely enamored of Carrie. He would not consider Perry an impediment or a disgrace for her to live down. He could take them back to Europe, away from the hate and bigotry in this country.

They could educate Perry in European universities. That was a bitter thought to accept, but as he rode to his lonely cabin late that night, he turned his son's future over in his mind. Here Perry would always be branded as a half-breed's bastard, given as little chance to fit in as his father. But Perry was only one-quarter Cheyenne. He had no ties to the People, would never know of them. He could grow up with none of the divided loyalties that tore at Hawk. Hawk should give up his son, let Carrie take him abroad. They could build a new life in an old land.

God knew she was morose enough about having him sit at the table tonight, he thought bitterly. As if he should expect a welcome-home from her! For now, he was needed to coordinate the handling of the two huge ranches. In fact, he would doubtless do so after she and Perry were gone. He had discovered on the Chicago trip that he had a real flair for dealing with businessmen. He had always been a fine stockman, and now even the brief time he would have to spend in eastern cities no longer repelled him. It would be a life, better than getting shot as a hired gun. Grimly he turned Redskin toward town. He needed to get drunk.

CHAPTER 26

Hawk rolled over in the big bed, only one turn, but it felt as if he'd been keelhauled. Sweet Lord, his head hurt! Very carefully he opened his eyes to the blinding October sunlight bathing the room. Agony. He shut them again quickly and that hurt, too. He lay still, flat on his back and tried to orient himself and recall what had happened last night after he left the ranch.

A shrill burst of off-key singing in Spanish immediately jarred his memory and his throbbing hangover. Carlotta Hernandez swished brightly into the room. "Querido, you are finally awake! Here, I have made coffee for you." Sitting down on the edge of the bed, she offered him the mug and snuggled against him as he unwillingly sat up. She rubbed her large breasts against his arm while her red satin robe hung loosely off one shoulder. Was everything she owned red? God, it hurt his eyes!

He closed them and took a pull on the coffee. Christ! She made even worse coffee than Carrie. Forcing down the urge to spit it back into the cup, he swallowed. "Guess I was drunker than I thought last night," he said noncommittally.

She laughed. "Ah, no, querido, you will not get out of our bargain so easy as that." She snapped her fingers in front of his face, and he was sure at least one if not both his eardrums shattered.

"What bargain?" His voice was cautious.

She pouted and then took the cup from him, sitting it on the bedside table. "Why, I am to be your housekeeper, cook, and, most important of all," she punctuated her remarks with light, teasing kisses to his face, neck, and chest, "your woman, here." She spread one little hand across the bed expansively.

It did not take much convincing to get him to lie back down. Then she began to work her most skillful wiles on him. Soon he forgot about the coffee, even about the hangover.

Gossip always traveled fast, and if it dealt with the Sinclairs, it traveled fastest of all. Within two days everyone in town and on Circle S knew that Hawk had the whore who came with him from Chicago ensconced in his cabin. He went about his business as usual, running the ranch and dealing with the men. He did not take his meals in the big kitchen any longer, though in truth Feliz's cooking was far to be preferred to Lottie's. He had successfully avoided Carrie, or in point of fact, she had avoided him for the past week. Feliz looked at him with sorrowful eyes, but made no comment. Kyle, however, was downright hostile.

"Yew got no right lettin' thet female live in yer ma's place. Ain't fittin', I tell ya." He invited Hawk to his cabin to go over the month's tally books, but they had no more than sat down at the kitchen table when the Texan launched into his friend. "Bad enough Carrie 'n' thet ferrin' feller sashayin' 'round town, but at least it's respectable. He don't invite her ta spend th' night at K Bar!"

"She's made her choice, Kyle, and I can't say I blame her. You know I'm no monk. I have to live, too." His face was bleak and closed. "I don't want to talk about it."

Knowing that tone of voice, Kyle subsided with a few inventive oaths and turned to the business at hand.

Carrie spent a great deal of time riding by herself in the next weeks. Autumn deepened and the rolling prairie grasses rustled, whispering that frost was near. The days grew shorter and the evenings cooler. It was the mating season for deer and elk, the last of the garden vegetables grew ripe and juicy, and apples were dropping from overladen branches in orchards kissed by the warm fall sun. Everywhere she went, Carrie saw the richness and beauty of the land, her land. Montana with its open sky, tractless grasslands, and bitter winters was her home; despite all its harshness she would never leave.

But how can I stay and watch him with that woman? It tore at her heart, and she hid herself from him, not wanting him to see her pain, to pity her. Even a whore was a better substitute for his dead wife than Carrie Sinclair. Sobbing, she kicked Taffy in the sides and rode toward the ranch.

It was nearly lunchtime, and she had promised to help Feliz with the bread baking that afternoon. When she slid off Taffy, she realized she had unconsciously been scanning the stable area for signs of Redskin again. But Hawk had his own "cook" now and did not eat with them. Doggedly she trudged into Feliz's aromatic kitchen.

Perry was eating small bits of steak with his fingers. Sitting on a kitchen chair with a large block of wood for a booster seat and a belt holding him secure, he could just reach the table. He was growing so rapidly that his high chair was already too small. The new one had not yet arrived, so Kyle had rigged up the block as a stopgap measure.

"Why did you give him whole pieces of meat, Feliz? He might choke!" Carrie moved to take the plate from the boy, who put up such a fierce squall she relented, watching carefully as he chewed the tiny pieces doggedly with erratically spaced but sturdy little teeth.

"Hrumph. He has been eating solid meat for weeks," Feliz retorted.

"I've never fed it to him. Neither have you, before this!"

"His papa has been sharing his breakfast steak with the little one for a month or more. Only the other day I caught them, and he confessed. See how well he can chew it? It does no harm." She kneaded a large slab of dough as she spoke, watching Carrie's reaction at the mention of Hawk.

"I thought his ladylove took care of feeding him breakfast! He doesn't eat his other meals here." Her voice was petulant, and she knew it.

"He must see his son, Carrie. Maybe he wishes to cause you no embarrassment, so he comes when he knows you are not here."

"If he wishes to cause me no embarrassment, then why does he keep that—that vulgar woman living with him!" There, it was out; she had said it, sobbed it in truth.

Feliz kept pounding the bread dough relentlessly. "So, you don't like it that he has a woman. You, of course, can have your young baron over here every evening, meet him in town, go riding with him. Everyone says you will marry with him."

"Well, Hawk certainly needn't bother marrying that trashy little baggage from Chicago," she shot back. "Anyway, you know I won't marry Wolf. I don't love him."

"I know, but does Hawk?"

"I doubt he cares or has even noticed." Try as she might, she could not keep the hurt from her voice.

"Carrie, you cannot expect Hawk to go without a woman from June to October while you make up your mind. He has not touched you—or has he?" Her compassionate brown eyes became assessing as she watched Carrie flinch at her shrewd sally.

"One time, last August," she replied, her voice choked and low.

"At the lake?"

Carrie nodded, cheeks flushed.

"And you, or course, turned on him and accused him afterward." Feliz's voice was gentle, but the accuracy of her description cut deeply.

Dashing back tears, Carrie said, "I told him he was just like Noah. Oh, Feliz, that was a lie, a lie. . . ." She sobbed. "I didn't mean it."

"Did you mean it when you called him a filthy savage that day in Iron Heart's village?"

Carrie crumpled onto a chair by the table and put her head down, continuing to sob. "No, no, of course not. I was tired and scared. He looked so different. . . ." her voice

faded as she subdued her crying. Then she raised her head
as the thought struck her. "How did you know...?"

Wiping her hands, Feliz walked over to Perry, who had
finished his luncheon and was fussing to get to his toys in
the corner. Lifting the child down, she said, "He told me
late one night, not long after it happened, out of a well of
pain so deep it had no bottom. If he had not been
borracho—very drunk—he would never have let even me
see this hurt. He thinks you do not love him, that you see
him as others in town do, as most white people have
always seen him—a half-breed, a savage."

"That's not true! Oh, God, it's not. I love him,
but—"

"No buts," Feliz interrupted. "If you want him, you
are going to have to fight for him. Tell him how you really
feel. All his life he has been an outsider. If you want to
belong with him, Carrie, you are going to have to convince him. You have outlasted Don Noah and showed the
whole town your courage. Are you brave enough to show
the man you love?"

Was she? Early the next morning she rode over to
Hawk's cabin, escorted by a grinning Kyle Hunnicut and
José Mendoza, Feliz's eldest son. Soon she would have the
answer to her question. When they got to the cabin, she
hopped off the wagon and gave Kyle a small, tremulous
smile. Then she walked to the door and pushed it open.
Hawk was gone for a long day on the south range and
would not be home until dusk.

Carlotta was there, however, just as Carrie expected.
But she did not expect the filthy, debris-strewn room that
confronted her. The once immaculate shrine for Marah
Sinclair was now a pigsty. Standing with hands on her
hips, Carrie experienced a wave of strengthening anger as
she looked about the main room where dirty clothes
littered the floor and food-encrusted dishes spilled over the
table and cabinets. Every piece of old-fashioned oak furniture, lovingly oiled before, was now piled high with
ashtrays of stale cigarillos, cups, and glasses. The room
stank!

A trail of lacy underwear and silk stockings led Carrie to

the bedroom door, which she kicked open unceremoniously. The loud noise roused the dozing Lottie, who lay sprawled across the big bed in a seductive and indolent pose on her stomach. Head still down, she said petulantly, "Querido, you do not have to be so noisy, por favor!"

"Ah, querida, but I do!" With that Carrie ripped up the bed covers and tossed them to the floor, exposing an indecent length of bare legs and a black-silk-clad derriere.

"Aaah! Who are you? How dare you break into my house?" Lottie's accent thickened as she scrambled from the bed and grabbed her red satin robe from a welter of clothes on the floor.

"For your information, *your* house sits on *my* land and I'm evicting you."

"Only Don Hawk can do that, and he is not here. I am his woman." Her black eyes shot sparks and her chin lifted in obvious pride.

"Not anymore. I'm replacing you!" Carrie advanced on her menacingly.

Carlotta Hernandez had been raised on the St. Augustine waterfront. She had learned to roll drunks and fend off attackers with a knife before she was ten. Quickly she reached behind her to the bedside chest, opened a drawer, and grabbed a wicked blade. "Now we see, you skinny gringa with ugly red hair!" She snorted in triumph, her face twisted in scorn. So this was the one he cried out for in his dreams, his Firehair! Why, she was too tall for a woman, flat-chested and washed-out. Carlotta would make short work of her!

Without waiting for the malevolent woman to wield her knife, Carrie turned and strode quickly into the main room, her eyes darting about for a weapon. Immediately they took in a wealth of ammunition, since every heavy pot, pan, and utensil in the place was lying out, dirty. She seized a medium-sized iron skillet and whirled just as Lottie came up behind her, intent on prodding her into a hasty retreat with the knife.

The collision was blurringly fast and ended with Carrie's skillet coming out uncontested winner over Lottie's stiletto. She struck the shorter woman roundly on the skull and the knife clattered to the floor. Lottie crumpled in a sexy heap of dishabille. Putting down the skillet, Carrie walked briskly to the door and called to Kyle. "Bring in my things and, oh yes, get rid of this trash for me, please."

Kyle's eyes lit up at the sight of the half-dressed female sprawled at Carrie's feet. "Yes, ma'am. My greatest pleasure."

He scooped Carlotta up, all the while assessing her obvious charms. Carrie tossed a bag of coins onto her midsection, now securely in Kyle's grasp. "This should pay her for services rendered, which obviously didn't include housekeeping. Take her back to Clancey's Place."

José brought in several boxes and a small trunk, which he placed uncertainly in the bedroom. His big brown eyes, so like his mother's, were round as saucers at the exotic display of women's unmentionables strewn across the place.

After they were gone, Carrie set to work. It was going to be a busy day. She gathered all Lottie's things and dumped them in a sack. Tacky, sluttish taste, she sniffed. Then she attacked the bedroom, stripping the bed, gagging on the cheap, heavy perfume the *puta* had doused the bedcovers with. She made up the bed with clean sheets and a soft quilt that she found in a bottom drawer of the oak chest in the room. Probably Marah had sewn it herself.

She dusted the furniture and swept the floors, then scrubbed the planks until they were clean but lacking the luster of polish, which she had no time to apply today. Next she attacked the encrusted dishes and cooking utensils, soaking and scouring until every knife, pot, and pan gleamed and each piece of crockery was stacked neatly on the shelves. Finally, she was ready to begin supper. Opening the basket brought from the house, she took out a small venison roast, a sack of dried peaches, a canister of flour, some yeast, and an assortment of other seasonings and vegetables.

By early evening, she had the venison larded and roasting in a heavy Dutch oven over the fire, light rolls rising in a pan on the hearth, a flaky-crusted peach pie cooling in the back window, and a big pan of freshly snapped beans ready to cook with fragrant tarragon. Thank God she had spent so much time helping Feliz in the kitchen over the past two years! Judiciously, she decided to let Hawk make the coffee.

Carrie took a long, cooling soak, all the while smelling the fragrances wafting from the kitchen. While she cleaned and refreshed herself she had more water heating for Hawk's bath. Then she turned her attention to a simple toilette.

Because the evening was warm for October, she put on a cool muslin dress. It was a bright rich yellow, and as she smoothed the straight, simple skirt, she recalled how Hawk had admired redheads in yellow so long ago. *Please, let him still think so.*

The neckline was rounded and scooped low and the sleeves were cut just below the elbow. All in all, it revealed a good deal of honey-gold skin. She brushed her hair until it crackled and glowed, then tied it back simply with a yellow ribbon. Flat-heeled soft-tan slippers completed the outfit. She wore no jewelry, but remembered to use her wildflower perfume.

Nervously, she went to check on the progress of his bath. The pot in the fireplace was bubbling. She began the arduous task of carrying several buckets of cool spring water to the tub, then added the boiling water from the fire to it until it was nicely warmed. After that she returned to the main room and set the table. A pretty cluster of yellow and white chrysanthemums were placed gracefully in a small earthen jar for a simple centerpiece.

Turning her back on the table, she went to lay out towels in the bedroom, next to the bath. Then she heard familiar footsteps falling lightly on the porch. Her heart began to hammer when the front door swung open, and that low, vibrant voice said, "What smells so great? Lottie, what the hell did you do to this place? You must have—" He froze in his tracks, staring at the lovely, yellow-clad woman in the bedroom door. He watched her through narrowed eyes as he struggled to gather his scattered wits.

I will be calm. "Hello, Hawk. There's warm bathwater

in the tub and clean clothes laid out on the bed. Supper will be ready by the time you're through." Without giving him a chance to say more, Carrie whisked across the room and began stirring the coals beneath the fire. Then she placed the rolls in the back, over low coals on a grate where they would bake to crisp brownness.

Hawk stood for a moment staring at the fiery cascade of curls tumbling down her back as she worked. In wordless perplexity, he went to the bedroom to do as she had bid. Quickly he shed his dusty gear and dropped into the warm soothing water. Tired, dirty, and starved, he could not remember when a bath had felt so wonderful or food had smelled so good. Quite a welcome change from the tawdry mess he'd been coming home to with Lottie every night.

Then the thought struck him. "Where the hell's Lottie?" He had voiced it aloud without really realizing it until a sweetly musical voice on the other side of the door replied.

"Gone back to Clancey's Place."

He mulled that over, considering various scenarios, none of which convinced him the lazy little slut would have gone willingly. While listening to the sounds of Carrie bustling about the kitchen, he quickly washed and shaved, then donned the white shirt, dark pants, and moccasins that had been laid out for him.

When he came soundlessly through the door, she was placing a beautifully browned venison roast on the table, surrounded on the big platter by potatoes and carrots. She looked up and said briskly, "I know I don't make good coffee. Would you?" She motioned to the granite pot filled with water and the jar of freshly ground beans.

As he measured coffee into the pot and placed it over the fire, he said, "Did you have Kyle and a dozen hands hogtie Lottie and haul her back to town?" He quirked an eyebrow at her, aggravated at her high-handedness, but, in spite of himself, glad the troublesome tart was gone.

"It only took Kyle to carry her out."

"Carry her?"

"After I flattened her with this." She hefted the skillet sitting on the sink. As his eyes widened in amazement, she hurried on to explain, "She came at me with this," Carrie pulled the long, wicked-looking blade out of a drawer, "so I grabbed the nearest weapon I could find. I didn't hit her too hard—I don't think. She was coming around when Kyle and José pulled away in the wagon."

Standing there, she looked so matter-of-fact and beautiful that he was struck speechless. Carrie was afraid to go on, yet knew she must hold the initiative, so she sat down and said, "Dinner's getting cold. Let's eat; we can talk afterward."

She was far too nervous to enjoy the food, but he was famished, not having had a decent meal in weeks. Lottie's cooking had been even worse than his own. If it hadn't been for an occasional breakfast in Feliz's kitchen, he would have starved to death.

"Could you always cook like this?" he asked as he bit into a juicy slab of venison and sopped up the rich gravy with a light, crunchy roll.

"Only since I came to Circle S and Feliz let me work in her kitchen. The Pattersons had a cook. All I got to do there was scrub pots and pans after her."

"Something I've never been very attentive to, as you might have noticed," he said ruefully.

"You're not much of a cook either. Every pan had food burned to the bottom of it."

He shrugged. "But I do make good coffee," he said, hefting his cup as she placed a generous slab of peach pie in front of him.

"As you once said to me, I didn't come here to make rotten coffee." She swallowed the nervous lump in her throat. For a while as they were eating, it almost felt as if they were a comfortable married couple, enjoying bantering conversation and the simple pleasure of one another's company. She hated to break the mood, but she had to speak her piece before her courage totally evaporated.

"Then what, Carrie? Why all this?" He gestured around the cheery, immaculate room to the remnants of the superb dinner. "Even a yellow dress."

She felt the heat flood her cheeks as she replied, "I remembered that you liked women in yellow."

"Redheads in yellow," he corrected, then waited, his fathomless obsidian eyes giving away nothing of his feelings.

"It ought to be pretty obvious, Hawk. I'm showing off all my domestic skills. I wouldn't make a man a bad wife. I—"

"A man like Wolf Krueger?" He interrupted her angrily. Why was she doing this? "Surely he's asked you."

She shook her head in mortification. "Yes, he's hinted at it. I know he would, if I let him, but I'll never marry a man I don't love."

"You sure did once," he shot back.

Her eyes blazed at his cruelty, goading her. "Yes, I did, much against my will, as a stupid terrified girl! That's what bothers you, isn't it? I was your *father's* wife—no matter that I bore your child!"

"It should never have happened between us, Carrie, and you know it," he said defensively.

"You mean you're sorry Perry was born?" She stood, her anger making her forget all the reasonable, conciliatory speeches she had rehearsed.

"No! How the hell do I know what I mean with you! All we ever do is get under one another's skin, hurt one another."

"Like that day at the pool last summer?" Her voice had softened now. "You're nothing like Noah. I never meant what I said, then or at Iron Heart's village. If I could call back those stupid words, I would give anything. I'm sorry. I was frightened and—"

"And you finally saw me as I am, or as a part of me is. I really am half Cheyenne, not just some exotic-looking white man, Carrie. I've lived their life, by their laws, and I honestly believe many of their ways are better."

"And their women are better, too!" Tears burned her eyes now. So this was the truth of it, what she had always dreaded. "You wanted to stay with her—your Cheyenne wife. I was just an encumbrance. You only came back with me because of Perry—because she was dead. You loved her—"

He cut her off furiously, standing up and knocking over

his chair. "I never loved her! I couldn't! God knows I wanted to, I tried!"

"I—I don't understand," she said brokenly, feeling his anguish, fighting down the urge to reach out to him, sensing he would reject her overtures.

He looked at her with blazing, accusing anger. "Don't you? I'll never forgive myself because all I thought of, dreamed of, was you! I couldn't love Wind Song because of you. She loved me with her whole heart, and I could never return that love. She knew it when she died...." His voice trailed away as the long-suppressed memories surfaced once more to tear at him.

"Hawk, I didn't know." It sounded so pitifully inadequate to her own ears. "Kyle told me about the banishment, what it meant—"

"Could you ever know?" he countered, facing her once more, the pain and guilt of a moment ago once more transformed into anger. "Could you ever imagine how it is to grow up belonging nowhere, to no one? Always being an outcast, spit on behind your back by polite society everywhere you went?"

"Yes, I can. Only they weren't afraid of me—they spit on me right to my face!" Her voice was surprisingly calm for all the turmoil inside her. "I've just spent two years as a branded adulteress, white trash who loved an Indian and bore his brat. How do you think the good people in Miles City treated me, Hawk? What do you think Noah did when he found out—oh yes, he found out, over a month before Perry was born, thanks to Mrs. Thorndyke. He would have killed us both if he'd lived to see your son! All the men were quitting, everyone but Feliz and her children. I was left with Caleb Rider for protection. Cy Cummins wouldn't even sell me supplies on credit anymore. If Kyle hadn't come back when he did, I'd have lost Circle S, lost our son's birthright!" She watched his stricken face, then plunged ahead.

"You bet I've learned what it is to be an outsider! At least they respect you—or your guns. They fear you, and you're a man. The rules are a little different for a woman, in case you never thought of it. I'll always be the worst sort of harlot to them—a white woman who betrayed her race and her husband.'' Her shoulders slumped, and she turned from his frozen, expressionless face. ''And you blame me, too. You don't want me.'' She began to move toward the door, not thinking or caring where she would go. His touch on her arm, as gentle as his voice, stopped her.

''Carrie, why did you tell me all this, come here and do all this? Just to marry me, so you could give Perry a legal father? If you married Wolf and took Perry abroad for an education, he'd be just as respectable, even more accepted than he'll ever be here.''

She did not turn around, but choked out the words in a tear-thickened voice. ''I'll never do that. I'll never take him away from his father, from the land that's his birthright. I'm proud he is my son and I'm proud you are his father.''

He pulled her around and into his arms slowly, then tipped her head up so she had to look at him. ''And what about love, Firehair? I know you love Perry, but you've never said you love me.''

''You've never given me a chance. You read everything I do wrong, no matter what I say—oh, Hawk, of course I love you! More than anything in life!'' She burrowed her head against his chest, holding him around the waist tightly, crying in great, wracking sobs as he stroked her bright hair and kissed the top of her head.

''What a fool I've been! Oh, Carrie, Carrie, my love. I've always been so afraid you turned to me that night in the garden out of loneliness and desperation, as an escape from Noah's cruelty. You needed gentleness and, yes, physical satisfaction, too. We both were drawn by that from the first minute we laid eyes on one another. I knew it even though I fought it, but you were so naive, so innocent.'' He kissed her upturned face gently, brushing away the tears with his lips.

She said softly, ''I never realized what a carnal creature I was until that day in the pool when I watched you undress.'' Her face flamed, but her lips curved into an incredibly seductive smile as she reached them up to his.

He groaned and kissed her with fierce passion now, letting all his defenses and inhibitions down. "I love you, Firehair," he growled hoarsely. She responded, pressing boldly against him, starved for his body after so long an abstinence.

"Tomorrow we'll go to town and get Judge Benton to marry us," he said, scooping her up and heading for the bedroom.

"Tomorrow," she repeated, renewing the kiss.

He slid her feet to the floor inside the bedroom door, still holding her tightly around the waist. Neither wanted to let the other go as they clung together, swaying in a dizzying kiss that spoke of so much longing, so much love, long denied. His tongue teased her lips, brushing the soft insides, then skimmed across her teeth. When she boldly followed his lead and pressed her eager tongue against his, he growled and twined them together in a swirl of rioting sensation.

Carrie kissed him back, returning caress for caress, her starved senses clamoring for every touch, every sensation she had remembered on all the long lonely nights of the past two years. She ran her hands up his shoulders and neck, curling her fingers in his thick, coarse black hair. It was growing longer again and she loved the feel of it, taking fistfuls and pulling his head closer to hers in the embrace.

He moved his devouring mouth off hers and slid it hotly down her cheek to the slender column of her throat. She threw back her head and bared it to his rapacious kisses, licks, and love bites, gasping and softly moaning his name.

He reached one hand up to the buttons on the front of her dress, unfastening them one at a time, pausing to lower his mouth to each bared inch of flesh as he pulled the dress off her shoulders. His lips brushed her shoulder, her collarbone, the valley between her breasts until she thought she would scream with the pleasure. Her breasts throbbed for his touch. Ever so slowly he continued the exquisite torture, freeing first one, then the other high, pointed peak. She arched against him, desperate for the heat of his mouth on her sensitive nipples. He teased and enveloped one, then the other, alternating between them like a starved man at a banquet until she held on to his shoulders, reeling in frenzied pleasure.

She could feel his hands, still busy with the fastening of her dress. When he had it freed, he stood back and she helped him pull it off her arms and drop it over her hips to the floor. The thin chemise was wadded around her waist, and she hastily unfastened it and tossed it down as he slid his large, dark hands over the white pantalets, easing them off her long, slim legs. He knelt and slipped her shoes off, then stood up once more, never taking his eyes from her willowy, golden body.

"You are the most beautiful woman I've ever seen," he breathed, running his hands up her thighs to span her slim waist and then slide over her rib cage to heft and cup the upthrust young breasts.

"I'm not changed? I mean since Perry was born?" she whispered, looking into his glowing eyes, which reflected her naked image on them.

"Maybe a little larger here." He pulled softly on a breast, sending ripples of pleasure shooting down to her toes and back up to lodge in the core of her.

She reached up and began unbuttoning his shirt. "Now my turn," she said in breathless concentration as she peeled the soft cotton off his broad shoulders and pulled it free of his pants. He shrugged it off and returned his hands to work their blistering magic on the hardened points of her breasts. With trembling hands she ran her fingers through the thick black hair of his chest, then pressed her face against its hard surface, feeling the sharp imprint of the medallion that gleamed in its usual place. "How long I've wanted to do this," she breathed. She inhaled the scent of him, male and vital, clean and enticing as her hands followed the pattern of his body hair downward to the waistband of his pants.

With a wicked chuckle she began to unfasten the straining buttons, slowly, as he gasped in pain and pleasure at being freed from the tight confinement. When she eased the pants down his straight, hard thighs, his shaft stood proud and straight.

He kicked pants and moccasins off hurriedly while she knelt and reached one hand out to hold a hard narrow buttock. The other hand cupped him experimentally. The sensation was electric, and now it was his turn to moan in need. "You'd better stop that, or I won't be able to control myself!"

He pulled her up into his arms and they both reveled in the sensation of naked breast and belly pressed tightly together, rubbing sensuously, smooth and silky against hard and hairy. Once more he picked her up and carried her the few steps to the bed, then dropped her onto its inviting width and followed her as they rolled, arms and legs entwined, to the center.

"The sheets smell like violets," he breathed into her hair.

"Big improvement over how they smelled before," she retorted, nipping playfully at his face and neck.

"Oh, Firehair, it smells like you now, all soft and clean, like wildflowers." He rolled on his back and pulled her on top of him for a long, languorous kiss, all the while running his hands up and down the delicate bones in her spine, cupping her delectable buttocks and massaging her silky flanks.

Carrie writhed against him, loving his hard, long body and his hands roaming over her. After a minute more of such close contact, she raised her head and looked into his eyes. "Please, Hawk, now. Love me now."

With amazing gentleness, he rolled them over and poised above her, looking down at her flushed, beautiful face with its plea for fulfillment. Ever so carefully he slid into her velvet warmth, concentrating with all his strength on going slowly to wait for her. It was as if he had been without a woman for as long as he knew she had been without a man.

Slowly he thrust and she arched, recalling the wonderful ballet of love they had played out that night in his room at the big house. Then she had never been made love to before, but it all came back to her now in such poignant

sweetness that it took her breath away. She opened her
eyes, focusing them after the initial haze of ecstasy, to
look up at him as he stared down at her. Jade and jet, their
gazes locked as all the love and vulnerability in their souls
rushed out and intermingled.

All too soon the slow cadence became frenzied as
Carrie's hunger drove her to pull him closer, to urge him to
move faster and harder until she made one final convulsive
arch, crying out his name. He watched her as his own
body blazed with the heat of a thousand stars, and then he
collapsed, shuddering, on top of her. Carrie locked her
legs around him and held him fiercely to her breast, never
wanting to let him go.

He caressed her neck with soft, nuzzling kisses, saying
in a laughing whisper, "I was afraid I couldn't hold back
for you!"

"It's been so long. What did you expect after two
months?" She buried her face against his neck.

"Mmm," he murmured in her ear, "then you admit you
enjoyed my savage lovemaking at the lake?" His face
darkened in self-condemnation. "I didn't want to hurt you,
my beautiful Firehair, but I was so jealous, so—"

She cut him off with a kiss. "You were right—I wanted
you. Oh, Hawk, I've always wanted you, always loved
you. Never doubt it. I couldn't bear it if you left me
again."

"No, no, never. I'll never be that big a fool again." He
rolled over and sat up, then reached for the medallion
around his neck. He took it off, saying, "I believe this
belongs to you, Firehair." With that he slipped it over her
head, gently lifting her hair to place it around her neck so
that it nestled between her breasts.

They snuggled beneath the covers and she caressed his
cheek softly, saying, "You belong to me, Hunting Hawk or
Even James Sinclair, both sides of you that I've seen, and
any I haven't, it doesn't matter. And I belong to you."

"Fate, the white man says, or destiny. I never thought it
was as poetic or as caring as the Cheyenne way. Let me
tell you about my medicine dream, Firehair, when I
received my name."

As he told her of the vision he had in that broiling-hot medicine lodge high on the Dakota mountainside, Carrie's eyes widened. He described the hawk and the wolf, the stolen cub, and the blazing, sun-streaked sky. Forgetting her nakedness, she sat up in bed. "You dreamed that the summer you were fourteen? And I was seven, back in St. Louis! It was hot and I awoke from my nap crying for my mother. That was the first time," she whispered, her hand reaching out to caress his cheek, awe in her voice.

He took her hand and kissed the soft palm. "I know. When you told me that day by the lake, I was stunned. I didn't understand what to make of it because I was so sure you hated me. It's strange, I never was certain whether the sun was rising or setting in the dream. Now I know it was rising."

"The beginning of a whole life together," she breathed as he sunk his fingers into her thick, flaming hair, scorched with the heat and beauty of it. He pulled her down in a fierce, sweet kiss.

Just as in the medicine dream, he had at last captured the sun here in his arms. He would hold her fiery love in his hands and in his heart forever.

Epilogue _____

Yellowstone County, 1886

The sun blazed across the summer sky, arching its golden light even through the dense foliage of the trees where Kyle waited with Carrie and her children. Perry sat proudly on his own small pony. He was five years old, and already his legs were long and his face serious. Even if he was three-quarters white, he looked Cheyenne. The boy controlled his mount with the inherent skill bred into the horsemen of the plains. Kyle held Ferris, Perry's three-year-old brother, who squirmed and fussed, eager to be down and exploring the strange new sights and sounds around them. Carrie sat on the ground, crooning to her two-month-old daughter Carolina while the baby dozed on her lap.

She looked worriedly over at Kyle. "Are you sure Iron Heart is still alive? That the council will let Hawk see his grandfather? I couldn't bear for him to be hurt again."

Just then Hawk rode away from the two men he had been conferring with, toward the hill where Carrie waited. As soon as he drew near she could tell the news was good.

"See, I jist had me a feelin'," Kyle said, grinning at Perry.

"You always seem to 'have a feeling' when anything turns out good, Uncle Kyle," Perry said, returning the smile.

Hawk escorted his family proudly into the encamp-

400

ment, smaller now than it had been four years earlier. The ravages of disease and harsh winters had shrunken the population even further. But Iron Heart lived.

"I would see my grandson once more before I die." He had spoken to the council, who had honored his wishes and rescinded the exile of Hunting Hawk after four years.

His sharp old eyes, still bright despite his advancing years, studied the woman. Daughter of the Sun, Little Otter had called her. It was a good name for the proud, beautiful wife of Hunting Hawk. She stood calmly with her children, waiting for him to speak. They were all gathered inside his lodge for this private reunion. There would be feasting with the whole village tonight, but now the old man searched their faces in silence.

"It is good you have returned, Hunting Hawk and Daughter of the Sun." He looked at them with love and pride in his usually impassive face. "And how are my great-grandchildren called?" He looked at Hawk, who knelt with his sons.

"The eldest, who you met when he was a babe, is Peregrine, an English name for the hunting hawk." The tall, black-eyed child looked gravely at his great-grandfather, awed by such age and majesty, but sensing a kinship to that austere, yet kindly face.

"This is Ferris; his name means iron." Iron Heart studied his namesake, whose thick black hair and coppery skin proclaimed his Cheyenne heritage. However, he had his mother's clear, bright-green eyes. He squirmed in his father's restraining grasp, eager to explore the mysteries of the lodge.

"And this is Carolina," Hawk said proudly as he exchanged his son, taking his daughter from Carrie's arms. "She is named for her mother, whose name means One Who Is Strong." Caro watched her father with liquid-gold eyes, listening to the low, familiar cadence of his voice. Her dark curls were burnished with red and her eyes were a golden brown, but her skin was as dark as her brother's coppery hue. Without a doubt, however, the delicate features were Carrie's.

"They please me greatly," Iron Heart said simply to Hawk. "I am content now, for I can see that the prophesy has been fulfilled and an old man's meddling has not changed what was meant to be."

"You mean our dream?" Carrie questioned quietly, taking Ferris into her arms.

Iron Heart's eyes looked puzzled. "Hunting Hawk's dream, yes, daughter. His medicine dream. He has told you of it?"

"We share it, Grandfather. Carrie had the same dream I did, at the same time. She told me of hers before she knew of mine."

For a moment the old man's eyes flashed with amazement; then he nodded. "So, it was doubly fated to be."

Iron Heart watched the subtle interplay between husband and wife and knew that it was right this time for his grandson. "I once wanted to keep you here with the People, but in my heart I knew it was wrong. I, too, pondered your medicine dream, which said you would take something from He Who Walks in Sun—his land? His woman? Or the son he thought to have?"

Hawk and Carrie exchanged glances. Then Hawk said, "Does our love and our firstborn displease the Powers?"

"No, I do not think so. I angered them when I urged you to wed Wind Song and live here. I knew the dream; I should have let it fulfill itself. Because of my meddling, much unhappiness followed; but now, I have lived to see things set right. The Powers are kind to a foolish old man."

"Then you are truly pleased with your great-grandchildren? It—it does not bother you that they are more white than Cheyenne?" Carrie's voice was uncertain, yet hopeful.

Hawk looked at his grandfather and smiled, for he knew what Iron Heart would say.

"One of our great chiefs said almost a lifetime ago, 'We were a small people and good captives made us more, so now there is scarcely one among us who is not a foreigner by blood!' You did not come to my grandson as a captive, Daughter of the Sun, but your blood has enriched us all the same. You are a part of the People. When we are gone and our way of life has vanished, we will live on in your children and their children."

Shirl loves to hear from her readers.
You can write to her at
P.O. Box 72,
Adrian, Michigan, 49221.

SENSATIONAL ROMANCES

☐ **AUTUMNFIRE** by Emily Carmichael
(D34-717, $3.95, U.S.A.)
(D34-718, $4.95, Canada)
Autumnfire, an Irish American beauty who was
raised by Indians, is captured by handsome
cowboy Jason Sinclair who rouses her heart and
stirs her desire.

☐ **GOLDEN LADY** by Shirl Henke
(D30-165, $3.95, U.S.A.)
(D30-166, $4.95, Canada)
Amanda's past was one filled with burning
shame. Now she wonders whether she dares to
risk losing the one man who claims her heart by
revealing the dark secrets she's kept hidden.

☐ **THE BAYOU FOX** by Helene Sinclair
(D30-219, $3.95, U.S.A.)
(D30-220, $4.95, Canada)
Bethany vows revenge on the gambler she
believes cheated her father of all he owned. But
when she plans a daring deception to beat the
man at his own game, she finds herself losing
her heart to him instead.

**Warner Books P.O. Box 690
New York, NY 10019**

Please send me the books I have checked. I enclose a check or money
order (not cash), plus 75¢ per order and 75¢ per copy to cover postage
and handling.* (Allow 4 weeks for delivery.)

___Please send me your free mail order catalog. (If ordering only the
catalog, include a large self-addressed, stamped envelope.)

Name _____

Address _____

City _____ State _____ Zip _____

*New York and California residents add applicable sales tax.   307